ISLE of WRATH

NEW YORK TIMES BESTSELLING AUTHOR
CLAIRE CONTRERAS

Copyright © 2026 by Claire Contreras

All rights reserved.

No part of this book may be reproduced in any form or by any electronic or mechanical means, including information storage and retrieval systems, without written permission from the author, except for the use of brief quotations in a book review.

Edited by: Gina Licciardi
Formatted by: Champagne
Cover Design: Hang Le
Maps: To The Moon and Back Design
Endpages: Angela Rizza

DEDICATION

To those who have never quite belonged anywhere.

Don't ever let anyone's view of you determine your self-worth.

You are a beautiful, resilient dreamer,

and you belong *everywhere*.

In the end, nothing will matter, except everything.

QUICK EXPLANATION GUIDE

Government:

Sages of Veritas: control the town of Veritas. 3 Sages per kingdom are chosen by Ignata, the Creator, to watch over her Undying Flame and keep ancient secrets/texts safe. Typically, they do not involve themselves in politics, but after years of strife, they worked alongside the Council to form the government and create the Veritas Treaty. They are in charge of the House of Truth.

The Council: headed by Constantine, it is a 3-person system. They banished mention of the gods, outlawed magic (which comes directly from the gods), and replaced the temples that existed with the House of Justice, House of Knowledge, House of Trade, and House of Truth. ★The Council is not allowed in Veritas without permission from the Sages.

Character name pronunciations:
Ada Temperance Acevedo = Ay-duh
Temperance = Temp-uh-rens
Acevedo = Ah-seh-veh-do
Jordi = Jor-dee
Elías = Eh-lee-us
Naima = Nah-ee-muh
Margot = Mar-goh
Margarita = Mar-gah-ree-tuh
Anala = Ah-nah-lah

Freida = Free-duh
Sara = Ser-ruh
Veneficia = Veh-neh-fee-sia
Malachi = Mal-uh-kai
Bain = Bayn
Jacobi = Jac-O-bee
Draven = Dray-ven
Kage = Kayj★★★
Yoshioka = Yow-shee-oh-kah
Constantine = Kon-stuhn-tyne
Nicolas = Nik-o-las
Arlo = Ar-loh
Casimir = Cass-ih-meer
Bastian = Bas-tee-ahn
Neith = Knee-th
Runerth = Roo-n-earth

Gods:
Ignata (Ig-nah-tah) = Creator
Noktelum (Nock-tuh-lum) = Creator
Together, Ignata and Noktelum created the oceans, land, darkness, light, infinity (time and space).
They had four children who are known as the original gods. People get their gifts directly from these gods.
Sulara (Soo-lah-rah) = goddess of day, fertility, wisdom, healing, rebirth
Mortiana (More-tee-ah-nah) = goddess of night —but not the moon, trickery, fate, time, death
Fidus (Fee-doos) = god of the ocean, fishing, sailing, sea storms, protector of sailors

Thalon (Tha-lun) = god animals, sea creatures, protector of beings
Maia (Mah-ee-uh) = goddess of thunder and lightning, war, chaos. Married to Sulara.
Lugal (Loo-gal) = god of the underworld, protector of afterlife, war, fertility. Married to Mortiana.
Luna (Loo-nah) = goddess of the moon, fertility, alchemy. Married to Fidus.
Maredor (Mar-eh-door) = god of magic, abundancy. Married to Thalon.

Other pronunciations:
Raffin = raff-inn
Serephony = seref-anee
Alatus = ala-dus
Lyrionne = lih-ree-on
Duende = doo-en-deh
Adhoranelo = ad0re-ah-neh-lo

*** The accurate pronunciation of Kage is "Kah-geh". It's how it's pronounced in the east (Arusha, Mizu, etc.), but in the west (Tenebris, Lyrionne, etc.) people pronounce it "kay-j" (or "cage").

LETTER TO ALL MOON FESTIVAL VISITORS

Three hundred years ago, the Kingdom of Tenebris was cursed, and the Shroud, a darkness manifested from that curse, ensured that Lunaris, once a famed port city, was severed from the kingdom.

For fifty years, Lunaris, known as "the Isle" to its inhabitants and the "lost city" to the rest of the continent, has been ruled by two powers.

The Sages, guardians of truth, who worship the goddess Ignata and encourage the gifts the gods bestow.

And **the Council,** who have rewritten history to serve their own agenda and banished all mention of gods and gifts.

Both promise safety from war and freedom from poverty and pain.

Both demand memories in exchange for asylum.

But while the residents of Lunaris may not remember their lives before, or the prophecy, or the curse that lurks beyond their walls, prophecies do not forget.

And the curse is waking.

My advice? Keep your memories and stay away.

Signed,
A Renegade

ISLE of WRATH

CHAPTER ONE

We all live in a cage.

Some are gilded. Some are iron. And others, like ours, are made of nothing but silence and the weight of what we're forbidden to remember. My brother's obsession with this concept borders on madness—like everything else he finds remotely interesting.

It's one of the many things we have in common. Along with the womb we shared, our caramel skin, dark curls, and the incessant curiosity that has gotten us both into trouble more times than I care to count. But even my obsessions have limits. Or perhaps, as Jordi likes to remind me, my limits are set by the cage I'm kept in.

As if I've summoned him with the thought, I feel his presence. That familiar hum of restless energy, sharp and frantic, pressing against the edges of my awareness. One of the gifts the gods blessed me with is the ability to sense others nearby, and Jordi's is always the easiest to find.

My eyes flick from the cages lining my workspace to the door, then to the injured raven on the table. I grab it just as the door slams open. It lets out a guttural croak as Jordi rushes inside clutching fistfuls of maps.

I open my mouth to reprimand him for not knocking and for bringing those damned maps here again, but the words die on my tongue. My brother, who presses his clothes each morning and keeps his hair cropped, looks unrecognizable. Disheveled. Unshaven. With shadows carved beneath those bloodshot hazel eyes I've always been jealous of.

The dull ache that has made a home in my chest these last two years deepens into something sharper. *Gods.* If I could turn back time, I would go to our first day at Veritas University, when we were eager students who didn't yet understand the weight of what we'd been given. When we were simply grateful not to be laborers, hauling stones to expand the Council's already massive amphitheater.

I would find a way to avoid whatever drove this wall of secrets and resentment. It's a futile dream, but I still wish for it each time I see him. But the gods didn't grant me the gift to turn back time. They blessed me with curses instead.

"This must be one of your emergencies," I say flatly.

Rather than answering, he stomps across the worn stone floor and unrolls his maps across my worktable, scattering vials and dried herbs and the careful order I'd spent the morning maintaining. The raven hops sideways to avoid being buried, letting out an indignant croak.

"I know you said you don't want to get involved—"

"Understatement of the century."

He pins me with a look. The same one he's been giving me since we were children, when he'd unearth some new mystery in the library's restricted texts and drag me along whether

I wanted to go or not. Neither of us says anything as I check the wrap on the raven's wing, running my fingers along the bandage. When I release it, it hops across the maps, leaving tiny smudges of dried blood on the parchment.

Jordi eyes it warily. "What happened to it?"

"Silent guards attacked it. The parrots, not the people."

"Ironic."

My lips twist in disgust. The Council may have banished mention of the gods from Lunaris, but they do love to take pages from their books. Black ravens like this one are said to report our deeds to the goddess Mortiana. The Council's gray parrots, with their small green amulets glinting at their throats, do the same for their masters.

As far as we're concerned, only one of the birds is worthy of fear, and it isn't the one on my table. At least the Veritas Treaty keeps them out of our town. The Sages made certain of it.

Jordi exhales, the sound too loud in the silence of my workspace. I look up and finally meet his eyes.

"Do you agree that the Shroud has been volatile lately?"

My jaw clenches. I know from experience that each question I answer will only pull me deeper into his labyrinth. He builds them so carefully with breadcrumbs for questions and revelations that lead further from the exits. And I'm always the idiot who follows. I guess it's the curse of being a sibling.

"Everyone knows the Shroud's been volatile," I say after a moment. "But that doesn't change our agreement. No maps and no theories until—"

"*After* the Moon Festival," he says before I have a chance to finish my sentence. "When you finally get your coveted title and tell me why one of the most skilled alchemists in Veritas has been stuck in a never-ending apprenticeship."

I scowl. "I'm not 'the most skilled' at anything."

"It's sad that Mother has made you believe that."

I glare at the maps and bite my tongue hard enough to taste copper. It's the only thing keeping me from speaking about Sara Veneficia. She's not our mother. Not by blood, anyway. She's known as Sara the All-Knowing, or the High Sage, to most of Veritas, but the orphans she raised call her Mother. She's the reason the town of Veritas exists, and why I've been pushing my brother away for the last two years.

"I should burn these maps," I mutter.

"I'm surprised you haven't."

My eyes snap to his. "Don't tempt me."

He presses his lips together to fight a smile, but the dimples in his cheeks betray him. Despite everything—the silence, the resentment, the words we can never take back—seeing that almost-smile loosens something in my chest.

Gods, I miss him.

It's a cruel thing, missing someone who stands right in front of you. Someone who shares your blood and your face and every memory of a childhood spent whispering secrets in the dark. It's crueler still in a place like Lunaris, where everyone arrives alone and siblings are as rare as starlight through the clouds.

The raven hops onto a sketch of a raffin half-buried beneath the maps, and Jordi tilts his head.

"Interesting that he chose that spot."

I laugh despite myself. "If you think this is a sign he's trying to wake the raffin, I will summon my fire."

"It's illegal to summon fire indoors."

"It's illegal to steal from the vault, but here we are."

He chuckles, low and warm, and I feel it in my chest. For a moment, we're children again, sneaking into the library after dark, shoulders pressed together as we pored over forbidden texts by candlelight.

"You have to admit," Jordi says, his voice turning wistful, "it would be nice if all it took to wake the raffins was birds pecking at their stone shells."

I snort. "You think it would be 'nice' to wake a creature with a thirty-foot wingspan, poisonous talons, and the ability to summon lightning from a three-hundred-year slumber?"

He scowls. "Maybe it would only take out the Council."

"That's not how it works. They'd wipe us all out."

"Either way, the curse would be lifted."

I stare at him for a moment. "I can't believe we're having this conversation again."

"It's more important than ever."

"I doubt that." I turn to the row of iron cages behind me, their bars casting thin shadows across the floor. "Maybe instead of dreaming about all of us dying for the supposed greater good, you should focus on small changes you can actually make. Like taking this raven home and healing him."

He scoffs. "And keep him caged?"

"It's a big cage, and it's only for a few hours." I reach for the largest one and set it on the table with a heavy thunk. "Besides, once the healing tonic kicks in, he'll be too out of it to know the difference."

"You just described all the residents of Lunaris."

The words land like a blow to the chest. I cast him a

sideways glance, keeping my face carefully blank. "That's not fair."

"I agree. It's not fair that they're all in the dark."

"They seem happy enough."

"Happy or surviving?"

I scoff. "Is there a difference?"

He frowns. "You can't possibly believe that."

I bite back a response and focus on the cage. The iron bars. The rusted lock. Anything but the disappointment carved into every line of his face.

"Can you please just look at the maps?" he asks quietly.

"And that's it? Only look at them?"

"Yes."

It's the resignation in his voice that makes me stop fiddling with the lock. I look at the map. My eyes land on the thick wall of darkness known as the Shroud. Even rendered in ink, it seems to pulse with something almost alive. It stretches across the north of our forest—a rift between Lunaris and the kingdom it once belonged to—like a wound that refuses to heal. Veritas scholars believe it's a manifestation of the curse placed on Tenebris, but no one can explain why our island was spared.

Both the Veritas maps and the Council's are titled "Isle of Lunaris," but that's where the similarities end. The Veritas maps show the continent above. The kingdoms, mountains, and rivers none of us will ever see. The Council's maps show only Lunaris itself, as though nothing else exists. As though nothing else ever did.

Just as well. You can't miss what you don't remember. And none of us remember anything from before we arrived.

Memories for asylum. That's the price everyone pays to live in Lunaris. The cost of the perfect society. The price of freedom.

Here, we are free from war, famine, and pain. Or rather, free from the memory of such things. Free from the grief and terror that drove people to seek refuge on these shores. We still hurt, of course. Still bleed and break and lose the ones we love. But the old pain doesn't follow us here. Not the way it once did.

I know this because I've felt the grief, the loss, the terror trapped in the golden brown memory stones. I'm sure if he could experience it, he'd understand why people choose to part with those memories and start a new life here. The times I've been foolish enough to touch them, I've ended up in the healing chamber for hours. Weeping for people I've never met. Mourning lives I never lived.

Besides, at least they got a choice. They seek Lunaris. Choose to live here. We never did. We were children when we arrived alongside twenty-three other orphans, all under sixteen. Too young to have manifested our gifts. Too young to understand what we were giving up.

Jordi refuses to acknowledge any of it. Refuses to accept that we had no say in the matter. It's almost as maddening as him refusing to leave with me when I begged him to. Almost as bad as him standing here, showing me all the things we can't change about this place.

The way I see it, things could be worse. We could be residents of the town below, where the Council rules supreme. At least the Sages give us choices. The freedom to learn, speak our minds, hone our gifts. The Council forbids all of that, and then some.

I look at the map the Sages commissioned Jordi to draw, which shows the continent above as it appeared three hundred years ago. It's impossible to draw anything accurately without a current reference, and even the merchants from neighboring islands can't get past the Shroud to the kingdoms above. But at least the continent is there. At least someone acknowledges it exists.

The older map bears a small flame where the Temple of Ignata once stood. A monument to the goddess we're taught to revere. The one who lit the Undying Flames in every kingdom and appointed Sages to guard her ancient secrets. Most of the Veritas maps still honor that ground, but it's missing from the map Jordi recently finished.

The biggest difference isn't the missing flame, though. It's the Shroud. On the older map, it looks more like a shadow. Less like a wound and more like a fading scar.

And cutting through the darkness ... a path linking Lunaris to the land above. My heart climbs into my throat when I check the date in the corner. Circa 280 A.S. Twenty years ago. My eyes snap to Jordi's.

"What does this mean?" I whisper.

"Notice there's no mark where the temple once was." He points at the empty area in the forest and pulls out the map commissioned a few years ago. "This one has it."

He lays out more maps. One after another in quick succession. The flame appears and disappears across the years like a guttering candle. Finally, he sets his recent map beside the twenty-year-old one.

"There's nothing there," I say. "And as the Sages graciously pointed out when they extended my apprenticeship and granted you the title of *Official Mapmaker for the Veritas Order*, the temple was there until the Council demanded it be torn down, *as per the Veritas Treaty.*"

Jordi scowls. "You know Freida and Anala had nothing to do with your apprenticeship being extended two years. That was *all* Mother, and I will never understand why you continue to roll over and take her lashings instead of fighting back."

I scoff. If he knew the extent of my defiance, he'd be proud rather than annoyed. But it's best he doesn't. Mother's ire is a hurricane. I'd rather shove the people I love into its eye than let them be torn apart by its winds.

Two years. That's what she promised. Even she can't go back on her word. Not when I made her repeat it in front of the other Sages.

"It doesn't matter. My two years will be up at the end of the Moon Festival."

"I know, but you could speak to Anala and Freida—"

"No." The word cuts through the air. "Last time I tried that, I ended up teaching alchemy to first years. I just need to keep my head down until the Moon Festival is over." My gaze drifts back to the map. To the Shroud. To the path that shouldn't exist. "No matter how curious I am about this."

"What about the Undying Flame? Do you really think they moved it?"

I shoot him a bewildered look. "You've sat in front of that Flame enough times. You know it's there."

He slams his hands on the table. The raven and I both jolt. "You've sat in front of it! I've sat beside you, sick to my stomach, praying you heal quickly because they demand too much of your emotive gifts."

The words hit like a fist to the chest. I swallow hard. "At least we know we have gifts. The Council's residents wear their amulets day and night. They don't even know what they're capable of."

He scoffs. "*Most* of our gifts."

My spine stiffens.

"The year we arrived was a Reckoning year. I think that's why the temple isn't marked on it," he says suddenly.

The mention of the Reckoning gives me pause. I frown as I study the map again. It occurs every ten years and is the only time the curse on the kingdom of Tenebris can be lifted. It should be important.

Instead, our texts gloss over it like an afterthought. Maybe it's because the Reckoning is marked by the blood moon, and in Lunaris, the sky belongs to the clouds. We get eight hours of sun before the darkness rolls in. We've never seen the stars, and the moon is little more than a rumor, glimpsed through brief tears in the gray.

The only acknowledgment of the Reckoning comes at the Veritas Ceremony on the first night of the Moon Festival. But the festival is annual. It just happens to coincide with when the blood moon supposedly rises.

"Are you saying this is a Reckoning year?"

"Yes."

I point at the lighter Shroud on the twenty-year-old map. "And this was one too."

"The Shroud shifts. I've read texts about it. Old ones, buried in the restricted stacks."

I flip through the maps beneath. "Where's the one from ten years ago?"

"Gone. Forty years ago, too." His jaw tightens. "They're hiding something. Either the Reckoning itself, or they don't want us near the Shroud right now. Probably both."

"They have scholars who study the Shroud."

"From afar. And they're forbidden from going near it in the months before the Moon Festival." He taps the map. "During the Reckoning, the trees within the Shroud move. That's how the pathway forms."

"Wouldn't we have felt it? The ground would tremble."

His lips twist. "That's what Naima said."

I huff a laugh. "Goddess strike me, Jor."

"The laborers have seen strange lights in the sky."

"What kind of lights?"

"I don't know. I haven't—"

The door crashes open. The raven croaks. Two students barrel in, still wearing their maroon houndstooth skirts and white knee-highs, hands pressed to heaving chests. Soot streaks their faces. Twin expressions of horror.

I glance from Mara to her quiet friend with the blue hair. "What happened?"

"The Shroud," Mara gasps. "The guards … come quickly!"

I grab my healing kit. Jordi shoves the maps into the bottom drawer where I keep my things.

We run.

CHAPTER TWO

"Did you see Arlo anywhere?" Jordi shouts over his shoulder, nearly colliding with Lenora.

My mentor presses her back against the wall and lifts the cage in her hand over her head. The small white owl inside tilts its head to eye us curiously as we rush past them.

"What's going on?" she calls out.

"The Shroud!" I shout back. "There's a loose raven with a bandaged wing in room four!"

Panicked gasps follow us as we crash through the front door. We skid to a stop on the sidewalk. Thick clouds swallow the afternoon sky, and fog has already descended on the streets, turning everything beyond a few feet to shadow. Somewhere ahead, a shriek splits the air. The four of us look in every direction, then bolt left toward the road at the edge of the forest.

"Did you see Arlo anywhere?" Jordi repeats as we run. "Arlo the Undefeated, Master of—"

"Bow and arrows. No, we didn't," Blue says. "A woman with a House of Justice patch screamed for us to get help. There was a guard on the ground. He looked…"

"Lifeless," Mara finishes.

My stomach hollows. Arlo trains new guards at the border in the afternoons. If anything's happened to him, I'll kill the Sages myself. They're the ones who sent him and Cas to the Dueling Estate. They're the reason our friends wear the Council's uniform now.

"Margot went to the … Sages," Mara pants.

"Where did you see the fallen guard?" Jordi asks.

She points a shaky finger ahead.

"Near the Noxbridge Library!" Blue shouts.

I stumble when I spot movement in the fog. Jordi throws out his arms and halts. We crash into him just as a blur of Lunarian green and Veritas maroon breaks through the haze, storming toward us.

Their fear hits me first. Then their panic. A wave of it, slamming into my chest before I can brace myself. I fist the back of Jordi's cloak, squeeze my eyes shut, and fight to keep it out.

It's not your fear. It's not your panic. It's not your fear. It's not your panic.

It's rare for me to lose my grip like this. But with this many people, this much terror, and without an amulet to keep my gifts contained, I shouldn't be surprised. My mind snags on that last thought for a beat. We're stepping into the Council's territory and I'm not wearing my amulet. The consequences of that are nearly as terrifying as whatever we're running towards. The thought vanishes as people run past us screaming.

"Run!"

"A Shroud demon took a guard!"

"We're going to die!" Mara's cry near my ear makes my eyes fly open.

I turn, grab Mara's shoulders and tune out everyone else. "Do you have water on you?"

Her hands shake as she pulls out a glass container. I address both students. "Take off your amulets. Wet your hands like you learned in class. If anything tries to grab you, channel your water."

"What about compulsion?" Blue asks, yanking off her purple amulet.

"No. No compulsion. No serephony. Not with these things." I hold her gaze. "We don't know if they can use it against you."

She nods rapidly.

I set a hand on each of their shoulders and squeeze. "Go."

"Professor," Mara whispers, wide-eyed. "What about the two of you?"

"Don't worry about us. Get back to Veritas and make sure everyone stays inside. Go!"

They give a sharp nod, turn towards the fleeing crowd, and run. I let out a shaky breath and turn back to Jordi.

"Deny it all you want," he says as we rush down the sidewalk. "You make a good professor."

I scoff. "That siren's hair turned blue two weeks ago during my truth serum lecture. She still hasn't figured out how to go blonde again."

The sound of footsteps makes us freeze. We slam our backs against the brick wall and watch two men in labor uniforms sprint past. I'm about to push off the wall when a cold breeze skates down the back of my neck. I go rigid. Yank Jordi back when he tries to move.

"Wait," I hiss, staring at the darkening fog.

I watch it spread slowly, creep closer, and nearly jump out of my skin when Jordi's hand closes around mine. I squeeze back, the way we used to when we were children, when the dark felt like something that could swallow us whole. In front of us, the fog ripples. A dark shape moves within it.

I can't make out what it is, but I swear I see wings. We don't breathe. We don't move. We just watch as the Shroud creature drifts past us.

Once it passes, Jordi slides along the wall, pulling me with him toward the edge of the sidewalk. He lets go when we reach the light post at the corner, and I press my palms against it, trying to draw heat from the metal. I don't know what my fire could possibly do to those creatures, but I'd rather be overly prepared than not.

"The fog looks different here," Jordi says. "Does it feel different to you?"

Something in his tone makes my hackles rise. I press my hands harder against the warm metal. "I don't know."

"Maybe you can just check to see which way it's moving?"

Everything inside me stills. I gape at my brother and cross my arms to contain the shiver that rocks through me.

"Jordi."

"At least try to see if you can sense where Arlo is," he pleads.

I turn to the fog. Toward the Shroud that pulses somewhere beyond it. The thought of reaching out with my serephony. Of letting it sense me back—

I shake my head and look at him. "You don't know what you're asking."

"I'd do it myself if I could!"

The sigil on my chest burns. "Of course you would. You're reckless!" I jab a finger toward the fog. "Those things are attracted to emotive gifts like serephony. What if I open myself up and they sense me?"

He scowls. "Only one person made that claim! He didn't even explain why."

I look away. "Let's just keep walking. Maybe we'll find them."

"And if all we find are more Shroud creatures?"

I shut my eyes and exhale.

"I'm not asking you to channel those things." His voice softens. "I'm asking you to find our friends and pull back. That's it."

"Gods." I uncross my arms and shake them at my sides, trying to loosen the tension coiled in my muscles. "This is the stupidest plan you've ever had."

His eyes brighten. "I'll be right here. If you start acting strange, I'll shake you until you open your eyes."

I shoot him one last glare before I close my eyes and try to center myself. He wouldn't ask this if he truly understood. Everyone in Lunaris loves to act tough when they talk about the Shroud. But that's all it is.

Talk. None of them actually walk into the pit of darkness. Most won't even get near the Shroud mushrooms.

That's the thing about darkness. We're all drawn to it. We like to look at it, talk about it, and wrap ourselves in the safety of its mystery. But few are willing to fully immerse themselves in it.

Myself included. Especially when it comes to the Shroud, because it's not just the darkness that makes it terrifying. It's not even the creatures. It's the lack of life.

The silence. The stillness. The kind of stillness that people fear more than the darkness itself. On my next exhale, I let Jordi's energy fade.

I picture myself drifting down the street, searching each corner and alley. Nothing. I reach further. Still nothing. The only thing I sense is the Shroud's void. Its quiet hunger, lurking just beyond the edges of my awareness. Waiting.

All at once, I stop drifting. I'm standing at the edge of the darkness, right beside the Shroud mushrooms that grow just outside of it. The damned mushrooms that are partly responsible for the stagnant state of my life.

A whisper curls through the darkness. A gust of cold wind hits the back of my neck and slithers down my spine. I turn my head in that direction. Nothing.

The whisper comes from my right this time. Closer. Heart in my throat, I turn my head again. Still nothing. I shake it off and try to focus on finding Arlo's calm, steady energy, but there's another sound. Waves crashing against the cliffs. I decide it's enough. If this is happening anywhere near the cliffs, it means the creatures are moving in the opposite direction. I start pulling back, and then ... *there.*

Something ripples in the darkness. I follow it to its source and find myself staring into a pair of glowing eyes. A burst of warmth rushes through me, chasing away the cold. My body starts to shake.

My eyes fly open. I'm back on the sidewalk. Jordi's face is inches from mine.

"Ada!" He shakes my shoulders. "What happened? Look at me!"

I sag against him on the exhale. He catches me, both arms tight around me.

"Goddess strike me. You're shivering!" His voice is rough. "What happened?"

I swallow. "I couldn't find him. But the creatures ... I think they're moving toward the cliffs."

His arms tighten. "Gods. This has never happened before! I didn't think ... did they ... did you—"

"No." I pull back enough to meet his eyes. "Nothing happened. I'm fine."

He starts to apologize, but a shriek cuts him off.

CHAPTER THREE

The Shroud has torn through the Noxbridge campus like a storm. Through the fog, I make out students, staff, and guards wandering in a daze. Bags and books litter the ground. What I can see of it, anyway.

My breath hitches as I catch sight of the wall. One of the Council's four coats of arms has been painted over. Red letters streak down the stone.

Curiosity is a poison that must be contained.

I grab the back of Jordi's cloak and pull him toward the alley. We stop at the edge and stare. Jagged lines of red drip from each letter, over the closed eye that represents the House of Truth on the crest, and accumulate on the sidewalk in a sanguine puddle. The illusion it creates will probably enrage the Council more than anything else.

They're nothing, if not particular, about spilled blood. A gray parrot glides through the alley, the green amulet at its throat glinting. My grip tightens on Jordi's cloak as we watch it pass. No doubt taking mental notes to report back to the Council like a good little silent guard. Once it's gone, I turn back to the words on the wall.

Curiosity is a poison that must be contained.

I recognize the words. The Council gives every resident a book at the welcoming ceremony, and this phrase is on the first page. But seeing it painted here, like this, feels like a taunt. Which makes no sense.

Lunarian residents don't grasp the concept of indoctrination. They don't know about the Council's erasure or censorship. So who wrote this? I drift closer to the wall without meaning to. I'm so lost in thought that I don't notice the bag on the ground until I trip over it.

"Goddess strike me!" Jordi rushes over.

I turn, expecting him to help me up, and see the horror on his face. Not a bag. A body. I yelp and scramble back as I stare at the man. His green eyes are wide, and his mouth is open as if he was frozen mid-scream. A scream that never came.

"Oh my ... *Is he dead*?!"

"There's another behind you!" Jordi crouches and tears off his cloak. "Give me your supplies."

My head whips around. Another laborer. Same uniform. Same frozen expression.

"Supplies!" Jordi snaps, and I force myself to move.

My hands shake as I tear open the bag and set it between us. I examine the laborer I tripped over. No pulse. No blood. No signs of attack.

I glance up at Jordi. He wears the same confusion I feel. Without looking at me, he leans in and yanks off the man's green amulet. I hold my breath.

A year ago, Jordi became convinced our amulets were linked to our memories. That the memory stones were linked to the Shroud. He talked about it endlessly—at the library, the tavern, the dining hall—until we gave him enough reasons why it was impossible.

If it were true, we'd have flashes of memories every time we removed our amulets. We'd dream of our pasts. We don't. Even so, I'm not sure what good taking off a dead man's amulet would do. Nothing happens. I let out a breath.

"What could have caused this?"

"I don't know! How would I know?" I look up, pulse rushing to my ears again when I see two more fallen men, also wearing laborer uniforms, in the middle of the alley.

"*Gods.*" Jordi glances over his shoulder to follow my line of vision and looks at me again. "You interned at the Hall of Reflection. The Whispering Ponds. You must have seen something like this!"

"I've never seen anything like this!" I don't bother pointing out that while I did intern at those places, my specialty lies in avian creatures, not people. "What about you? All those books in the vaults?"

He frowns and shakes his head. "The closest thing I've read is the book about the Shroud and the memory stones. The one I tried to show you."

I open my mouth to respond, and shriek when the man in front of Jordi inhales sharply and shoots upright. His hands close around my brother's throat. I lunge forward, shouting, pulling at the man's arms. He doesn't let go.

"My daughter!" the man screams. "Give me back my daughter!"

Jordi gasps, clawing at the hands around his neck.

I let go of his arms and wrap myself around his torso

instead, pulling as hard as I can. A wave of desperation slams into my chest. Fear. Heartache. Not mine.

The man's arms drop suddenly, as the fight goes out of him. He falls limp, crashing back on top of me and knocking the wind from my lungs. Jordi pulls him off. I scramble back, chest heaving, and stare at the lifeless man.

"What ... was that?" I pant.

Jordi grips his throat, still staring at the body. "I don't know."

The fog is thickening around us again. I check the man for a pulse I know I won't find and look up in time to see Jordi yank off the next man's amulet.

"What are you doing?" I hiss.

He steps back. The laborer inhales sharply and shoots upright. This one doesn't attack. He looks around wildly, then his shoulders sag and he begins to cry.

"Don't let them take me!" he sobs. "Please. Don't let them take me!"

My throat closes when I notice the three marks on the side of his neck. The only indication of just how young he is. While age isn't a topic of conversation in Lunaris, new arrivals whose gifts just manifested are marked by three red dots on the side of their necks. The mark remains there for about a year, which means he hasn't been here very long and he can't be much older than seventeen.

There's a lot I disagree with in Lunaris, but I've always admired our ability to take pain away from asylum seekers. Yet something about the way these men woke feels wrong. Are they remembering their most painful memories? There's no way to know. But watching him, so young, so frail, the color draining from his face … I move toward him.

"What are you doing? Don't!" Jordi shouts.

I kneel beside the boy and grab his hand. Tears stream down his face as he looks at me. "Have you seen my mother?"

My throat tightens. I shake my head. I can't speak. I just squeeze his hand while he cries. Then he goes still. Slumps over. And I feel him vanish completely. My chest squeezes painfully as I let go of his hand and bury my face in my hands to breathe through the lingering grief.

"Temp." Jordi's voice is soft. I lower my hands and look up at him. "I'm not sure if there's a connection between the Reckoning and what I found, but—"

He inhales sharply. I frown as I stare at his face, which has gone slack, mouth hanging open. Everything slows. Something whizzes beside my ear and I watch in horror as a green-tipped arrow barely misses Jordi's head.

Then I see it. The arrow in his torso. Blood bubbling through his gray tunic. Another whoosh cuts through the air as a third arrow splits the fog, missing his head as he falls to his knees.

My scream rings through the air as I rush toward him, reaching him just before he slumps over. I cradle my arms underneath his head to cushion the fall before it lands on the cobblestone, and set my hands on either side of where the arrow is sticking out. Through my blurred vision, I see the blood that immediately coats my hands, and scream again, looking around wildly. It's impossible to see anything through the thick fog. His body jerks underneath me, pulling my focus back to him.

23

"Jordi!" I shriek as his eyelids begin to close.

Focus, Ada. Focus. Breathe. Stay calm. You can do this. You've done this.

But I haven't. Not really. I've done this to an alatus hit by an arrow. Not a human being. Not my twin brother.

A sob rattles in my chest. I force it down and grab my scissors.

They catch on the fabric once, twice, three times. I hurl them against the cobblestone and rip the material with my hands. Water first. Then alcohol.

He groans and arches off the ground when it hits his skin, but I do it again. I look at his face and nearly stop breathing. His eyes have rolled back.

"No. No!" I slap his face with a bloody hand. "You stay with me, you little bastard!"

He coughs. Good sign. I wipe around the arrow to assess the damage. My stomach drops at the sight of the black lines spiraling from the wound. Poison. *Oh gods.* I move faster, setting both hands on the arrow and pulling as hard as I can. Blood bubbles out of the wound. I soak a new cloth with water and alcohol and press it there. Jordi shakes again as I search my kit for the only thing I know can reverse the effects of the poison.

Finally, I find the small vial of purple liquid. I uncap it with my teeth and pour it into the wound. I wipe his clammy forehead, leaving a streak of blood, and pry open each eyelid. A sob rattles through me. His eyes are still rolled back.

How? This is the strongest anti-venom I make. Godsdamn it. I'm never making the poison that coats these arrows again. If Jordi dies because of this—

No.

I squeeze my eyes shut and go over every step. I did everything correctly. I know I did. His pulse flutters weakly beneath my fingers. My hands shake harder. I look around again, trying my damndest to open my senses to anyone nearby.

Shouts in the distance. People running. But nothing close by. No one can see me. I look down at my brother and make a decision.

"I'm about to sign my own death sentence for you, Jordan Elías, so you better not die." I squeeze his hand, shut my eyes, and breathe to center myself.

Centering was the first thing the Sages taught me when my gifts manifested. The second, once they discovered my natural-born healing gift, was to lock it away and throw away the key. After reading what happened to healers throughout the kingdoms, that's exactly what I did. I've been tempted over the years. Never enough to act on it. Until now.

Magic is an exchange of power between us and the gods. A lot of people in Veritas won't even remove their amulets for fear their gifts will feed the wrong gods. As if there is such a thing. Everyone knows the gods aren't merciful or benevolent.

But then, neither are we.

I take one more breath and start my plea to Ignata. I've never done it this way before, but I don't know how to heal someone, and right now, I need all the help I can get.

Please, Goddess Ignata. Creator. Kiskeya. Mother of all land. I beg you to help me heal my brother. Please. I don't know how to do this. I can't do this without your help.

Nothing. No spark in my chest. No tingling in my

fingertips. I let out a shaky breath and repeat it once more before I move on.

Please, Goddess Sulara. Daughter of Ignata. Goddess of day, health, life, and rebirth. I'm begging you to help me heal my brother. I'll do anything. Please.

Nothing. I was so sure this gift was linked to Sulara. It's healing. It has to be. But my second plea goes unanswered, and I'm forced to move on.

Just thinking about the next goddess makes the sigil on my chest flare. Not with defiance. Something else. A warning to stop. A dare to keep going. It feels like standing at the edge of the Shroud.

The thought almost knocks me off center, but I squeeze my eyes shut and concentrate harder.

Please, Goddess Mortiana. Daughter of Ignata. Goddess of night, time, and death. I beg you to help me heal my brother. I'll do anything you ask. Take on any task you give me. Just ... save him. Please.

Nothing. I repeat the words, shouting them inside my own head. And then I feel it. Discomfort blooms in my chest.

Not the warmth I feel when I summon my fire. This burns. Scorches. It spreads through me until my throat closes and my eyes sting. Unbearable. Intense. I struggle to cut the connection, gulping for air. And then I'm yanked underwater.

CHAPTER FOUR

I GASP AWAKE. My arms swing wildly, expecting water, but my feet are on solid ground. Dim orange lights flicker in the darkness. It takes a moment to realize where I am.

Or where I think I am. The cavernous tunnels beneath Lunaris. I haven't been down here in years, but the scent of burning eucalyptus is unmistakable. The Veritas torch binders use it.

I turn and stumble back when I find myself in front of a massive archway. I reach for the torch resting beside the column. I summon my fire, light it, and raise it to the stone. Ravens are etched into the columns.

Above, a massive raven head crowns the entrance. But the stone is colorless, so I can't tell whose temple this is. Mortiana's ravens are black. Sulara's are white.

Either way, one of them answered. Pulse roaring, I step inside the chamber and freeze. A pit sits at the center. Identical to the Undying Flame in the Temple of Veritas.

Jordi's words flash through my mind: *Do you really believe they moved the Undying Flame from its original location?* My heart pounds harder. He's been trying to tell me something. Could he have found the lost temple?

I shake my head. None of this makes sense. I was just outside the Noxbridge Library. Jordi was dying in my arms.

I have no choice but to approach the pit. Each step echoes in the vast chamber. Inside, I find pieces of chipped stone, ancient and crumbling. Beneath them, the faint pulse of an ember. Waiting.

I move to drop the torch inside. My hand trembles and stops right above it. The Undying Flame is never supposed to be re-lit by mortal hands. The texts are clear on this.

But nothing about this moment is right. Nothing about any of this is real. I've already shattered a dozen laws tonight. What's one more? I have to save Jordi.

I toss the torch.

A column of flame surges toward the vaulted ceiling, so bright it sears my vision. I lift a hand to shield my face and stumble back, trip, and hit the stone hard. From my elbows, I watch the Flame climb and writhe, casting wild shadows across the ancient walls. Then it settles. Contracts. Expands again. As if it's breathing. As if it's alive.

"Your name," it hisses.

My blood turns to ice. "Ada."

"Full name."

I try to push myself up. My hands tremble, slipping against the stone. I make it to my knees and wipe the sweat from my forehead, staring up at the Flame.

"Your. Name." It roars the words, impatient flames licking the vaulted ceiling.

"Ada Temperance Acevedo."

The Flame contracts. Settles. When it speaks again, its voice is almost soft.

"State your bargain."

Heart rattling, I sink back on my heels. The Flame towers above me, ancient and patient, and I have never felt so small.

I have no idea what I'm supposed to say. I've never made a bargain in my life. The Veritas Order forbids them. Stories of those who bargained with gods and lost everything are whispered like warnings in the dark.

"Your bargain," the Flame repeats. The words slither through the chamber.

"I want to ..." My voice breaks. I swallow and try again. "I need to save my brother. I'll do anything. Please."

The Flame swells. Contracts. A sound escapes it, low and rumbling. Almost like laughter.

"That is a foolish way to make a bargain with a god."

Cold dread pools in my stomach as the weight of my words settles over me. *I'll do anything.* I've just handed this creature a blade and bared my throat. But it doesn't matter.

There is no sacrifice too great. No cost too high. Not for Jordi. Desperation is its own kind of madness. And I am drowning in it.

The Flame sways, slow and hypnotic. Its heat caresses my skin like a warning.

"Such gifts in one vessel." The voice curls through the chamber, ancient and knowing. "Empathy. Serephony. Flame-summoner."

A pause. The fire crackles. Waits.

"And the one you've buried so deep you've almost forgotten it exists."

My blood goes cold. The air in my lungs thins.

"The Sages taught you to lock it away." The Flame flickers, and I swear I feel it looking at me. Into me. Through me. "But you cannot bury what you are, child. You cannot outrun your own blood."

It stills. The silence that follows presses against my ears like a hand over my mouth.

"Interesting." The word is barely a whisper now, soft as ash. "What are these Sages playing at, I wonder."

Something in its tone makes my skin crawl. As if it knows things about me that I don't. As if it's been waiting for me to stumble into this chamber all along.

"I don't—"

"Has your brother told you what he's done?"

The question lands like a stone in still water. I clasp my hands tighter. Shake my head.

"Speak, child," it roars.

I flinch. "No."

The Flame sways again, slow and entrancing. I feel myself leaning toward it without meaning to. Toward the warmth. The light. The answers it's dangling just out of reach.

"Would you like to know before you make this bargain?"

I force myself to look away. "It wouldn't make a difference."

The Flame flares. Shadows twist along the walls, reshaping themselves until an image bleeds across the stone. Flickering. Alive.

My breath hitches. Jordi. He walks down a hill shrouded in mist, his figure small against the darkness. He passes through an archway like the one outside this chamber.

Ancient. Waiting. He steps inside and moves toward a light that pulses like a heartbeat. The cave looks like one near the cliffs, but wrong somehow. Older. Sacred.

A beam of pale light pours from above, illuminating something floating over a stone platform. A blade. Long and slender. Hovering in the air as if held by invisible hands. Like an offering. I rise on my knees to get a better look. It looks like the ceremonial swords the Veritas blacksmiths forge for the Moon Festival.

Like a—

No.

Oh gods, no.

A god scepter.

Each god has one. A scepter forged from one of their bones. Some accounts claim they're swords. Others say they're keys to doors no mortal should open.

But every story agrees on one thing: the scepters choose their wielders. And the unworthy are cursed. Destroyed. Unmade. Not right away, but over time. I hold my breath as Jordi's hand stretches toward the light. The image shatters into smoke.

My eyes snap back to the Flame. It watches me. Waits. A predator savoring the moment before the kill.

"Would you still bargain for his life?" The fire crackles, sparks drifting upward like dying stars. "If you knew your brother was deemed unworthy? If you knew his blood was already turning black with the curse?"

The words carve through me. I think of the poison spreading through his veins. The black lines I watched spider across his skin. Was that the arrow, or something older? Something he did to himself in that cave?

It doesn't matter.

"Yes."

"Even if it means you'll be indebted to me? Even if the price is more than you can fathom?"

I don't hesitate. "Yes."

The Flame stills. The chamber falls so silent I can hear my own heartbeat, wild and desperate, echoing off the ancient stone.

"Why?"

The question cracks something open inside me. All the years of pushing him away. All the secrets and silence and distance I built between us because I thought it would protect him. And now he's dying in my arms and none of it mattered. None of it kept him safe.

My throat closes. My eyes burn. When I finally speak, the words come out shattered. "He's all I have."

"Not *all*," the Flame murmurs.

Soft. Almost tender. The gentleness is worse than the roaring. I wonder if it's referring to the Sages, my friends, or both.

"He's the only one who matters." A tear slips down my cheek as I say the words. "Please. I'll give you anything. Just save him."

The Flame swells. Once. Twice. As if breathing me in. As if tasting the desperation on my skin.

"The bargain is struck."

The words echo through the chamber, through my bones, through the hollow place in my chest where my heart used to be. For one fleeting moment, relief crashes over me. Jordi will live. Whatever this costs, whatever I've promised, he will live.

But the Flame isn't finished.

"I do not heal, child." Its voice drops to something low and ancient. Something that has watched civilizations rise and crumble to dust. "I take. That is my nature. That is all I have ever been."

The fire flickers. Shadows claw up the walls.

"You must seal this yourself."

"I ... but I don't know how—"

"You do." The words coil around me like a serpent, soft and suffocating. "You've always known. You simply chose to forget. Chose to bury the truth so deep you convinced yourself it wasn't there."

The Flame sways. I sway with it. I can't look away. Can't move. Can't breathe. The heat wraps around me like arms pulling me under.

"Return to him. Use what you've buried. Show me you're worthy of the debt you now carry."

"What do you—"

"My warrior will arrive soon." A pause. The flames dance, almost playful. Almost cruel. "To collect."

My eyelids grow heavy. The chamber blurs at the edges. I fight it, but the warmth is spreading through my limbs like honey, like poison, dragging me down into something soft and dark.

It doesn't matter. Jordi is safe. I saved him. I—

"You will save your brother." The voice is distant now. A whisper from the bottom of a well. "I never said he was safe."

I try to speak. Try to scream. My lips part but nothing comes out. I am frozen. Trapped in my own body as the darkness creeps in from the edges of my vision.

"Safety is an illusion, child." A hiss. A caress. A curse. "You, of all people, should know that by now."

I reach for the Flame. For answers. For anything. And the darkness rushes in and swallows me whole.

I gasp awake.

Cobblestones beneath my knees. Fog pressing in from all sides. My hands are still pressed against Jordi's wound. His blood is warm, bubbling beneath my palms.

His chest isn't moving. *No. No, no, no.* We made a bargain. I gave everything. I—

You've always known. You simply chose to forget. Use what you've buried.

The Flame's voice echoes through me like a command. Like a key turning in a lock. I squeeze my eyes shut. Take a breath. And stop fighting.

I reach for the gift I've kept locked away my entire life. The one the Sages forbade me from using. The one that guarantees my death in all eight kingdoms. I picture the box I've kept it in.

Rusted. Forgotten. Buried in a box in the darkest corner of my mind, my chest, deep in my gut where no one would ever find it. Where I convinced myself even I couldn't reach it.

Heat slams into me as I tear the box open. Not the

familiar warmth of my fire gift. This is different. Deeper. Older. Like something that has been sleeping inside me since before I was born, waiting for this moment. Waiting to be set free.

Like before, when I begged the goddess for help. But this time, I don't fight it. I let it consume me. Flames lick through my chest. Spread through my arms. Down to my fingertips. Up my throat. And finally, into my eyes.

They burn as if I'm staring directly into the sun. The world turns white and gold and blinding, and I can't tell if I'm screaming or if the sound is coming from somewhere else entirely. Beneath my fingers, I feel everything. The poison spreading through Jordi's veins.

His heart stuttering, slowing, giving up. The darkness traveling through his blood, claiming him inch by inch. And I pull. I pull, and pull, and pull. The poison resists, clings to his veins like it belongs there, like it wants him. I pull harder.

My eyes burn brighter. The heat roars through me, a wildfire tearing through me. Through the whooshing in my ears, I hear myself screaming. But I don't stop. I can't. I keep pulling until something shifts.

Jordi's chest heaves. Once. Twice. He coughs, a wet, ragged sound that might be the most beautiful thing I've ever heard.

My eyes fly open. I blink rapidly, the world swimming back into focus. The black veins are fading from his skin, retreating like shadows from the dawn. He's breathing. He's alive.

My entire body is trembling. I feel hollow. Empty. I look down at my hands and shake harder when I see that I'm covered in black, from the tips of my fingers up to my elbows. It's the last thing I see before my world tilts sideways and everything goes dark.

Like everyone else on this island, I have no memories of the five years of life before I arrived here. I've searched for them. Clawed at the edges of my mind, desperate for even a glimpse of *before*. But the furthest I ever go is waking up at the Veritas Estate, turning my head, and finding Naima and Margot asleep in their beds beside me.

But this time, something is different.

This time, I remember.

I remember opening my eyes to three faces hovering above me. The Sages. Their expressions tight with something I didn't understand then. Something I'm not sure I understand now.

"Are you sure this is them?" Mother's voice. Sharp. Urgent.

"I'm positive," Anala the All-Seeing responds calmly.

"How could she have survived this wound?" Mother asks. Beneath the sharpness, I see something else. Something that might have been fear.

"How could any of these children have survived the Shroud on their own?" Freida the Hunter asks.

A pause.

"Who says they did?" Anala replies.

"What are you saying?" Mother hisses.

Anala leans closer. Her fingers brush my chest as she speaks in a language I don't recognize. Ancient. Guttural. The words scrape against my ears like stone against stone.

Mother gasps. "How is that possible?"

"The Reckoning," Anala says simply. Her eyes meet mine, and I swear she knows I'm listening—knows I'll remember this somehow. "They were chosen. Sent for the Reckoning."

My eyes fly open.

I'm lying in a hammock. The familiar sway of it. The familiar scent of herbs and smoke and something faintly sweet.

The healing chamber. I'm back at the Temple of Veritas.

My body feels heavy. Wrong. Like it belongs to someone else. I turn my head slowly, and my gaze lands on the Undying Flame at the center of the room. It flickers. Dances. And for a moment, just a moment, I swear it's watching me.

Safety is an illusion.

The words drift through my mind like smoke.

As my eyes grow heavy again, as the darkness pulls me back under, I can't help but wonder who the Sages have been idolizing this whole time.

And what, exactly, did they raise us to become?

CHAPTER FIVE

I smell it before I see anything. Eucalyptus. The metallic tang of burning torches. The familiar warmth of hot stones seeping into my bones.

The healing chamber. I'm in the healing chamber. I keep my eyes closed, clinging to the darkness behind my lids. If I don't open them, I don't have to face what I've done. I don't have to remember. But then a memory creeps in. The Flame.

Use what you've buried.

My eyes fly open. I stare up at the shadows dancing along the vaulted ceiling, my heart pounding so hard I can feel it in my teeth. How long have I been here? Who brought me? What do they know?

I lift my hands to rub the sleep from my eyes. And freeze. My fingers are stained black. From the tips down to my knuckles, as if I dipped them in ink.

That only happens when I make memory elixirs, and I haven't—

The rest of the memory slams into me like a fist. Jordi. The arrow in his torso. His blood, hot and slick beneath my palms. The black veins crawling through his skin. The heat building behind my eyes until I thought they would burst into flames.

And then ... his wound closing. Skin knitting together beneath my fingers like it had never been torn at all. A dull ache pulses beneath my ribs. I suck in a breath as I press my hand to my own torso, to the spot where the arrow pierced my brother.

So that's how it works. I don't just heal. I take. The wound. The pain. The poison.

I instinctively set my hand against the much older scar on my torso. The one that's been there as far back as I can remember. That I have no memory of getting. I shake away the thought and try to focus on what matters now. Jordi is alive.

But I can't ignore the black stains on my hands, or that I'm lying in the Veritas healing chamber wearing a gray shift dress that isn't mine, smelling of the floral soap the Veritas Order makes. Someone brought me here. Someone undressed me. Someone saw.

Goddess strike me. The Sages. There's no way they don't know about this. I squeeze my eyes shut again, willing the world to disappear. I can be banished for this.

Expelling a breath, I open my eyes again. The pendulum clock on the far wall reads five o'clock, but through the small window near the ceiling, the sky is nothing but thick gray clouds. It could be dawn. It could be dusk. In Lunaris, it's impossible to tell.

It doesn't matter. I need to get out of here before someone comes. Swinging my legs over the hammock takes more effort than it should, but I manage to plant my feet on the ground without triggering the bells hooked to the ropes.

My eyes land on the pair of cloth maroon slippers with the gold Veritas signet embroidered on them and the folded pieces of paper beneath them. I grab everything and tiptoe toward the back of the chamber.

The mosaic map of Lunaris sprawls across the back wall—ancient tiles worn smooth by centuries of secrets. My eyes snag on the onyx temple in the upper corner. The object of my brother's obsession. My chest tightens.

I can't think about Jordi right now. I can't think about any of it. I press down on the temple. Wait for the click. Slip inside the wall. Darkness swallows me.

Veritas isn't as ancient as Lunaris or its labyrinth of tunnels, but the Sages built it with the same bones. The same secrets. Passages that snake through the buildings like veins, hidden from the eyes of anyone who doesn't know where to look.

I stand in the darkness for a moment before I summon a small fire in my palm. It sparks to life immediately thanks to the warmth of the hot stones that hum beneath my skin. The flame casts long shadows against the narrow area as I reach for the latch that leads into the hall. I close my fist around the fire as I step into the dim orange glow and start walking.

Voices bleed through the stone. I freeze, heart climbing into my throat as I press against the wall and squint into the peephole beside the next latch. The domed rotunda yawns open below me. At its center, flames lick the edges of a stone pit—a replica of the Undying Flame that burns in the healing chamber I just left.

The curved seats are nearly full. A sea of maroons and dark grays and golds, Moon Festival finery catching the firelight like scattered jewels. I search the crowd for familiar faces, for Naima or Margot, but before I can find them, the chatter in the room stops.

My gaze snaps to the top of the chamber. Freida the Hunter steps into the firelight first. Veritas armor clings to her towering frame—maroon cloth draped over leather and iron plates. Her fiery red hair is wound into two thick braids pinned behind her elegant, pointed ears. She surveys the room the way a predator surveys a field of prey.

Anala the All-Seeing glides in behind her. Her maroon gown flows like dark water, gold flowers embroidered across the fabric catching the light with every step. Her thick dark hair crowns her head in an intricate braid, and her eyes sweep the room as if she can see through every wall. Every secret. Every lie. I barely breathe as I watch Mother appear.

She's wearing a dark green gown. The Council's colors. She wears a variation of these gowns every time she meets with them, which is more often than not these last few years. Gold armor caps her shoulders in the shape of wings, but unlike the legion's ceremonial flourishes, hers taper into razor-sharp points.

The kind that could impale with a careless turn. Her corset is forged from the same gilded metal, cinching her waist before giving way to a skirt that pools like spilled ink across the stone floor. The Sages taught us that to understand the world, you must understand power. How it moves. How it breathes. How it makes people kneel without ever asking them to.

Anala doesn't need her gift of foresight to make everyone in this room second-guess their own thoughts. Freida doesn't need her stature or her shrewd, warrior's eyes to make them wither. And Mother doesn't need her sharp tongue.

They certainly don't need theatrics to remind everyone that they're in charge, but they use it anyway. They use everything from their posture—shoulders back, chins held high—to where they stand in a room, underneath lights that help accentuate their sharp cheekbones and arched ears. The Council does the same, of course, but they hide behind propaganda and carefully constructed lies.

The Sages don't hide. They take every awful thing that's ever been said about them and use that as well. They wield weapons out of the narratives meant to destroy them.

"I'll get right to it." Mother's voice cuts through the silence. "This year's Veritas Ceremony will be postponed until further notice."

Gasps ripple through the chamber. Whispers rise like smoke.

"I also want to address the legion guards some of you have seen near our borders." She pauses, letting the dread settle. "They will not set foot inside Veritas. The treaty stands. They will remain in their territory."

Another wave of whispers. Mother silences it with a look.

"Yes, Tilda?"

"Any news on Ada and Jordan?" she asks, "Are they still recovering?"

"They are both perfectly fine."

"Then why is Jordi at the Hall of Reflection instead of the Whispering Ponds?"

I go still. The Hall of Reflection is run by Veritas healers, but it's primarily for the Council's guard and the duelers. Veritas residents always go to the Ponds.

"Jordan doesn't require the Whispering Ponds," Mother says smoothly. "He's resting at the Hall alongside a few others recovering from minor injuries."

Minor injuries. I exhale a relieved breath.

"Are you going to address what I saw Ada do?" Ronnie's voice slices through the chamber. My breath catches. "I know what I saw! I saw her heal him!"

The gasps that follow are deafening. Whispers crash against the domed ceiling like waves against rock. I press my palms flat to the stone wall, lowering my head, willing my heart to slow. Ronnie has always had it out for us, but hearing the accusation, watching his envy take shape like this ...

All at once the room goes silent. I look through the peephole and see the Sages' eyes flash silver, like blades catching the light before it strikes. It's what happens when their emotions slip past their iron control.

The room seems to hold a collective breath when Freida steps forward. Her footsteps thunder across the stone floor as she crosses to Ronnie's side of the chamber. Everyone on that side of the room shrinks back when she stops in front of them. My own shoulders stiffen.

"Ada is an alchemic healer," she says quietly. "She carries potions with her at all times. That is what she used on Jordan's wound." She leans closer to Ronnie, and I watch him flinch. "I suggest you stop making dangerous accusations, Ronald. Unless you'd like to discuss the implications further. With me. Alone."

"We all know how much you hate us!" Naima's voice

rings out from across the chamber, sharp and furious. "But to accuse her of that is low, even for you!"

My throat tightens at the sound of her defense—at the fire in her voice, the loyalty. Murmurs of agreement ripple through the crowd. Another housemate of ours speaks up in agreement. Those of us who were raised at the Veritas Estate should have forged unbreakable bonds, but the Sages only chose seven of us to mentor and a few of the others, like Ronnie, never seemed to forgive us for it.

"That's enough!" Mother's voice is a whip crack. "Ronald, I will see you after I'm finished."

He says nothing.

"Details about the Moon Festival will be in the daily announcements. But there is one final matter—the reason I called you here," Mother says as her gaze sweeps through the room. "The Council will be holding a speech at the square shortly. Everyone is expected to attend. That includes all of us in Veritas."

More gasps. More whispers. The dread in the room thickens like fog.

Mother sighs. "Yes, Margarita?"

I press my face harder against the wall as I try to find Margot in the chamber.

"Bas says the Council is looking for whoever's been leaving messages on the walls," she says. "He mentioned a potential uprising."

Freida scoffs. "Bastian said this?"

"He says they're calling them renegades."

"And what was your part in this conversation?" Mother asks sharply.

"I asked him what he meant by uprising."

"You don't know what the word means? Should we be concerned about your education?"

A lesser person would crumble or stay silent, but Margot was one of the seven the Sages chose to mentor. Worse, like me, she's one of the few who have defied them. She's used to Mother's ire. I can't help but smile when I hear her voice grow stronger.

"I know what it means," she says. "I just don't understand why they're using it—especially when the messages are just the Council's own manifesto."

"Mocking the Council's manifesto," Mother corrects. "Which they view as a threat."

"I'm concerned about our residents," Margot responds. "You said the guards will stay outside our walls. But Bas says they might send them in. To take people for questioning."

The words land like a blow. I inhale sharply—so does everyone else. Then the chamber erupts. Voices rising, overlapping, crashing against the domed ceiling.

"Enough!" Mother's voice cuts through the chaos. "Our residents, Margarita? Do you remember what I said to you when you decided to go behind our back and add your name to that marriage list?"

Margot's quiet for a moment. "Yes."

"What did I say?"

A pause. Then—"You said the moment one of us is appointed a legion guard to marry, our mouths are metaphorically stitched shut. We become the ears of the Veritas Order."

"Precisely." Mother's smile is a cruel, beautiful thing.

"Since you'll be married to a legion guard by the end of this year's festival, I suggest you start practicing now."

She turns to address the room again, and her voice hardens to iron.

"Their guards will remain outside our gates. Whatever uprising they discuss—whatever messages appear on their walls—is *not* our concern."

Voices swell again, but I've heard enough. I peel myself from the wall and keep moving. My legs are unsteady. My hands are shaking. The black stains on my fingers seem darker in the dim light of the passage, like shadows are seeping into my skin.

Memories crash over me in waves. Jordi's blood soaking my palms. The glowing eyes in the Shroud. The red letters dripping down the wall like fresh wounds.

The Flame's voice curling through my mind. *Use what you've buried.* The god scepter. The laborers. The way the Council's guards looked at us like we were already guilty of something. I run.

CHAPTER SIX

Something is wrong. I feel it in my bones. In the pit of my stomach. A wrongness I can't name, can't shake, can't claw out of myself no matter how hard I try.

I strip off the gray shift dress and stand before the bathroom mirror. The new scar glares back at me—a reddened slash across my lower abdomen. Jordi's wound. Now mine. I smooth healing elixir over it, letting my eyes fall shut as the soothing mix of aloe and mint seeps into my skin. When I open them again, my gaze catches on the other scar. The faded jagged line that looks like someone slashed me with a scythe.

A token from a past that simply exists with no memory of how I got it. Most days I forget it's buried beneath the gold-threaded lines and sigils the Sages marked my skin with. For protection, they said. I glare at the sigil between my breasts that burns each time my anger rises.

I've learned to ignore that as well. I've learned to ignore a lot of things. I unfold the letters that were left underneath the slippers and read them while I dress.

Temp—

I'm sure you'll worry when you wake, so a few things: your purple potion worked. They're keeping me at the Hall to make sure the toxins are "fully out of my system." (They are. But they want me to rest, just in case.)

Anala says we're expecting more visitors than usual for the festival. The inns will fill quickly, so I told Draven his friends can stay in my quarters until his guest rooms are ready. If they're anything like him, you won't even notice they're there.

I love you, J

I pull on my black stockings, slip into the short maroon-fringed dress, and reach for the next letter.

Temp—

Arlo says you're still sleeping. It's been two days. We're worried.

I'm still at Reflection—long story. I need to see you before Constantine's speech at the square.

—J

P.S. Give Draven the books in my bag if you get a chance.

Two days.

I stare at the words. Then at my hands. The black stain has faded. Only my fingernails remain darkened, the way they've been ever since the Sages tasked me with making the memory elixirs.

Two days. I was asleep for two days. I pull my hair into a quick ponytail and clasp my amulet around my neck. The Hall of Reflection sits on the border between Veritas and Lunaris, and I don't want to risk going over there without it again.

When I glance back at the letter, the words are gone.

Godsdamn it. I unclasp the amulet. Watch the words bleed back onto the page. Jordi refuses to write on regular paper.

He's convinced the Council will find it. As if he's plotting some elaborate coup. Margot's words echo back. *Uprising. Renegades.*

I shake it off. My brother is many things, but he's not a fool. He knows something like that would get him banished—or worse. I unfold the last letter.

If I'm not here by the time you come, know this was meant to happen.

I saw it.

Trust me.

—J

The blood drains from my face.

I saw it.

If the Flame hadn't shown me that vision of my brother's hand closing around the scepter I might have overlooked those three words. Might have dismissed them as Jordi being dramatic. But I did see it. And this is Jordi. My hands grip the edge of the counter until my knuckles go white.

Foresight is not a gift men are given in this realm. It's why so many of them have enslaved women who possess it. Caged them. Used them.

Wrung visions from their minds like water from cloth. The only other way for a man to see the future is to bargain for it. And only one god is said to grant that bargain. But Lugal doesn't have a scepter. Not that I know of.

Did Jordi somehow use Mortiana's scepter to bargain with her consort? That's the only explanation I can think of. But *why*? Why would my brother willingly enter a bargain with the god of war? What could possibly be worth that price?

That thought is what finally gets me moving. I slide into my patent shoes, grab my cloak, my keys. Yank the door open and freeze. The sconces in the shared space between my quarters and Jordi's have been snuffed out.

Every nerve in my body screams as I turn to lock my bedroom door behind me. I try to reason with myself that maybe I didn't turn on the lights when I arrived, but I remember it vividly. I strain to hear movement, but there's nothing. A prickle of awareness skates down my spine and spreads through my chest. I may not hear or sense anyone in the dark, but I know something is there.

I feel them watching me. Heart in my throat, I reach for the iron poker beside the fireplace. I grip it tight and turn slowly, lifting the poker toward the dark like a blade. I feel ridiculous. But I'd rather look like a fool than die as one.

"What, exactly, are you going to do with that?" The voice is deep. Quiet. Laced with something that might be amusement. I go still. Then I tighten my grip and swing the poker into the dark.

"Who's there?"

Low laughter ripples through the shadows and curls into the pit of my stomach.

"Who is there?" I call out, my voice wavering. "What do you want?"

I lift a trembling hand and summon fire. The flame that answers is small and shaking. Pitiful. But it's enough to see the outline of a massive figure lounging in one of the wingback chairs at the center of the room. Long legs stretched out. Arms draped over the rests like a king on a throne. His amusement washes over me, unbidden.

"Nice trick," he murmurs.

I grip the poker tighter. "Who are you?"

He doesn't answer. Instead, every sconce in the room flares to life at once.

I flinch against the sudden blaze of light, blinking hard as my eyes adjust. When they do, I study the intruder. A dark hooded cloak swallows most of him. Everything but the sheer size of him.

He's built like Jacobi Draven, my brother's mentor, a former warrior turned scholar. But Draven would never sit like that. Sprawled in the chair like he owns it. Like he owns the room. Like he owns *me*.

The thought leaves a sour taste in my mouth. It could be one of his friends. If this is how he greets strangers, by lurking in the dark and laughing at their fear, we're going to have a problem.

My eyes dart around the room. Land on Jordi's satchel behind the chair. If the scepter is in there—No. There's no way I'm getting within arm's reach of this man.

I can't fight him. I'm not sure I can fight anyone. The Sages made us take combat lessons, so in theory I know how to punch, kick, stab. In reality, my skills lie in avoiding those things even when it comes to people my size.

"Who are you?" I bite out, keeping the poker pointed at him as I take a step toward the door.

"Why don't you have a seat?"

"Tell me who you are."

"Sit down, and I will."

"No." I take another step toward the door. "Who are you, and why were you sitting here in the dark?"

He tilts his head. Just slightly. Like a predator deciding whether to pounce. "Waiting for you, of course."

The poker trembles in my hands. I adjust my grip, but my palms are slick with sweat.

"What does that mean?"

A pause. Then, slowly, he rises from the chair. "I was sent to collect a debt."

The poker slips from my fingers. It clatters against the stone floor, and I don't move to pick it up. I don't move at all. I can't with the Flame's words echoing through my skull, over and over, drowning out everything else: *My warrior will arrive soon to collect your end of the bargain.*

I stare at my collector.

And he stares back.

CHAPTER SEVEN

"I DON'T LIKE TO REPEAT MYSELF."

There's no mistaking the quiet demand or the arrogance in his tone. Both of which I immediately don't like. I've dealt with enough arrogant merchants at the clinic and the taverns around Veneficia Alley to know how much of a pain they can be. I take a breath and remind myself that I don't have to like him. He's here to collect a bargain, not propose marriage.

"Who are you?"

"Sit and I'll tell you."

"I can't even see your face."

"What difference does that make?"

"I don't know. Just humor me."

His annoyance is unmistakable in my chest, but there's also a hint of amusement underneath that I'm unsure what to make of. I watch as he pulls the hood away from his face, exposing a dark, unkept beard and a curtain of wavy, unruly dark hair. From the little I can see underneath all of that, he has warm brown skin, full lips, a straight nose, and thick eyebrows that are currently furrowed as he takes in my attire.

I can't see his eyes since he has them lowered, but from what I can see, I know this man could never walk around here unnoticed. The Lunarian Council puts a lot of importance on physical beauty. All of their residents—especially their duelers and legion guards—are in top shape and always well-groomed, with cleanly shaved faces. Hairstyles are the only thing they don't seem to monitor.

Draven has long ropey locs. Arlo has straight blond hair. Casimir and Bastian have short hair. Either way, the man in front of me wouldn't qualify as good-looking in Lunaris. The Veritas Order, by contrast, teaches that beauty is internal. Beauty lies in the mind, in the heart, and on the tongue. We portray what we feel, and thus, feeling beautiful makes us beautiful. It's a concept that can get tricky when dealing with delusional, arrogant people, of course, but the Veritas Order has a way of dealing with them as well.

When he finally lifts his gaze to mine, I stop breathing. At first glance, I immediately think of the golden brown memory stones that haunt my waking days and sleepless nights. But then something else comes to mind. I think of the golden sunrises I watched from the cliffs back when I still thought new days meant new opportunities. It's an oddly comforting thought.

Something akin to surprise flashes in his eyes when I decide to step away from the door and find out what he's here for. I'm smart enough to know I can't outrun a debt, especially one owed to a goddess. I pick up the things I dropped, set everything down at the edge of the table, and sit in the chair furthest away from him. Safety may be an illusion, but it's one I'll cling to as long as I can.

"What is your name?" he asks once I'm situated.

I clear my throat. "What's yours?"

The corner of his mouth barely lifts, but I feel a hint of amusement in my chest again. "Malachi. You may call me Mal if you'd like."

So proper. Maybe not like some of those merchants, after all. I sit with that information for a moment. The majority of the residents don't keep the names they arrive with. The Veritas Order is very particular about name choices, and I can't imagine they'd approve of any name that begins with *Mal*.

"Ada. You may call me Ada," I say after a moment. "What do you want from me, Malachi?"

"What do *I* want?" He raises an eyebrow. "What a question to ask a man like me."

His response gives me pause. I look away quickly. I remind myself that my carelessness with words was what got me into this situation to begin with, so I need to be very careful with what I say and limit my questions. Something bitter flares in my chest, beckoning my attention back to his face.

"I can taste your fear," he comments.

"I can feel your disgust," I shoot back and bite my tongue, but it's too late to take the words back.

Shrewd golden eyes narrow and study me for a long moment. His eyes remind me less of the memory stones and sunrises now and more of an eagle with its sights set on its prey.

His lip curls. "You're an empath."

I bristle at the disapproval in his tone, and get angry at myself for my reaction. Empaths are always ridiculed for being "too emotional," which is ironic, considering we shoulder the weight of everyone else's feelings.

"You're not supposed to talk about gifts," I snap.

He raises an eyebrow. "Why not?"

I can't say I'm entirely surprised by the question. There's no way a man this size could escape the guards who welcome new ships by the docks. There's also no way they'd let him walk out of the House of Justice looking the way he does, though, which means he definitely arrived another way. The Shroud instantly comes to mind, but this is Mortiana's collector. She could have dropped him from the sky, or dug him out of the ground, for all I know.

"I'm not here to hurt you," he says after a moment.

My lips twist. "That would be more reassuring if you'd knocked on the front door."

He studies my face. "Why can't I ask about your gifts?"

"If you'd gone to the House of Justice, which you obviously didn't, you'd know the mention of gifts is forbidden in Lunaris. Everyone receives a crystal amulet to wear that prevents them from using their gifts here."

He straightens in his chair. "Magic is forbidden? How long has it been that way?"

I shrug. "Since the Council deemed it so."

His brows knit slightly. "Who is the Council?"

My eyes widen. I know in my bones he's not some silent guard the Council sent after me, but I still look around to make sure I'm not being watched. It's nonsensical paranoia. The Council doesn't even know I exist. Up until the day Jordi was given his apprenticeship with the Keeper of the Vault, the Sages forbade us from stepping foot in the Council's territory at all.

My eyes sweep the room from the small windows near

the ceiling, where the dark early evening clouds hang over the sky, to the kitchen. Finally, my gaze lands on Jordi's satchel and remains there for a moment. Could he have already gone through it? Probably. My pulse races as my eyes dart around each crevice of the room again. It occurs to me that this is how the Council's residents live every day. Looking over their shoulders and not fully trusting the people around them.

"I already told you I'm not here to hurt you," he says gruffly.

His obvious annoyance makes my sigil flare and straightens my spine.

"I'm sure this will be difficult for you to believe, being favored by the goddess of death and looking like that." I wave a hand in his direction. "But you're not the most fearful presence in Lunaris. Why don't you just tell me how to repay my end of the bargain?"

He stares at me for a moment. "Who is the Council?"

Without knowing anything about him, I know I'm going to be stuck here for hours if I decide to answer that question. He's very obviously an outsider. One who doesn't know anything about this place and will surely have countless questions. It's not uncommon whenever we get new visitors during the Moon Festival.

It's worse, since, unbeknownst to them, the amulets they wear during the festival make it so that the moment they leave, their memories of this place begin to fade. The merchants are spared from that fate since they only stick around Veritas. But the festival guests don't know any better, which makes them incredibly annoying to deal with since they ask the same stupid questions every single time they visit. My knee starts bouncing as I try to figure out what I can possibly say to get out of this.

"Can we do this later?" I finally blurt out.

"No."

Again, my spine stiffens. "Look, I know the gods don't wait for anything, and I mean no disrespect to Mortiana, nor am I trying to make excuses or get out of my debt, but I really need to—"

"No."

I blink. "You didn't even let me finish speaking."

"The answer is no."

"But you haven't even … you didn't let me … you haven't even heard my argument!" I sputter.

"I don't need to. The answer will still be no. I do not have the time nor the patience to continue this later."

A sharp laugh leaves my lips. "*You* don't have the time or the patience?"

"Who is the Council?" The quiet demand makes the hair on the back of my neck stand up.

I bite my tongue as the faint remnants of the compulsion vibrate through my chest. Someone else may not have noticed, but I was raised around too many sirens and endured too much training not to recognize it. And Malachi … the way he just used it, he either didn't mean to *or* is so powerful that people don't typically notice.

"That won't work on me."

He merely stares.

"The compulsion." I swallow. "It won't work on me."

He clears his throat, frowns, and glances away

momentarily. In the time it takes him to regroup, I decide to answer his questions so I can get out of here quickly.

"The Council is a group of people who have been in charge of Lunaris for the last forty years, give or take."

"Give or take?"

"The Veritas Treaty was signed forty years ago, so I guess it's been that long."

"Who is the treaty between?"

"The Lunarian Council and the Sages of Veritas."

"So Lunaris is ... split between them?"

"Yes, but they work together." I glance at the clock, knee bouncing incessantly. "Look, I don't mind answering your questions, but this is a complicated topic and I really need to leave."

"Is magic also forbidden in Veritas?"

My jaw clenches when he doesn't even acknowledge what I said, but I answer anyway. "No. That only applies to the Council's territory."

He nods like he expected that answer, which makes me think he must know about the Sages, at least. I guess it's not surprising since there are Sages in each kingdom and everyone knows about them and the Veritas Order. I'm about to say once more that I need to leave, but he pins me with a hard stare.

"And their residents accept that?"

I take a breath and expel it slowly. "They don't know any better. The Council banished mention of the gods and the gifts they grant us with. Their residents are told their amulets are what keep the Shroud from rotting our land and the creatures from coming in, so they wear them at all times."

He stares at me for a long moment as he processes that. "How can no one challenge them? Are they claiming to be regents?"

I frown. "What do you mean?"

"Are they claiming the king gave them the power to act on his behalf?"

I search his eyes. How could the goddess' collector not know the answer to *that*?

"There is no king here," I say after a moment. "In Veritas, the monarchy is mentioned, of course, but we mostly focus on ancient civilizations. I doubt the Council's texts mention them at all."

"What about the older residents? Surely they must challenge the Council's ignorant teachings."

I shake my head slowly. "No one in Lunaris has memories of their lives before they arrived here."

"How?" he whispers.

"Everyone trades their memories for asylum."

He stares at me, unblinking, for so long that I almost question if he's a demon, after all. But then I feel a low thunderous rumble vibrate in my chest, and I realize it's his anger. My breath catches as it builds, and I force myself to sever the tie to his emotions before it takes hold.

"They trade their memories?" he asks in a soft voice that sends a chill down my spine. He glares at me when I nod, like *I'm* the one working for the goddess of Noktemore and sneaking into people's private quarters. "Why would you agree to that? Why would *anyone*?"

My sigil burns as a swift wave of anger rushes through me. It's on the tip of my tongue to tell him that I didn't have a choice in the matter, but I think better of it. I don't have to defend myself, or any of our residents' choices, to *him*. I glare at him as I stand up and start picking up my things.

"Safety, food, purpose. The promise of life in a perfect society. That's why."

A loud thump in my brother's quarters makes our heads whip in that direction. Somehow, Malachi doesn't make any noise as he stands up, but his large figure is impossible to miss in the corner of my eye. I hold my breath as the door to my brother's private quarters opens, and let it out in a relieved exhale when Draven steps in wearing a dark green cloak with intricate gold stitching. His thick eyebrows lower and his long locs sway as he looks between me and Malachi.

Finally, his gaze lands on him. "I told you not to leave the private quarters."

I gape at him. "You *know* this man?"

"He's a friend. Your brother said he could stay at his place for the time being."

"Ada was telling me some very interesting things about Lunaris," Malachi says, narrowing his eyes at Draven, who merely shakes his head.

"Not now, Bain."

My eyes fly back to my collector. "*Bain?*"

"It's my middle name," he says. "It's what my friends call me."

"*Oh.*"

Malachi Bain. *The Sages would never approve of that name.* But it certainly suits someone who works for the goddess of death. I look at Draven, wondering how much he knows about that, then at Malachi. And then I start pulling on my cloak and head toward the door.

"Have you spoken to Sara?" Draven asks behind me.

"No. I need to go see Jordi." I start putting on my amulet as I head to the door.

"Who's Jordi?" Mal asks.

"Jordi can wait. You need to see Sara. There's a lot happening that you don't know about. It may not be—"

"*She* can wait!" I snap, whirling around to face him as I open the door and let it rest against my shoulder.

"Very well." Draven shrugs. "Just make sure you don't go to the square."

That gives me pause, but I'm momentarily distracted by the man beside him. I return Draven's glare. "Instead of worrying about me, maybe you should make your friend look presentable. *If* that's even possible."

Malachi's brows lower. "Where are you going?"

"We'll finish our conversation later," I say and move to step out.

"You can't leave," he growls.

I freeze again and glance back at him. "I *can't* leave? There are many things you don't know about me, Malachi Bain, but perhaps the most important is this: I only take orders from a handful of people and *you* are not one of them."

With that, I let the door shut behind me and run to the stairs. If everyone is supposed to attend the Council's speech, this is the perfect time to see my brother.

CHAPTER EIGHT

The bridge is a nightmare. A sea of visitors clogs the path, their chatter rising around me like gnats I can't swat away. Most of them wear purple cloaks with winged serpents pinned to their chests. Lyrionne. They've likely been here before.

"Don't you find it odd that there are no children here?" someone asks.

I groan. Not that anyone can hear me over the noise.

"They're not allowed to have children," a man responds.

"Why?"

"To prevent overpopulation."

"Is it even an island?" someone whispers.

"Mind your mouth. They gave us strict orders," the man hisses.

I feel his eyes on the back of my head. I cross my arms tighter and keep walking past the visitors who have stopped to gossip about the river flowing beneath us. A small, vicious part of me wishes I could shove them into the River of Sorrows they're so fascinated with. Let them discover firsthand whether the curse is real.

I bite back a laugh, picturing Jordi's horrified face if I said that aloud. I can only make those jokes in front of a handful of people. The ones who know I'd never actually do it. I made the mistake of voicing something similar in front of the Sages once. They made me read texts about empaths who lost control and did terrible things. I never joked about it again.

"The man at the inn said they register their names and wait to be assigned a spouse," a woman says, her voice light. Amused. "Like a marriage lottery."

My jaw clenches as the sound of tinkling laughter rings out across the bridge.

"Good gods. They don't even choose their own partners?"

"Matched by temperament, apparently. And they never part, which is more than we can say in Lyrionne," another responds.

We reach the end of the bridge.

"Is that the Council's flag? I rather like it."

My stomach turns as I glance up at the dark green banner hanging from the building ahead. The fabric ripples in the wind, making the eye that sits inside the heart look like it's blinking. Beneath it, the words: *The Everlasting Endures Your Pain.* A shortened version of the full mantra: *The Everlasting endures your pain so you don't have to.* I glare at the eye one final time before I pull my hood over my head and break free from the crowd.

The alley swallows me, dark and narrow, the walls pressing close as I run into it. I skid to a halt as I round the corner and see a black carriage pulling away from the Hall of Reflection. I turn toward the building, ready to go inside, when a face in the carriage window catches my eye. My heart stops. Jordi.

I yank my hood down and run after it. "Jordi! Wait! Stop!"

The coachman glances back but doesn't slow. "Take it up with the Council!"

I stumble on a raised cobblestone. Keep running. "The Council? Where are you taking him?"

"To the Keep! As we told the woman inside, we're just following orders!"

"What orders?" I scream. I reach the carriage and slam my palm against the window. "Jordi!"

His head whips toward me.

He looks slightly better than he did the other day, but still not well enough.

"Godsdamn it! Stop the carriage!" I shout, forcing myself into a sprint.

My fist connects with the window. Jordi doesn't speak. He just looks at me with that tired, lopsided smile. The one he thinks is comforting. I hit the window again.

"Jordi! What are you doing?!"

The carriage slows as it nears the turn. It has to. The corner is too sharp. I slam both palms against the glass. The blond guard inside startles, then glares as he opens the window slightly.

"Stop this carriage! Now!"

"We have orders!" the guard shouts.

"Temp, it's okay," Jordi says, his voice calm. Too calm. "It's only a few questions."

My eyes snap to him. I open my mouth to scream, but something white glints in his lap. Manacles. His wrists are bound. I stumble.

"This is against the Veritas Treaty!" My voice cracks. I slam my fists against the side of the carriage. "Stop!"

"Take it up with the Council!" the guard shouts as the carriage turns onto the street.

I know I won't catch them. I know it's useless. But I keep running anyway, lungs burning, legs threatening to give out. Jordi looks back over his shoulder. Our eyes meet for half a breath. Fear flickers across his face. Then grief. Resignation. And beneath it all, determination.

Maybe that's why I stop.

I watch the carriage vanish into a wall of fog. Watch my brother vanish. The pressure in my chest builds and builds until I'm forced to double over, hands on my knees, and scream. The sound rips out of me.

Raw. Ragged. Endless. I don't know how long I stay like that. Gasping. Shaking. Replaying his notes. The vision of him grabbing the scepter. The look in his eyes as the carriage carried him away. His wrists in those strange white manacles.

It's almost as if he knew he'd be taken. As if he wanted to be. It doesn't make sense, but when it comes to Jordi … I don't know what to think anymore. I remind myself that he's a grown man, free to make his own choices, but gods, how idiotic can one grown man be? I force myself to breathe as I turn into the alley. And stop when my feet hit a red puddle.

My eyes follow the sinuous red lines to the words

scrawled over the Council's signet. *In the end, nothing will matter, except everything.* I don't recognize the phrase from the Council's pamphlets, but something about it tugs at me. The same blocky handwriting as before. The same strange x's dotting the i's.

I force myself to turn away and head toward the only place I can think of to look for answers.

CHAPTER NINE

I drift toward Veneficia Alley in a haze, barely registering the vendors setting up their festival tents, the bright fabrics and glittering wares blurring at the edges of my vision. My hand lifts in absent greeting as I pass familiar faces, but my mind is elsewhere. Lost in fog. Lost in the image of my brother's bound wrists disappearing into the mist.

My name cuts through the noise. I whirl around. Naima is waving from the far end of the alley, her dark brows furrowed into a determined scowl as she shoulders through the crowd. She glances back, speaking to someone behind her. My spine stiffens when I see the man walking beside her. An outsider.

Of all the impossible things I've witnessed today, this might be the strangest. The Sages raised us to fear outsiders, and none of my friends took that lesson to heart more than Naima. She'll befriend the occasional merchant who shares her features, hoping to learn something about where she came from, but this is different. This man is no merchant.

They share the same sleeveless tunics, the same muscular arms on full display. But that's where the similarities end. The outsider has fair skin and straight black hair pulled into a knot at the crown of his head. When Naima pauses to shoot a flirty smile at a woman in a purple dress, he rolls his eyes with the practiced exasperation of someone who has witnessed this a thousand times.

The familiarity between them unsettles me more than anything else.

As they draw closer, I take in the details. His tunic is black, longer in the back, cinched at the waist by brown leather straps that hold twin daggers at his hips. The hilt of a sword peeks over his shoulder.

Weapons. That's something he and Naima have in common, though she's always preferred wielding them to forging them. If they'd allowed women at the Dueling Estate, Naima would have followed Arlo and Casimir without hesitation. Thank the goddess they don't.

I've already lost two friends to the Council. I couldn't bear to lose her as well. When they reach me, I open my gift. Just a crack. Just enough to taste the stranger's emotions. Anguish and frustration, tangled together. And beneath it, fragile as glass, hope.

He feels me. Dark glittering eyes pin me in place, and the connection snaps shut like a door slammed in my face. I blink, startled. No one has ever noticed when I reach for their emotions. No one has ever pushed me out.

His lips curve slightly, amused by my reaction. I study him more carefully now, taking in the contradictions of his face: soft and sharp, delicate and dangerous, arranged into something close to perfection.

"My gods, Temp." Naima's arms wrap around me, pulling me into a fierce embrace. "We've been so worried."

I exhale and let my eyes fall shut, sinking into the comfort of her. The warmth. The steadiness. For a moment, I let myself pretend everything is fine.

Then we pull apart, and the words spill out of me. "Jordi's gone."

Her expression falters. "I know. We were there when the silent guards took him."

"Silent guards?" I search her face. "Are you certain?"

"I wouldn't have noticed if Kage hadn't pointed out the SiGA letters on their patches." Her jaw tightens. "I told them it was a violation of the treaty."

My gaze swings to the man beside her. He's watching me with a quiet smile, as if he finds this entire situation mildly entertaining, which is wildly annoying.

"Oh gods, I forgot." Naima waves a hand between us. "Ada, this is Kage Yoshioka. He rented one of Tilda's rooms that faces the forge."

I nod slowly as the pieces begin to slide into place.

"Kage, this is Ada. Jordi's sister."

His brows shoot toward his widow's peak. "You're Jordi's sister?"

My gaze snaps back to Naima, and she laughs, shaking her head. "It's a long story. He's Draven's friend. He was supposed to stay at Jordi's, but I convinced him otherwise."

Kage scowls at her. "You told me she was hideous and mean."

"She *is* mean."

"But not at all hideous." He turns to me with a slight bow and offers his hand. I take it. "It's a pleasure to meet you, Ada, though I wish the circumstances were different."

"Likewise." I study him a moment longer, thinking of Malachi, of Draven, of the tangled web forming around me. Then I push it aside and turn back to Naima. "They violated the treaty."

"That was my first thought, but we don't actually know what the treaty says about the silent guards. They didn't exist when it was signed."

I realize she's right. Back then, there were only the gray parrots with their glinting amulets, watching from rooftops and windowsills. SiGA came later. Around the time our gifts manifested, if I remember correctly.

"I can't believe they do this job without compensation," Kage says quietly.

My mouth twists. "They believe if they report enough people, the Council will notice them. Promote them to legion guards."

"Has that ever happened?"

"Never."

"Because they don't have the gifts the legion guards have?"

I frown. "What do you mean?"

He holds my gaze for a long moment, something unreadable flickering behind his eyes. Then he shakes his head. "It doesn't matter. I was going to stop those guards, but your brother told me not to get involved."

"It was like he was okay with it," Naima whispers. "Like he wanted to go. Why would he want that?"

I swallow past the tightness in my throat. "I don't know. But we can't just let this stand."

"What are we supposed to do?" She spreads her hands.

"The Council is at the square addressing the first wave of arrivals. The Sages will be with them all night."

"Can we go to the Lunarian Keep?" Kage asks.

"No," Naima and I say simultaneously.

"The Council isn't allowed to visit the Veritas Estate without permission," she explains, "And the Sages have made it clear we're not to visit the Keep, either."

He raises an eyebrow. "Even if they broke the treaty first?"

Naima and I exchange a look. I shake my head. "Even then. We'd need to speak to Arlo or Cas first. Or find one of Jordi's maps of the Keep and try to sneak in."

"You have his maps?" Kage's voice lifts with hope, and my eyes narrow.

"You said you're Draven's friend."

"I am."

"How do you know him?"

"We fought together in the war. In Vinadriel."

"Kage is here for the Reckoning," Naima says. "That's why he needs a current map of Lunaris." She laughs at whatever expression crosses my face. "That was my reaction as well."

I study Kage with new eyes. "What exactly are you hoping to do here?"

His chin lifts. "Lift the curse."

"He's dedicated his life to it," Naima continues. "Him, Draven, and ..." She glances at Kage.

"Bain."

The name lands in my chest like a stone. I was

expecting it, but hearing it spoken aloud makes it real in a way I wasn't prepared for.

Kage notices my surprise. "You know him?"

"He's ..." I clear my throat. "He's staying at Jordi's."

Kage's face transforms. The guarded wariness melts into something bright and almost boyish. "So he is here."

I stuff my trembling hands into my cloak pockets. "How do you know it's a Reckoning year? And why come here, of all places?"

"Because the sprites that mark the Reckoning led me here."

"The sprites look like red lightning," Naima adds. "They've been appearing every night."

My eyes snap to hers. "You saw them?"

She nods, her expression grave.

I press a hand over my pounding heart. Jordi was right. About the sprites, about the Reckoning, and probably about far more than I ever gave him credit for. I think of Malachi again. His golden brown eyes. His quiet arrogance. How can he be here for the Reckoning and to collect the bargain I struck with the goddess? The two don't fit together, and I can't ask Kage without revealing what I've done.

"Doesn't the blood moon mark the Reckoning?" I ask. "We don't even see the moon here."

Kage casts me a sideways glance. "You would have seen it ten years ago, if they hadn't kept you indoors during the festival."

My brows snap together. I look at Naima, and she nods slowly. "When our gifts manifested."

Ten years ago. The year everything changed. The year the Sages locked us inside and told us the outside world wasn't safe. A roar of cheers erupts around us, shattering the moment. Naima grabs my hand before I can process what she's said.

"We need to move."

CHAPTER TEN

"I can't believe you brought me to the square," I hiss as we shoulder past a sea of dark green cloaks.

The crowd presses in on all sides, suffocating, the air thick with perfume and anticipation.

"Everyone is supposed to be here tonight," Naima mutters back.

"Draven specifically told me not to come."

One of the Council's residents shoots me a silencing glare. I bite my tongue and keep moving. The crowd's attention is fixed on the man speaking from the stage. I can't see him, but his voice drifts over the square, low and honeyed. Together. Unity. Peace.

Naima leads us up a set of stairs, and we each claim a step overlooking the square. My eyes land on the man on stage. Constantine. Even from here, his presence commands the square the way a spider commands its web.

I've only seen him twice, both from a distance, but he's impossible to forget. His skin is pale as bone, his features so symmetrical they seem carved rather than born. Silver hair falls past his elbows, gleaming under the torchlight. He looks like the portraits of the old aristocrats that hang in the Veritas archives, the ones the Sages warn us about. The ones who ruled through fear and called it order.

He wears a dark green cloak with thick gold brocade at the shoulders, a matching doublet stitched with gold thread, and shoes polished to a mirror shine. Every detail is calculated. Every thread is a statement of power.

"This Moon Festival will be the biggest we've ever hosted," he announces, his voice carrying effortlessly across the square. "And the longest."

The crowd erupts in cheers. Constantine grins, drinking it all in. "Our usual esteemed guests have already arrived, most of whom are here tonight. But there are many more to come."

The gold ring on his pinky catches the torchlight as he gestures, the glint of a tiny amber stone catches my attention before I turn back to the crowd. I watch the way they lean towards him, their faces upturned like flowers seeking sun. There's something hypnotic about the cadence of his voice. Something that slips beneath the skin and settles there. It reminds me of a compulsion, but this is subtler. Softer. The kind of poison you don't taste until it's already in your blood.

"Of course, that means we must remain vigilant," he continues. "Any outsiders who enter without reporting to the House of Justice will be dealt with accordingly."

The threat lands softly, but it's a threat all the same. I scan the stage behind him. Freida and Anala sit in dark red cloaks, their faces unreadable. Mother and Draven are beside them, still wearing the green I saw earlier. The other two Council members flank them, their features obscured from this distance. I've never seen them up close. I'm not sure I want to.

I scan the crowd near the stage, searching for Arlo and Cas. For Malachi, so I can point him out to Kage. The handful of Veritas residents near the front stand out like drops of blood in a field of green. A few purple and pale blue cloaks cluster on the far side, visiting merchants or dignitaries from distant courts.

Every face is tilted toward Constantine as though he's delivering prophecy rather than the same tedious reminders they recite every year. *Wear your amulets at all times. Adhere to each evening's color theme. Duels at the amphitheater are free but require a ticket.* I could recite it in my sleep.

A flare of warmth blooms in my chest without warning. The sensation of being watched. I turn instinctively toward the field on the far side of the square, where three massive alatuses graze underneath the dark clouds above. Their wings stretch and fold in slow, languid movements, casting long shadows across the grass.

And there, standing near them, is a hooded figure. Tall and broad, still as stone. I can't see his face, but I know it's Malachi. And I know, with bone-deep certainty, that he's staring directly at me.

Naima's gasp yanks me back. I turn toward the stage and stop breathing. Casimir and Arlo step closer to Constantine wearing dark green coats with gold brocade at the shoulders. The same gold brocade Constantine wears. The same gold the highest-ranking officers of the Lunarian Legion are granted when they've proven their absolute loyalty to the Council. Gold wings. They've been given gold wings.

"Oh gods," Naima breathes beside me.

She sounds as horrified as I feel by this sudden promotion.

We knew it was a possibility, of course. We figured it would happen eventually, with the way the Council has taken interest in them. But seeing them in those uniforms makes it real in a way I wasn't prepared for. Murmurs ripple through the crowd. Gasps. A few scattered cheers and whistles from Lunarian residents.

"Most of you have had the pleasure of watching Casimir the Handsome and Arlo the Undefeated duel in our amphitheater," Constantine says, grinning as the crowd roars its approval. "I'm proud to announce that after years of loyal service, they have earned their gold wings."

Gold wings. The words echo in my skull. The gold wings are not just a promotion. They're a chain.

Once you wear them, you belong to the Council completely. You follow their orders without question. You hunt whoever they tell you to hunt. You kill whoever they tell you to kill.

Arlo and Cas have just become weapons. And the Council now holds the blade. The cheers are deafening. I press my hands over my mouth, unable to look away, unable to breathe.

"Their first task," Constantine continues, his voice cutting through the noise. "Will be finding the renegades."

Another wave of cheers. My stomach turns.

"Whoever is leaving these hateful messages on our walls, mocking our ideals and threatening our peace, will be punished." He steps to the edge of the stage, and his pale eyes seem to sweep the entire crowd at once. "There is nowhere on this island you can hide from us. We will find you. We will protect Lunaris!"

The words settle over the square like the Shroud itself, dark and foreboding and inevitable.

He gestures toward Arlo and Cas. "You've seen their skills in the arena. Come the final evening of the festival, anyone deemed a renegade will face their wrath!"

The crowd erupts. The sound is distant, muffled by the drumming in my ears. My gaze flies to the Sages. They're whispering amongst themselves, their expressions unreadable.

Mother's jaw is tight. Freida's hand rests on the arm of her chair, knuckles white. They didn't know. I'm certain of it. They didn't know this was coming.

I look at Arlo and Cas again. My oldest friends. My family, in every way that matters. Cas was my first everything.

My first kiss, my first heartbreak, the first person outside the Estate I ever trusted completely. And Arlo has always been as much a brother to me as Jordi. I would die for either of them. I thought they would do the same for me. Now they stand on that stage in gold wings, and I don't know what they are anymore.

When they became legion guards a few years ago, they swore their loyalty to the Veritas Order would always come first. They promised us. They promised me. But I've heard the stories.

The Council has ways of breaking people. Of twisting their minds until they see enemies in the faces of the ones they love. Until they believe betrayal is righteousness and cruelty is duty. I stare at Arlo and Cas, standing in their gold wings, and I wonder if I've already lost them. If I lost them the moment they stepped onto that stage.

CHAPTER ELEVEN

The three of us are split up in the current of people. At some point, I stop fighting and allow myself to move with the herd rather than looking for them. They'll go to Siren's anyway. It's where all the locals end up after the festivities, and where my friends and I hang out most nights.

I'm so lost in thought, replaying Arlo and Cas in their gold wings, that I don't realize I've been walking in the wrong direction until I find myself standing across from the northernmost bridge. I close my eyes and force myself to breathe. The universe, it seems, has other plans for me tonight. I swallow my irritation and decide to make use of the detour.

I stop by the clinic to check on the birds and grab the maps Jordi left behind. I'm not sure what Kage hopes to do with them, or why Draven hasn't provided his own, but my brother would want to help. He always wants to help. The thought of him brings back the image of his face in the carriage window.

That look of determination. As if he knew exactly where he was going and why. I don't know what he's up to, but I need to speak to the Sages. If anyone has answers, it has to be them. But then I remember the looks on their faces when Cas and Arlo were on that stage and Naima's words come back to me.

Between the Reckoning, the sprites, the blood moon we were never allowed to see, I don't know what to believe anymore. I hear music and people chattering nearby, but thankfully the bridge is empty when I reach it. I tip my head back as I walk, but all I find are the usual thick, dark clouds that coat the sky. Still, I stop at the center of the bridge and rest my hands on the parapet to scan over it again.

Nothing happens, but I stay a little longer, listening to the faint rush of water below, the River of Sorrows murmuring its secrets to the dark. I'm staring down into the darkness, thinking of all the times I met Cas here in the middle of the night to sneak kisses, when a flash of light pulls my gaze upward.

It vanishes before I can track it, but I hold my breath and wait. My breath catches when the lamps around me flicker, and again when a flash of red light splits the sky above the forest. At first, I think Naima is right, it looks like lightning, but when it disappears and returns, what I see are roots. Or branches clawing upward from invisible soil in the sky.

The light blinks out quickly and returns. Six of them now, larger, closer, burning against the clouds like wounds. The lamps around me stutter and dim. The sprites disappear and reappear in a heartbeat.

Bigger. Closer. My pulse hammers against my ribs as I stare. They don't look like roots at all now. They look like limbs. Like red-winged figures suspended in the sky, looking down at me.

This time, when the sprites disappear, they take the lights

around me, plunging me into complete darkness. I stand frozen. Barely breathing. Waiting for the sprites to return, for the lamps to flicker back to life.

Nothing happens.

I turn slowly. Every lamp is dead. The bridge, the streets, the buildings beyond. Lunaris has gone dark.

My hands tremble as I raise them and summon fire. The flames that answer are small and wavering. Abysmal, Mother would say. The memory of the word brings another with it.

The crack of a wooden ruler against my lower back, my stomach, my thighs, teaching me to focus through pain. My shoulders snap back. The flames grow taller, steadier, casting long shadows across the stone. I start moving, slow shuffling steps toward the end of the bridge, counting as I go.

Forty-seven steps from one side to the other. I've walked this bridge a thousand times. I'm already at twenty-three. Twenty-four. Twenty-five. Twenty-six. Something moves in the darkness ahead. I freeze.

My flames shrink and sputter as I sweep them left, right, then forward again. From the corner of my eye, I catch a ripple in the dark, but there's nothing there. I force myself to breathe. In through my nose. Out through my mouth. Focus. Then I notice the silence. The lack. Even the river has stopped flowing.

A light, cool breeze passes through. So light it barely makes the flames in my palms waver, but I feel it. The hairs on the back of my neck rise just before the stillness arrives. Fear seeps into me slowly.

So slowly that by the time it settles in my bones, my flames have already died. I shake my hands at my sides, desperate, as if friction alone could reignite them. But I'm not a match. I'm a conduit who has lost her focus. Worse, I'm a conduit who has lost her belief.

I squeeze my eyes shut and reach for my gift, but doubt floods in instead. Ignata. Mortiana. The Flame I bargained with. Which god have I been praying to all these years? Which one am I supposed to search for now? It doesn't matter. None of it matters if I'm dead. And if the Shroud creatures are near, death is exactly where I'm headed.

I force myself to focus. Find the source of the stillness. Figure out which way to run. A sob builds in my chest when I locate it. I swallow it down, careful not to make a sound as I clench my fists and open my eyes. A pair of glowing eyes stares back at me from the darkness. Then I scream. And run.

For all the stories, all the warnings, all the training, I am completely unprepared for this encounter. I scream again when something cold grazes the back of my neck, and trip on a raised cobblestone, but I keep running. Goddess, I don't want to make another bargain, but I don't want to die, and I'm not sure which fate is worse. As if one of the gods heard my thoughts, the lamps at the edge of the bridge flicker to life. Hope surges through me. Then the lights die again, and the hope dies with them.

"We remember you, empath," a voice hisses in my left ear, scratchy and wrong.

I scream and stumble. This time, I go down hard, hands and knees slamming into the cobblestones. Adrenaline forces me to push up, to keep moving, but before I can rise, a cold weight crashes onto my back. I'm slammed face-first into the stone.

The weight presses down, pinning my chest, my knees, the side of my face against the cold, damp ground. I can't move. I can't breathe. I thrash beneath it, trying to twist free, but the weight shifts and pins me harder. The sob I've been holding breaks loose as a whimper. Those glowing eyes appear inches from my face.

"You were ours to claim," it rasps. "You are ours to claim."

I try to refuse, to scream, but the sound comes out muffled and broken. Cold air slides down my throat, thick as smoke, choking off my voice. I brace for it to take my soul. It doesn't.

It just stares. The accounts say the Shroud creatures can be killed, so I assumed they were made of flesh, but the thing in front of me is all smoke and shadow. Formless except for the faint outline of a face. Soft features. Almost delicate. Almost beautiful.

My eyes fall shut as the cold sinks deeper. Into my spine. Around my heart. Through my lungs.

In the darkness behind my lids, I see everyone I love, flashing through my mind like pages torn from a book. Jordi's face. Hear Naima's laugh. See Margot's knowing smile.

Feel Arlo's hand squeeze mine. Casimir's arms wrap around me. Mother's stern expression. The arguments we've had, the words I never got to say aloud. Freida's fierce embrace. Anala's warm smile.

The thoughts shatter and suddenly I feel myself being pulled upward, outward, somewhere else entirely. Weightless. Untethered. Floating in a void that has no beginning and no end. Then, a flash.

My eyes open. I'm no longer on the bridge. I'm standing before the Undying Flame in the Temple of Veritas, warmth flooding my face, two hands clasped in mine. Anala's voice reaches me, distant but clear.

"Your gift is precious and singular. That's why you must stay behind closed doors, away from outsiders who would use it to harm you."

A memory. One I'd buried so deep I'd forgotten it existed.

"You were ours to claim," the voice scrapes through it, dragging me back. "You are ours to claim."

Another voice joins the first, layered over it like an echo. "We know what you are. What you hide. He unmade us with that gift." Cold fingers trace my jaw, and I shudder. "But you… you, healer, could undo it. You could undo him."

My heart seizes. They can't know that. No one knows that. Unless … unless they saw me heal Jordi? Ronnie did. But why not take me then? I open my mouth to scream, but the cold pressure on my lungs is too much.

"Ours," the voices hiss in unison. "Ours to—"

Heat punctures through me suddenly. My eyes fly open and I gasp as the warmth travels through me, thawing my lungs and flooding my limbs with strength. The weight vanishes. I shove myself upright.

The lamps ahead flicker to life, wild and stuttering. I run toward them. A cold tendril grazes my neck, and a massive shadow swallows my own on the cobblestones below. I stumble again. My knees hit the ground hard. Before I can rise, something wraps around my torso and hauls me off my feet.

I scream and kick, thrashing against the grip, but it only tightens.

"Stop moving!" a voice roars, and the sound cuts through my panic like a blade.

My entire body goes taut. "Mal … Malachi?"

He grunts in response. I twist, trying to see him, but he has me pinned against his side like a sack of grain, my back pressed to his ribs, my feet dangling uselessly.

"I said stop moving!" He whirls us around, and my scream dies in my throat.

Three pairs of glowing eyes hover in the darkness before us.

"What are you doing?" My voice is raw, shredded from screaming. "You need to run!"

"Shut up," he seethes, and begins chanting under his breath.

The words are foreign, ancient, a language I almost recognize but can't quite name. He's casting. I catch a glimpse of movement as he raises his other arm. A massive sword arcs into view, the blade longer than my body. Red and gold glyphs blaze to life along the steel, pulsing brighter with every word he speaks, until the weapon is glowing.

The air crackles with energy, sharp and electric, lifting the hairs on my arms and rattling my teeth. Then Malachi surges forward, toward the creatures, and my stomach drops.

I squeeze my eyes shut. An inhuman shriek splits the night. Then another. Then silence.

He pivots sharply and marches us off the bridge. When I open my eyes and look around, the creatures are gone. The streetlamps burn steady and warm. The fog has thinned to wisps. I sag against him, trembling.

"Did you kill them?" My voice comes out hoarse, barely a whisper.

"What do you think?"

The sharpness in his tone makes me bristle. "You can put me down now."

He scoffs. "And risk having to chase you again? Not interested."

"What?" I frown and try twisting again. "You just saved my life! Why would I run?"

"I don't know, Ada, because you're a fucking menace!"

"I …" I blink, momentarily at a loss for words. "Maybe so, but I'm not an idiot!"

"That's highly debatable," he mutters.

My spine goes rigid. Menace, I can accept. Reckless, fine. But an idiot? Absolutely not.

"You act like I wanted to be attacked! I just hap—"

He drops me without warning. I stumble, throw my hands out to catch myself, and hiss when my raw palms slam into the wall. I shove off the stone and whirl to face him, fists clenched despite the pain.

"What is wrong with you?"

"What's wrong with me?" He yanks his hood down and glares at me, golden eyes blazing. "What the fuck were you thinking?"

I open my mouth to respond and stop.

The scowling man staring back at me looks nothing like the brute I met earlier. The thick beard is gone, trimmed to light stubble that reveals a sharp jaw and high cheekbones. His hair is shorter, no longer wild but swept back from his face. He wears a navy blue cloak now, gold armor gleaming at his shoulders, a matching tunic molding to the broad planes of his chest. He cleaned up. He cleaned up well.

"Not that I mind you staring, but you'll have plenty of time to ogle me inside."

My eyes snap back to his face. "*Ogle*? The last time I saw you, I almost mistook you for a talking yak! I'm just making sure you're the same person."

He presses his lips together and cocks his head. "Right."

I ignore his skepticism and step toward the streetlamp, scanning the streets beyond the river.

"Who are you looking for?"

"My friend Naima." I glance back at him. "And Kage Yoshioka."

His entire body goes taut. "Kage is here?"

"He said he's here for the Reckoning." I turn back to the empty streets. "They should be at Siren's by now. Assuming they didn't encounter any of those creatures."

"If she's with Kage, she's safe."

"How do you know?" I look up at him. "Does he have one of those glowing swords?"

His brow arches. "I don't think Vida would appreciate that description."

"Who's Vida?"

"My sword."

"You named your sword Vida?" I almost laugh. "As in *life*?"

"It seemed fitting." He shrugs. "What is Siren's Call?"

"A tavern. Brothel. Gambling den. Dance hall." I point toward the docks. "Past the last bridge, corner of Veneficia Alley."

"And where will you be while I'm searching for this den of sin?"

"Home."

I should explain that I just need to change and clean my wounds, but something tells me he'd follow me upstairs, and I need a few minutes alone. A few minutes without his presence pressing against my senses like a hand around my throat. But instead of going in the direction I pointed, he turns towards my building.

"Where are you going?"

He stops. Turns. "You said you were going home."

"*I'm* going home. Alone." I cross my arms. "Why don't you just tell me what my debt is so we can get this over with? Then you can go find your friend and do whatever you came here to do."

He points at me, the gesture almost accusatory. "We are sticking together from now on."

"Why would we—"

The words die in my throat as he stalks toward me, his expression dark and furious, and I find myself backing up until my shoulders hit the wall.

"You could have died on that bridge." His voice is low, rough, barely controlled. "Do you understand that? Do you understand that when I heard you screaming, I felt like I was going to lose my fucking mind?"

My heart lurches. Confusion and something else, something I refuse to name, wage war inside my chest. None of this makes sense. Not his admission. Not the way my pulse quickens to hear it.

A thousand thoughts crash through my mind, but one

rises above the rest: the bonding elixir. The one I've refused to make for two years. The reason I'm still trapped in my apprenticeship, still under Mother's thumb, still fighting for a freedom that seems further away with every passing day.

Logically, the connection makes no sense. But it's the only explanation I can find for the way his emotions slam into me even when I'm not reaching for them. The way he found me on that bridge. The warmth that flooded my chest when I was drowning in cold. My knees threaten to buckle. I grab the lamppost to steady myself. No. It can't be that.

"How did you find me?" The question comes out smaller than I intend.

"Because the goddess bound us together."

The words hit me like a physical blow. I stare at him. "What ... what do you mean?"

"You don't know what bound means? Linked. Tied. Connected—"

"I know what the word means!" My sigil flares, and for once, I'm grateful for the burn. "I just don't understand why you'd think—"

The air crackles, sharp with the same energy I felt on the bridge. My chest flares with anger that isn't entirely my own. I see it mirrored in his eyes. The lamp above us flickers. I realize, with dawning horror, that I'm not afraid of him.

I *should* be. Every instinct I have says I should be. But the fear never comes. I shake my head, sorting through everything I know about bonds. I've been fascinated by them since childhood, since I first read *Mystical Bonds* in the Veritas library. Back then, they seemed romantic. Magical. Now it feels like a trap closing around my throat.

According to *Mystical Bonds*, the Creators forged bonds after the unicorns were hunted to extinction, a safeguard to protect the remaining avian creatures of the realm. Before the bonds, the dreki, wyvern, and unicorns were treated as tools. Weapons. Beasts of burden to be used until they broke and then discarded like rusted blades.

The unicorns were poached for their horns and the healing magic within. The dreki and wyvern were conscripted into transport and war. All of them, along with the raffin, were put into a deep slumber by the curse, turned to stone until someone finds a way to lift it. The alatuses are the only avian creatures that escaped that fate, and no one knows why.

In Lunaris, we don't have natural bonds. But the Council requires the alatuses to be bound to their legion guards through an alchemized elixir meant to mimic the real thing. Shame curdles in my stomach as I look down at my fingernails. Still stained. A permanent reminder of every elixir I made, every bond I helped forge against nature's will.

I stopped making them two years ago, much to Mother's dismay. But refusing to continue doesn't erase what I've already done. Maybe this is Mortiana's way of making me pay. Retribution, after all, doesn't expire.

Yet, I refuse to accept that after years of wondering what it might feel like to share a bond with one of the majestic creatures of this realm, to feel that ancient, sacred connection, this is what I'd get. Not an alatus, or a dreki or a wyvern.

Him. Of all the creatures in this realm, I get *him*.

It's absurd. All of it. But I force myself to breathe and remember one crucial detail: bonds must be accepted by both parties. That'll be my way out.

"You felt my panic through the bond," I say slowly, testing the theory aloud. "That's how you found me. Which means if I'm injured, you'd feel it. And vice versa."

Surely no warrior would want that. To be tethered to an empath, to feel every flash of fear. It's unheard of. Unnatural.

He tilts his head, something unreadable shifting behind his eyes. "It's more nuanced than that."

"How?"

"What do you know about ravens?"

I frown. "What do ravens have to do with anything?"

"You have ravens here," he says impatiently. "What do you know about them?"

"I'm an avian healer. I'd like to think I know enough."

His expression shifts. The anger drains away, the frustration, the barely leashed impatience. What's left is something I haven't seen on his face before. Shock.

Pure, unguarded shock. His eyes roam over my face like he's seeing me for the first time, like I've just rearranged myself into something he didn't expect. I'm so busy trying to piece together what ravens have to do with any of this that I almost miss the shift. The way his shock hardens into something else. Something calculating.

A cold shiver traces down my spine.

"You're a healer?" he asks.

His voice is quiet. Too quiet. The kind of quiet that precedes a trap snapping shut. I bite my tongue and keep my face blank. I was trained for moments like this.

If I can survive Mother's interrogations, Freida's cold dissections of every lie I've ever told, I can survive this man's scrutiny. I shove my fear down and reach for something else.

Anger isn't ideal, but it's close to the surface, banked and ready. I let it rise.

"I'm an alchemic healer," I say, stepping away from the lamppost. "I specialize in winged creatures. Now tell me what ravens have to do with any of this."

His eyes narrow, but he doesn't look away. "You know they mate for life."

"Of course."

"And the raffin? Did you study them as well?"

I cross my arms. "Are you going to quiz me on avian biology all night, or are you going to say something useful?"

He presses his lips together as if I'm the one wasting precious time. "Unlike ravens, raffin are soul-bound to their mates."

"Some would argue that ravens are soul-bound as well, since they mate for life and all."

"People like to argue many things. That doesn't mean they're right."

I raise an eyebrow. "But you are, apparently."

"Most of the time."

I barely suppress an eye roll and turn my mind to everything I know about the raffin. They were created by Lugal, the god of war, bred to combat the massive avian predators of enemy kingdoms. Smaller than the dreki, but no less deadly. Poisonous talons.

The ability to summon lightning from clear skies. And when it comes to their mates, they are utterly, violently territorial. Our history books are filled with accounts of cities reduced to ash after a raffin's mate was killed. Scholars call it the furia, a rage so consuming it doesn't end until everything around them burns. Not exactly the bond I dreamed of as a girl.

My eyes narrow. "You're saying this bond is like the raffin's bond with their mates?"

"Mortiana bargains souls." He says it like it's obvious. Like I should have figured it out by now. "It makes sense that she'd bind ours. Considering what I felt when you left earlier. And when I heard you screaming on that bridge."

The scowl on his face deepens, as if the memory still burns.

"But we're strangers," I whisper.

He shrugs, though the gesture is anything but casual. "Soul bonds don't care about logic."

My pulse roars in my ears. Repaying a debt is one thing. Being soul-bound to a stranger, tied to him in ways I don't fully understand, vulnerable to a rage that could burn cities if something happens to me? That's something else entirely.

"I can't do this." I shake my head. "I can't accept this bond."

"Accept?" He barks out a laugh. It's a cruel sound. "You think this is a choice? You think I want this?" He steps closer, and the air between us crackles. "I was promised a fair chance at breaking the curse, and instead I ended up in the lost kingdom, bound to an empath."

He spits the last word like it's poison on his tongue. My jaw drops. Then my anger surges, hot and bright, and I shove it right back at him.

"You think *I* want to feel the ridiculous emotions of overgrown men? To be bound to one?" I step forward, matching his energy. "I'd rather be bound to one of those stone raffin than spend another moment tethered to you."

"Ridiculous?" He seethes, closing the distance between us until I'm forced to step back.

My shoulders hit the wall. He keeps coming, caging me in with his body, his fury radiating off him like heat from a forge.

"You gave up your memories," he growls, his face inches from mine. "You traded your entire past for a place in this godsforsaken city, and you have the nerve to call me ridiculous?"

I bristle, fists clenching despite the raw skin of my palms. I should breathe. I should calm down. Anger has its place, and this isn't it. But his judgment, his arrogance, the way he looks at me like I'm the one who's done something unforgivable, it makes it impossible to stay silent.

"You're collecting bargains for the goddess of death!" I snarl, tilting my chin up to meet his glare. "Don't lecture me about impossible choices!"

The lamp above us flickers wildly. His eyes bore into mine, golden and furious, and for a moment, I think he might do something terrible. Or wicked. I'm not sure which would be worse. Then he steps back. Turns away. Gives me his broad back and the silence that follows. The light steadies. I take one breath. Then another. When I'm certain my voice won't shake, I speak.

"How do we break this bond?"

He turns to face me again, and something in his expression has shuttered. "I assume it ends when you deliver your end of the bargain."

"Which is what, exactly?"

"You're going to help me lift the curse."

I stare at him. "The 300 year old curse? The one that's turned every raffin, dreki, and wyvern to stone? The one no one has been able to break since before my grandmother's grandmother was born?"

"Is there another I should know about?" he asks.

The arrogance in his voice makes my fingers itch for his throat. I clench my fists tighter.

"According to your friend, you've tried before. Multiple times." I hold my ground even as he takes a step closer. "What makes you think this time will be different?"

He doesn't answer. Not with words. He just keeps coming, slow and deliberate, until he's close enough that I have to tilt my head back to hold his gaze. My breath catches when he lifts a hand to my face. His fingers splay along my jaw, warm and rough, and his thumb finds the hollow of my throat where my pulse beats wild and frantic.

I should push him away. I should burn him where he stands. But I'm frozen, just like I was on that bridge, and some traitorous part of me doesn't want to move at all.

His lips curve into a slow, wolfish smile. He lowers his face until his lips hover a breath from mine. Close enough that I can feel the heat of him, the promise of something I refuse to name.

"It's different," he murmurs, "because I didn't have you before, Menace."

Then he drops his hand and pulls away. Turns without another word and walks toward my apartment like he owns it. Like he owns me. I stay pressed against the wall, heart in my throat, long after he disappears inside.

The night air is cold against my flushed skin. The moon remains hidden behind the endless clouds. And somewhere deep in my chest, in the place where the bond has taken root, I feel a flicker of something warm.

I tell myself it's anger.

I almost believe it.

CHAPTER TWELVE

I CLEAN MY CUTS AND CHANGE MY CLOTHES, BUT MY SKIN STILL crawls with the memory of cold fingers on my jaw. My private quarters suddenly feel too small, so I grab Jordi's maps and notes and tell Malachi we're leaving. It's what my brother would do, after all. Hunt for answers instead of hiding from them.

We take the backroads to avoid the flood of visitors, and I focus on the faint sounds of waves crashing against the cliffs and the calming scent of the ocean breeze.

"What happens when the curse is lifted?" I ask after a stretch of silence.

"The rot will stop. The land will grow rich again, the lakes and streams will run pure, and the Shroud …" He pauses, something flickering across his face. "The Shroud will cease to exist. It may take time, but the kingdom will finally begin to heal."

"And Lunaris will rejoin Tenebris."

"Yes."

I frown. "What will happen to the residents here?"

"What do you mean?"

"The people who live in Lunaris came from elsewhere. They wanted peace. A life without pain." I swallow. "That's why they traded their memories."

He raises an eyebrow, and the judgment in that single gesture makes my hackles rise, my sigil flares hot against my skin.

"You may not believe that, but it's the truth."

"I believe that's what you believe."

The condescension in his voice makes me want to hit him. I bite my tongue and force myself to breathe. "Either way, what will happen to them?"

"I don't know." He shrugs, and even that gesture feels dismissive. "I don't understand how the memory trade works, and I don't know enough about this place to give you an answer."

We walk in silence. The night presses close around us, thick with salt air and the distant murmur of revelry from the square. When I speak again, my voice sounds smaller than I intend.

"You already have Draven and Kage. Technically, you don't need me for anything."

"*We* are bound together until Mortiana deems your debt paid."

I nod, conceding that much at least. "Have you ever been bound to anyone before?"

He scoffs. "No."

"So you don't know what will happen to me if we fail?"

He casts me a sideways glance, sharp and assessing. "You didn't think to ask that before you made the bargain?"

"I was desperate." The admission scrapes against my throat.

"Nothing good comes from desperate bargains."

I cast him a bland look. "Trust me, that's becoming clearer by the second."

His expression doesn't change, but amusement flickers through the bond, warm and unexpected. He clears his throat as if to dismiss it. "Mortiana is the only one who can answer that question."

"Well, it's not like I can summon the goddess of death for a chat." I shoot him a look. "How do you even know this is how I'm supposed to pay my debt?"

"Mortiana told me before I left Noktemore."

My head snaps toward him. "You were in Noktemore? How?"

"I live there."

I stop walking. Face him fully. "*How*? You're not even a…" I trail off, realizing how little I actually know about the realm of the dead.

He raises an eyebrow. "I'm not even a what?"

"I don't know. I thought only spirits lived there, and demons, maybe." I study his face in the lamplight. "You're not a spirit, and I don't think you're a demon. Then again, that would be the least shocking revelation of the day."

He huffs out a surprised laugh. "I'm not a demon. But I suppose that's better than a yak."

"Slightly."

He shakes his head, and we start walking again. "Noktemore is hidden, but it's a kingdom like any other. Many sought refuge there when the curse fell. Others, like me, remain until our bargains are fulfilled."

"So you're stuck there."

"For now."

The answer gives me pause. I don't know if it's his size or his arrogance or the way he carries himself like a man who has never known captivity, but the idea of him being trapped anywhere feels wrong.

"For how long?"

"Until I break the curse." His jaw tightens. "Each Reckoning, I'm given an opportunity. Usually I end up in Vindariel, where it all began, or one of the nearby kingdoms. This is the first time I've been sent to Lunaris." He glances at me. "And the first time Mortiana has given me instructions. Which is why I believe you're the key to ending this."

"Right." I try to resign myself to the fact that there's no escaping this. "Your friend mentioned it's the final Reckoning. I didn't realize there was a time constraint."

"You might, if you hadn't traded your memories."

I shoot him a withering look. "What exactly did Mortiana tell you?"

"She told me someone who owed her a debt would help me break the curse." His golden eyes find mine in the dark. "And then I woke up here, tethered to you."

"I don't understand why she'd bind you to someone who knows nothing about this curse."

"Mortiana is fair, but she's still a goddess." His voice turns bitter. "To them, we're pawns in a game that never ends. If she wanted to make this easy, she would have bound me to a mercenary or a scholar. Instead, she gave me you."

The words land strangely. Not quite an insult. Not quite anything else.

"A mercenary," I repeat dryly. "Does lifting the curse require you to kill people?"

He frowns like he's never even considered that and I breathe out a tired laugh. Of course, he wouldn't. He named his godsdamn sword Vida.

"What can I possibly help you with?" I ask after a moment.

"You've lived here your entire life. You know the streets, the people, the secrets this place keeps." He ticks off points on his fingers. "You'll help me find the artifact I need. You'll teach me everything about Lunaris: the Council, the Sages, the residents, the visitors who come and go." His eyes meet mine. "Everything. I want to know all of it."

I snort. "That's a tall order."

"And one you will fulfill."

My brows shoot up. "Do I need to remind you that I don't take orders from you?"

"Do I need to remind you that a goddess bound you to me?"

"She bound you to me as well." I hold his gaze. "Does that mean you'll let me order you around?"

Something shifts in his expression. His eyes gleam under the streetlamp, golden and dangerous. "That depends." His voice drops lower. "What would you have me do?"

Warmth pools low in my stomach, unbidden and unwelcome. I tear my gaze away, disturbed by my own reaction. We're headed to Siren's Call, where the air is thick with compulsions designed to awaken every vice and hunger. If this bond is truly anything like the raffin's, I'm walking into a trap of my own making. It's going to be a very long night.

"My brother would be better suited for this," I say after a moment, the ache of his absence sharp in my chest. "He knows more about the curse than anyone."

"The goddess bound me to *you*, Ada."

I look up at him. "Only because I was the one who made the bargain."

"That's not how it works." His voice is quieter now. Almost gentle. "When you enter a bargain with a god, you give them access to your entire life. Everyone in it. If Mortiana wanted your brother to repay your debt, she would have bound me to him instead." He holds my gaze. "She chose you, Ada. Specifically."

My stomach drops.

The Sages warned us against bargains, but they never told us this. I think of the people who refuse to use their gifts, who wear their amulets every moment of every day, and wonder if they somehow know. Goddess strike me. How many people have endangered everyone they love without realizing it?

"You don't know me," he says after a moment. "I don't expect you to trust me. But we're bound whether we like it or not, and honesty is one of the few weapons we have."

"Weapons against what?"

"The bond itself." He runs a hand through his hair, and for the first time, he looks almost uncertain. "If we can be honest with each other, we might be able to trick it into thinking we've accepted it. That would prevent ... complications."

"The furia."

"Exactly." His eyes find mine. "I'm not saying it will be easy. But I think we can survive this if we start with honesty."

I bite my lip, turning his words over in my mind. I wasn't

exaggerating when I called it a tall order. The Veritas Order thrives on secrecy. It's how we've survived while other organizations crumbled to dust.

Mother forced me to end things with Cas the moment he became a dueler, terrified the Council would notice him and, by extension, notice me. At the time, it seemed paranoid. Excessive.

Now, standing here soul-bound to an outsider, I'm beginning to think she wasn't paranoid enough. Gods, I don't want to think about what Mother would do if she discovered this debt before I can repay it. Banishment is rare, but I wouldn't put it past her. Not for this.

Still, I can't deny that his suggestion makes a certain kind of sense. The music from Veneficia Alley grows louder as we approach, fiddles and drums and raucous laughter spilling into the night. Despite everything, I feel some of the tension in my shoulders ease.

"Fine," I say as we near the entrance.

"Fine, you agree to honesty?"

"To honesty." I stop a few paces from the door and extend my hand. "But it goes both ways."

"Of course." His fingers wrap around mine, warm and rough, swallowing my hand entirely. "Honesty."

We hold there a moment too long. The bond hums between us, quiet but undeniable, before we finally let go.

He pulls open the door, and Siren's Call rushes to greet us. Lively music and laughter, the clink of glasses raised in celebration, dominoes striking polished wood, the warm haze of pipe smoke and candlelight. For the first time in days, I take a breath that actually fills my lungs.

I slip off my cloak and drape it over my arm. The gold-feathered dress beneath catches the light, the hem brushing high on my thighs. Behind me, I feel Malachi's gaze land. Linger. Surprise flares through the bond. Then appreciation, slow and molten, before he wrenches it away. Heart in my throat, I glance over my shoulder and look at his face.

"Malachi."

His gaze snaps to mine, and something unreadable flickers there before it's gone. "Please don't mention the bond to my friends."

"You have my word." The answer comes without hesitation. I want to trust it. I'm not sure I have a choice.

Kage and Malachi claim a corner table, spreading Jordi's maps between them and speaking in low, urgent tones. Naima, Margot, and I take the booth beside them, nursing our ales and trading whispers about everything that's happened.

"I'll be back," Naima says after a moment, her eyes fixed across the room.

I follow her gaze to where Sylvie sits with her friends, dark hair tumbling over one shoulder as she laughs at something.

"Try not to insult anyone this time," I quip and bite back a laugh when she casts a murderous look my way.

"She really likes her," Kage says.

"I can't imagine why," Margot mutters beside me. "Sylvie

is basically Bas in female form, and all Naima does is insult him."

"Ah, Bastian the betrothed." Kage glances at Malachi across from him. "Did you know the only way out of the Veritas Order is to sign your name on a list and wait to be matched with a legion guard?"

"Why would anyone do that?"

"Because Mother can be suffocating. Some people prefer marriage to a stranger over staying under her control," Margot comments.

"Mother?"

"The High Sage," Kage supplies before I can answer. "She raised them. All seven."

"How did that happen?" Malachi asks. His tone is casual, but his gaze has sharpened, tracking every detail.

Margot clears her throat and sets her hand over mine. "I'm sure Kage will fill you in. Ada and I need some air."

I stand, and Malachi's eyes follow the movement. They trace the line of my dress, the hand Margot keeps clasped in mine, and finally settle on my face. The weight of his attention prickles against my skin. I turn away before I can read what's in his expression.

"He's the friend staying at Jordi's?" Margot waves a hand through the cloud of cigar smoke as we weave through the gambling den toward the back.

"Unfortunately."

The terrace greets us with clean air and the crash of distant waves. Most of the crowd has gathered on the far side, so we claim the corner by the railing, where the shadows are deepest.

I rest my forearms on the worn wooden railing and exhale, taking in the view: the dark tangle of trees beyond, the lit patio below where no one ever lingers. People prefer to conduct their questionable business in the dark, not under lamplight.

Margot clears her throat. "He's…"

"Handsome?"

She laughs, startled. "I was going to say intense. But yes, he's gorgeous, if you're into the rugged aristocrat type."

I snort. "When was the last time you saw an aristocrat in Veritas?"

"Last Moon Festival." Her green eyes glint with mischief. "When you threw one out of your bed at three in the morning."

"If you thought that man looked anything like Mal, you weren't paying attention."

Her brows shoot up. "Mal?"

Heat creeps up my neck. "You're an idiot."

Her soft laughter coaxes a reluctant smile from me. Margot knows I hate discussing these things. Not out of prudishness, but practicality. Casual encounters with festival visitors are likely the closest I'll ever come to a relationship, unless I want to follow her path. And that's not something I can see for myself.

"You're right," she says after a moment. "There's rugged, and then there's Bain. But there is something almost regal about the way he carries himself."

"Did you bring me out here to warn me off him, or tell me you're interested, or …"

"What? No. Gods." Her face twists. "There's a reason this arrangement with Bas works for me."

"That's one way to put it," I murmur, turning back to the dark trees.

We both know the truth neither of us says aloud. If not for the law requiring marriage approval from the House of Justice, she and Naima would have been together years ago. But the Sages declared them incompatible, and the Sages are never wrong about these things.

They could be together without the title. Share a home, share a life. But Margot craves the word wife the way I crave the title of Veritas healer. I don't fully understand it, since we don't bear children or raise them like the families in the ancient texts, but I've learned that fulfillment takes different shapes for different people. I respect her choice, even if it breaks something in me to watch her settle.

"What will you do about Jordi?" she asks after a moment.

I sigh. "Go to the Sages. What else can I do?"

She hesitates. "Do you think they already know?"

I straighten, crossing my arms as I turn to face her fully. "Why would you say that?"

"I don't know." She shakes her head, looks away, then meets my eyes again. "I don't know how else to say this, so I'm just going to say it."

My shoulders tense. I recognize that look. She wore it the night we were girls sharing a room at the estate, and she stumbled upon Freida and Anala kissing in an alcove. We'd been so young, so confused. The Sages never ate, never drank, barely blinked. We'd assumed they had no human wants at all.

"What is it?" I ask, though part of me doesn't want to know.

"Bas told me something." She swallows. "He said the elixirs have been weaker. For the past couple of years."

My heart stutters. I bite my tongue and force myself to breathe before I speak. "How would Bas know that?"

"A Council member took him somewhere." Her voice drops to barely a whisper. "A pleasure garden. At the Keep."

I go very still. "Pleasure garden."

"For emotions. Not..." She shakes her head. "The Council member, Nicolas, told him the elixirs are too weak now. So they take the newer residents to the garden, give them the cloud potion, and remove their amulets." Her voice cracks. "Then they watch. They call it 'letting them enjoy the little life they have left.'"

The breath I try to take gets stuck somewhere in my chest. I think of the laborers Jordi and I encountered in the tunnels. The way they screamed when their amulets were removed. The raw, animal grief that poured out of them.

That's what the Council watches for entertainment. I wrap my arms around myself to stop the shaking.

"Why would he take him there?" I whisper.

"He ..." She pauses to clear her throat. "Nicolas and Bas were together for a time."

The words land wrong. Everything about this lands wrong.

"For a time," I repeat, my mind reeling.

Bas was intolerable at the Veritas Estate, with his haughty attitude and anger issues. The Sages thread a small flame symbol on the women in Veritas—a sigil that reminds us to calm down each time anger rises. But the men are simply sent to the Dueling Estate to unleash their anger on sparring partners. When our gifts manifested, Bas' anger got worse, which is part of the reason he was sent there for good.

Arlo and Casimir soon followed, but they always returned to Veritas. Even after they became legion guards, they claimed their loyalty to the Veritas Order. Bas only returned when his presence was required and acted like it was a chore and we were all beneath him. Margot claims he's changed. I've never seen the evidence.

But I've heard enough from Arlo to know what happens to handsome young duelers who catch the Council's attention. The thought of anyone being used that way makes my sigil burn.

"Did Bas have a choice?" I ask carefully. "In the arrangement?"

"Yes." She says it quickly, defensively, then lowers her voice. "I think he loves him. Bas does."

Gods. I don't know if that makes it better or infinitely worse.

"When did he tell you this?"

"A few days ago. You were at the healing chamber, so I couldn't ..." She presses a hand to her chest. "I can't stop thinking about it. The way he described it. It sounded like a nightmare dressed up as mercy."

I swallow hard, fighting the urge to reach for her. One of the first things the Sages taught us: empaths cannot comfort other empaths. The word they used was cataclysmic. And I remember the ache in my chest during those early lessons, when we tried anyway. When holding each other only made the pain echo louder.

"When did he go there?" I can't bring myself to call it a pleasure garden. "What exactly did he see?"

"After the last Moon Festival." Her voice wavers. "He said they remove the amulets and just… watch. Watch them cry, laugh, grieve. Feel everything they traded away when they came here." She bites her trembling lip. "And the Council calls it mercy."

The words land like a blow to the center of my chest, right where the dull ache has taken root. I look away, swallowing against the grief climbing my throat. When I speak, the words feel like they're being dragged out of me over broken glass.

"And they just watch. Like they're … " I can't finish. I press a hand to my throat as if I could hold the horror in.

"Like they're entertainment," she whispers. "Like duelers bleeding for a crowd." She turns to me, and I feel the weight of the question before she asks it. "Have the ingredients for the elixir changed?"

I can't look at her. I shake my head.

It's not a lie. The ingredients haven't changed since the treaty was signed.

The only thing that's changed is me. Two years ago, I stopped making them.

And now people are suffering because of it.

CHAPTER THIRTEEN

An entire day passes with no word from Jordi. By the time I drag myself home, exhaustion has sunk into my bones like lead. All I want is to bury my face in my pillow and forget the world exists.

Instead, I open my door to find Naima, Kage, and Malachi crowded around my dining table, maps and ancient texts spread between them like the remnants of a war council. They look up in unison. I press my back against the door and study their faces: Naima's furrowed brow, Kage's knowing grin, Malachi's careful blankness. I close my eyes and sigh.

"And here I thought you'd be thrilled to find me waiting for you," Kage says.

A tired laugh escapes me despite everything. I open my eyes to find Malachi and Naima both shaking their heads at him.

"That bad?" Naima asks softly.

I let my head fall back against the door. "The Sages have been gone all day. No news about Jordi. And the interns at the clinic left the atrium door open, so I spent half the morning chasing birds and the other half trying not to strangle anyone."

She winces. "If it helps, one of the forgery interns dropped a hammer on her foot. Had to be carried to the Whispering Ponds."

I sputter a laugh. "How is that supposed to help? That's terrible."

"How long do people intern before they're given permanent positions?" Malachi asks.

"Depends on the trade," I say, pushing off the door and heading toward my room. "Could be months. Could be years."

"It was different for us," Naima adds behind me. "We arrived as children. We interned everywhere before our gifts even manifested."

Their voices blur into background noise as I shed my coat and shoes. My bed calls to me, soft and inviting, but I force myself to turn away and rejoin them at the table.

"Did you eat?" Naima asks as I sink into my usual chair.

"Lenora made coconut fried fish."

Her mouth drops. "Lucky."

"It was the only enjoyable part of my day."

"Do you want to know another thing I find fascinating about this place?" Kage asks.

"You start every sentence with that question," Naima mutters.

Malachi's brow arches. "Can you blame us? Lunaris was part of Tenebris before the curse. It's been lost for three hundred years." His gaze sweeps over the room, the maps, the windows overlooking the dark street beyond. "Even if that weren't the case, this place is ... "

"Strange," Kage finishes, sliding an old map toward us. "It's my understanding that as part of the treaty, the Council banished any mention of all the gods and repurposed the temples." He places a newer map beside the first. "If this older map was truly drawn before the treaty, this building shouldn't exist on it."

I lean forward to see what he's pointing at. "The Hall of Gratitude?"

"Why wouldn't it be there?" Naima frowns.

"Because that's where the Shadow Guild meets," Malachi says quietly.

"You think the Council is part of the Shadow Guild?" I stare at the map as if it might rearrange itself into something that makes sense.

Malachi nods. "Specifically, the faction that worships the Everlasting."

I sink back in my chair. Naima looks as stunned as I feel.

The Shadow Guild and the Veritas Order have been enemies for as long as either has existed. The atrocities the Guild committed against the Sages were the reason our Order was created in the first place. The idea that the Council could be aligned with them, that we've been living alongside our oldest enemy for decades without knowing ...

It shouldn't be possible. And yet.

"Do you know how the Shadow Guild formed?" Kage asks.

"The basics." I fold my arms. "Ignata chose three Sages

per kingdom. For balance, Noktelum was supposed to choose three Mages. But Ignata had a vision, something terrible enough to stop them after the first three were already selected. Those three Mages didn't take kindly to being abandoned by their god." I shrug. "So they founded their own order. The Shadow Guild."

Kage nods. "The Mages needed a place to meet, so they sought out a cave rumored to hold strange power." His voice takes on the cadence of an old story, well-worn and often told. "There were tales of a dead man left in that cave who walked out alive three days later. Another of a man who sheltered there and wished for wings. A week later, he emerged with them growing from his back."

Naima leans over to bump my shoulder. "Like those romance books you used to devour about the winged hero who—"

"Naima." I bump her shoulder hard enough to send her rocking back in her chair.

She cackles, head thrown back, the gold clasps on her braids tinkling like bells. I bite the inside of my cheek to keep from laughing. If I encourage her, she'll never stop, and my face is already burning.

I turn back to Kage. "Ignore her. Continue."

"I have to admit," Malachi says, and I can hear the smirk in his voice, "I'm very curious what this winged hero did to earn such a reaction."

I glare at him. His amusement pulses through the bond, warm and infuriating.

Kage grins. "I'm also curious."

"Just tell us what happened in the cave."

"They found a stone," he says. "Amber, like many in those caves, but larger. The resin had trapped twigs in the shape of a heart, and at the center of that heart … " He pauses. "An eye. Perfectly preserved. And it blinked."

A chill traces down my spine. "That's…"

"Impossible?" Kage shrugs. "I've never seen it myself. But enough people have, across enough centuries, that I believe the accounts. They called the stone the Everlasting."

"The Everlasting," I repeat slowly. "The Council's symbol. The mantra they chant. It's all about a stone?"

"Not just any stone."

"The Mage who found it mounted the stone in a scepter," Kage continues. "The other two Mages were furious. They saw it as blasphemy against Noktelum."

"Because only gods are supposed to have scepters," Naima says.

"Exactly. That's what split the Guild. One faction stayed loyal to Noktelum. The other followed the Mage with the Everlasting, worshipping the stone like a deity."

"Back then, people still referred to the stone as the Everlasting," Malachi says, his voice low. "But one of the Mage's followers murdered him and took the scepter. That man eventually became king of Arusha." His jaw tightens. "And he took the name for himself. The Everlasting."

My stomach turns. "Cato. You're telling me Cato, the man who cursed Tenebris, is the Everlasting? That's who the Council worships?"

"I'm glad you know enough about him to be disturbed," Kage says.

"I don't know much." I shake my head. "But I know

enough to be horrified by anyone who isn't a god demanding worship."

"That's fair."

"Isn't this enough proof?" Naima presses. "And wouldn't Draven have known? He's been here for years."

She catches my eye, and I see the question she can't ask aloud. *Do the Sages know? Have they always known?* I give her the smallest nod. They must. I just can't fathom why they would allow it.

"That's complicated," Kage says slowly. "Draven doesn't remember Cato. He remembers everything else we've asked about, every detail of his life before Lunaris, but mention Cato and there's just... nothing. A blank space where the memory should be."

I stare at him. I didn't know that was possible. A single memory, surgically removed, while leaving everything else intact? What kind of power would that require?

"Is there a way to find an older map?" Malachi asks, cutting through my spiraling thoughts.

I nod at the yellowed parchment. "Older than this?"

"One from before the Hall of Gratitude existed."

"I've never seen one that old. But if anyone can find it, it's Draven." I pause. "He's the Keeper of the Vault. If such a map exists, he'd know."

Malachi shakes his head. "He avoids the vault during the festival. Says the Council has been unusually vigilant these past weeks. Watching everything. Everyone."

My stomach twists. What if Draven is the reason Jordi was taken? What if he's connected to the renegades? What if they both are? I shove the thought away before it can take root. One crisis at a time.

"Why does the original matter?" Naima asks.

"Because we need to know what temple stood there before," Malachi says. "What power it held. What the Council might be using it for now."

She frowns. "Why would that change anything?"

"Because the merchants from Lyrionne call Constantine something interesting." Kage's voice drops. "The Keeper of Memories."

"He has nothing to do with the memory collections." The words come out sharper than I intend. "Nothing to do with the stones or the ceremony. The only thing he does is show up and say a few words on behalf of 'the Everlasting' and take the credit. He's a farce."

Kage raises an eyebrow. "Then who does collect them?"

"No one collects them." I spread my hands. "The Veritas healers conduct the ceremony. The Sages attend. But the memories themselves are stored in individual stones. No one receives them. They're just... kept."

"Each person gets their own stone?"

"Yes. And in exchange, they're given an amulet." I touch my chest where mine usually rests. "The amulets are supposed to protect us. From the Shroud, from our own emotions, from everything we traded away."

Kage exchanges a look with Malachi. "Those are the amulets I mentioned. The ones that supposedly keep the Shroudmaidens at bay and prevent the Shroud from spreading."

"Shroudmaidens?" The word feels strange on my tongue. Wrong.

Malachi's gaze finds mine. "The creatures you encountered on the bridge. That's what they're called outside these walls."

"Where are the stones kept?" Kage asks.

"They call it the Wall of Memories, but no one knows its location. Jordi used to think…" I have to stop and swallow past the sudden tightness in my throat. "He thought they were stored beneath the House of Truth. But there are thousands of stones. Maybe tens of thousands. I can't imagine they're all in one place."

Kage and Malachi exchange a look that makes my pulse stutter.

"What?" I demand. "What is it?"

Kage's eyes lock onto mine. "The amulets and the memory stones. Are they connected?"

I nod, throat too tight for words.

"Why does that matter?" Naima whispers.

"The Sages would never allow the stones near the Hall of Gratitude." Kage's voice has gone thin. Afraid. "Right? They wouldn't let them anywhere near that place?"

"I don't know." My voice sounds strange to my own ears. "Would it matter?"

Kage laughs, but there's no humor in it. "Would it matter? The Everlasting is a siphoner, Ada. Cato can drain gifts from others and use them as his own. Why do you think the seers went into hiding? Why do you think healers were hunted to near extinction?"

My stomach lurches. A siphoner. Someone who can

steal gifts, consume them, wield them as weapons. I think of Jordi's theories about the amulets and memory stones. His conviction that they're connected to the Shroud somehow, feeding it, sustaining it. I think of the laborers screaming in the tunnels. Malachi must feel my panic through the bond, but I can't bring myself to care.

"Is Cato the siphoner, or is it the stone?" Naima's voice is barely audible. "Is it him, or the scepter?"

"There are theories," Kage says carefully. "Some believe the Mage's gifts were transferred into the scepter when Cato killed him. That the weapon itself holds the power, and Cato is just the one wielding it."

I force myself to swallow. "What do you believe?"

"I think it's the scepter," Kage says. "Cato relies on compulsion more than any other gift, and there are records of his eyes flashing amber when he uses it. The stone is amber. It can't be a coincidence."

I stare at him. "His eyes flash? Like the Sages?"

"Similar. The Sages' eyes flash silver because they were blessed by Ignata, who commands lightning. Cato's flash amber because his power comes from something else entirely." Kage's expression darkens. "Something older. Hungrier."

"I didn't know anyone else's eyes flashed," Naima breathes.

"It's rare, but not unheard of." Kage shakes his head. "But that's a tangent for another time."

"Agreed." I press my palms flat against the table to stop them from trembling. "Right now, I need to understand what the Council is doing with the memory stones. And what it has to do with this Everlasting."

"Does it truly matter?" Naima's voice rises, desperate. "Cato has never set foot in Lunaris. The Everlasting is just a name the Shadow Guild gave a rock. That doesn't make it a god. That doesn't make him one either."

I shake my head slowly. "That's not entirely true."

"How do you figure?"

"The Sages teach that everything is energy," I say slowly, piecing the thoughts together as I speak. "Our breath, our magic, the fabric of our being. Ancient cultures believed the same. Everything is cyclical. The circle of life. We are energy, and energy cannot be destroyed, only transformed."

"Right." Naima shrugs. "That's what Ignata's teachings are based on."

"Then consider this." I lean forward. "The only difference between a concept and a god is the energy we give it. One person's belief is just an idea. But gather a community around that idea, worship it together, build temples in its name, and suddenly that idea has power. Real power." I meet each of their eyes in turn. "And in this case, they took over an already existing temple that already had its own energy baked into it."

I let that sink in.

"Which is why we need the original map," Malachi says quietly. "We need to know what temple stood there before. And whether the memory stones are anywhere near it."

I nod, but my mind has already drifted. Back to the bridge. To the Shroudmaidens and their rasping voices. *We remember you, empath. You were ours to claim.* To the laborers dying in the tunnels, screaming for families they'd forgotten.

To Margot's voice cracking as she described the pleasure gardens. The Council watching grief like entertainment.

A shudder tears through me, violent enough that Naima reaches for my hand. If Jordi is right, and the Shroud opens during the Reckoning, and Cato finds a way through … *Gods*. Repaying my debt will be the least of my worries. Surviving will be the only thing that matters.

And I'm not sure any of us will.

CHAPTER FOURTEEN

Sleep evades me for the third night in a row. Every time I close my eyes, the nightmares find me. My brother's manacled wrists. Glowing eyes in the dark. Whispers layered like echoes, crawling beneath my skin. The cold pressing into my spine, filling my lungs, dragging me under. The third time I jolt awake, gasping, I give up on sleep entirely.

I ease my door open, careful not to make a sound, and freeze when I see the outline of a figure in one of the wingback chairs. Large. Still. Watching the darkness like it might have something to say. The bond flares with awareness before I can retreat. He knows I'm here.

"Nightmares again?" His voice cuts through the silence, low and rough, and I still flinch despite expecting it.

The question makes something in my chest tighten. I force myself to move, crossing toward the bookshelf as if I had a destination in mind.

"I wasn't aware I had any before tonight."

"You did. Last night. And the night before."

"I'm glad you're keeping count," I mutter.

I don't look at him as I pass, but I feel the weight of his

gaze on my back like a physical touch. My fingers trail along the spines of books I'm not actually searching for until I give up the pretense and turn. His eyes are on me. On the shapeless black camisole and shorts I sleep in. He doesn't bother to hide it.

I should say something cutting. Instead, I'm too busy noticing the absence of his shirt, the firelight playing across the planes of his chest, the shadows pooling in the hollows of his collarbones. An open book rests on his lap. A bottle of wine and a half-empty glass sit on the table beside him. When my gaze finally returns to his face, something knowing glints in his eyes.

"Should I do a twirl for you?"

A low chuckle rumbles from his chest, and the sound warms something in mine that I refuse to examine.

I nod at the book. "What are you reading?"

His eyes never leave my face as he recites, "Where you find logic, you will find truth. Where you find truth, you will find knowledge. Where you find knowledge, you will find power."

My eyebrows rise. "The Sages don't hold open auditions, but I'm sure they'd be impressed by your interest in their order."

"Perhaps you can arrange an audience." He tracks my movements as I cross the room and sink into the chair diagonal from his. "Considering how close you are to them."

"Naima must have left out the part where I fell from their good graces."

"She did." He closes the book and leans back, studying

me with an intensity that makes my skin prickle. "How did that happen?"

"It's a long story." I cover a yawn with the back of my hand.

"You're exhausted."

"Another long day." I sink deeper into the chair. "Another day of nothing going right."

"I assume your visit with the Sages didn't go well?"

"It didn't go at all." I stare at the wine bottle, wishing it were closer. "They weren't there. Again."

He searches my face. "Are they usually this difficult to find?"

"No." I meet his eyes. "But nothing about this festival is normal."

He nods slowly. "The nightmares. Were they about the bridge, or something else?"

My shoulders stiffen at the question. Instead of answering, I reach for the wine, pour myself a glass, and take a long sip. The sweetness spreads across my tongue, warm and welcome, loosening the knots in my muscles.

"Where in the north are you from?" I ask when I open my eyes and find him still watching me.

"Vindariel."

A thread of anguish bleeds through the bond before he wrenches it away. Vindariel. Where the curse began. I've read texts that describe its cliffs and mountain ranges, its rolling countryside and crystalline lakes. But those texts predate the curse by centuries. I can't imagine any of that beauty survived. I don't say that. Some wounds don't need salt.

"We don't have nightmares in Lunaris," I say, setting

the glass on the table between us. "We're not supposed to, anyway."

He picks up the glass without asking. "Part of the memory trade?"

I nod. "Dreams can be memories in disguise. Or worse."

"Foresight." He takes a slow sip. "One of many gifts forbidden across the kingdoms."

That gives me pause. "I didn't realize it was forbidden. I thought seers went into hiding because they were hunted. Like healers."

"It's astounding how someone raised by women who claim to value knowledge above all else can know so little about the world beyond these walls."

"Your arrogance is what's astounding," I say, snatching the glass from the table and draining what's left. "Especially considering how much you're expecting me to help you with."

He pours another glass and claims it before I can. "How is it that someone raised by the Sages is so easily baited?"

"I'm not easily baited. You just happen to naturally annoy me." I lean back in my chair, matching his posture. "Which does not bode well for our current situation."

"Some would argue that means you care what I think."

I raise an eyebrow. "People like to argue many things. That doesn't mean they're right."

He huffs a surprised laugh and sinks deeper into the chair, sprawling like a king on a throne. Legs extended, wine glass dangling from careless fingers, golden eyes watching me like I'm a puzzle he hasn't quite solved.

I remember what Margot said at Siren's and wonder, briefly, if I have a type I never knew about.

I extend my hand, palm up, signaling for the glass.

He tilts his head. "I'm sure you have more in the kitchen."

"Oh, I'm sorry." I press a hand to my chest in mock offense. "I didn't realize sharing my wine, from my favorite glass, in my own home, was somehow inconveniencing you."

I don't actually have a favorite glass, but watching the emotions flicker across his face makes the lie worthwhile. Surprise. Consideration. And finally, amusement, breaking through like light through storm clouds.

He laughs. It's a deep, husky sound that doesn't last nearly long enough, but it warms something in my chest all the same. His eyes are bright when he finally hands over the glass.

"Thank you." I take a sip and pass it back.

He drinks, watching me over the rim. "What does 'Temp' mean?"

I snort. "It's what my friends call me. Unlike you, who claim only friends call you Bain, yet everyone seems to use it."

His eyes gleam. "Is that jealousy I'm sensing?"

"I'm merely pointing out the hypocrisy."

"Hypocrisy." He considers the word like he's tasting it. "Temper?"

I laugh despite myself. "No."

His expression shifts, the playfulness draining away. "Let's talk about healers."

My pulse kicks. I pray he can't feel it through the bond. "What about them?"

"You said you thought seers were hunted the way healers were."

"Are you saying they weren't?"

"Not everywhere. Not by everyone."

"But they were hunted," I say carefully. "When they still existed."

"Do you know why?"

"I've read accounts of kings collecting them. Imprisoning them." I keep my voice steady. "I assume Cato was one of them."

He sets the glass down with a deliberateness that makes me go still. "Cato doesn't just imprison them."

Something in his voice raises the hair on my arms. "Then what does he do?"

"He drains them." He stares at the wine bottle, but I don't think he's seeing it. "The Everlasting scepter weakens each time it's used. It needs to be regenerated." His voice drops. "That's what the healers are for. That's why he's gone through so many of them. Kept them chained beneath his palace like livestock. Drained them until there was nothing left."

The room tilts. I grip the armrest hard enough to hurt, fighting to keep my expression blank while my heart slams against my ribs. The pleasure gardens. The Everlasting being fed. The Shroudmaidens on the bridge.

"It's why he has hunters searching constantly," Malachi continues, oblivious to the way my world is cracking apart. "Even now. Even after all these years."

He takes a long drink, watching me over the rim. "Do you know what the Sages' original purpose was?"

I force myself to breathe. "To tend the Undying Flame. Guard the ancient texts. Reveal the fates of newborns."

"The last one is perhaps the most important." He lets the glass dangle from his fingers again. "Their gifts compel them to seek out certain newborns and reveal their fates. People travel for months just to bring their children to the Sages' temples, hoping their child will be deemed worthy of a revelation."

I stare at the wine glass, aching to reach for it, but my hands won't stop trembling. I curl them into fists instead. "What's your point, Malachi?"

His brows rise, surprise or amusement or both flickering across his face. "My point is that Sages don't take in twenty-five orphaned children out of the goodness of their hearts. And they certainly don't choose seven of those children to train as their own, years before their gifts manifest, without reason." He tilts his head. "You have to admit, it's rather peculiar."

The word hangs between us. Peculiar. As if my entire childhood, my entire identity, is simply a curiosity to be examined.

"Perhaps they were bored," I say with a lightness I don't feel. "You seem to have opinions about everything. What's your take on it?"

"I'm not certain yet." His eyes search my face in the dim light. "There are many things about Lunaris I can't quite reconcile."

"Like the memory trade."

"Among other things." His mouth curves, but his gaze remains intent. Probing.

He leans forward to set the glass on the table, and I catch it: the tightening of his jaw, the subtle hitch in his movement. It's the kind of tell Cas and Arlo used to wear when they came home from the Dueling Estate, trying to hide wounds they thought made them look weak.

"You're injured."

He goes still. "I'm fine."

"You don't move like someone who's fine."

His eyes meet mine, guarded now, the openness from moments ago shuttered away. "It's nothing."

I shrug. "If you want my help, you know where to find me."

He nods, and we let the silence stretch between us. It should feel awkward. It doesn't. It feels like something settling into place, quiet and unexpected.

"You still haven't told me about the artifact," I say. "The one you need my help finding."

"Right." He leans back. "Have you heard of god scepters?"

The question hits me like cold water. The image the Flame showed me flashes through my mind: the scepter floating in darkness, light pouring down on it like a blessing or a curse. Is that what he's searching for? Has he already torn apart Jordi's quarters looking for it? Searched my room while I was gone?

My panic must show on my face, because he laughs. The sound is dark and smoky, curling through the room like incense.

"If I didn't know better, I'd think you used Mortiana's scepter to make your bargain."

My eyes narrow. "How do you know I didn't?"

His lips curl into something slow and cunning. "Because we can't both have it."

"You have it?" My mind races. If he has Mortiana's scepter, whose did Jordi find? Lugal's? But Lugal isn't one of the four. He's a consort, a god by marriage only. As far as I know, he doesn't have a scepter of his own.

"Care to explain that reaction?"

"Not particularly."

The sconces flicker. "Tell me."

Compulsion threads through the words, wrapping around my throat like fingers. My teeth clench. "Can you not use that on me?"

He exhales sharply, closing his eyes. "I didn't mean to."

"Do you not have control of your gifts?"

When his eyes open, there's something strange flickering in them. Something that looks almost like fear. He blinks, and it's gone.

"It's complicated."

"You're not going to explain?"

"I'd rather discuss the scepter."

I study him for a long moment, then relent. "The Flame showed me something. My brother, reaching for a scepter in a cave. Light pouring down on it like it was the only thing in the world that mattered."

"What did the scepter look like?"

"I don't know. The vision wasn't clear." I shake my head. "I assumed it was Mortiana's."

He frowns and looks away, something troubled crossing his face.

"If you already have Mortiana's scepter, why do you need another?"

"I need Sulara's to lift the curse."

"How would a scepter lift a curse?"

"By driving it into the roots of the Bratus tree."

I stare at him. "The Bratus tree. The one that was cursed."

"Yes."

A thousand questions crowd my tongue. How would we get there? How would the scepter heal anything? How is any of this supposed to work?

"Sulara's scepter has healing properties," he says before I can settle on which question to ask first.

"Healing properties." I turn the words over in my mind. The scepters are made from the bones of their gods. "Does that mean Sulara's bones can heal?"

His mouth twists into something bitter. "If they could, I would have lifted the curse centuries ago."

My brows rise. I shouldn't be surprised. He's from Vindariel. He's dedicated his entire existence to breaking this curse. Of course he would have tried everything.

I force myself to refocus. "How does it have healing properties?"

"It's made from one of Sulara's bones and the horn of a unicorn." He raises an eyebrow. "Don't tell me you thought unicorns were a myth."

I give him an unamused look. "I know they were real. I thought they'd been poached to extinction."

"They were."

The words leave a sour taste in my mouth. I'm beginning to understand why some people refuse to use their gifts at all. Why they'd rather live diminished than feed the gods.

"Sulara is supposed to be the goddess of life and healing." I frown. "How could she allow unicorns to be poached?"

"Who says she allowed it?"

"Then how does her scepter have a unicorn's horn?"

"It truly is astonishing how little you know."

"And yet you're relying on me to help you." I don't bother hiding my irritation. "Strange, isn't it?"

"You say that as if I had a choice."

"You act as if I have any choices at all." My voice rises despite my efforts to control it. "As if I asked for any of this."

He exhales slowly and looks away. "Let's agree to stop reminding each other that neither of us chose this."

"Only if you agree to stop repeating how little I know about everything."

"I don't mean for you to take offense. It's just surprising considering who raised you," he argues.

"Just finish telling me about the scepters," I mutter.

"The Creators made the scepters as punishment for their misbehaving children. They took a bone from each of them." His voice is flat, reciting facts he's known so long they've lost their horror. "A bone can regrow. It hurts, but it heals. So the Creators demanded something else as well. Something that couldn't grow back."

"Their familiars," I whisper.

He nods.

My stomach churns. Even if I weren't an animal healer, even if I hadn't spent my life caring for wounded creatures, this would horrify me. What kind of parent demands such a price from their children? What kind of god does that make them?

"Why would they do that?"

"The same reason they forced the gods to marry mortals." He shifts in his chair, and I catch another wince he tries to hide. "To ensure they never forgot how fragile life is. How easily it can be taken."

The words settle over me like a shroud.

"How did you learn about scepters in the first place?" he asks, steering the conversation away before I can dwell on it.

"Everyone knows about them. We have books with depictions and accounts of people finding them and being cursed by them. They're a cautionary tale of sorts, which is probably why the Council allows those stories to remain unchanged. Where is the account about the scepter being brought here?" I ask, looking at the bookshelf.

"It's an old legend."

I stare at him. "You're basing all of this on a *legend*?"

"It's a legend, not a fairytale."

"And that's supposed to make me feel better?"

"Legends should be taken seriously." His frown deepens. "More seriously than most things."

I laugh before I can stop myself, raising my hands when he glares. "I'm sorry. You just don't strike me as the type to chase old stories across kingdoms."

His expression shifts into something I can't quite read. "Someday, legends will be the only thing that remains of any of us. The only proof we ever existed at all."

I consider that. It's not like I expect my name to be remembered anywhere. "But legends change. They get twisted over time."

"Stories change," he says quietly. "Legends don't. Legends are only written once a story is over. The way they're told might shift, but the core remains. The truth of it endures."

"I don't see the difference," I admit. "History is told through stories, and those change constantly."

"Legends are bones. They hold their shape." He tilts his head. "Stories are living things. They grow and shift."

"And that's supposed to be okay? You wouldn't care if stories painted you as a coward? A villain?"

He laughs, low and humorless. "Who says they don't already?"

I go still. It hadn't occurred to me that he might exist in our histories. That somewhere in the vault or the Noxbridge Library, there might be accounts of a man named Bain, painted as hero or monster depending on who held the pen. Jordi told me once that Draven's name appears in books scattered across the vault and the Noxbridge Library. Always painted as a hero, which means little in Lunaris, where the Council decides who deserves that title and history rewrites itself to agree.

It occurs to me that we're bound regardless of whether he's a hero, a coward, a villain, or all three. But something else nags at me, something softer than curiosity.

"Does it bother you? The way the stories paint you?"

"Should it?"

"I think it would bother me."

He studies my face for a long moment. "Has it occurred to you that they might be telling the truth?"

"I'm not asking if it's true." I hold his gaze. "I'm asking if it hurts."

Something flickers in his expression. He looks away, toward the bookshelf, toward the darkness beyond the window.

"It used to."

"What changed?"

"My perception." He's quiet for a moment. "History is written by whoever survives long enough to hold the pen.

There's never been a hero who hasn't been villainized, just as there has never been a villain who hasn't been deemed a hero. I guess I learned to live with it." He looks at me again. "Tomorrow's stories shouldn't diminish today's actions."

The words settle into me, finding a home somewhere near my ribs. Jordi would appreciate this man, I think. The way he sees the world. The weight he carries without complaint. We sit in silence for a long moment, comfortable and strange all at once.

Finally, I stand. "I'm going to try to sleep."

He nods but doesn't move. I feel his gaze on my back as I cross the room, warm and steady through the bond.

"Goodnight, Menace."

His voice follows me into the darkness, wrapping around me like smoke, like a promise I'm not ready to examine. I close the door behind me and lean against it, heart beating too fast for reasons I refuse to name.

CHAPTER FIFTEEN

Three days and still no word from Jordi. No mention of him in the daily announcements, no explanation for the extended festival, no indication of when the Veritas ceremony will take place. The silence feels deliberate. Calculated.

But Mother's newest assistant let slip that she'll be at the estate this evening, and I intend to be there waiting. As soon as I can figure out how to secure this godsforsaken corset.

I wrestle with the ribbons until my shoulders burn, then give up. Margot's shop it is. I hate the waste of time, but this is the only thing I own that Mother will deem appropriate, and I refuse to give her ammunition. A loose corset, a wrinkled hem, a single hair out of place, and she'll spend the entire conversation picking at it instead of answering my questions.

I smooth the gold chiffon skirt that pools at my feet when I walk, fasten the thick gold bracelet Naima forged for me, a feathered cuff that hides a thin dagger in its hilt, and open my bedroom door. I freeze when I find Malachi standing on the other side. He steps forward, filling the doorframe. His black sleeveless tunic is torn and streaked with dirt, and his expression could curdle milk.

"Goddess, Mal!" I press one hand to my galloping heart and the other to my corset to keep it from sliding off entirely.

"Where have you been?" The words come out low. Almost a growl.

I blink, caught off guard by his hostility, and by the way my pulse kicks when I catch the heat in his gaze as it sweeps over me. It's there and gone in a heartbeat, replaced by something harder.

"You were looking for me?"

He raises an eyebrow. "Does that excite you? Were we playing a game of hide and seek I wasn't informed of?"

My eyes narrow. "I'm not excited. I'm annoyed."

"Annoyed by your own excitement, perhaps."

I stare at him for a moment. "If you're going to be insufferable, you might as well make yourself useful," I say, one hand clutching the corset and the other lifting my hair off my neck as I turn and walk back to the mirror. "Help me with this."

He follows without comment, and I watch in the mirror as he studies the mess I've made of the ribbons. His frown deepens. "You barely tied this at all."

"My arms gave out. I was going to walk to Margot's shop and have her fix it." I gasp when he tugs the ribbons sharply. "Gods! Not that tight."

"You were going to walk across town with this falling off you?"

"I would have held it."

"People are half-drunk thanks to those wine dispensers

on every corner. It's not safe to walk around like this." He begins unlacing what I've done, his movements careful despite his irritation.

"Like what?" I ask, though I'm only half listening. I'm too busy watching the way his biceps flex with each pull of the ribbon, the controlled strength in his hands.

He lifts his head just long enough to give me a withering look, then returns to his task. "Where were you earlier?"

"The clinic. And then I wanted to see if the rumors about legion guards on every corner were true."

His hands still. "By yourself?"

"No, with my lover," I deadpan.

He tugs the ribbon hard enough to steal my breath. I gasp.

"Goddess strike you, Malachi Bain!" I glare at him in the mirror. "What is wrong with you today?"

He stops lacing entirely, his glare meeting mine in the mirror. "What's wrong with me is that we overheard someone say Shroudmaidens were spotted near the clinic. And when I went to find you, you weren't there."

Something warm blooms in my chest despite the fear his words should inspire. I bite my lip to keep from smiling. "So you were looking for me."

He exhales, something between frustration and amusement. "Yes. I was worried and I was looking for you."

His admission makes my stomach dip. "But you knew I was fine. Because of the bond."

I say it because I want to know if he's been reaching for it the way I have. If he finds the same strange comfort in it that I do. It's maddening to admit, even to myself. The bond is a reminder of everything I owe, everything I can't escape.

And yet, in the chaos of the last few days, it's become an anchor. The one certain thing in a world that's falling apart around me. He doesn't answer. But he doesn't look away either.

"Did you and Kage actually search for the artifact today," I ask, forcing lightness into my voice. "Or did you just roll around in the sand?"

His lips twitch. "We conducted our search before we went to the Dueling Estate to roll around in the sand."

"The Dueling Estate?"

"Draven arranged a tour. The place was empty." He resumes lacing, his touch gentler now. "Apparently there's a match at the amphitheater tonight."

"They hold them twice daily during the festival." I frown. "Though I'm not sure how that works if the festival keeps extending." I catch his eye in the mirror. "When exactly is the Reckoning supposed to begin?"

"When the blood moon rises."

"And if it doesn't?"

"It will."

"You really believe we'll be able to see it? The sky here is never clear. The Shroud swallows everything."

"The sprites will stop. The sky will clear. We'll see it." He says it like a man who's repeated the same words to himself a thousand times. "We just have to wait."

I don't believe him. But I'm tired of arguing about things neither of us can control. "Are you satisfied with your search? Convinced the scepter isn't at the estate or temple?"

"It's not where we looked. But if it's here at all, those are still the most likely places."

"You are the most stubborn person I've ever met," I mutter.

The look he gives me in the mirror suggests he could say the same.

"I can try to search the estate tonight," I offer. "I'll be there anyway."

"Is that where you're going?"

I nod and straighten my spine as he continues to work the ribbons.

"You seem to know your way around a corset."

The moment the words leave my mouth, something uncomfortable twists in my stomach. It takes me a moment to recognize it as jealousy, another to realize it's bleeding through the bond, not quite mine but not quite his either. I close my eyes and shove it down.

"My older sister made sure of it."

My eyes fly open. "You have an older sister?"

"Why does that surprise you?"

"I don't know." I study his reflection. "It's hard to picture you as someone's little brother."

His eyes flick to mine. "Little is a stretch."

"Younger, then," I correct with a smile. "Is she in Vindariel?"

His hands still on the ribbons. A thread of anguish bleeds through the bond, sharp enough to make my breath catch.

"She's not," he says finally.

"You don't have to talk about her," I say softly.

"I haven't. Not in a very long time." He exhales, and his hands resume their work, slower now. Careful. "She was… is… funny. Kind. Insufferably bossy." Something almost like a smile touches his mouth. "She's the reason I became a warrior."

"To protect her?"

He huffs a quiet laugh. "To be like her."

"Oh." My brows rise. "She must be extraordinary, then."

His expression softens for just a moment before grief shutters it away. The ache of it reaches me through the bond, raw and old and deep. I don't know if it's my empathy or the bond or some tangled combination of both, but I hate that I can feel it. Hate that I can't do anything to ease it.

He tugs the final ribbon into place and steps back. I let my hair fall over my shoulders and turn to face him properly for the first time. He looks me over. His brows crease. His throat bobs as he swallows.

I bite my tongue to keep from asking what he's thinking. Pull back from the bond to give him privacy, in case his thoughts are still with his sister. But when his eyes finally lift to mine, there's no grief in them. Only hunger, dark and undisguised, and it sets something in me ablaze.

I tell myself it's the bond. The raffin instinct bleeding through. But I don't care. The way he's looking at me right now, like I'm something worth devouring, something worth keeping. It feels like an eternity before either of us moves.

Anticipation coils tight in my chest. I wait for him to speak, to close the distance, to do something. Instead, he turns and walks out of my bedroom without a word. I stare at the empty doorway for longer than I should before I force myself to gather my thoughts and remember why I'm doing this and move.

My steps slow as I exit my room and find him studying

the maps and notes scattered over the dining table. He doesn't look up or say anything, so I continue my walk to the front door. I set a hand on the door knob and stare at the wood as I speak.

"Thank you. For helping me."

"Were you really with your lover?"

My heart stutters, then slams against my ribs. I turn to face him and find his eyes honed on me. I shake my head.

"Do you have one?"

I swallow. "Would it matter if I did?"

He tilts his head slightly. "What an interesting way to phrase a question."

A shiver traces down my spine. It takes me a moment to find my voice. "I don't have anyone." I hold his gaze. "Do you?"

Amusement flickers through the bond, threaded with something that feels almost like loneliness. He shakes his head slowly. "No."

The word hangs between us, heavy with everything neither of us is saying. I should go. I need to go. Mother won't wait forever, and I have questions that need answers. But for a long, suspended moment, I can't make myself move. Finally, I mutter a goodbye and slip out the door before I can do something foolish. Like stay.

I knock three times on Mother's office door, then enter before she can tell me to wait. The sight of her stops me short.

She's wearing maroon tonight, a low-cut gown that makes her look less like a Sage and more like the aristocrats who ruled before the treaty. After weeks of seeing her in Veritas green, the change is almost jarring.

Her eyes flash silver as she looks up from the papers on her desk. When she notices it's me, they fade back to brown, though the warning in them doesn't. My gaze drifts to the portrait behind her of a woman in crimson, face buried in a book, enclosed within a bubble, within another bubble, within another still.

Freida painted it years ago and hung it while Mother was away. I still remember the fury in Mother's voice when she discovered it. And yet, she never took it down. I've always wondered what that means. Whether it's a reminder of something she wants to remember, or something she refuses to forget.

"Close the door."

I do, then cross the room and stop on the opposite side of her desk. A supplicant's position. You'd think I'd be used to it by now considering how often I've stood here over the years, but I hate it. I hate that every time I stand before her I feel like a scared little girl. Mother likes to say she's respected, not feared, by the residents in Veritas, but I don't think she can differentiate the two.

"Sit."

"No, thank you." I clasp my hands in front of me to keep them from shaking. "Where is Jordi?"

She sets down her pen with the same deliberate calm she uses for everything, the calm that says she has all the time in the world and you have none.

"You know how I feel about stupid questions."

"And you know how I feel about being lied to." I hold her gaze even as her eyes flash silver, even as every instinct screams at me to look away, to bow, to apologize. I swallow and force my shoulders back. "Did you know they were going to take him?"

"I knew they would want to question him."

"And you allowed it?"

Something flickers across her face, too fast to read. "Jordan is exactly where he needs to be."

"Did you know they took him in manacles?" My voice rises despite my efforts to control it. "That's a violation of the treaty. They sent silent guards, not legion, not anyone the Order could recognize. They did it while the city was distracted. That's not questioning, that's an abduction."

"The treaty," she says, folding her hands on the desk, "is more nuanced than you understand."

My sigil flares, heat spreading across my chest like a brand. I breathe through it. Shove the anger down the way she taught me, the way all Veritas women are taught.

"When will he come home?"

"When it's time."

"What does that mean?"

"It means your brother is safe." Her voice is perfectly even. Perfectly controlled. "The situation is being handled. That is all you need to know."

I close my eyes. Breathe. When I open them, she's already returned to her papers, as if the matter is settled. As if I've been dismissed.

"Fine." I keep my voice steady through sheer force of will. "Then tell me about the laborers. Why are they dying the way they are? Why are they remembering things they traded away?"

Her jaw tightens. The movement is subtle, barely there, but I've spent my whole life learning to read her.

"That is none of your concern."

I stare at her. "How can you say that? I've seen them. I've watched them scream for families they were never supposed to remember."

She looks up, and her eyes flash silver. "Weren't you the one who refused to continue making the elixirs?" Her voice could cut glass. "I think it's a little late to start caring about those laborers now. Don't you?"

I knew she would say it. I've been waiting for it since I walked through the door. It still lands like a knife between my ribs. Without thinking, I reach for the bond. Malachi's presence flickers at the edge of my awareness, warm and steady, and I breathe a little easier.

"So, to be clear," I say, keeping my voice controlled. The way she taught me. "You won't tell me where Jordi is. You won't acknowledge that the Council violated the treaty. You won't explain why they sent silent guards instead of legion, or why they did it while the city was looking the other way, or why my brother was dragged off in chains like a criminal."

I study her the way Malachi studies me, searching for cracks in the stone. Her eyes are hard. Her jaw is clenched. But she doesn't look away, and she doesn't answer. Fine. If she won't give me answers, I'll give her truths.

"Come to think of it," I continue, "you've always been good at diverting our attention when something important is happening. The Council learned that trick from someone."

Her eyes flash silver. A warning.

I don't stop.

"Perhaps you taught them. Or perhaps you learned it together."

"It seems to me," she says, her voice dangerously soft, "that you came here with all the answers already in hand. You merely wanted to give me a piece of your mind."

"No." My voice cracks, and I hate it. "I came here hoping I was wrong. Hoping you didn't know about Jordi. Hoping you would be as outraged as I am that the Council broke the treaty, that they took one of us, that they—" I have to stop. Swallow the knot forming in my throat. "I came here for help, Mother. The way I've always come to you for help."

She says nothing.

"But I see now that was foolish of me."

She rises from her chair with the slow deliberateness of a predator. She's only a few inches taller than me, but at this moment, she seems to fill the entire room. The power radiating off her is almost visible, silver flickering at the edges of her irises. I release my clasped hands and lift my chin. Hold my ground. Even as every instinct tells me to kneel.

"Everything I have done," she says, "and everything I do, is to protect you. To keep you safe."

"From what?"

"From things you do not need to know about."

I lower my gaze to the desk between us. The papers covered in her elegant script. The seal of Veritas pressed into wax. I think about what Malachi said about gods treating mortals like pawns.

About games that never end. It clicks, then. The thing

I've always known but never let myself name. To Mother, we will always be children. Pieces to be moved. Minds to be shaped. She calls it protection, but protection and control wear the same face when you're the one being protected. We obey because she raised us to believe we have no choice.

This isn't a new realization. The seven of us have whispered about it in dark corners since we were old enough to question anything. But it's never felt this sharp. This urgent.

Mother was never warm like Anala, never gentle like Freida. But she was the one who claimed us. Named herself our guardian. Taught us to embrace our gifts, pushed us to reach our full potential. But what is potential, really, when you're only allowed to grow in the shape of a cage?

It takes everything I have to lift my head again. When I do, I find her seated once more, reading a foreign newspaper as if I've already left. As if this conversation is finished. As if I'm finished. My sigil burns. I'm not.

"I have done everything you asked of me." My voice shakes despite my efforts to steady it. "We all have. We followed your rules. We stayed in our territory. We kept your secrets and swallowed your lies and pretended this cage was a home."

Her eyes lift to mine. Cold. Assessing. I don't stop.

"You promise outsiders safety and acceptance. You tell us to honor the treaty, to stay away from the Council, to trust that you know what's best. And yet when they take one of us, when they drag one of your own to the Keep in chains, you sit behind this desk and do nothing."

My voice breaks. I hate it. I keep going anyway.

"When someone you raised, someone you claimed as

family, disappears for three days without a word, you do nothing. You know nothing. You say nothing." I take a breath that feels like swallowing glass. "What else will you allow, Mother? How much more will you let them take before you decide it matters?"

She's quiet for a long moment. When she speaks, her voice is softer than I've heard it in years. "You have to trust that I have your best interests at heart. That everything I do, I do for you." She meets my eyes. "Your brother is safe. I give you my word. Is that not enough?"

Her word. The same word she's given us a thousand times. The word we were taught to treat as law. I laugh. The sound is shaky, cracked, nothing like humor.

"Not anymore."

I turn away from her. My pulse roars in my ears as I cross to the door, every step feeling like a small rebellion. The Council's doctrine echoes in my head, painted in red letters across the walls of the Keep. *Curiosity is a poison.*

I pull the door open. If curiosity is poison, then truth is the only antidote. And I intend to find it, no matter what it costs me.

CHAPTER SIXTEEN

A SHARP THUMP TEARS ME FROM SLEEP. I JOLT UPRIGHT, disoriented, heart pounding. Afternoon light still streams through the windows. The clinic. I'm at the clinic.

The pounding comes again, urgent and relentless. The cages behind me rattle as I shove back from the desk and rush to the door. When I wrench it open, I find Draven on the other side, and the look on his face stops my breath.

His dark eyes are wild. He pushes past me without waiting for an invitation, scanning the room like he expects to find enemies hiding in the corners. I shut the door and watch him, unease coiling in my stomach.

His locs are tied back loosely, and he's dressed for movement: sleeveless tunic, dark trousers, boots meant for running. I've never seen him like this outside the training grounds. Never seen him look afraid. That's what makes my gut clench. Draven doesn't do *afraid*.

"Is it Jordi?" My voice comes out sharper than I intend. "Did something happen?"

"I know as much as you do." He whirls to face me, and those dark eyes pin me in place. There's always been something otherworldly about the way he looks at people, like he's seeing through skin and bone to whatever lies beneath. "I'm looking for Bain."

"Oh." I reach for the bond instinctively, exhale when I find it warm and intact. "The clinic is warded. If that's what you're worried about."

He shoots me a questioning look.

"I assume you're worried about silent guards." I gesture at the high windows near the ceiling. "Unless you expect Malachi to come crashing through those?"

The corner of his mouth quirks. "That would be a sight."

"Not for the one who'd have to rebuild the wall."

He shakes his head, a ghost of a smile crossing his face. He's quiet for a moment, then: "Do you remember the argument you and—"

Pounding on the door cuts him off. I hold up a finger and turn to answer it. Malachi fills the doorway. The afternoon sun catches him from behind, gilding the edges of his dark hair, throwing the planes of his face into sharp relief. He's wearing a short-sleeved tunic the color of deep water, and his arms are bare, all golden skin and corded muscle. Something in my chest tightens at the sight of him.

His gaze drops to what I'm wearing. The sheer ivory blouse. The decorative wings cascading from my shoulders to my hips, gold and ivory lace catching the light. His eyes trace down to my leather pants, my boots, and back up again, lingering on the wings like he's trying to commit them to memory.

Behind me, Draven clears his throat pointedly. I step aside to let Malachi in. He doesn't look away from me as he crosses the threshold. I exhale and shut the door behind him.

When I turn, Draven and Malachi are pulling apart from a brief embrace, the kind warriors share. Draven's attention returns to me immediately.

"As I was saying. Do you remember the argument you had with Jordi at the estate when he first started his apprenticeship?"

I raise an eyebrow. "You'll have to be more specific."

"It was after dinner. We were outside." His eyes glint with something like mischief. "You were wearing a red leather dress. Gold earrings."

Malachi's head snaps toward him. "How do you remember what she was wearing?"

"It was a memorable dress," Draven says, slow and deliberate.

The glare Malachi levels at him could melt iron.

"What was the argument about?" I ask, biting back a smile at the tension radiating off Mal.

Draven's expression sobers. "You said you believed in the society the Council and Sages built here. That it was worth protecting." His eyes search mine. "Do you still feel that way?"

The question catches me off guard. "I've always had issues with Lunaris. But it's safe here. Stable. There's no violence outside the dueling arena, and even those matches aren't meant to kill."

"Unless there's an execution," Draven says quietly.

"Those are rare. Once a year at the festival, and usually it's banishment, not death." I cross my arms. "I hate the control. I disagree with nearly everything the Council does. But I don't hate living in Veritas." I pause. "For the most part."

Malachi's quiet laugh sends warmth through the bond. "For the most part."

"The Sages say I'm a contrarian with a problem with authority." I shrug. "I'd probably find something to complain about anywhere."

Amusement flickers through the bond, bright and warm.

I turn back to Draven. "I've never gone hungry. I've always had shelter. I've never feared for my life." I pause, considering my own words. "Until recently, anyway. So yes, I value what Lunaris provides. Even if I hate how it provides it."

He nods slowly, something unreadable in his expression.

"Why are you asking me this?"

"I was wondering if your perspective had shifted," he says. Before I can respond, his tone sharpens. "You remember how to access the tunnels?"

I blink. "Is this about the vault?"

He nods, then turns to Malachi. "Cato's hunters have arrived."

I stare at him. "Hunters? Who are they hunting?"

"His heir." Draven's jaw tightens. "Cato believes his son is here. In Lunaris."

"He believes he may be here?" My brows rise. "He doesn't know for certain?"

"Apparently not."

Something clicks in my mind. The memory trade. The selective erasure. "Can I ask you something personal?"

Draven nods.

"I've heard you retained most of your memories from before Lunaris. Everything except Cato." I study his face. "Do you know why? Or how that's even possible?"

"Freida told me my incantation was different from the standard ceremony. Different words, different intent." He shakes his head. "I couldn't tell you what that means. But there are journals in the vault, written by the scholars who created the elixir. If answers exist, they'll be there."

Different incantations. Different intent. It's always been the missing piece, the thing none of us could explain about the welcoming ceremonies. Why some residents forget everything while others retain fragments. Why some lose themselves entirely.

I file the information away, another thread in a tapestry I'm only beginning to see.

"Kage and I discussed it," Malachi says, his voice shifting into something harder. More commanding. "We think it's best if you go ahead of us. Back to Vindariel."

Draven goes still. "With all due respect, I have to refuse." His voice is careful, controlled. "The last time I left you behind, I ended up trapped here for a decade. This is the final Reckoning. We cannot afford mistakes."

"You think I don't know that?" Malachi's scowl deepens. "If Cato's hunters found their way here, it means the wards in Vindariel may be compromised. If they fall, the others will need reinforcement."

"Vick has held the line for three centuries. I doubt my presence will tip the scales."

Malachi sets a hand on his shoulder. The gesture is firm. Final. "I am asking you to go."

Draven's eyes narrow. "Asking."

"I wouldn't if I didn't believe it was necessary."

Draven's jaw clenches. The silence stretches, taut as a bowstring.

I watch them, fascinated despite myself. Draven is broader and more imposing than even Malachi. The kind of man who commands attention simply by existing. And yet, there's no question who holds authority.

Malachi's hand on Draven's shoulder isn't a request. It's a reminder of rank. Whatever hierarchy exists between them, Malachi sits at its peak. Finally, Draven exhales. Something in him yields, though reluctance still lines his face.

"I don't like it. But if that's what you need, I'll wrap things up here and leave as soon as I can."

Malachi clasps his shoulder once, then turns to me. "Are you ready?"

I think of the blood oath I swore. The tunnels I've never taken an outsider through. The secrets I'm about to betray. I give a sharp nod. "Ready as I'll ever be."

Seven red doors are scattered across Lunaris, tucked between shops and homes, unremarkable except for the faded Veritas signet carved into the stone above each one. Most residents walk past them without a second glance. A few notice. Fewer still wonder what lies behind them.

I've heard the speculation. A hidden burial ground. A repository of Veritas secrets. A passage to the underworld itself.

All of it is partially true, but none of it captures the

whole. And since those of us with access have sworn blood oaths to keep silent, the full truth will likely never surface.

My steps slow as we approach. The red door looms before us, ancient wood weathered by salt air and time. I stop in front of the small bronze dish mounted beside it and stare at it for a long moment. Freida told me once that these dishes predated the streetlamps.

In the old days, they were lit to illuminate the keyholes for travelers arriving after dark. A kindness, disguised as function. But the dishes beside the red doors serve a different purpose. They're not illumination. They're keys.

"What is it?" Malachi's voice is low beside me.

I look up at him. "When I was granted access to these doors, I swore a blood oath. Never bring outsiders into the tunnels. Never speak of what lies within." I swallow. "I'm about to break both."

He's quiet for a moment. "What happens if you break it?"

"I don't know." I laugh, but the sound comes out thin. "I suppose we're about to find out."

His expression darkens. "That's not funny, Ada."

"I know." I meet his eyes. "But the alternative is staying in the dark, and I'm done with that."

I exhale and turn back to the dish. Beneath it, a small compartment holds shards of something dark, flint or obsidian, ancient and sharp. I catch them as they fall, arrange them in the dish, and summon fire to my palm.

The flame catches. Holds. The lock groans, a sound like old bones shifting. "I need you to—"

Before I can finish, Malachi surges forward, bracing the door before it can seal us out. I extinguish the fire against my palm and scrape the shards back into their compartment, then follow him through. The darkness swallows us whole. The tunnels open before us, vast and cathedral-like.

Ribbed vaults arc overhead, supported by pointed arches that march into the darkness like sentinels. The air is cold and still, carrying the faint mineral scent of ancient stone. Old texts claim the founding family wanted their burial chambers to mirror the city they built above, a kingdom beneath a kingdom.

They succeeded. But how they expanded from a few crypts beneath the university to this labyrinthine network that stretches beneath all of Lunaris remains a mystery. Some scholars believe the tunnels were built to transport wine from the docks without taxation. Others say the founders used them to move valuables past bandits on the northern roads. A few darker accounts suggest the tunnels served a different purpose entirely: hiding things that should never see daylight.

"My brother used to say these tunnels stretch all the way to Vindariel," I murmur as we walk, our footsteps silent on the ancient stone. "That somewhere beneath the Shroud, there's a passage to the outside world."

"Do you believe that?"

I glance at him. "If I did, I wouldn't still be here."

"You would leave?"

The question catches me off guard. "Why does that surprise you?"

"No. I suppose it doesn't." He tips his head back, studying the vaulted ceiling. "There's no echo."

"The Order's doing. Some enchantment woven into the

stone." I shrug. "I've had it explained to me a dozen times. I still don't understand it."

"How do you navigate without a map?"

"Practice." I trail my fingers along the wall as we walk, feeling the grooves worn smooth by centuries of hands doing the same. "The first 'important task' the Sages gave me was ferrying texts from the House of Truth to the vault. I was young enough to think it was an honor."

"How old were you?"

"I'm not sure. We lose track of age in Lunaris. The residents who arrive already have their gifts, and those of us who came as children..." I shrug. "We mark time by festivals, not years."

"But you have some idea."

"If we were truly five when we arrived, then I'm twenty-five. Give or take." I glance up at him, curiosity getting the better of me. "How old are you?"

He huffs a laugh, but there's something hollow beneath it. "That's ... complicated."

The way he says it makes me wonder just how complicated. Centuries, he'd said. The curse has lasted three hundred years, and he's been trying to break it since the beginning.

I decide not to push.

"To answer your question," I say, "I was too young and naive to care what the texts contained. Which is probably exactly why they chose me for the task."

"Who does it now?"

"The luminaries, I think. Initiates waiting for full membership. They're too focused on proving their loyalty to question what they're carrying." I pause. "Mother relies on that.

On people being too afraid of disappointing her to ask dangerous questions."

"Sounds like a High Sage."

"You've known others?"

He nods, his expression unreadable. "A few."

We turn right at a fork in the tunnel and emerge before the first burial chamber. Malachi slows to study it: marble columns flanking iron doors twice his height, the metal worked with symbols I've never been able to decipher.

"Have you ever been inside?"

"A few times." I smile despite myself. "Arlo was terrified of the hupia legend when we were children. Convinced the spirits of the dead would drag him into the crypts if he got too close. Once, I hid inside and jumped out at him." The memory surfaces, bright and warm. "I thought he was going to die of fright. Or murder me on the spot."

"Arlo." Malachi's voice is carefully neutral. "The legion guard."

"Yes." The word scrapes against my throat. "He's my best friend. Or he was." I swallow. "He was raised in Veritas with us. By the Sages."

He says nothing, but I feel his attention sharpen. Another piece of the puzzle, clicking into place in that calculating mind of his.

I keep walking. Past the other chambers. Past the stairs that spiral up to the Noxbridge Library. Toward the massive torch that burns at the end of the hall, its flame casting dancing shadows on the ancient stone.

I stop beneath the archway and study the three staves mounted on the wall. The central one burns eternally, its flame blue-white and unwavering. The flanking torches remain dark, their braziers cold.

"I've never actually opened the vaults," I admit as Malachi comes to stand beside me. His presence is warm at my back, solid and grounding. "But I understand the mechanism is similar to the doors. Fire and intention."

"Similar enough." He moves past me, close enough that I catch his scent, cedar and rain, and surveys the hall. "Which side is the Veritas vault?"

"The right." I watch him take the torch from its bracket and light it from the eternal flame. "The left was meant for the Council, but they have no access to the tunnels. Part of the treaty. Their vault is in the House of Knowledge."

"Interesting," he murmurs, and I can practically hear him filing the information away.

I watch the door, expecting a click, a groan, something. Nothing happens.

Malachi crosses to it without hesitation. He sets the torch into the cradle beside the frame and turns it, slow and deliberate, until something within the mechanism catches. Then he presses his palm flat against a dark square of stone I hadn't noticed, and holds.

The door sighs. There's no other word for it. A sound like ancient lungs releasing centuries of held breath. Then it swings inward, revealing only darkness beyond.

"How did you do that?" I whisper.

He glances back at me, firelight dancing in his eyes. "Magic."

I snort, but my heart is racing.

I follow him in. The door swings shut behind us, and the

darkness is immediate and absolute. I can't see my own hand in front of my face. Jordi always told me fire was forbidden inside the vault, the risk to the texts too great, but standing here in the black, I don't know what else to do.

I open my mouth to ask, and then the lights begin.

One by one, sconces flare to life along the walls. Blue-white flames, cold and strange, climbing from darkness to illuminate the space around us. They spread in a slow wave, circling the rotunda until the entire chamber glows.

I gasp. I can't help it.

The flames burn without heat, without smoke, without any fuel I can see. Some ancient enchantment I couldn't begin to understand. The lantern above the archway ignites next, then the lights in the chamber beyond, a cascade of illumination that feels almost like a welcome.

"Incredible," I breathe, and start forward.

The second rotunda steals what's left of my breath.

Books. Thousands of them. They line the walls from floor to domed ceiling, leather spines and cloth covers and materials I don't recognize, stacked and shelved and organized in ways that suggest centuries of careful curation. Spiral stairs climb both sides of the chamber, leading to a second level where glass cases hold artifacts that glint in the strange blue light. At the center of it all sits a round table surrounded by eight chairs, as if scholars might return at any moment to resume their work.

"Jordi's descriptions don't do it justice," I whisper.

This isn't just a vault. It's a temple to knowledge itself. And it's been hidden beneath Lunaris this entire time. We find the maps with surprising ease, organized by era and region.

I pull a stack of books from the shelves labeled "Lost Histories" and "Pre-Treaty Records," then settle beside Malachi at the table. We work in companionable silence. Him spreading maps across the worn wood, me turning brittle pages with careful fingers. The weight of centuries presses down around us, but it's not oppressive. It's almost peaceful.

A splash of color catches my eye. I look up to find Malachi unrolling a map unlike any I've seen: creatures swimming through painted oceans, winged figures soaring through illustrated skies, the cartography itself a work of art.

"Is that a forgery, or genuinely ancient?"

He squints at the script along the bottom. "It's around 350 years old, by my estimation."

I lean closer, bracing myself on the table's edge to study an island marked near the coast of Arusha. The script beside it is elegant, deliberate.

"The Island of Larimar," I read aloud. "I've never heard of it."

"Your maps are limited by design." He traces the island's outline with one finger. "And Larimar no longer exists."

My stomach drops. "The way Lunaris 'no longer exists'?"

"No." His voice is quiet. Final. "Larimar is truly gone. Cato destroyed it." He meets my eyes. "That's where the original healers came from. It was their homeland."

"What?" I sink back into my chair, the room tilting around me. "What do you mean?"

"The full history is probably in those books." He nods at the stack I pulled. "The short version is this: Cato wanted to marry Larimar's princess. She refused him. So he sent his army to slaughter everyone on the island and take her regardless."

The words are so simple. So matter-of-fact. And so utterly horrifying. For years, I've heard that healers were hunted to extinction. That unicorns were poached until none remained. I never understood how such things were possible. How an entire gift could be erased from the world.

Now I understand.

People like Cato made it so. He destroyed an entire civilization, murdered every soul on an island, because one woman denied him. *Gods.* That poor woman. To watch everyone she loved murdered, and then be taken by the man who ordered it.

For a moment, I almost understand the appeal of the memory trade. The mercy of forgetting something so horrific. But then I remember that the Council worships this man. That they've built their entire system around his ideology. And the nausea that rises in my throat has nothing to do with mercy.

I think of the Sages. How they forbade me from speaking about my gift. How they've always insisted I stay far from the Council's notice. They know, I realize.

They've always known what Cato is capable of. They've never put much importance on the last three hundred years of history, but there are things that transcend time, civilizations, and borders. Cruelty is one of them. The erasure of powerful women and people deemed "less than" by those in power appears in every culture I've ever studied.

It's a pattern as old as civilization itself. And yet. For every tyrant who rises, opposition rises too. It may be quieter. Less visible. But it endures. I hold onto that thought like a lifeline.

"Pia came from a long line of powerful women." Malachi turns toward me, his voice heavy with something that sounds like grief. "Her mother was the greatest healer of her generation. Her grandmother was a sorceress feared across three kingdoms. Her sister was a Sage."

"Is that why he wanted her?"

"He knew her gifts would be extraordinary. Even before they manifested." His jaw tightens. "She was thirteen the first time he visited Larimar. Seventeen when he returned to take her by force. She hadn't even come into her full power yet, and he was already certain she could restore his Everlasting scepter."

Thirteen. A child. And a monster had already marked her as his.

"That's what he wanted her for?" My voice comes out rough. I have to look away to blink back the tears threatening to form. "And people just allowed it? No one stopped him?"

"Allowed?" His eyebrows rise. "What do you think the war between Tenebris and Arusha has been about for three hundred years?"

The question lands like a blow. The war. The curse. All of it spiraling out from one man's obsession with one woman who refused to be owned.

"She fled to Tenebris," I say slowly, piecing it together. "And he followed. And cursed the entire kingdom because they gave her shelter."

"Yes."

Another thought surfaces, darker than the rest. "The child. The one Cato's hunters are searching for." I meet his eyes. "Please tell me it's not hers."

He's quiet for a long moment.

"They say he is."

I press a hand to my stomach, fighting the urge to be sick. "Gods. That poor child."

"He was hidden before Cato could find him. Raised in secret. The goddess showed some mercy there, at least."

I stare at the books without seeing them. "If the curse was cast three hundred years ago, wouldn't the child be…" I do the math, then stop. "Over three hundred years old?"

Malachi raises an eyebrow. "And how does aging work in the realm of the dead?"

Right. Noktemore. Time moves differently there, or not at all. A child hidden three centuries ago could still be a child. Or something else entirely.

"If Pia escaped him three centuries ago, maybe the Everlasting has lost its power by now." I cling to the hope. "Three hundred years is a long time without a healer to restore it."

"It would be, if people weren't still worshipping him across the kingdoms." Malachi's voice is grim. "You know what they say. Every thought you give someone is energy. Every prayer, every fear, every whisper of their name. It feeds them. We believe this about gods." His eyes meet mine. "The same is true for those who fancy themselves gods."

The implication settles into my bones like ice. All those residents in Lunaris, chanting the Everlasting's name. Bowing to his symbol. Feeding power to a monster they've never even seen. I close my eyes. Let the horror of it wash over me.

"There's more," Malachi says quietly. "Long before Cato set foot in Larimar, he served as one of King Runerth's advisors. He was stationed in Lunaris for a time."

My eyes fly open. "Here?"

"Here. Which means if the Hall of Gratitude was built on the site of an older temple, and if Cato himself was involved in its construction…"

He doesn't finish the sentence. He doesn't have to.

"That's terrifying," I whisper and frown as another question arises. "Cato wasn't born into royalty?"

"Gods, no." He scoffs. "Arusha was a queendom for thousands of years before he seized power. He overthrew an entire matriarchal dynasty. It was unprecedented."

"And no one stopped him?"

"They tried." He begins gathering the maps, his movements careful, reverent of their age. "But as you know, the Everlasting is a siphoner. What the Sages and Council accomplished here with elixirs and memory trade, Cato achieved in Arusha through the Everlasting and his voice alone."

His words. His compulsion. I wrap my arms around myself, suddenly cold despite the strange warmth of the enchanted lights.

"I don't know what's more disturbing," I say quietly. "That bloodlines and birth order determine who rules, or that someone like Cato can rise from nothing and crown himself king through sheer brutality."

Malachi's quiet laugh is unexpected. It fills some hollow place in my chest, just enough warmth to steady me. I look at the stack of books on the table. The lost histories. The erased truths.

"I'm taking these," I say, and it's not a question.

He doesn't try to stop me. One more defiant act. One more step away from the cage I was raised in. I tuck the books under my arm and follow him back into the dark.

CHAPTER SEVENTEEN

We take the stairs up to the Noxbridge Library. Malachi wants to search for the scepter, and I don't argue. I've always been fascinated by this place, though I've only been inside twice. Unlike Veritas University, which the Sages built from nothing, Noxbridge was constructed by the founding family of Tenebris itself, back when they still called Lunaris home.

"You should consider recruiting students here once the curse is lifted," he says, that infuriating lilt in his voice. "You'd be excellent at it."

"If you knew how much effort it takes not to strangle you every time you use that tone, you'd never speak again."

"Or I'd speak more." He winks. "Just to watch you try."

Heat rushes to my cheeks and settles somewhere lower. I look away, hoping to hide my reaction, but his low chuckle tells me I've failed. I sigh and shake my head. When I glance back, his attention has drifted to the decorative wings cascading down my back.

I can't help but laugh. "You can touch them, if you want."

His eyes find mine, searching, as if gauging whether I mean it. I turn my back to him and cross my arms, waiting. The first brush of his finger down my spine steals my breath. He does it again, slower this time, tracing the path of the decorative feathers.

A shaky laugh escapes me. "I don't think I've ever met anyone whose fascination with wings rivals my own."

He hums, the sound vibrating through the space between us. "You haven't met anyone who's actually had them, then."

I go still. The words repeat in my head. Had them. Actually had them.

I whirl around. "What?"

I search his face for answers, but he offers none. My mind races through everything I know about winged beings, which is far less than what I know about wings themselves. I devoured books about winged warriors as a girl, but those were romances, fiction dressed up as history. What I know for certain is that in Iredell, wings are a mark of royal blood.

Not every bearer sits on a throne, many are generations removed from power, but the bloodline runs true regardless. Malachi must be one of those distant heirs. He fought in the war alongside Draven and Kage, which tells me enough. The royals I've read about prefer to start wars from the safety of their palaces and let others bleed in their name.

They don't bargain away their freedom to goddesses of death. They don't spend centuries trapped in Noktemore, fighting to break curses they didn't cause. Whatever Malachi is, he's not that kind of royal. When I look at him again, his eyes are bright with amusement. He's enjoying this.

"Your curiosity almost tastes as sweet as your anger," he

murmurs, and the low rumble of his voice does something dangerous to my pulse.

"I hope you know I won't be able to focus on anything else until you answer every question I have."

He opens his mouth to respond, then snaps it shut. His head turns sharply toward the front of the library. Before I can ask what's wrong, his hand closes around my arm. He pulls me into a row of towering shelves as footsteps echo through the silence, growing closer with each second.

Another sharp turn, and he's pressing me into a shadowed alcove, my back flat against cold stone, his body blocking the entrance. The footsteps stop somewhere close. Too close.

"Did you hear about the crew they captured?" A gruff voice, unfamiliar.

"The ones who scaled the cliffs near the Keep?" Another voice, higher. "What did they want?"

"They claim to be searching for the heir. Cato's heir."

Silence. Then—"I can't imagine Lord Constantine took that well."

A snort. "He did not. Last time he visited Lyrionne, he had half the kingdom convinced he was the heir. Probably believes it himself by now."

"He probably believes Cato will thank him for taking Tenebris, too."

Malachi goes rigid against me, every muscle coiled. From the corner of my eye, I see a sconce flicker, and without thinking, I fist my hand in his cloak and pull him closer. His nose brushes mine. His breath ghosts across my lips. Neither of us moves.

"That'll never happen. Though I suppose this would be a good place to hide, if the heir even exists."

"The seer saw a son. Twenty years ago. And she saw him arrive here."

"Seers have been wrong before."

"You want to be the one to tell Cato his seer was wrong?"

Laughter, fading as they walk away. I hold my breath until the footsteps fade entirely. Twenty years ago. A good place to hide.

A lot of people arrived that year, but narrowing them down wouldn't be impossible. Unless Constantine doesn't want to find the heir. Unless he'd rather believe he is one. The thought stops me cold. Is that why he's so invested in the memory trade? So no one can prove otherwise?

"Well, they have weapons that can kill the Rooks. Between you and me, I hope they don't succeed. We don't need more of Cato's …"

The lights flicker. Through the bond, I feel Malachi's fury spike, sharp and sudden. We've been careful about keeping our emotions contained, but this is different. This is personal. He moves to step out of the alcove. I catch his arm and hold tight. He frowns down at me.

"You can't fight here," I whisper. "You can't spill blood in the Council's territory. Not unless you want both of us dead."

Something flickers in his expression, frustration or understanding, I can't tell. He nods once, scans the shadows, and signals for me to follow. I do. Quickly. Quietly. The stolen books in my bag press against my ribs, a reminder of everything I have to lose.

We slip out the side door and freeze.

Four men in legion uniforms stand in the alley, blocking our path. For one suspended moment, everyone is still. Then someone shouts, and the world erupts into chaos. Malachi moves before I can blink.

He seizes the man nearest him, twists his arm at an angle that shouldn't be possible, and drives him into the wall with a crack that echoes off the stone. The second man lunges. Mal catches him by the collar, drives an elbow into his face, then kicks him backward with enough force to send him crashing into the opposite wall. I only see those two before instinct takes over.

A third man charges at me from the left. My heart slams against my ribs, but I don't run. I plant my feet, wait until he's close, and drive my knee up hard. He doubles over with a grunt. I bring my foot up and catch him across the jaw.

He goes down. I pray he stays there. Movement in my peripheral vision. A fourth man, emerging from the shadows while Malachi is occupied.

"Mal!" I rip the blade from my cuff, but I'm too slow.

The man drives a dagger into Malachi's side.

The scream that tears from my throat doesn't sound human. I lunge forward, but hands grab me from behind, wrenching me backward. I don't think. Fire blooms in my palm, hot and bright, and I twist free and drive my blade into whoever's holding me without looking. They release me with a cry.

Please don't be dead. Gods. I hope I don't know them. I spin around. The man clutches his arm, blood seeping between his fingers, but he's alive. I turn back to Malachi.

He's clutching his side, staring at the blood-soaked blade

171

in the man's hand with an expression I can't read. Confusion. Disbelief. Something darker beneath.

The man who stabbed him grins, blood on his teeth. "I knew this Rook killer would come in handy."

My sigil flares so hot I can feel it searing through my blouse. I'm moving before I can think. Blade high. Arm extended.

I drive the steel into the man's bicep. He snarls and wheels toward me, the dagger rising. Mal is faster. He rips the weapon from the man's grip and opens his throat in one fluid motion.

The man's eyes go wide. So do mine. Blood sprays in an arc as he crumples to the cobblestones. Someone screams.

I think it might be me, but my ears are ringing and my body is shaking so hard I can't tell where I end and the world begins. I tear my gaze from the body and look around wildly. This is the same place. The exact same place where I healed Jordi.

Where the laborers died screaming for families they couldn't remember. And now this. More blood soaking into the same stones. I scan the rooftops for gray birds. The windows for watching eyes. Any sign that we've been seen.

Warmth floods through the bond, sudden and deliberate, and I gasp in a breath I didn't know I needed. Then I'm hauled off the ground. I register Mal's warmth, strong arms, and the feel of his breath against my temple, but I can't seem to stop shaking or take my eyes off the carnage around us.

"Bloodshed equals banishment," I whisper, the words pulled from me without thought.

The first law of Lunaris. The one the Sages always warned

us they couldn't protect us from. And I've just broken it in the Council's own territory. These men were wearing uniforms.

Someone will come looking. Someone will find out. I'll be banished. Gone. I'll never see Jordi again. Never help him get home.

Some distant part of my mind whispers that none of this will matter if we succeed. If we break the curse, if the Shroud falls, the Council's laws will mean nothing. Lunaris might not even exist anymore. But all I can think about is what I'll lose.

The chance to fix the elixir. To undo the harm I've caused. To find a way for the residents to remove their amulets without losing themselves to grief.

"Menace." Mal's voice in my ear breaks through my thoughts. "Look at me." My eyes find his face, blurred despite how close we are. "You did nothing wrong."

I nod and try to breathe. Try to feel anything beyond the cold numbness spreading through my chest. My gaze darts back to the bodies. Are they all dead?

Did I kill any of them? I was careful. I soaked my blades in white poppy this time, not wolfsbane. They should only wound, not kill.

But the man Malachi stabbed, his throat is sliced and his eyes are open. Fixed. The blood pooling beneath him is already going dark.

"Eyes on me," Mal says sharply. "Ada. Look at me."

I force myself to focus.

"These aren't legion guards." His voice is steady, certain. "They're Cato's hunters. They would have killed us both without hesitation." He scans the alley. "They probably murdered real guards to get those uniforms."

A shudder runs through me. Arlo probably isn't on duty tonight. But still. Legion guards are like the laborers: no memories from before, no thoughts of their own. They do what the Council tells them and believe what the Council wants them to believe. Easy targets for men who needed uniforms.

"How do you know they're Cato's hunters?" I whisper.

"No amulets. And legion guards don't carry that mark."

I follow his gaze to the nearest body. On the inside of the man's forearm, black ink stands stark against cooling skin: an eye inside a heart. The Everlasting. My stomach drops.

Malachi turns to leave. I struggle against his grip.

"You're hurt," I hiss. "Put me down."

"I'll be fine."

"We don't know how deep it went. Let me down so I can—"

He stops walking and fixes me with a look that steals the words from my tongue. "Will you just let me have this?"

I stare at him for a long moment. Then I stop fighting. I let my head fall against his shoulder, let my body sag into his arms. He exhales, and I feel the tension drain from him too, as if my surrender has given him permission to breathe.

For the first time since I made the bargain, I wonder what I'll feel when the bond is gone. If there will be a hollow place where his presence used to be. I don't let myself think about the answer.

Whatever fragile peace we found shatters the moment we reach my apartment.

The door hangs open. Inside, chaos. Books scattered across the floor like fallen leaves. My brother's bag, gone. The table where he drew his maps lies on its side, one leg snapped clean off.

My eyes catch on the bookshelf. It's been shoved aside, exposing the hidden alcove behind it. The entrance to the Veritas hallways, the secret we've guarded for as long as I can remember, laid bare.

I don't know what terrifies me more: that someone who knew about this passage betrayed us, or that the Council finally found it on their own.

Either way, nowhere is safe anymore.

CHAPTER EIGHTEEN

MY FIRST THOUGHT IS THAT SOMEONE KNOWS ABOUT THE scepter. My second is they're looking for anything to condemn Jordi as a renegade. Either way, I'm rattled. More rattled than I already was, which shouldn't be possible. I force myself to breathe, to push everything aside as I wash my hands and gather my supplies.

"Take off your tunic."

He raises an eyebrow, then flinches as he shifts toward me.

"Take off your tunic," I repeat. "And keep your infuriating comments to yourself."

Something dark flickers in his eyes. It hits me somewhere deep, somewhere I refuse to acknowledge right now. I force myself to look away. He starts to pull the tunic over his head, and I lunge forward when I see the fabric catch on the wound.

"Stop!"

He freezes, arms half-raised. "What now?"

"I need to cut it away from the wound. Just …" I scan the apartment until my eyes land on my brother's open doorway. "Let's do this on the bed."

He huffs a laugh. "Menace, if you wanted to get me into bed, you could have just—"

"Finish that sentence and I'll use the scissors on something other than fabric."

He laughs, the sound cut short by a hiss of pain. "Such excellent bedside manner."

"Be quiet and move."

I brush past him and pause in the doorway to Jordi's room.

The bed is made. Everything in place. Neater than my brother ever kept it. And it doesn't smell like him anymore—his particular blend of ink and the herbs he kept dried in his pockets. Now it smells like Malachi. Cedar and rain. I didn't expect that small detail to hurt as much as it does.

I swallow hard and focus on what needs to be done. I spread a towel across the mattress. Malachi lowers himself onto it without comment, watching as I cut the ruined fabric away from his wound. When I'm finished, he sits up just enough to toss the remnants aside.

When I look up, he's watching me, gauging my reaction to his scarred torso. The marks crisscross his chest and arms, pale lines against golden skin, too many to count. I keep my expression neutral.

We all carry scars. Mine don't speak of war, but they have their own stories. Some of which I don't even remember.

The dagger rests beside him on the mattress, its blade gleaming white in the lamplight.

"What is that made of?" I ask as I clean the wound.

He lifts it, turns it in his hand. "I'm not certain. Ivory,

perhaps. Or bone." His jaw tightens. "Whatever it is, it incapacitated me instantly."

My hands still. "He called it a Rook killer."

"He did."

I raise an eyebrow and hold his gaze as I dab alcohol into the wound.

He hisses through his teeth. "Remind me to hire you if I ever need someone interrogated."

"You're a warrior."

"You already knew that."

"I did." I lighten my touch on the wound. "Are you a Rook?"

"Yes."

The word settles into me with unexpected weight. "But Rooks are bound to raffins. Or they were."

His eyes crinkle at the corners. "We are."

I turn that over in my mind as I begin stitching the wound. Freida used to tell us stories about the Rooks, Lugal's chosen warriors, bound to their raffins through blood and magic. "They're barely leashed until the furia takes hold," she'd said once, her voice dropping low. "And then they're ruthless. Unstoppable."

I glance at Malachi's face. Calm. Patient. Waiting. I try to reconcile that image with the man bleeding beneath my hands.

"I thought you said you had wings."

"I did."

"Then why would you need a raffin?"

"Raffins fly higher than any winged being can reach. And they carry their own gifts." He's quiet for a moment.

"More importantly, the raffin chooses its rider. Mine chose me. I accepted."

I nod slowly, turning those two words over. *Chose. Accepted.* A bond built on mutual consent, not force or transaction. Unlike everything else in this godsforsaken city.

"I'm done," I murmur, tying off the final stitch.

He sets the dagger aside and sits up slowly. The movement brings his face close to mine, close enough that I can see the flecks of amber and gold in his eyes.

"I need one more favor."

My pulse kicks. "What?"

"My back." His voice drops. "It doesn't usually bother me. But since I arrived here, it's been ..."

He doesn't finish.

I bite back a smile. "And you're too stubborn to ask for help, even after I offered."

His eyes darken. Something low in my stomach tightens in response. We're so close that if I leaned forward even slightly, my lips would meet his. I don't lean forward. I force myself to stand instead, creating distance neither of us asked for.

"Let me see."

He shifts on the bed, turning his back to me. I have to press my hand to my mouth to keep from making a sound. I don't know what I was expecting, but this wasn't it. Never this.

I've assisted Lenora twice when she's had to amputate alatus wings. Both times left a mark on me that took months to fade. But those were clean procedures, done with care and precision. This is something else entirely.

The scars stretch across his shoulder blades in ragged arcs, as if someone took a blade to his back and carved out the wings in pieces. The skin is puckered and angry, healed wrong. Stitched carelessly.

"That bad?" His voice is light, but I hear the strain beneath it.

"Mal." My voice comes out rough. "What happened to you?"

I reach out, and the moment my finger touches the unmarred skin beside the scars, he hisses and arches away from me.

"I haven't even touched them yet."

His laugh is bitter, hollow. "I know."

"How can this possibly hurt more than the stab wound?" I reach for the balm, trying to keep my voice steady. "How long ago did this happen?"

"A few Reckonings."

"Is it always this bad?"

A pause. "I don't think so."

"I can give you something for the pain. The same compound I used for the stitches—"

"No."

The sharpness in his voice makes me stop. "Mal—"

"No." He doesn't look at me. "Numbing these scars will only make the pain worse later. It's part of the bargain."

I stare at the ruined landscape of his back. "What bargain demands that?" The implication hits me slowly. Then all at once. My eyes widen. "You bargained away your wings."

"Yes."

I try to wrap my mind around it. A god who would

accept wings as payment. Who would strip someone of flight and then forbid them from numbing the memory of what they lost.

"And you call her fair."

"I said she was fair." His voice is quiet. "I never said she wasn't cruel."

I don't have an answer for that. I begin applying the balm instead, working it carefully into the edges of the scars. The muscles beneath my fingers twitch, but he holds himself still.

"Wings are supposed to be a divine gift. Given to bloodlines the gods deemed worthy." I keep my touch as gentle as I can manage. "A goddess can't just take back a gift."

"She didn't take them. I offered them."

"So you made a bargain. Lost your wings. Lost even the mercy of numbing the pain." I shake my head. "And you still ended up trapped in Noktemore."

"That was a different bargain." His voice carries an edge of frustration. "And the cost of a debt is always steeper than the gain."

The words settle into me with an uncomfortable weight. I think of my own bargain. What I asked for. What I might still owe. A goddess saved my brother's life. In exchange, I'm supposed to help save an entire kingdom. The scales don't balance. They never have.

"Was it worth it?" I ask softly. "Whatever you bargained your wings for?"

He's quiet for a long moment. "I hope so."

"Will lifting the curse bring them back?"

"Lifting the curse won't bring back any of the lives lost." His voice is flat. Final. "I doubt it will restore what I gave up."

The words carve something hollow in my chest. In Lunaris, we speak of the curse in abstractions. The Shroud. The outsiders who flee here seeking safety. The rotting soil in distant Tenebris.

We never discuss what it means to live under that curse. What it costs the people who couldn't escape. The Council and Sages frame it as charity: they take in refugees from a broken kingdom. But we never hear from those kingdoms directly. We only know what we're told.

"Why are you still an apprentice?" The question cuts through my thoughts.

I huff a surprised laugh. "Have you been asking about me?"

"Yes." He glances over his shoulder, eyes gleaming. "Imagine my surprise when everyone described you as level-headed. Patient. A few students mentioned you were a harsh grader, easily annoyed, but otherwise—"

"The students are obnoxious."

"They also said you were the most attractive professor in Lunaris."

I snort, adding more balm to his shoulder. "At least I have that going for me."

"No one could tell me why you're still an apprentice."

"That's because no one knows."

"No one?" His gaze sharpens. "Not even your friends? Your brother?"

"No one."

"Why?"

I'm quiet for a moment, choosing my words carefully. "In

Lunaris, information is currency. And sharing certain things carries consequences I'd rather not invite."

He's quiet for a moment. "Will you tell me?"

I pull my hands away and meet his eyes. "If I tell you, you have to agree to wait until I'm finished before you unleash your wrathful judgment."

He raises an eyebrow. "Wrathful judgment sounds a bit harsh."

"Have you forgotten how you react every time the memory trade comes up?"

His eyes narrow. "I'll listen."

I give a nod and focus on the balm. "Do you have alatuses in northern Tenebris?"

"No. The surrounding kingdoms have similar creatures, but they call them pegasi."

"Pegasi are different." I shake my head. "Alatuses stand twenty-four to twenty-eight hands. Much larger. And they have venomous canines capable of killing a man in minutes."

"I guess you'll have to add animals to the list of things you have to teach me about," he says with a hint of amusement in his tone.

"Alatuses aren't native to Lunaris." I continue working the balm into his scars. "Neither are bonds. But although alatuses don't require bonds to accept riders, the Council deems they must be."

"The Council deems it," he mutters.

I ignore him. "An elixir is used to bind rider and alatus together. An alchemized bond."

"That's not how bonds are supposed to work."

"It's how ours work."

He shoots me a look. "That's different."

"I thought we agreed you'd withhold judgment."

He faces forward again. "The Creators forged bonds that allow those creatures to choose their riders. Choice is built into the magic."

"How can something forged be natural?"

"Forged doesn't mean forced." His voice softens slightly. "The rider can refuse. Walk away. The bond only holds if both parties consent."

"That's not how it works here."

He doesn't argue. But I feel his frustration bleeding through the bond.

"Natural bonds don't exist here," I say finally. "At least not anymore."

"Would you know if they did?"

The question gives me pause. "You think the memory trade severs bonds."

"I thought you didn't want my wrathful judgment?" He jolts and shoots me a bewildered look when I poke him in the ribs. "Is this how you treat all of your patients?"

"My patients are animals," I say sweetly. "They don't talk back."

His eyes warm as he studies my face, but he shakes it away as he says, "I think the memory trade could sever bonds, yes."

I swallow. "For years, the Sages tasked me with making the bonding elixirs."

"And you did it?" he asks, his voice deceptively soft.

"You act like I had a choice."

"Everyone—" He stops mid-sentence, brows furrowing.

He turns towards me again and searches my face. He doesn't ask, but I answer anyway.

"I was five when I arrived here. Five when I partook in the memory trade. Many of us arrived before our gifts manifested. As far as I know, it was the only year it happened. So, no, I didn't have a choice. Not then, and not when my gifts finally did manifest and the Sages discovered I could work with the Shroud mushrooms."

He swallows. "Gods, Menace."

He lifts a hand but I pull my own hand back before he can reach it. If I let him touch me right now, I'll shatter. I'm barely holding myself together as it is. If my refusal stings, he doesn't show it.

"When did you stop making it?" he asks, setting his hand back on the bed.

"A couple of years ago," I whisper. "I stopped making the memory elixirs too."

His eyes search my face. "And now they're punishing you."

I nod. "I knew there would be consequences. I didn't expect them to be this severe. But that's the nature of choices, isn't it? We never know what they'll cost until after we've made them."

Silence stretches between us as I finish. He doesn't move, even after I set the balm aside and wipe my hands clean. The weight of everything unsaid presses down on us both. I'm about to stand when he speaks again.

"Mortiana and Lugal keep me in stasis while I'm in Noktemore."

My breath catches. "Is that why you weren't sure if the

pain is always this bad? Because you're not fully conscious between Reckonings?"

He turns to face me. "I was 28 when I made my last bargain with Mortiana. That's when Lugal convinced her to grant me stasis."

I study his face, the way the lamplight catches the sharp planes of his jaw, the shadows beneath his eyes. "How long ago was that?"

Something flickers through the bond. Grief, old and worn smooth by time. "I was born the year Tenebris was cursed. I went into stasis 28 years later."

Three hundred years. Give or take.

"You've been in stasis that entire time?"

He nods. "Unless there's a Reckoning, or other tasks I need to complete."

"Is it like sleeping?"

He's quiet for a moment. "It feels like… restless nothingness. Aware but not awake. Existing but not living."

I have to look away. The weight of it presses down on me: his wings, his raffin, three centuries suspended in nothing. Too much. Too much for one person to bear.

"I'm sorry," I whisper. "For everything you've lost."

"It was a long time ago."

"That doesn't make it less awful."

He watches me for a long moment. "Do you regret it?"

"The bargain?"

"Choosing not to make those elixirs."

My first instinct is to say yes. I regret it every day, but that's not quite true. I think about the Shroud and what I suspect may be happening. The mushrooms.

The dying laborers. The pleasure gardens where the Council watches residents weep for memories they were never supposed to have. The guilt has been crushing lately. But regret?

I think back to the night it started. The half-dead alatus dragged into my clinic, an arrow wound turning septic because no one at the arena had the antidote. I remember the creature's pain, not for itself, but for its rider, who lay recovering somewhere in the Hall of Reflection. I remember how that rider replaced the alatus the following week. As if nothing had been lost.

I think of the laborers screaming for families they weren't supposed to remember. The pleasure gardens where grief becomes entertainment.

"No," I say finally. "I don't regret it."

"What about the bargain you made with the goddess? Do you think you'll regret that?"

"Which part?" I stand and begin gathering my supplies. "Our bond? Or agreeing to help lift a curse I barely understand?"

"Both."

I consider it as I work. Healing Jordi was never a choice. I might have worded the bargain differently, might have been more careful. But make it? I'd make it again in a heartbeat.

I meet his eyes. "Ask me again after we lift the curse."

His eyebrow rises. "You sound certain we will."

"I am." I start toward the door.

"Weren't you the one who pointed out how many times we've failed?"

I glance back, a smile tugging at my lips. "Weren't you the one who said you didn't have me before?"

Something shifts in his expression. Surprise, maybe. Or something softer. I don't wait for a response. I slip out of the room and close the door behind me, leaving him with the mess and the silence and whatever thoughts are churning behind those golden eyes.

Sleep doesn't come.

Every time I close my eyes, I see the scars on Malachi's back. The ragged arcs where wings used to be. I think about Larimar burning, and Pia taken, and the hunters in the alley with the Everlasting branded into their skin. I think about what Malachi said, about bonds being severed, about nothing in Lunaris being what it seems.

That thought is what drives me out of bed. I retrieve the books I took from the vault and spread them across my desk. Among them, a slim volume bound in black leather, unmarked. I don't remember taking it.

I don't even remember seeing it on the shelf. I open it anyway. The first line stops my heart. I slam the book shut. My heart hammers against my ribs. My hands shake around the leather cover.

There have been only a handful of moments in my life when I've stood at the edge of something that would change me completely. Irrevocably. This is one of them. I lift the book with trembling hands and study the cover.

The Veritas symbol is etched into the leather, so faint I nearly missed it before. That symbol used to mean truth. Valor. Justice.

It used to mean everything. I let myself mourn the girl who believed that. Just for a moment. Then I open the book again.

In the end, nothing will matter, except everything.

CHAPTER NINETEEN

A *Study in Darkness: The Shroud Accounts kept by Lenora Bromwell for the Veritas Order of Tenebris in the city of Lunaris Year: 250 A.S.*

I am not a scribe, but my predecessor advised us to keep our own account of our findings in the event the forgetting elixir is used against us.

After years of unrest and no formal government due to the absence of King Runerth and Queen Neith, a new arrival has caught the Sages' attention.

Constantine "The Just," a solar Duende from a small town between Mizu and Arusha, claims to have an answer to Lunaris' problems. The forgetting elixir.

The Sages are wary. Constantine is part of the Shadow Guild, and we all know what Cato has done with that elixir and that stone.

Yet Anala the All-Seeing's visions cannot be ignored. She saw Larimar burning. She saw Pia fleeing. She saw Constantine, the curse, and the evil lurking at our door.

Thus, the Veritas Treaty has been drafted and the forgetting elixir included, despite our concerns.

My predecessor warned them of two things:

A loud thump tears me from the page. The book slips from my fingers. My knee cracks against the desk as I jolt upright, and my sigil flares hot beneath my blouse.

"Godsdamn it." I shove back from the chair and storm to the door, yanking it open with more force than necessary.

Malachi and Kage stand in the hallway, eyebrows rising in unison as they take in my expression.

"Someone woke up on the wrong side of the bed," Kage murmurs.

"I was reading," I snap.

Malachi lifts a black leather book. "Kage brought this."

"And this." Kage dangles a brown paper sack between us. The scent of Milly's bakery wafts out, butter and sugar and something sweeter beneath.

My stomach growls, loud enough for both of them to hear. I exhale and step aside. "Fine. You're forgiven."

Kage chuckles as he follows me to the table. "I will never understand why men think women are unpredictable."

"The wise words of an eternal bachelor," Malachi says flatly.

I bite back a laugh as I pour passion fruit juice into three glasses. But my amusement dies when my gaze catches on the bookshelf across the room. We put it back in place. Organized the books. Made it look untouched.

But someone was here. Someone went through our things. And they either used that hidden passage or discovered it. Either way, we're exposed.

"I got into the Keep," Kage says, pulling out the chair across from me. "Found your brother."

My knees nearly give out. I sink into my seat before they can. "And?"

"Exhausted. But unharmed." He nods at the black book on the table. "He asked me to bring you that."

"You're certain he's not hurt? They haven't—"

"I asked. He hasn't been touched." Kage meets my eyes. "Not physically, anyway."

"Thank you." The words come out unsteady. I reach for the book, but Malachi's hand closes over mine.

"Eat first."

The concern in his eyes makes something in my chest tighten. My stomach growls again, betraying me, and I decide not to argue.

Everything else fades when I tear off a piece of the warm, flaky bread and find melted guava inside. I close my eyes and let myself have this one small moment of sweetness. When I open them, both men are watching me with undisguised amusement.

I look at Kage. "You bought these?"

He nods, wary.

"I've never given marriage much thought," I say, reaching for another piece. "But between news of my brother and Milly's guava bread, I'd marry you tomorrow if you asked."

Kage throws his head back and laughs, the sound rich and startled. Through the bond, I feel a flicker of annoyance from Malachi, quickly smothered by reluctant amusement.

"I was the one who sent him to the Keep," Malachi says, a glint in his eyes that makes my pulse stutter. "And told him to bring the food."

I shrug, reaching for another piece. "Then you can be a contender."

He barks a surprised laugh. "You're going to make us compete for your heart?"

"My heart?" I raise an eyebrow over the rim of my glass. "I thought we were discussing marriage."

Kage chokes on his bread.

"You don't think you can have both?" Malachi asks, his voice dropping into something more serious.

"I do. I just wouldn't expect you two to care about the distinction."

"What makes you say that?" Kage manages between coughs.

"Outsiders have a different view of marriage."

Malachi's eyebrow rises. "As opposed to the High Sage, who selects your partners for you?"

I shoot him a look but don't take the bait. "The merchants who come through Siren's talk about marriage in terms of legacy. Heirs. Bloodlines. They don't see their spouses as people. They see them as warm bodies to share their beds and raise children who'll carry their names forward." I take a sip of juice. "The entire institution is clouded by the obsession with what comes after."

"And how do you view it?" he asks quietly.

"We don't have children in Lunaris. Marriage isn't about legacy here. It's about partnership." I turn the glass in my hands. "Companionship. Comfort. Emotional security." I meet his eyes. "We have our own work, our own income. We're not looking for someone to provide for us. We're looking for someone to weather the storms with."

Kage makes a sound of quiet surprise. Malachi's frown deepens, as if the concept of marriage is entirely foreign to him. I suppose it is. Three centuries in stasis doesn't leave much room for thinking about partnership.

"Would you want children?" Kage asks. "If you could have them?"

The question catches me off guard. "I've never thought about it."

His eyes widen. "Never?"

I shake my head and let my gaze fall to their hands. Scarred. Calloused. Hands that have held weapons, drawn blood, survived things I can only imagine. Hands that have lived.

Even Malachi, frozen as he's been, had 28 years of real life before stasis. Different kingdoms. Different struggles. A world beyond these walls.

Those of us raised in Veritas have only ever known this. It's one of the things Jordi used to argue about, late at night when we couldn't sleep. How can we know what we're missing if we've never had it?

In light of everything I've learned, I can see how I may have been wrong about a lot of things. I always believed the memory trade was merciful. The incantations let people keep their cultures, their food, their music, the fabric of who they are. The trade only takes the pain.

That's what I told myself, even after I stopped making the elixirs. But maybe that's only true in Veritas. How would I know what happens in the rest of Lunaris? I can't shake what I saw in those laborers. The way they screamed.

And the pleasure gardens, where grief is turned into

spectacle, make everything worse. Outside of Arlo, Cas, and Bas, I don't know anyone who lives under Council rule. And even they were raised in Veritas. Do they count? Does Bas, who I barely recognize anymore?

Fear of the silent guards keeps us from even trying to know them. Everything I've heard about Council residents is secondhand. And when I sort through those scraps, I realize how empty they are. I've never heard anyone describe a Lunarian as funny.

Or creative. Or kind. Only functional. "A new guard training near the Shroud." "A dueler who can flip mid-air." Descriptions of what they do. Never who they are.

Gods. I made those elixirs for years and never once questioned whether the incantations were the same for everyone. The words are kept locked away in the House of Truth. Only the healers who perform the ceremonies know what they say.

But Draven said Freida told him his incantation was different. Different words. Different intent. What if the ceremonies aren't the same at all? What if Veritas and the Council use entirely different incantations?

The painting behind Mother's desk surfaces in my mind. The woman in crimson, trapped inside bubble after bubble after bubble. We call ourselves the guardians of truth. The keepers of ancient knowledge.

Our texts span thousands of years and countless cultures. But what is knowledge without experience? What good is truth if you can only read about it, never live it?

I clear my throat and force myself back to the present. "How did you get into the Keep?"

"Can't reveal all my secrets." Kage winks. "Not if we're to be married."

Malachi makes a low sound in his throat. I pretend I don't notice.

"Your brother wanted me to tell you something," Kage says as I slide the book toward me. His voice has gone serious. "He said he was trying to spare you from this. And that you shouldn't blame yourself for what's inside."

My stomach turns. Whatever sweetness the bread brought is gone now. I think of the other book, the one still sitting on my desk with its gold-inked warning. Then I take a breath and open this one.

The Council's signet is embossed on the first page. I flip past it and find columns. Row after row after row of them, filling every page.

Names. Hundreds of names.

"What is this?" My voice comes out barely above a whisper.

"A ledger," Malachi says quietly. "Duelers. Laborers."

"Jordi said there are more like it," Kage adds. "This is just the one he could get to."

I scan the columns. Names in the first. Gifts in the second, healer, seer, fire-wielder, empath. The third column stops me cold. Prices.

Each person has a price.

I press a hand to my mouth. There has to be another explanation. There has to be. My hands shake as I flip through the pages. I search for Arlo. For Cas. For Bastian. None of them appear.

Understanding sinks in. They wouldn't be here. They

arrived as children, the same year I did, and were raised in Veritas. This ledger is something else. Something worse.

I look up at them. My voice shakes. "All of these people were purchased."

It's not a question. I can see the answer in their faces. In the careful pity they're trying to hide. Warmth reaches through the bond, Malachi trying to steady me, but I wrench myself away from it.

Sever the connection before it can take hold. I can't accept comfort right now. Not for this. Not when I made the elixirs that kept these people compliant. Not when I helped build the cage they were sold into.

CHAPTER TWENTY

I leave the pretty dress hanging in my wardrobe. Tonight calls for something else. I pull the Veritas armor from my trunk. I've only worn it twice, both times ceremonial, but tonight it feels right.

Necessary. The pleated black leather skirt sits high on my waist. The silver chest plate fits like a second skin, scalloped shoulder guards curving over my arms. I clip the round medallions into place, the Veritas symbol etched into each, and fasten the maroon cape and hood.

Finally, I secure the silver cuffs on my forearms and pull on my boots. When I catch my reflection in the mirror, I look like I'm ready for war. Good.

Malachi turns toward me when I walk out of my bedroom. His gaze travels slowly from my boots to the crown of my head, lingering in places that make heat rise to my cheeks.

"Did you enter a dueling competition I wasn't informed of?"

"No." I brush past him toward the door. "But you've just reminded me to enter you in the annual jester competition."

His low chuckle follows me out.

We take the back routes, but tonight I lead us down a path most outsiders never find.

"How are your injuries?" I ask as we walk. "Both of them."

"Better. No pain on my side or my back."

I turn to stare at him. "You're serious?"

"Why wouldn't I be?"

"Because that weapon was designed to kill you. And those scars looked like they'd been hurting for centuries."

"Well." His mouth curves. "I am being treated by the finest alchemic healer in Tenebris. Possibly all of Iredell. Perhaps even—"

I bump his side with my shoulder. "Okay, I believe you!"

He chuckles. My laughter fades as we approach the live oaks that flank the narrow path. Someone has strung lights through the branches, hundreds of them, glowing soft and golden against the dark.

Neither of us speaks.

By day, these trees form a canopy of twisted trunks and trailing moss, beautiful in an ancient, overgrown way. By night, the path usually feels foreboding, shadows pooling between the roots. But tonight, bathed in this borrowed starlight, it's something else entirely.

I turn to say something, but the words dissolve before I can speak them. Malachi walks beside me with his hands in his pockets, his stride unhurried for once. The golden light softens the sharp edges of him, and he looks less like the terrifying warrior I've come to know and more like ... something else. Someone who might have existed before the curse. Before the bargains. Before everything was taken from him.

"What is this place called?" he asks softly.

"It doesn't have an official name." I look up at the canopy above us, where the branches from opposite sides of the path reach toward each other, intertwining like fingers laced together. "The students call it Union Street. Because the trees look like they're trying to hold on to each other."

I don't know why my voice drops. "There's something almost tragically romantic about it, don't you think?"

He's quiet for a moment. "There's a word in the old tongue. Adhoranelo."

"Adhoranelo," I repeat softly. "What does it mean?"

"It doesn't translate directly." His voice is low, thoughtful. "It describes a feeling of deep longing. A soul-deep ache for someone, or somewhere." He glances at me. "The kind of ache that never fully goes away."

"That sounds unbearably sad."

"It's not meant to be." Something soft enters his expression. "The elders say the ache settles in your chest as a reminder. That somewhere in the world, there's a place you belong. Or a person you're meant to find."

"I suppose that's slightly less devastating."

The corner of his mouth curves.

"Some cultures believe it means you have a bonded mate out there, waiting." He laughs quietly when he sees my expression shift. "Would that be so terrible?"

I glance at him sideways. "I've never even considered children. You think I've spent time contemplating bonded mates?"

"Then we have that in common."

Something in my chest tightens. It's a strange, complicated feeling. Part of me wants him to say he wishes I were his true bonded mate. The other part aches for the fact that he's never allowed himself to imagine having one at all.

We emerge from the canopy into the glow of Veneficia Alley. Music drifts from somewhere ahead, lively and bright, at odds with the weight of our conversation.

"What happens if you're already with someone when you meet your bonded mate?"

"I imagine you'd have a difficult conversation ahead of you. Assuming you chose to pursue your bonded mate." He pauses. "Though I suspect the conversation would be uncomfortable either way."

"So you don't have to accept your bonded mate?"

"Of course not. Both parties have to choose. The bond only holds if both sides consent." He shoots me a pointed look. "Our current situation notwithstanding."

"What if one chooses and the other doesn't?"

"Then one of them spends the rest of their life carrying the ache alone."

"That sounds dramatic."

His lip twitches. "Perhaps. But imagine knowing the person the gods chose for you is living happily with someone else. That you could have had them, and chose not to."

"What if someone has multiple bonded mates?"

His eyes glint in the lantern light. "Not in this realm. Though I've heard it works differently elsewhere."

"Fascinating," I murmur.

"Could you handle multiple mates?"

I scoff. "If it's anything like what we have? Absolutely not." I meet his gaze. "And I wouldn't want to."

His chuckle dies abruptly. His gaze snaps to something

in the alley ahead. Before I can see what caught his attention, he's pulling me off the main road and into the shadows of a side street. His grip on my arm is tight. Urgent.

"Go straight to Siren's. Tell Kage to meet me here."

"What is it? Who did you see?"

"I'll explain later." His eyes are hard. "Go. Now."

I nod and rush towards Siren's. I find Kage laughing with a stranger in the middle of the street. The moment I relay Malachi's message, all traces of humor vanish. He heads toward the alley without a word.

I stand there, torn between following and continuing on. The door to Siren's opens before I can decide and Naima steps out. We both freeze when we realize we're dressed identically—the same armor, the same cape, the same silver cuffs. For a moment, we just stare. Then we're laughing, pulling each other into a tight embrace.

"I needed this right now," she breathes against my ear and holds me tighter when I stiffen. "Jordi's fine, as far as we know, but Arlo came to deliver other concerning news. He doesn't want all of us seen together, so he's waiting in a private room near the stairs. When we go inside, smile, wave, and act natural. There are people in there we need to avoid."

My heart pounds as she drapes an arm over my shoulders and guides me inside. I paste on a smile and play along, waving at familiar faces, pretending nothing is wrong as she leads me to the private room. It's the performance of my life.

The room is small and dim, lit only by a single sconce. Arlo stands near the window, dressed in his new uniform—dark green with thick gold epaulettes and gleaming buttons.

His blond hair is tied back, revealing his arched ears. For a long moment, neither of us moves.

I study the sharp lines of his face. The cheekbones, the jaw, those soft green eyes that haven't changed since we were children. I don't know who moves first. One moment I'm by the door. The next, I'm in his arms, and we're both crying into each other's shoulders like the world is ending. Maybe it is.

In this moment, I forget about his uniform, the Council, the ransacked apartment. He's just Arlo. The little blond boy with the lisp who broke my naive heart when he confessed he was in love with my brother. Who became my brother in every way that mattered.

I push away every fear, that the Council has changed him, that we've lost him, that we'll never get him back. Instead, I hold onto the memories. The way he held my hand in the healing chambers when Jordi couldn't bear to go. The way he always knew when I needed space, and when I needed someone to pull me out of myself. The way he never judged me for either. I hold him tighter, trying to thank him for all of it without words.

"Gods, Temp." His voice cracks. "I wanted to see you. It's been impossible."

"I know." I pull back, wiping my face. "I saw your ... promotion."

He flinches. "You were there?"

"Yes." I manage something like a smile. "I hate your new uniform."

He laughs, the sound watery. "You hated my old one too."

My lip trembles. I pull him into one more hug before

stepping back. "This must be urgent if you braved the tunnels. With all those Hupia spirits lurking."

He sputters. "I'm a champion dueler!"

"And that means you're no longer afraid of ghosts following you home?"

He rolls his eyes. "I'm a very fast runner."

That startles a real laugh out of me. His eyes warm.

"I missed you, Temp."

"I missed you too, Lo." The lightness lasts only a moment. "Have you seen Jordi?"

"No. It was difficult enough getting there before. Now it's impossible." His expression darkens. "That's why I'm here. To warn you."

My stomach drops. "Warn me about what?"

"The Council knows." His voice is low, urgent. "They know the Sages raised children in Veritas. They don't have names yet, but they're looking."

"How do they know?"

"I don't know. But I overheard Constantine and Nicolas. They've sent guards everywhere, claiming they're hunting renegades. But I think they're trying to identify us. Find out who the children were." He hesitates. "Cas was assigned to search your quarters."

The air leaves my lungs. "Cas did that?"

"He didn't have a choice. He had to make it look thorough."

"The hidden passage was exposed, Arlo. That's not thorough. That's deliberate."

Pain flashes across his face. "You really think Cas would

betray us? What would he have to gain? He was raised alongside us!"

I look away and swallow. I hate that I don't have answers to those questions. That I even have to doubt him at all. I force myself to breathe and look at him again.

"Why does Constantine even care? We're not children anymore."

"It would be a treaty violation. The Sages weren't supposed to raise anyone. Not without Council approval."

"And arresting the Veritas mapmaker isn't a violation?"

His jaw tightens. "We might see it that way. But the Sages haven't retaliated."

"Why would they want the Sages to retaliate?"

"I don't know." He runs a hand through his hair. "All I know is Constantine is furious that the Sages raised children without his knowledge. The visitors keep mentioning an heir—Cato's son—and Constantine keeps insisting he's the heir. But behind closed doors, he's obsessed with the children the Sages raised." His eyes meet mine. "It's only a matter of time before they discover you were singled out. That there were seven."

My heart plummets. There are so many threads to follow here, so many dangers. But one terrifies me more than the rest. "Lo. Three of you are in their territory. In their fold."

"We were young when we arrived at the Dueling Estate. The Sages provide housing for some duelers. It wouldn't seem strange that we went home on weekends." His smile is sad, resigned. "Besides, we're too popular now. Hurting us would hurt their image."

"That's not protection, Arlo. That's leverage." I press a hand to my forehead. "Gods, I hate this. All of it."

"Just be careful what you say around the visitors. The Council is more vigilant than I've ever seen them."

I think of the hunters in the alley. The Everlasting branded into their skin. I keep my face neutral. The lights flicker. A wave of discomfort floods through the bond—not mine. Footsteps in the hallway. We both turn toward the door. I realize too late that I never locked it.

"I have to go." Arlo snatches his cloak and moves toward the large mirror at the back of the room.

I rush to him, pull him into one last embrace as he swings the mirror open.

"Please be careful."

"You be careful." He grabs my face, presses a hard kiss to my forehead and slips into the darkness beyond.

The mirror swings shut behind him. The mirror hasn't finished closing before the door bursts open behind me. I spin, heart in my throat. Malachi fills the doorway.

His eyes sweep the room, land on the mirror, then snap to me. He steps inside and kicks the door shut behind him, the lock clicking into place. The look on his face makes my breath catch. Gone is the man who walked with me under the oaks, speaking of bonded mates and ancient words. This is the warrior. The Rook. Every line of him is coiled tight, dangerous.

"Did something happen?" I whisper.

His eyes narrow on my face. Even knowing he'd never hurt me, I feel the weight of his attention like a physical thing. I've seen him angry before. This is different.

It takes me an embarrassing moment to identify what

I'm feeling through the bond. Not his anger, though that's there too. Jealousy. Sharp and primal, clawing at the inside of my ribs.

I square my shoulders. "Mal. Did something happen? Outside?"

"No." The word is clipped. Final. His voice is so low and controlled it raises the hair on my arms.

The air between us crackles. I can feel the tension in my teeth. "Then what are you doing here?"

"Looking for you." His voice drops. "As usual."

The intensity of his stare makes it hard to think. "How did you find me?"

"Your friend told me you were in a private room."

The way he spits the word tells me what he thought I was doing in here. My pulse kicks up.

"And you thought interrupting me was a good idea?"

"No." He shakes his head, pushing off the door, advancing toward me with slow, deliberate steps. "I knew it was a terrible idea. Probably my worst yet."

My heart pounds harder with each step he takes. "But you did it anyway."

"Yes."

"Why?"

I step back. He keeps coming. I step back again, and again, until my spine meets the wall.

His eyes darken. "It's my turn to ask questions."

I nod, not trusting my voice.

"This need I feel through the bond." His voice is rough. "Is it for the person who just disappeared through that door?"

"No." I hold his gaze. "Of course not."

"Of course not?" He's close enough now that I can see the gold flecks in his eyes. "It's a rather intense need."

My breath shallows. "It is. But it's for you."

He closes his eyes. When he opens them again, they're molten. "Is it you? Or the bond?"

I stare at him. "You can't be serious."

The look he gives me says he absolutely is. Something snaps in my chest.

"Is it the bond when you stare at me across a room like I'm the only person in it?" I step toward him, closing the distance he created. "Is it the bond when you watch my lips like you're dying to know how they'd feel against yours? When you angle every glass we share so your mouth lands exactly where mine was?"

Another step. He doesn't retreat.

"When you choose the chair closest to mine, every single time? When you find excuses to brush your hand against mine over maps we've already memorized?" My voice drops. "Should I continue?"

His eyes blaze. He closes the final distance between us, and suddenly my back is against the wall and he's everywhere, one hand cupping the back of my neck, his calloused thumb tracing the line of my jaw. My pulse is a drum.

My hands find his cloak, fisting the fabric, pulling him closer. I tilt my face up, eyes closing, waiting. He doesn't close the gap. I make a sound of frustration and yank him toward me.

"Tell me what you want." His voice is a low rasp against my lips.

"Right now? I want to kill you."

"Right now," he breathes, "I just might let you."

And then his mouth is on mine.

The kiss is slow. Devastating. His tongue traces the seam of my lips before sliding inside, exploring with a precision that makes my knees weak. A soft brutality.

A careful conquest. As if he's been imagining this for weeks and refuses to rush a single second of it. I try to match his pace. The hunger burning through me makes it impossible.

His hands slide down my sides, my hips, and settle on my thighs. I try to deepen the kiss, to chase him when he pulls back. He breaks away just far enough to search my face. His eyes are dark and wild, storm clouds over a churning sea.

Through the bond, I feel hesitation. A question. My voice won't come. So I answer in a different way. I slide my hands down his arms, feeling the muscles coil beneath my touch, and dig my nails in.

The lights flicker. He hoists me up in one fluid motion, lifting me against the wall. His hands slide beneath my skirt, rough and warm, and a shiver races through me as I wrap my legs around him.

He settles between my thighs, but not close enough. Not where I need him. I lock my ankles behind his back and pull. The motion forces him forward, pressing him exactly where I'm burning for him. The sound he makes is low and raw. His mouth crashes back into mine.

I rock against him again, and he growls into my mouth, a sound that vibrates through my entire body. I try to get closer, always closer, but it's not enough. He grips my hips and drives forward, hitting exactly the right spot, and I gasp, breaking the kiss. My head falls back against the wall. I've never felt so completely out of control. I don't want it to stop.

Some distant part of my mind notes that we're wearing far too many clothes. Then his mouth finds my neck, and I stop thinking entirely. His teeth graze my pulse point. His tongue follows. When he sucks hard enough to leave a mark, I forget my own name.

My fingers sink into his hair, gripping, pulling him closer. "Gods, yes—"

"*Fuck*," he breathes against the hollow of my throat.

He pulls back suddenly, and I make a sound of protest before I can stop myself. "Look at me."

I do. And the air leaves my lungs. No one has ever looked at me the way he's looking at me now. Like I'm the only thing in the world that matters. Like he'd burn kingdoms to keep me.

"You're the most beautiful thing I've ever seen." His voice is guttural.

Before I can respond, his mouth claims mine again. I dig my nails into the back of his neck. He bites my lip in response, and the sound I make is shameless. His hips surge forward.

I meet him thrust for thrust. The kiss turns savage. All teeth and tongue and desperation, flames consuming everything in their path.

"Bain!" Kage's voice cuts through from the other side of the door.

The lights flicker violently. We wrench apart, chests heaving, both of us turning toward the sound.

"Temp." Naima's voice. Urgent. "This is important."

"Be right there!" I manage.

Malachi presses his forehead to mine, breathing hard. "What was it you said? Bloodshed means banishment?"

I choke out a laugh as I untangle myself from him, smoothing my skirt, trying to make myself presentable on the way to the door. My hands are still shaking as I open it, but the expressions that greet me kill whatever warmth was left in my body.

Naima. Kage. And behind them, Margot, pale as death, eyes wide and glassy. Kage pushes past me without a word. The others follow. I barely manage to shut the door behind them.

"This better be a godsdamn emergency," Malachi says, still breathing hard.

Margot meets my eyes. "I had a vision."

Three words. The room goes cold.

I look at Naima, who looks as terrified as I feel. We both know what those words mean. In Lunaris, seers are hunted. Visions are a death sentence. And Margot just admitted to having one. In front of outsiders.

"What did you see?" My voice comes out barely audible.

"You. And Bain. At the welcoming ceremony." Her voice shakes. "You have to be there."

"Why?" Malachi demands.

Margot shakes her head. Tears pool in her eyes, threatening to fall. "I don't know," she whispers.

My stomach hollows. I've never seen Margot like this—trembling, tears threatening to spill, terror written across every line of her face. I start toward her, but she raises a shaking hand to stop me. Naima tries next. Margot stops her too. Whatever she saw, she needs to get it out before she falls apart.

"I saw the blood moon rise over the ceremony." Her voice fractures. "And I saw... I saw Bas. Publicly executed. By the Council."

The words hit me like a physical blow. "At the ceremony?"

"No." Her lip quivers.

This time, Naima surges forward and wraps her arms around Margot from behind before she can stop her. Margot crumples. A sob tears through her, raw and broken, and she grips Naima's arms like they're the only thing keeping her upright.

"Margie." Naima's voice is soft, steady. "Is all of this happening at once?"

Margot shakes her head. "Not at once, but it's all connected."

Naima nods and gently pushes the hair from Margot's tear-streaked face. She looks at me over her shoulder. The expression on her face cracks something in my chest. I press my hand to my mouth, fighting to keep the wave of emotion from crashing over me.

Warmth pulses through the bond, steady and grounding. I feel Mal move closer but don't look away from Margot as she takes a shuddering breath and meets my eyes.

"Bas ... it happens at the amphitheater. And ..." She bites her trembling lip. "And you. I saw you get taken, Temp."

The floor tilts beneath me. Malachi's hand closes around my arm as I stagger, but I can't look away from Margot.

"Taken?" I whisper.

"By who?" Mal growls.

"I don't know," she sobs quietly.

I've never known my friend to be a liar, but there's

something she's not telling us. I can feel it in my bones. I think of Jordi in the Keep. Arlo's warning about the Council hunting us. The ledger full of purchased people. And now this. But if Margot dared to reveal her gift in front of outsiders, if she risked everything to tell us this much ... why wouldn't she just say everything?

"Temp." Naima's voice cuts through the chaos in my head. "The welcoming ceremony. It's happening right now."

Right now. Which means Margot's visions start tonight.

CHAPTER TWENTY-ONE

THE WELCOMING CEREMONY HAS ALWAYS BEEN HELD IN WHAT was once Sulara's temple. That knowledge used to comfort me. I told myself that even though the Council erased the goddess of rebirth from history and built the House of Truth over her sacred ground, something of her remained. That she was still here, guiding new residents toward their own rebirths. Their freedom.

Now, as I reach the door to the hidden passage within the temple walls, I wonder if I had it backward all along. What if she's been cursing us? What if every rebirth has been a new cage?

The door swings shut behind us, and darkness swallows everything. My hand opens instinctively. Fire blooms in my palm, casting dancing shadows on the ancient stone. I use the flickering light to guide us to the nearest latch—a small iron hook set into the wall.

I've only witnessed the ceremony twice, both times from this exact vantage point. Mother insisted on it. By the time the Council departed and I was allowed to descend, everyone had gone. Only the stones remained. The stones always remain.

I hold my breath, slip my finger into the hook, and extinguish my flame. The brick slides into the hollow beside it with a soft scrape of stone on stone. Orange light floods my vision. I blink against it, eyes adjusting.

Below, three figures in dark green hoods sit in a semicircle. A fourth stands beneath the open dome at the center of the rotunda. Two more figures in maroon flank the table. Veritas healers, here to perform their part.

The table holds the instruments of transformation. A small vial of clear elixir, and two green velvet pillows. One cradles a memory stone. The other, an amulet.

My stomach twists. Part of me hoped I'd witness a Veritas ceremony—gentle, respectful, the version I've always believed in. But Margot's vision brought us here. This is exactly what I'm meant to see.

I hadn't yet learned to make the elixir when Mother first brought me here. I was too young to understand what I was watching. I'm not too young anymore. I close my eyes as Malachi moves closer, his presence steadying me.

Then I open my serephony gift and let the room's emotions flood in. I find Anala immediately. Her familiar warmth, her steady resilience. I almost tune her out of habit.

Then I feel something else. Something that doesn't belong. Guilt. My eyes fly open. I can't see her face from here, but I search for it anyway. The Sages carry many emotions. Guilt is not one of them.

Movement below pulls my attention away. A hooded figure approaches the table and lowers their hood. From this angle, I can only make out short black hair. Warm brown skin.

They're instructed to turn. To face in our direction. I stop breathing. The resemblance is impossible to ignore.

The same skin tone, the same arched ears peeking out of the mop of brown hair, the same pillowy lips and sharp cheekbones. A younger version, but unmistakable. He looks exactly like Cas.

They instruct him to kneel. He does, slowly, as if the motion costs him something. And then I see his hands. Scarred. Trembling.

My gaze snaps to the Veritas healer beside Anala. I wait for her to ask the question that should come first. *Are you here by choice?* She doesn't ask. No one does.

I turn my gift toward the boy and let his emotions in. The agony hits me like a blow to the chest. I stagger backward. Malachi's arm around my waist keeps me upright. His presence steadies me enough to breathe. But I don't close the connection. I need to feel this.

Constantine's voice echoes through the rotunda. "One drop of blood, freely given. All memories surrendered. The price of sanctuary is trust."

The words are ceremonial. Sacred. They should mean something. And I guess they do. It's just not what I always thought they meant. One of the Veritas healers steps forward.

She carries the vial, the blade, and both stones on their velvet pillow. Her approach is slow. Calm. The same way I approach injured animals at the clinic. *I won't hurt you. Trust me. I want to help.* And like those injured animals, this boy doesn't seem to have a choice.

She kneels before him. Sets everything down with gentle

precision. I don't know what I expected. Something violent, perhaps.

Something that matches the horror coiling in my chest. But her voice is soft as she begins the incantation, too low for me to hear. The words the healers speak are never written down. Never shared. The only text available to read is Constantine's. I'm beginning to understand why.

I focus on his emotions again, forcing myself to stay open. The sadness. The grief. They pour through me like ice water.

This is what the ceremony promises to remove. I just wish I could take it from him without him having to surrender anything in return. But beneath the grief, I feel something else. Resistance. Defiance. And anger. Gods, his anger burns through my sigil as if it were my own.

He takes the vial with a shaking hand. The damned elixir. He drinks it in one swallow and sets it down so hard the glass should shatter. His hands stop trembling.

His emotions begin to dim, but the defiance is still there, clawing at the walls closing in around it. Something clicks into place. A realization so heavy I can barely hold it. I push it down. I can't afford to fall apart yet.

The healer takes his hand, turns it palm-up, and draws the blade across his skin. The boy flinches but doesn't make a sound. Blood wells in the wound, dark and gleaming. The memory stone is pressed into his bleeding palm.

The amulet placed atop it. Another incantation, soft and inexorable. His body begins to tremble. Malachi's arm tightens around me.

"Breathe, Menace," he whispers in my ear.

I bite my tongue and nod as my eyes fill with tears. I can't breathe. I can't. I don't deserve to.

Not right now. I hold onto the boy's emotions, his defiance, and then all at once everything stops. His trembling. His defiance. All of it is sucked into the stones in his bleeding palm. Gone.

The healer rises and helps him to his feet. He turns toward us again. This time, when I reach for his emotions, there's nothing. A hollow where a person used to be.

Constantine's voice slices through the silence. "On behalf of the Everlasting, I, Lord Constantine, receive your truth."

He stops mid-sentence. Someone gasps. The Veritas healer looks up, yanking her hood down. Constantine does the same. Others follow—green cloaks, maroon cloaks, figures emerging from shadows I hadn't noticed. All of them staring upward. Malachi goes rigid against me. I follow their gaze to the open dome. The clouds are moving. Parting. Sprites, I think. But no …

Red spills across the parting clouds, and then I see it.

The moon.

Not a sliver. Not a glimpse through the Shroud. The full, perfect sphere of it, hanging in the sky. And it is red.

Red like a wound. Red like fire. The tears that were banked in my eyes trickle down my cheek as I look at it. I've never understood why ancient cultures built temples, wrote prophecies about it, and killed in its name. I do now. It is terrifying and beautiful.

Below, more gasps. I force myself to look away from the moon and find Anala. Her entire body is shaking. Freida moves to stand behind her, hands closing on her arms to steady her.

The gesture is practiced. Familiar from all the times Anala has had visions in the past and Freida has been there to catch her. Anala's head snaps back. Her eyes snap open and pure, burning silver eyes shine through.

No pupil, no iris, just light as she stares up at the blood moon. When she speaks, the voice that emerges is not hers. It is deeper. Darker. Ancient. It echoes through the rotunda as if the temple itself is speaking through her.

"When the blood moon rises and does not fall, the caged shall answer the kingdom's call. One year the red eye watches from above. One year to choose between duty and love. From the drowned island, the flame still burns. What was taken must be returned. The healer's hands will break the chain, but the price of freedom is all she contains. When the last stone shatters and the Shroud falls, the blue flame will answer the kingdom's call."

Then, silence. Below, Constantine raises his hands like a conqueror claiming victory. He says something, but I don't hear it. I can't hear anything except those words, echoing in my skull.

The healer's hands will break the chain.

But the price of freedom is all she contains.

Sleep won't come. I toss and turn until the sheets are tangled around my legs, then give up and reach for the journal.

The name at the top still makes my stomach clench. Lenora Bromwell. My professor. My mentor. My boss. Another person who lied to me. I keep reading.

My predecessor warned them that the elixir has only ever been used for people on their deathbeds. It was meant to alleviate temporary suffering. Not to be administered to the healthy. They also warned that the mushroom typically used has been contaminated by the curse. Sara's response: "In the end, none of this will matter if we do not act now."

Three gifts necessary: Siphony (specifically landsiphoner), empathy, and serephony Ingredients: Shroud mushroom, water from the Whispering Ponds, dried sap from the commiphora tree Subjects tested: Maidens from the Valley of the Innocent

I stop reading. Maidens from the Valley of the Innocent. Tested. Did they volunteer, or were they taken the way the legion guards were?

Findings: When handled by three gifted individuals, the Shroud mushroom proves more effective than the red-capped variety.

Reversal: We've discovered that lion's mane may reverse the effects. Two years have passed, and the subject given the reversal elixir appears to retain her memories.

Our concern: What happens to the memories once extracted? A simple stone cannot contain them indefinitely. The emotions attached to those memories are even more concerning. Where will they go?

Update: This will be my final entry.

The state of Lunaris is grim. Everything appears fine on the surface. It is not. The society that promises freedom and peace is built on lies.

The memory stones are kept hidden in specific locations beneath Lunaris. The Shroud—which began as nothing more than dark clouds in the forest—has expanded into something far worse. The stones seem to be feeding it. All those suppressed memories. All that pain.

We must put an end to this. I am afraid of what will happen if we're caught. But I am more afraid of what will happen if we don't try.

I'm certain the High Sage was wrong about one thing.
In the end, nothing will matter, except everything.

I read it again. And again. And again. The stones contain memories.

But memories are just one part of what makes a person whole. What happens when you strip away the rest?

I think of the boy who looked like Cas. The emotions I felt in him before the ceremony. The resistance, the defiance, the desperate anger. I felt something similar once, years ago. It's impossible to fathom that I'd confuse the two, but everything is about perspective, and resistance can feel a lot like hope. But hope doesn't survive what they do to people here.

I look at my hands. My fingernails are stained black from years of work with the elixirs. Every vial I brewed. Every stone I touched. Every extraction I enabled.

I think of the laborers dying in the street, screaming for families they weren't supposed to remember. I think of the pleasure gardens, where grief becomes entertainment.

I helped build all of it.

I think about the Shroud. The Shroudmaidens. We've been told our whole lives to fear them. Soul eaters. Monsters.

But the Shroud feeds on stolen memories. On pain. On everything we've taken from people without their true consent. Maybe the monsters aren't in the forest. Maybe the monsters are us.

Maybe the monster is *me*.

The weight of it crushes me. I bury my face in my hands. I defended the Sages my entire life. They let us keep our gifts.

They helped us hone them. They gave us purpose. But every elixir I made fed the Shroud. Every stone I filled added to the darkness. I wasn't helping people heal. I was helping the cage grow stronger.

The door creaks open. I don't look up. The bed dips beside me. A hand settles on my back, warm and steady, and his thumb traces slow circles against my spine. I try to stop crying. His gentleness makes it worse.

"Menace." His voice is rough. Quiet.

I take a shaky breath and wipe my face. When I finally look at him, he's glaring at the journal in my lap. He picks it up and tosses it onto the table like it's poisoned. When he turns back to me, his jaw is tight. But his eyes are soft.

"What do you need?"

The question cracks something open in my chest. Not *what's wrong?* Not *why are you crying?* Not *what did you find?* Just, *what do you need?*

Gods, how many times have I asked people that question, and yet no one has ever asked me. Not my brother. Not my friends. Not the Sages who shaped my entire life. No one has ever considered that I might need anything at all.

I throw my arms around his neck before I can stop myself. He doesn't hesitate. His arms close around me, engulfing me in warmth, in safety, in something I don't have a name for. When the sobs come, he doesn't try to quiet them. He just holds me tighter.

I don't know how long I cry. Long enough for him to shift us both beneath the covers, to lay us down, to pull me against his chest. The sconces extinguish themselves, one by one. The door clicks softly shut—his magic, or mine, I don't know. His arms never leave me. For the first time in days, I sleep.

CHAPTER TWENTY-TWO

I STORM THROUGH THE BACK DOORS OF THE VERITAS ESTATE without acknowledging anyone. My mind is a hive of fury, and I have no patience for pleasantries. I nearly walk past Mara without seeing her. She's stationed outside Mother's office like a nervous sentry.

"Profess—I mean, Ada." She shuffles after me as I brush past. "The High Sage said she won't tolerate any disturbances."

"I'm sure she did."

"And this isn't even ... I'm supposed to be interning with Gerri, the High Sage's lead alchemist, but she told me to guard the door while she handled something, and she said if I let anyone disturb the High Sage, I'll be dismissed and I'll never get another opportunity like this, so please—"

She flinches when I spin to face her. The explosion building in my chest dies the moment I take a good look at her. At the fear in her wide brown eyes and the way she clutches her journal to her chest like a shield. I notice the gold Veritas pin on her lapel. The houndstooth maroon jacket, just like the one I wore at her age.

I've been so consumed with my own survival these past

two years that I never let myself see it. She's me. A younger, more hopeful version, still believing in everything I've stopped believing in.

Her brows furrow at my silence. I decide I hate her confusion more than her rambling. At least her rambling comes from genuine curiosity and the need to understand. It's her clinging to what's left of her identity after she made the memory trade.

I don't know what brought her to Lunaris. I only know she's from Lyrionne. Most sirens in Veritas are. I think of what Malachi said about the temples in Tenebris. How parents bring their children, hoping they'll be deemed special. *Chosen.*

And I remember something Tilda told me years ago. She said Siren's Call is the most hopeful place in Veritas. Not because of the tavern or the gambling hall or the brothel, but because it's where people come to see their loved ones. I never understood what she meant. Until now.

All those merchants who flood Veneficia Alley, who fill the seats at Siren's and order drinks they barely touch, they're not here for business. They're here to see the children they brought to Lunaris for a better life. Children who don't remember them. Who don't remember the sacrifices that were made for them.

"Ada?" Mara's voice is soft. Concerned. "Are you alright? You're…"

I touch my face. My fingers come away wet.

"I'm fine." I wipe the tears away with the back of my hand and force something like a smile. "Sara's expecting me." I clear my throat. "I don't know who Gerri is, but if she gives you trouble, tell her you're the best alchemy student I've ever taught. Tell her firing you would be a disservice to the Order." I hold her gaze. "And if that doesn't work, come find me. I'll handle it."

She stares at me, speechless. I don't wait for a response. I turn to Mother's office, grip the handle, and throw the door open without knocking. All three Sages turn toward me at once.

Their eyes flash silver in sequence, one after another, like a warning signal. In daylight, they look less menacing than they did in my childhood nightmares. It doesn't matter. I'm not afraid of them anymore.

"Ada." Mother's voice is exhausted. She sits behind her desk like a queen on a crumbling throne.

"Ada." Anala's smile is serene, almost peaceful. She perches on the edge of the velvet couch.

"Temp!" Freida grins from beside her, the only warmth in the room.

Despite everything, Anala's obvious relief and Freida's genuine excitement crack something in my armor. My lips twitch. They rise to embrace me, and I let them. Freida drags over a third chair so we can sit together facing the desk.

Diplomacy wasn't what I came for. On the walk here, I could only envision one outcome: burning this place to the ground. This is better. Probably.

"I went to the Hall of Truth last night." I cut off whatever small talk Freida was about to offer. "I watched the ceremony."

Anala nods slowly. "I thought you might."

"Because you saw it in a vision?"

"No." Her smile turns sad. "I just know you. I'm

surprised you didn't go when Sara extended your apprenticeship. But I knew this time would be different."

"Did you want me to see it?"

Freida answers before Anala can. "We knew it would crush you to witness what the Council does. We hated lying to you." She exchanges a glance with Anala. "But we understood why the truth had to stay buried."

My chest tightens. "The Veritas residents—are they—"

"All here willingly," Freida says quickly. Too quickly.

"What about Lenora?"

Silence. Anala's eyes flash silver. That's enough to answer.

"She's here willingly," Mother says after a long pause.

"Willingly." I let the word hang between us, ugly and hollow. If I hadn't been raised by these women, I might believe her. "Did you take her memories after she made the elixir? Or after she discovered what the Shroud really is?" I lean forward. "Was creating it your plan all along?"

Her eyes blaze silver. "We did not create the Shroud. It is a manifestation of the curse. It existed before the treaty was ever signed. We've never lied about that."

"But you took Lenora's memories." My voice shakes, and I hate it. I hate that this woman can still surprise me. Disappoint me. "You took her memories, and you've done nothing to get my brother back from those monsters."

"We did what we had to do."

My sigil burns beneath my blouse. "What are the Shroudmaidens?"

"We don't know." Her voice is flat. "That is the truth."

"But you do know the Shroud feeds on the memory stones. On all that stolen pain."

She straightens. "That is—"

"Stop." Freida's voice cuts like a blade. "It's too late, Sara. Everything you've done. Everything we've done." She shakes her head. "It's too late. You must see that."

Mother's eyes flash. "It is not too late. It will only be too late if—"

Freida slams her palm on the desk. "Just tell her the godsdamn truth!"

The room goes silent.

Mother turns to me. When she speaks, her voice is calm, but her eyes remain silver. Unnatural.

"You've studied ancient civilizations. You know that history doesn't repeat itself exactly—but the themes are cyclical. The patterns recur."

I nod slowly, uncertain where this is leading.

"The question is never who will break the cycle," she continues. "It's when. I thought sparing Lunaris from the truth of the last three hundred years was a kindness." She pauses. "But mostly, I knew it would keep you and your brother safe."

The air in the room shifts. "Safe from what?"

"From Cato." Her voice drops. "From his hunters. From everything he's spent centuries searching for."

I sink back in my chair. The prophecy. This is about the prophecy. I knew it the moment I heard Anala speak those words under the blood moon.

I felt it in my bones. But knowing something and having it confirmed are different creatures entirely. She went to all these lengths to … what? Prevent it from coming true? But why would she want to prevent—

"Because I'm a healer," I say slowly, the pieces clicking

into place. "A *true* healer. The prophecy says the healer's hands will break the chain. Is that why—"

"Because Cato is your father."

The words hit the air like a clap of thunder. They ring in my ears. Echo. Refuse to make sense.

My father.

Cato.

The Everlasting.

I shake my head. The denial rises to my lips, ready to be spoken, but it won't come. As if some part of me already knows.

Cato, who slaughtered the healers of Larimar. Who hunts seers and siphoners. Who stole a throne and cursed an entire kingdom when he couldn't have what he wanted. That monster is my father.

"No." The word comes out broken. "That's not ... how is that possible?"

Mother speaks before I can finish.

"Many years ago, Cato visited my homeland of Larimar..."

The room tilts. Mother's voice fades to static. Larimar. Pia's homeland. The drowned island.

From the drowned island, the flame still burns.

The last thing I see is Mother rising from her chair, her mouth forming my name.

Then darkness swallows everything.

CHAPTER TWENTY-THREE

"Ada?" A light slap against my cheek. "Ada?" Another. My eyes fly open. White dots dance across my vision. Beyond the haze, three faces hover above me. Pale skin and red hair. Brown skin and dark hair. Darker skin and darker hair still. All three have arched ears.

Their features sharpen as I blink. Blue eyes. Dark brown. Lighter brown. All filled with concern. Then a wave crashes through me. Not theirs. *Malachi's*. His worry floods the bond so powerfully I nearly choke on it. I close my eyes and push reassurance back toward him, then pull away before his presence overwhelms me completely.

"Goddess, Ada." Anala's voice is barely a whisper.

"Are you alright?" Freida frowns as I try to sit up.

"I'm fine." My voice comes out hoarse.

Anala presses a glass to my lips. I drink. Her dark eyes search my face. "Better?"

"Thank you." Another sip. A shaky exhale. "I'm fine. I won't faint again."

They step back, giving me room, but none of them returns to their seat until I'm sitting upright again.

I look at Mother behind her desk. Mother. The word feels different now. Wrong, somehow. "Are you my... am I your..."

"No." Her voice is gentle. "You are not my daughter." A sad smile crosses her face. "But if you'll allow me, I'll tell you how all of this began."

I take a breath and nod.

"The island of Larimar had a monarchy, but not like the kingdoms you've studied." She settles back in her chair. "The island was divided into sectors, each belonging to a different tribe. Each tribe had its own cacique, its own customs, its own way of life. King Elías ruled with his queen, but they worked alongside the caciques. Peace through cooperation, not domination."

She pauses. "It ensured no culture was erased. No traditions lost. Just because people share land doesn't mean they share beliefs. Larimar embraced that difference."

"That sounds ... fair." I rub my eyes, half-hoping I'll wake from this nightmare. "Why didn't you teach us about them?"

"Because teaching about Larimar means teaching about Cato." She closes her eyes briefly. "I hoped he would be dead before you ever learned his name."

"I read about what he did." My jaw clenches. "How he wanted Pia and when he was refused, he tried to enslave the entire island with compulsion. When that failed, he ordered the slaughter."

Sara's eyebrows rise.

"Where do Jordi and I fit into this? And Lunaris?" I ask.

She takes a long, steadying breath. Lets it out slowly. "Pia was your mother."

I recoil. "That's impossible. Tenebris has been cursed for three hundred years. Pia died shortly after."

"She did." Mother's voice is steady. "But she still gave birth to you and your brother." The words make no sense. I let her continue anyway. "It was only by Ignata's grace that I survived what Cato did to our people. I was taken to Asturyum, where the goddess Sulara allowed me to recover." Her voice tightens. "When I was strong enough, I tried to save my sister. The goddess would not permit it."

I close my eyes. "Your sister."

"Yes," she whispers. "Pia was my sister."

"Gods," I breathe, shaking my head.

"I was sent here with Freida and Anala to guard Ignata's Flame. We could not leave," she says, hands curling into fists on the desk. "I knew Pia was alive because of what Cato was doing. His atrocities. I knew he was using her gifts to heal that scepter."

"The siphoning scepter," I whisper.

"It drains the gifts of his followers and stores them for his use. But each time it drains, it needs to be healed. That's what he kept her for."

"Before the curse fell, I began having visions," Anala says softly. "I saw Pia escape. I saw Tenebris consumed by darkness. I saw the Shroud that would rise from that curse." She pauses. "And I saw children arrive here. Seven of them. The Flame told me they would need to be trained. Hidden."

"Constantine arrived shortly after." Freida takes Anala's trembling hand. "He brought the idea of the memory trade.

We didn't like it. But Anala's visions were too strong to ignore, and we don't believe in coincidences."

"Did you know he was Shadow Guild when he arrived? That he worshipped Cato?"

"Many in the Guild call Noktelum the Everlasting," Freida says carefully. "The distinction wasn't clear."

"We knew." Mother's voice is harsh. "I knew. I recognized the look in his eyes. I've seen that devotion before."

"And you let him stay? Agreed to work with him?"

"I thought it was better to keep him close. Watch him."

"Like King Elías did with Cato? Even knowing he was dangerous?"

Her smile is bitter. "I suppose I am my father's daughter, after all."

"Gods." I press my hands to my face and drop them as I shake my head. "Why not use the memory elixir against the Council from the start?"

"Because the treaty was signed," Freida says.

Mother eyes me curiously. "You think it's wrong to use it against others but not Constantine?"

"He's a monster!"

Her brows raise. "That's what every usurper says about the people they dethrone."

A harsh laugh spills from my lips. "Well, maybe I'm my father's daughter, after all."

She rears back as if I've slapped her.

"Ada," Anala breathes.

I ignore her and narrow my eyes on Sara. "Does Jordi know?"

"He found the prophecy in the vault. He asked if you

were the healer it speaks of." She meets my eyes. "I told him no. And that is the truth. Cato's sorceress wrote that prophecy about Pia. They knew she would eventually emerge from hiding to break the curse."

"There's a …" She trails off. Her expression twists, and she looks away.

My stomach clenches. I've never seen her falter like this. I glance at Freida, hoping for steadiness, but her eyes are glistening. No help there.

"There's a legend about Pia." Freida's voice is soft. "She obtained Sulara's scepter. She planned to drive it into the roots of the Bratus that extend to Tenebris. To break the curse herself." A pause. "She was heavily pregnant when she set out. And so very brave."

Her smile is sad. "But legends are only written when …"

"Someone's story ends." The words come out hoarse. Malachi said that to me once. "So she died."

"Yes. But not there. She was taken to Noktemore."

My heart stutters. The Flame. Its voice in my head. I was so rattled about Jordi that I barely absorbed what it told me.

"Pia was a follower of Mortiana," Anala explains. "When she was attacked on her way to the Bratus, Mortiana brought her to Noktemore. Put her in stasis. Tried to save her."

She shakes her head. "But saving someone requires a bargain. Everything requires a bargain. And there was no one to make one on Pia's behalf."

I have to bite down on the inside of my cheek to keep

from sobbing. That poor woman. Even in her final moments, she was alone. She must have felt alone her entire life. I can't imagine *that* kind of isolation.

"The gods went to their siblings," Anala continues. "All of them rallied together. That alone should tell you how much your mother meant to them. The gods barely tolerate each other. They never unite."

"But the Creators denied their request." Freida's voice is heavy. "They said saving all three would cost too much."

"Three people were too many to save?" My sigil flares.

"We believe it's because of how powerful the three of you would have been together." Freida's voice drops. "And how powerful Cato would have become if he ever got his hands on all of you."

My throat aches with everything I'm holding back. The grief. The rage. The horror. Warmth pulses through the bond. Malachi, still there, still steady. I lean into it without meaning to.

Then the realization crashes over me.

Malachi, Kage, Draven, and countless others have dedicated their lives to undoing the damage my father caused. The curse my mother triggered. I am the daughter of the people who destroyed their kingdom. The comfort I've been taking from the bond suddenly feels wrong. I pull back.

"Pia's sacrifice started a movement." Anala's voice steadies. "The gods created the Reckoning. Healers began emerging from hiding, traveling to the Bratus. Some went willingly. Others …"

"Were forced." My stomach turns. "Like the laborers here."

"The imbalance grew dangerous. So Mortiana waited. Two hundred and seventy-five years." Anala meets my eyes. "When the time was right, she brought your mother out of stasis and allowed her to give birth."

"But she died," I whisper.

"In childbirth. Yes."

The silence is suffocating.

I swallow. "Did they wait for us to survive? Or for us to have a chance at lifting the curse?"

"The prophecy is not yours!" Sara's voice cracks like a whip.

"We don't know that!" Anala's eyes flash silver. "The balance hasn't been restored, Sara. The gods won't let an entire kingdom die."

"Cato is waiting." Sara's voice is venomous. "He's waiting for his heir to reach the Bratus. For his hunters to find the son he believes will save his legacy. He has the princess of Tenebris in stasis. Kept in a glass case. Waiting for the day she wakes so he can cross the wards that keep him out." Her hands shake. "Everything is a waiting game. And we are running out of time."

"How would Cato know when the healer reaches the Bratus?"

"Sulara's scepter." Freida's voice is grave. "That's the key. They believe when the healer, the true healer, will drive the scepter into the roots and the curse will break. But the scepter has never been found."

"Is it here? In Lunaris?"

"The legend suggests it is. We've searched. Constantine has searched." She shakes her head. "Nothing."

"How do you know Constantine doesn't already have it?"

Her eyebrow rises. "We were here before he arrived."

Right. They searched before he ever arrived. Which brings me back to what I read in Lenora's journal.

"Lenora wrote about the memory stones. She believed they were feeding the Shroud. Keeping it intact." I watch Mother's face. "Is that true?"

"Yes," she says, no hesitation. "The Shroud grew after each Reckoning. When we learned about the sacrifices at the Bratus, we realized the connection. Pain feeds it. Grief feeds it."

"So you used the memory stones," I whisper. "You fed the Shroud deliberately. To keep it strong."

She nods. Sharp. Unapologetic. "The Shroud keeps us hidden. Cato cannot find us. His hunters cannot reach us. The only opening is during the Reckoning, and few are foolish enough to travel through."

My chest squeezes. You built a wall of stolen grief and call it protection." I blink rapidly, clearing the tears from my eyes as I look at the three of them. "The Moon Festival. You created it as a diversion. So when the Reckoning happened every ten years, no one would notice."

None of them denies it.

"People come here during the Festival. They beg to stay. They want to forget their pasts. Start over." I shake my head. "Why purchase anyone?"

"We have never purchased anyone," Sara snaps. "The treaty is signed in blood. We cannot question who the

Council admits. We cannot intervene in their ceremonies. The oath forbids it."

"Do not tell me what you can and cannot do!" My voice shakes with fury. "Your people were enslaved and you've allowed the Council to do the same to others! You can spin it whatever way you like and blame the blood oath, but it doesn't make it right!"

"I have been trying to keep you safe!" The roar tears out of her. "I couldn't save my sister. I have done everything in my power to protect her children!"

My sigil burns so hot I expect smoke to rise from my chest plate. But the anger shifts. Twists into something worse. Horrified disbelief. I stare at the woman who raised us. Who taught us so much. And yet so little.

"Your sister was kidnapped and enslaved, and the best you could come up with was to build a cage for her children and to trick us into believing that it was a safe haven?" I whisper. "Do you expect us to be grateful for that?"

She surges to her feet, slamming her palms on the desk. "I am not asking for your gratitude! I did what I had to do to keep you alive!"

"You used me!" I shoot out of my chair, sigil blazing with barely contained fury. "You pretend that letting us use our gifts is kindness. You sit here and talk about Cato draining your sister, but you used her daughter just the same! You made me complicit in all of this! You taught me to hone my emotive alchemy to make poison! You used my empathy …" My voice cracks on that word. I stop and take a breath. "You used my empathy to weld chains."

"You have no idea what you're talking about!" Her

eyes blaze silver. "You have no idea what Cato will do if he finds you. Why do you think your brother was willing to go to the Keep? To let the Council take him?"

My knees nearly give out. I catch myself on the edge of the desk. "What does that mean?"

"Jordi had a dream about your mother. He saw what Cato did to her. How he drained her to keep his scepter alive. He knows what will happen when Cato discovers he has a daughter. A healer. Just like Pia."

Not if. When. The air leaves my lungs. I grip the desk harder to stay upright.

"Cato is looking for a son. And Jordi let himself be taken to the Keep. Where Cato's most devoted follower is waiting." I shake my head. "How does that make any sense?"

"Right now, Constantine believes he's the heir. As long as he clings to that lie, it buys us time to—"

"Time?" I bark out a laugh. "You cannot be that delusional. The final Reckoning is happening. The cage you built is crumbling. Constantine already knows you raised children here. It's only a matter of time before he realizes you singled some out for special treatment."

"He already has three of the seven in his legion. And Jordi is in his Keep. You handed Cato's heir directly to his most loyal follower!"

"What are you saying? How would he know about the children we raised?" Freida's voice is barely a whisper.

"I don't know, but Arlo overheard Constantine and Nicolas. Those legion guards you've allowed to search Veritas? They're not hunting renegades." I swing my gaze to Mother. "They're hunting us."

I step closer. "So tell me. Where is all this *time* you think you have? Because I don't see it."

"May Ignata spare us," Anala breathes.

"Jordi thought he could find the memory stones before the curse broke. Prevent deaths." Freida's fear is plain on her face. "We told him not to go. When he was taken, I tried to get him out. But they moved him."

"Where?"

"Luisa believes he's in the Hall of Gratitude." Freida swallows. "Which is a problem. Because we can't get in."

"Because of the wards," I say, my mind already racing ahead.

"Yes."

"Luisa can't bypass them?"

"She's a known Veritas guard. The wards are keyed to names. That's what makes them effective. No registered Veritas resident can enter."

I mull that over. If the wards are keyed to names the Council knows, then only registered residents would be blocked. But the Council doesn't know about me.

Or Naima. Or Margot. And Malachi and Kage aren't residents at all. My gaze snaps to the blood-red sky beyond the windows. I'm moving before I've finished the thought.

"Ada!" Sara shouts. "Where are you going?"

I grip the doorknob and turn to her. "To get Jordi out of there!"

"You can't just storm in there," Freida says, bewildered. "You have to—"

I yank the door open. "I know what I have to do."

"You're wrong," Sara says.

I freeze in the doorway, sigil flaring, ready for another fight. But when I turn, she's smiling. Not the sad smile from before. Something fiercer. Something proud.

"You, Ada the Tempest, are unequivocally your mother's daughter."

CHAPTER TWENTY-FOUR

The walk home feels like wading through water. Every step is a fight. I cling to Sara's final words because the alternative is acknowledging the truth.

My father is a murderous tyrant.

My stomach turns. How am I supposed to live with that?

How am I supposed to look Malachi in the eyes? His kingdom is cursed because of my parents. Pia may not have intended it, but her flight to Tenebris was the catalyst. The match that lit the fire.

Gods. He must hate her.

They all must.

That thought hits harder than knowing who my father is. I slow as I reach my building, pressing my back against the wall to steady myself. Above me, the sky bleeds crimson. The blood moon hasn't set. It watches me like a wound that won't close. I shut my eyes and try to breathe.

I'll go inside. Find a map of the tunnels. Figure out the fastest route to the Hall of Gratitude. Malachi will ask questions, and I'll tell him the truth.

Part of it, anyway. My brother is there. That much I can say. The rest? I can't. Not yet. Maybe not ever.

The thought of how he'll look at me when he learns who my father is breaks something in my chest. A monster's daughter. Even if he could look past it, I'm not sure I could.

He gave up his wings. His raffin. His freedom. Three centuries of his life, suspended in nothing. Because of that curse. Because of my family.

My knees give out. I slide down the wall and pull my knees to my chest, making myself as small as possible. For once in my life, I feel like the child the Sages never allowed me to be.

I think of the boy at the ceremony. The one who looked like Cas. The way he resisted until the very end, until there was nothing left to resist with. Thousands of people have suffered that fate.

Maybe more. Because of me. My safety cost them their freedom. That's the cruelty of it all.

Even setting aside the elixirs I brewed for ten years, all of it still leads back to me. Not Jordi. Me. Jordi is Cato's son.

But I'm the one who inherited Pia's healing gift. I'm the one Cato truly wants. The key to breaking the curse. Or becoming his next victim.

A sob builds in my chest. I swallow it down. This is something I cannot hide from Malachi. I won't.

Not because I owe Mortiana a debt, but because I owe it to him. To Kage. To Draven. To all of Tenebris. They could have turned Pia away when she fled to them. They sheltered her instead. And they've been paying for that kindness ever since.

The healer's hands will break the chain, but the price of freedom is all she contains. I don't know what those words mean. Am I meant to die, like all the healers who tried before me? To be drained by my own father until nothing remains?

I take a breath. Another. I cannot fall apart. Not again. Not yet. I think of everything Pia endured. Everything she sacrificed. If she could face Cato while carrying his children, I can stand up and walk inside my own building.

I feel Malachi before I see him. His presence floods the bond, urgent and sharp. I lift my head. He's at the top of the stairs, silhouetted against the flickering lights. The moment he sees me, he moves, descending so fast his feet barely seem to touch the steps.

I tip my head back to look at him, and something in my chest tightens. He looks like a warrior standing in the aftermath of battle. The bleeding sky frames him like one of Freida's old paintings, the ones depicting gods and wars and terrible beauty. It feels like an omen.

My sigil flares, and I realize what I'm feeling isn't mine. His anger. Barely contained, burning through the bond like wildfire. I'd forgotten how it feels. Destructive. Unforgiving. Ready to consume everything in its path.

I haul myself off the ground and tip my head back to meet his gaze. *Gods.* Even scowling, he's devastating. Maybe more so. The rage suits him somehow, sharpening all those already dangerous edges. Not that I'd ever tell him that.

I'd never admit that I love the stubble darkening his jaw. Or how many hours I spent imagining what it would feel like to sink my fingers into his hair before I finally did. Or that I've memorized the flecks of brown and black in those golden eyes.

I'd never admit that when his jaw flexes like it's doing now, something low in my stomach tightens. Or that the same thing happens every time he says "fuck," even though the word still catches me off guard.

"Keep looking at me like that, Menace." His voice is rough. "And I'll send everyone home."

Heat floods through me, but I force myself to ignore it. I nod toward the building. "Who's here?"

"It doesn't matter."

The edge in his voice snaps my attention back to his face. "Why are you so angry?"

"Because you're in pain!"

I swallow. "It was a typical meeting with the Sages. I tried to close the bond so you wouldn't have to feel any of it. Next time I'll—"

"You think I'm angry because I felt it?" He steps closer. "I'm angry they made you feel that way at all. I'm angry they have wards around that property." His voice drops, dangerous. "Which is probably for the best. Because if I'd been able to get inside, the realm would be short three Sages right now. And goddess-*fucking*-forbid we upset the balance!"

I stop breathing.

"Oh," I manage.

"Yes. Oh." His hand lifts to cup the back of my neck, and he lowers his face until our eyes are level. "And now I'm furious that you tried to shut me out. That you thought you had to carry it alone."

A sob rises. I bite my trembling lip and force it down. Can't he see I'm barely holding on? That I'm unraveling with every breath? That I cannot share this particular pain with him?

"My torment isn't yours to carry," I whisper.

"No." His thumb traces along my jaw. "But it would be my privilege if you let me."

The sob escapes before I can stop it. I shake my head and try to pull away, but he holds me there, watching me with those golden eyes that see far too much.

"Why are you fighting this?" His voice is barely a whisper.

Another sob tears through me. "Because I have to!"

This time, when I pull away, he lets me go.

Somehow, that breaks me more than if he'd held on.

I hate this. All of it. And the bond makes everything worse. I can feel his concern.

His confusion. And gods, the doubt. As if he's questioning whether I want him as much as he wants me. If only he knew. If only I could tell him that wanting him isn't the problem.

I wish I could reach inside myself and tear it all out. The bond. The guilt. Everything.

"What changed?" He searches my face. "What did they tell you?"

The knot in my throat tightens. I want to scream that nothing has changed and everything has changed. But I can't. If I say that, I might as well say it all. And I don't know if I'll ever be able to say these words aloud. The shame is suffocating. Brutal.

I've never wished for anything outside of what the Veritas Order could give me. I stopped wanting things I couldn't have a long time ago. But if I let myself wish for something now, it would be him.

The thought makes another sob rise. I turn away, closing my eyes, searching for that place inside myself where I can shut everyone out. But I can't find it. The bond has invaded everything. He's everywhere.

"Ada."

"I can't do this right now, Mal." I keep my eyes closed. Coward.

"Look at me."

I squeeze my eyes tighter.

"Look at me!" The snap in his voice makes me flinch.

My eyes fly open. His gaze is so intense it feels like being pinned. The flickering lights make his eyes look like they're glowing.

"Whatever they told you about me," he says, voice low and controlled, "I can explain."

I blink. "About you?"

His brows furrow. He searches my face for answers I can't give. Before either of us can speak, Kage's voice bellows from the second-story window.

"We found it!" He holds up a rolled map, then frowns at the two of us. "Whatever's happening down there can wait. We found the map."

I exhale and head for the stairs. We climb in silence, neither of us speaking until we reach the apartment door. His hand closes around mine. He pulls me back. I turn, heart pounding, and meet his gaze.

"This conversation isn't over."

I nod. That's all I can manage.

I expected Kage and Naima. Maybe Margot. I didn't expect Draven.

All four of them are crowded around the dining table, maps spread between them, Lenora's journal open at the center.

"Gods, Temp." Naima nearly knocks her chair over rushing toward me. Margot follows, her expression mirroring the same concern.

I hold up my hands before either of them can embrace me. "I'm barely holding on," I whisper. "If you hug me, I'll shatter."

"You look like you've already been crying." Margot's voice is soft.

"So do you."

Her mouth twitches. Almost a smile.

"Was it that bad?" Naima searches my face.

"Worse."

Naima's eyes widen. Margot's expression, impossibly, grows sadder. I wonder again what else she's seen. What she's not telling us. I don't ask. Not now.

"Do you want to talk about it?" Naima whispers.

"I'm about to." I nod toward the table. They follow me over. I offer Draven a small smile as I sit across from him. "I thought you were leaving."

"I came to say goodbye." He studies my face but doesn't comment on whatever he sees there.

"You look awful," Kage says flatly. He shrugs at the glares he receives. "What? She does."

"Thanks for that." I exhale and focus on the map. "Where did you find it?"

"Lenora's journal. It was in the binding. Hidden," Naima says.

"You left it out this morning," Mal adds.

I frown, wondering why Lenora went through such lengths to hide the map. It's old. Ancient, maybe. The Shroud is barely a smudge at the edges.

The Temple of Veritas isn't marked. Neither is the University or the Estate. I search for the Hall of Gratitude. Instead, I find the Temple of Noktelum.

My hands start shaking. I tuck them under the table, pressing them against my thighs to still them. I force myself to examine the rest. The amphitheater is labeled *Malvorathis Amphitheater*.

The Keep is marked as *Neith's Palace*. In the bottom corner, faded script reads: *Zoila Veneficia, Map Maker of the Veritas Order, circa 1 A.S.* Three hundred years ago. Before Constantine. Before the treaty. Before everything went wrong.

"The Sages believe Jordi's been moved to the Hall of Gratitude." My voice is steadier than I expected.

Silence.

"What?" Naima breathes.

"How do they know?" Draven's eyes narrow.

"Freida tried to extract him from the Keep. He'd already been moved."

Draven leans forward. "Why that location? Of all the places they could take him?"

"Jordi got arrested on purpose."

Draven blinks. "He did what?"

"He wanted to move the memory stones underneath the Hall of Gratitude to prevent deaths once the curse is lifted." I swallow. "I can only assume he was caught trying to do that."

"Goddess strike me," Naima breathes.

"I suppose I'm staying another night," Draven says quietly.

"Can you get past the wards?" Margot asks.

He shakes his head. "I've tried."

"The wards only cover street level," Kage announces. "I checked last night while you were at the ceremony."

"*We* checked," Naima corrects pointedly. "And we saw something near the red doors. Shroudmaidens, maybe."

Kage sighs. "For the hundredth time, we didn't see Shroudmaidens."

"We saw very dark fog," Naima says through gritted teeth. "*Moving* fog. For all we know, the Shroudmaidens are down there."

"Do the Sages know how long he's been there?" Mal asks.

I shake my head, finally meeting his eyes. I'm grateful for the determination I find in them. He glances at the rest of the table.

"We're going to get him out tonight." He slides a newer map to the center of the table and hands charcoal pencils to Draven and Kage. He holds my eyes as he offers me the third. "Mark all the entrances to the tunnels that you know of."

"While we're planning our inevitable demise, we should

talk about secrets," Kage says, looking at me and my friends. "Naima's been forthcoming enough, but we need to know what gifts the three of you have."

Margot scoffs. "A little too forthcoming, if you ask me."

"Good thing no one asked you," he says, winking at her.

"We need to strike at midnight," Draven says, ignoring Kage. "That's when the Council's festivities get ... interesting. If we arrive at midnight and leave by half past one, we'll have a window. Sometimes they bring guests to the Hall. I don't know why."

I check the clock. Eight. Four hours to plan. I startle when Kage claps his hands together.

"As I was saying, I'd rather not walk in there and discover one of you can manipulate time or something equally useful that we could've planned around." He spreads his hands on the table. "Who wants to go first?"

My lips twist. "Why don't you start, since you're so eager?"

He shoots me a look. "We'll have to work on that attitude before the wedding."

A low warning sound rumbles from Malachi's direction. Naima snorts. I cast her a silencing glare.

"If that look held any magic, it would kill on contact," Kage quips.

"Yosh," Draven mutters. "Can we proceed?"

Kage exhales dramatically. "Fine. I can move through shadows. And ..."

He raises a hand. Dark smoke coils from his palm, serpentine and deliberate. It snakes across the table toward me. I lift a hand to bat it away, but the tendril wraps around my wrist and holds firm. I've seen his shadows before. I've never seen them grip.

"How?" I breathe.

He grins. "Imagine what I could do to you in the bed—"

The maps fly off the table and slap him in the face before he can finish the sentence. The shadow dissolves. My hand thumps down onto wood.

Kage glares at Malachi. "Godsdamn it, Bain. I thought you said all of your gifts weren't back."

"They're not."

"All your gifts?" Margot leans forward. "How many do you have?"

"Several," Kage says. "Unfortunately, the curse limits how long we can hold some of them."

"The curse affects your gifts?"

"Some of our abilities come from the creatures we're bonded to. With the creatures in a slumber, those gifts fade faster than they used to."

"Does using them bring you comfort?" I ask quietly. "Or does it just remind you of what you've lost?"

His smile turns sad. "I try to focus on the comfort it brings."

"What about your other gifts?" Margot presses.

"Some come from gods, as you know. Others from weapons. The scepters are the most powerful, but other weapons have divine powers as well."

I think of Malachi's sword. Vida. I wonder which god it belongs to.

"Before the curse, four out of ten people manifested

natural gifts from the gods." He glances at Draven. "Sound right?"

"Roughly. Maybe a little more than that."

Kage nods. "These days, almost no one in Vindariel is born with any. They can barely maintain basic sorcery. Most of their gifts are used to keep the water clean and the soil alive."

My chest tightens. Again. I've lost count how many times today. How many sacrifices have been made because of one man's greed? Kage slaps the table, pulling me back.

"All this to say, I understand you need to rely on elixirs and incantations for your gifts, but once the curse is lifted, you may get stronger gifts or not need incantations to summon them," he says.

Margot straightens. "Stronger gifts like what?"

"Like the one I just demonstrated."

"Oh." She looks disappointed for a moment. Then she raises her hand and produces her own tendril of smoke.

Light gray. It drifts to the center of the table, spiraling lazily, then vanishes when she closes her fist.

Kage gapes. "How?"

The three of us laugh. Draven chuckles. Malachi's eyes narrow, calculating.

"I can't make mine grip like yours," Margot admits. "It's more of a distraction. Probably useless in the tunnels."

"The Sages never taught you to solidify it?"

She shakes her head. "They don't have this gift. They did what they could with books, but some things can't be learned from reading."

Kage turns to Naima. "What about you? What are you hiding?"

"You know about the metal forging."

"That's all?"

Her smile is mysterious. "Maybe."

He shakes his head and turns to me. Before he can ask, I open my palm. Fire blooms there, steady and bright.

Kage looks at Malachi. "You knew she could do that?"

"I did," he says with a pride that makes my chest ache more.

Kage looks at the three of us again and shakes his head in disbelief. "Well, I guess that's yet another thing the curse didn't affect here."

"Can we get to planning now?" Draven asks, getting us back on track.

An hour later, we have something resembling a plan.

Naima, Margot, and Kage leave to gather supplies. Coats. Lanterns. Whatever else Kage insists we'll need.

Draven lasts approximately three seconds after they leave before announcing he needs to go home. I nearly beg him to stay. Anything to avoid being alone with Malachi before the mission. But Malachi just looks at my face and tells me to rest. He doesn't push. I'm out of my chair and through my bedroom door before he can change his mind.

"We're still having that conversation after we get your brother back," he calls after me.

I nod, shut the door behind me, and collapse onto my bed.

CHAPTER TWENTY-FIVE

Eucalyptus. The scent hits me before my eyes open. I'm on my hands and knees. The floor beneath me is slick, almost wet, and I grapple for purchase as I try to stand. My feet slide out from under me twice before I manage to rise. A third slip sends me crashing into a wall.

My eyes dart through the darkness. The vault? No. Different. I search for my last memory and find only fog. I must be dreaming. Whispers flutter through the air. I turn toward them and hold my breath.

Then the chatter rises. All at once, like a swarm of cicadas waking from a long slumber. The sound is deafening. I flinch and double over, pressing my palms to my ears.

My head whips in the direction of the light. I stagger towards it. I stop before a familiar archway. Through it, I see the Flame burning at the center of the chamber. Mortiana. My stomach turns.

I step into the threshold, and the Flame flares. *Ada Temperance Acevedo.*

I wet my lips. "Why am I here? I'm not making another bargain."

The Flame stills. *It's difficult to make another bargain when you haven't paid back your first debt. Then again, plenty of souls in my kingdom carry multiple debts.*

"Why am I here?" I repeat, crossing my arms to hide the trembling in my hands.

Because your debt is important. And my collector has been avoiding me.

My shoulders stiffen. I think of everything Malachi has given up. Everything she's taken from him.

The Flame flares, almost amused. *Is my warrior not treating you well?*

My sigil flares. I clench my jaw, trying to contain the anger, but those words burn through me. *My* warrior. As if she owns him.

Is this the bond? The Flame's tone turns condescending. *I know how territorial it can make people.*

I want to find a bucket of water and douse it. The thought gives me a flicker of satisfaction.

The Flame stills. Then flares. *Are these your emotions? A* pause, and then—*Well. That is unexpected.*

"What do you want?" I demand.

I wanted to give you a clue about the scepter you seek. But now I'm not so sure. The Flame sways. *You seem angry. Hostile. So unlike the girl who was willing to sacrifice everything for her brother.*

I close my eyes and force myself to remember that this goddess saved my mother. She gave Pia sanctuary when no one else would.

I open my eyes. "You need this curse lifted as much as anyone."

Oh? The Flame flickers with interest. *Have you been*

reading? Did you find the books the Sages hid from you? The history of your people? The truth?

My spine straightens. "I know the truth."

Since you're still standing, I assume you haven't told him. The Flame pulses. *Not when he's spent the last two centuries sacrificing healers to the Bratus.*

My blood turns to ice.

Of course, stasis has a way of obscuring memories. He may not remember. Or perhaps he does.

I shake my head. "No."

You don't believe me?

"No."

The Flame flares. *You do know he's a warrior. He has killed many people. Some deserving. Some not.*

Gods, I hate her. "I know what he is."

The Flame roars. *Do you?*

"What do you want?" I repeat.

Since this is the final Reckoning, I will give you two things.

"Wait." I step forward. "I don't want another bargain."

This requires no bargain. The Flame settles. *I offer you this kindness because I loved your mother. And because I love your people.*

I swallow. "Would asking if my mother is still alive require another bargain?"

The Flame goes still. *I cannot speak of the dead. But my warrior might, if he trusts you enough to tell you about his debt.*

The blood drains from my face.

He did not kill your mother. The Flame flickers. *But that does not mean he bears no responsibility for the healers who came before you.*

I can't breathe.

That is two kindnesses I'm giving you.

The third kindness is this: the Sages told you they feed the Shroud, but they do not know what lurks within it. That knowledge is crucial to lifting the curse.

I wait, barely breathing.

And the fourth: tell Malachi to bring you home. I will give you the scepter myself.

My ears ring. A thousand questions crowd my mind, but only one escapes.

"Is Noktemore my home?"

The Flame stills again. *It is your birthplace. But you, my child, have no home.* The words cut like blades. *Your homeland was destroyed. Your birthplace was merely that: a place of birth. The kingdom you belong to does not want you. The place that raised you does not value you.*

A sob rises in my throat. I bite my tongue hard enough to taste copper.

Why do you see sadness where there is hope? The Flame's voice softens. *Belonging nowhere gives you the freedom to belong anywhere. Everywhere.*

I swallow. Nod. For once, I'm grateful for the Flame's strange wisdom. "What will you want in exchange for the scepter?"

The Flame roars. Unmistakably, it's laughing. *My child, I already have your soul. What more could I possibly take?*

The kindness of moments ago evaporates. I narrow my eyes. "You had Malachi's soul too. You still took his wings."

The Flame roars, then goes still. *I did not take the warrior's soul. I took his wings. I took years of his life. But a soul is not your body. It is not your gift.* The Flame pulses. *A soul is everything.*

Every moment that makes you who you are. Every memory. Every love. Every loss.

My breath hitches.

You said you would give up anything. That is what I will collect if you fail to repay your debt.

The prophecy surfaces in my mind. Those words, in Anala's terrible voice. "The healer's hands will break the chain, but the price of freedom is all she contains," I recite. "Does that mean my soul?"

It does not. The Flame flickers. *The prophecy will take your memories.*

My heart stutters.

Unless we come to an agreement.

"What kind of agreement?"

A bargain, of course.

The hunger in its voice makes me want to run.

"What kind of bargain?"

Tell me what you want. I'll tell you the cost. The Flame stills, then flares with what might be amusement. *Oh, but you want so many things, my Tempest. You cannot lift the curse, save Lunaris, defeat your father, keep your memories, and keep your warrior.*

My chest tightens.

Not all of them.

I straighten my spine. "Why not?"

Because there is always a price.

"Did my mother's life mean nothing? Her sacrifices?" The words burst out of me. "She gave up everything. Her freedom. Her home. Her family. Her youth. Her gift. Her life. Her children."

My voice breaks on the last word. "Where was the balance then? Surely her sacrifice was worth something."

Hm. The Flame considers this. *You believe her sacrifices should grant you some freedoms?*

"And my brother's. Yes."

I admit, I find myself at a loss. That is a rarity. The Flame sways, almost thoughtfully. *Very well, Tempest. Let us make an arrangement. Someday soon, I will need you to do something. In exchange, I will give you a key to my kingdom.*

"To Noktemore?"

Yes.

"Why would you do that?"

Does it matter? The Flame flares. *Ah, but of course it matters. My Tempest is a fast learner.*

The Flame sways. *I foresee that someday soon, you will need sanctuary. Noktemore can provide it.* A pause. *As for why I would extend this offer to you ... let's say I'm settling a debt of my own.*

I don't question it. Margot's vision flashes through my mind. Being taken. If Cato finds me, if I lose my memories, I'll need an escape. Noktemore could be that escape.

"What do you need from me?"

When the time comes, I will need you to herald a message. You need only agree to deliver it.

My stomach twists. "What kind of message?"

I will tell you when the time comes.

"Will it harm anyone?"

Only the herald.

"Me?" The word comes out too loud. I force my voice lower. "Why would I agree to harm myself?"

The Flame roars. *What have I told you about safety?* It

hisses the word like a curse. *Nothing in existence is ever truly safe. Human, animal, land, or god.*

The Flame expands, almost like a sigh. *I like you, Tempest. For that, I will consider returning some of your memories. In time.*

"Heralding your message won't protect them?"

That cannot be helped.

"I won't remember my brother?" My voice cracks. "My friends?"

Would you rather lose your memories for a time and regain them later? Or lose your soul for eternity? The Flame pulses. *Herald my message. Accept the key to Noktemore. In time, your memories will return.*

I take a shaking breath and concede with a nod. "Tell me what I need to say."

Good. The Flame settles. *For that, I will grant you another kindness.*

All of you are my children. That is why I claim you as mine. The Flame flickers. *But the warrior is not yours. He belongs to his kingdom. He always will, unless he chooses otherwise.*

A pause.

He never has.

My chest aches.

My advice: move on. Find someone worthy of you. Someone less damaged. Less afraid. Less self-righteous. Another flicker. *Less weak.*

My sigil burns so hot I have to clench my fists to keep from screaming.

Do not tell me you've let his rugged good looks cloud your judgment. The Flame sounds almost disappointed. *Surely you see his faults.*

I bite my tongue until I taste blood.

Speak, child.

"I do not want less." The words tear out of me. "He may be many things, but he is not weak. He did not ask for this curse. He has given up everything for a kingdom that will probably never acknowledge his sacrifice!"

You're probably right. The Flame seems to consider this. *Though some call him a coward. Some call him evil.*

My sigil blazes. "Those people can rot in the pits of Noktemore."

The Flame flares. And flares. And flares again.

I glare at it, refusing to back down.

Oh, Tempest. Someday I will tell you why I find such humor in this. Alas, your passionate defense has roused my curiosity. The Flame pulses. *Choose a word. It will be your key to Noktemore. You will not remember it when you wake. I cannot have you telling your warrior.*

Before I can ask what the point is, the Flame roars. *Ask him about the healers who came before. Ask him about his debt. Tell him to bring you home, and I will give you my sister's scepter myself.*

I hold my breath.

If he gives you those answers and still refuses to bring you to me, I will consider telling him your key. So you can find each other in my kingdom. The Flame dims slightly. *When the time comes, I will tell you what to herald.*

The Flame vanishes.

Darkness. Complete and absolute.

The air shifts. A crackling energy replaces it, raising every hair on my arms, making my teeth ache. I stop breathing when I feel something behind me. Something close. Its breath ghosts across my neck.

What is your word, Tempest?

I whisper my word. Then I'm falling. Careening through the cold, endless dark. I land hard on my feet and immediately collapse to my hands and knees. Darkness still. But different. This time, the air smells of petrichor and something ancient.

My fingers curl in damp grass. They snag on something soft. Spongy. Frowning, I push myself up and lift my hand.

A Shroud mushroom.

That's when I feel it.

The stillness. Absolute and wrong. A rush of cold air at my back. The whispers rise again, countless voices overlapping.

We claim you. We claim you. We claim you.

My eyes fly open. I shoot upright in bed, fisting the sheets, gasping for air. The lights around my room flicker wildly. A moment to feel the concern flooding the bond.

Another moment to register the figure standing in my doorway. By then, I've already screamed.

CHAPTER TWENTY-SIX

Malachi storms through the doorway. All black. Vida strapped to his back. His expression is murderous as he scans the room for threats. When his eyes find my face, they soften.

But the Flame's words crawl back into my mind. *He's spent the last two centuries sacrificing healers to the Bratus. Stasis has a way of obscuring memories. He may not remember. Or perhaps he does.*

Countless healers have been sacrificed. The Flame said I need to understand what lurks within the Shroud. And I can't stop wondering if the Shroudmaidens were once like me. Healers led to slaughter.

Is that how Malachi sees me? Another sacrifice waiting to happen? I want to reject the thought. I can't. The Flame laughed at me, as if I were naive to think he could see me as anything else. When he discovers whose daughter I am, that's exactly what I'll become to him. A means to an end.

My stomach lurches. I scramble out of bed and barely make it to the bathroom before my knees hit the cold tile. I retch into the toilet. Nothing comes up, but my body heaves anyway, trying to expel something it can't name. The thought of Cato makes me double over again.

I flinch when I feel him behind me. His hands gather my hair, holding it back from my face. My eyes squeeze shut. The gesture is so gentle. So at odds with everything the Flame told me. I want to summon Mortiana and curse her for what she said about him. I remind myself that she's a trickster. She lies.

For all I know, she was lying about the healers. She must know that's the one thing I could never forgive. I can't even forgive myself for the damage I caused unknowingly. How could I forgive him for doing it on purpose?

I sink back onto my heels. His hand moves to my shoulder, warm and steady.

"Better?" His thumb brushes the back of my neck.

I shudder. Not from disgust. From how badly I want to lean into his touch despite everything. I manage a nod. He backs away, giving me space, but I feel the weight of his gaze as I rise and move to the sink.

I brush my teeth. Wash my hands. Wash them again. And again. I'm stalling, hoping he'll leave. He doesn't. He just stands there, silent. Watching. It's unnerving.

"Does that usually happen when you dream?"

I glance at his reflection in the mirror. He's watching my black-stained fingers as I scrub them for the hundredth time.

"I don't know. It used to happen when I made the elixirs." I shut off the water. Reach for a towel.

"It hasn't happened since I've been here." His eyes narrow slightly. "Not after dreams."

I hadn't noticed. Of course he would. I wonder if this is what happens when Mortiana summons someone. I wonder if he knows, and if he's waiting for me to admit it. I don't. That conversation leads somewhere I'm not ready to go.

I shrug and set the towel down. Turn to face him. "Maybe I woke up before it could."

"Maybe." He doesn't sound convinced.

Loud pounding at the front door breaks the tension. Malachi's expression darkens as he moves to answer it. I exhale in relief and finish dressing.

The tunnel descends far deeper than any I've traveled before. My ears pop as we take the stairs down. And down. And down.

When we finally reach the bottom, I realize the depth is only the beginning of what's wrong. The Veritas tunnels are clean. Well-lit. Maintained.

This place is none of those things. The air is cold and thick with something I can't name. A disquiet energy that prickles along my skin. I can't shake the feeling that something is watching us. Waiting.

I lift my lantern toward the ceiling. The vaulted stone glistens with moisture, pale ridges arching overhead like ribs. Like we're walking through the carcass of something massive. Something that died here long ago and never fully decomposed.

Warmth pulses through the bond. Deliberate. Reassuring. My head turns toward Malachi.

He's nodding at something Kage says, but his eyes are on me. I can't help but wonder if he knows what I am. Has he known from the beginning? From the moment he appeared in my life, or rescued me on that bridge?

I remember his expression when I first told him I was a healer. There was a gleam in his eyes. Recognition? Hunger?

I push the thought away. He's helped me. Protected me. Countless times. Because of the bond, that voice whispers. Unease coils tighter in my gut. I force myself to look away.

"Are you alright?" Naima appears at my side, bumping my shoulder. I flinch.

"Fine." The lie tastes sour. "I just want to find Jordi. This place feels wrong."

"I'm taking the rear." Kage falls into step beside us.

I frown. "Shouldn't you lead? You have the shadows."

"That's what I said." He pitches his voice louder. "But lover boy wants me back here. Ready to hide you in my shadows if things go wrong." A grin. "I'm not sure why he trusts that I won't try anything."

"I trust that you don't want to die in these tunnels after everything you've survived," Mal responds without looking back.

My stomach swoops.

Draven shoots Kage a bewildered look. Kage just laughs.

Margot leans toward Naima. "Told you I would have won that bet."

Naima snorts. "Why do you think I never took it?"

I gape at them, but don't say a word.

Draven glances back. "Next right. Then we hope for the best."

"Why are these tunnels so different from the ones in Veritas?" I ask quietly.

"Hard to say. These were built first. Centuries before the others." He pauses. "Some texts claim they stretch all the way to Vindariel."

"Jordi mentioned that." I keep my voice low. "Do you think it's true?"

"It's a long way north. But anything is possible."

"Gods." Margot shivers as we round the corner. "Imagine making that journey through here."

This passage is different. The air shifts. It's not the same stillness as the Shroud, but it's close. By the way everyone slows, I know I'm not the only one who feels it.

Cold brushes the back of my neck. I freeze.

We've been waiting for your return, empath. The voice is inhuman. It speaks directly into my mind.

I bite my tongue to keep from screaming. My eyes lock on Malachi and I yank on the bond. Hard. He stops instantly. Everyone stops with him.

He turns. His eyes sweep the tunnel before landing on Kage. A nod passes between them. Malachi holds my gaze for a moment, then he turns and keeps moving.

Something lands on my back. I barely swallow my shriek.

"Just me," Kage breathes against my ear. "Give me your lantern. Walk straight to Bain. I'll guide you." His shadow settles over my shoulders like a cloak. "Don't look back. Don't touch the walls."

Heart pounding, I nod and surrender the lantern. The shadows guide me forward, threading me between my friends until I reach Malachi. He doesn't look at me. He simply lifts his arm and tucks me against his side. The motion is swift. Sure. As if we've done this a thousand times before.

"Did you see this?" Draven's voice is barely audible as he lifts his lantern to the wall.

We all stop and turn towards it.

"What the … " Naima raises her own light. "Are those memory stones?"

"Something's growing over them," Draven murmurs. "Vines, maybe."

I stare, trying to make sense of it. Memory stones. There are hundreds of them, maybe thousands, embedded in the wall. And covering each one, thin black lines spreading outward like veins. Margot pokes my back and points down.

My breath catches. The black lines cover the floor. They spread in all directions like a spiderweb. Or the roots of a tree. They climb the stairs leading up to the Hall of Gratitude. They snake down the dark hallway to our left.

They're everywhere.

Everyone swings their lanterns toward the hallway.

The light reaches the darkness. And the darkness reaches back.

CHAPTER TWENTY-SEVEN

My friends scream. I can't make a sound. Two pairs of glowing eyes approach through the darkness. Four more blink open behind them.

The Shroudmaidens stop. One steps forward, separating from the rest. No one moves. I feel Malachi pass his lantern to someone behind him. See his hand drift toward Vida's hilt.

Through the bond, I feel the crackle of his energy. The restlessness coiled beneath his calm exterior. It reminds me of Jordi, but different. Jordi's energy is reactive, sharp movements born from contained anger. Malachi's is deliberate. Controlled. Honed by centuries of patient vengeance.

At the edges of my vision, Kage's shadows coil. Margot's gray smoke rises beside them. Both ready. Both waiting.

The Shroudmaiden lifts an arm. Extends a long, crooked finger. The limb shifts as I watch. First smoke, like Kage's shadows.

Then bone. Then flesh, cycling through colors: green-blue, gray, leathery brown like my skin, olive like Margot's. As if it's trying on bodies. Remembering what it was. None of us breathe.

"*We only want her.*"

The finger points at me.

Malachi's arm tightens around my waist. "You can't have her."

The Shroudmaiden's eyes pulse. It lowers its hand. Stares.

We stare back.

Malachi moves. So fast I don't register his arm leaving me until Vida is drawn between us and the creature, glyphs blazing along the blade.

"*She is not yours to claim, warrior.*"

Malachi begins to speak. Low, guttural words in a language I don't recognize. The Shroudmaidens shriek, the sound ricocheting off the stone walls. Margot's smoke surges around us, forming a barrier.

"*She. Is. Not. Yours. To. Claim.*"

The voices speak as one. Deep. Ancient. The memory stones in the walls flicker in response, as if awakened. The Shroudmaidens launch into the air.

Lanterns rise behind us. The light spreads, revealing what the darkness hid. The Shroudmaidens hover beneath the dome. But beyond them, the walls glow with countless memory stones stretching into an endless hall.

And between those stones, suspended in the air, more Shroudmaidens than I can count. My pulse thunders.

"Oh gods," Margot breathes. Her smoke barrier wavers.

Kage's shadows tighten around us, compensating.

The Shroudmaidens laugh. The sound is terrible. Wrong. It echoes off the walls like breaking glass.

One of them dives. Its smoke-body bends, and suddenly

a face materializes inches from mine. Glowing eyes. No features. Just light and hunger.

"*You fed—*"

Malachi's blade cuts through the air. The creature vanishes before it can finish.

Silence.

They're gone. All of them. As if they were never there.

I press a hand to my pounding heart and stare into the dark hall. I don't know what horrifies me more: the endless memory stones, or the accusation the Shroudmaiden started to make.

You fed, it said. Fed what? The Shroud? Them?

Naima's voice pulls me back. "That sword. What are those glyphs?"

"Wards against evil."

I frown at his answer. There's more to it. There has to be. But the narrow staircase looms ahead, and we're out of time for questions.

Kage sends a shadow upward with a lantern. The light climbs and climbs, swallowed by darkness long before it finds the top. When he lowers the lantern, I notice the steps more clearly.

Steep. Chipped. As if no one has walked them in centuries. That doesn't make sense. None of this makes sense.

Kage retrieves his shadow and turns to face us. He taps the side of his temple. "Dray?"

Draven dips his chin. Some code between them. I don't ask.

The plan is set. Draven and Margot stay below. Malachi and Naima search for the scepter. Kage and I find Jordi.

I should tell Malachi what Mortiana said about the scepter. That it's not here. That she'll give it to us herself. But the words won't come.

Kage gives Malachi the same signal, then moves toward the stairs.

"Wait." I catch his arm. "Naima should go first."

Malachi shakes his head. "We stick to the plan."

"What if the door is locked?"

"I'll pick it," Kage says.

"She doesn't need a key. She can just open it."

Kage's eyebrows rise as realization dawns on him. "Metal forger." He glances at Naima. "A *true* metal forger."

Her responding smile is small. Wary.

Another wordless exchange passes between Kage and Mal before Kage shrugs and allows Naima to take the lead. I glance back at Mal as we begin the climb and nearly collide with his face, inches from mine.

"Can you get inside people's heads?"

He stares at me for a moment. "If I say yes, will you let me into yours?"

"No."

I turn forward and freeze. The stairs aren't touching the walls.

"What?" Malachi asks.

"The stairs."

Everyone stops. The structure wobbles beneath us.

I stop breathing. "Oh gods. Oh gods, oh gods, oh gods."

"Calm down." Kage's voice is steady. "We're not that high yet."

I look down. He's right. A fall from here wouldn't kill us. But if the entire structure collapses while we're on it? That's a different story.

"This is the only way in," Naima says. "What are we supposed to do, use the front door?"

"We run," Kage suggests.

"*Run?*" I gasp. "Have you lost your mind?"

"If we slip, we're dead. Maybe not you with your fucking shadows, but the rest of us are!" My voice cracks. "And if the whole thing crumbles? Then what?"

Naima and Kage's eyebrows shoot up. Through the bond, I feel Malachi's surprise. My eyes widen as I register the word that just left my mouth. Not because of the curse itself. Because of how rare it is in Lunaris. Because I sound exactly like him. As if I needed another thing to process right now.

"Relax," Kage says softly.

I growl at him. Actually growl.

His eyebrow rises. "How did you not see this when I sent the light up?"

"You were the one who sent your shadow up! How did *you* not see it?"

The staircase groans. Sways. I make a sound that's embarrassingly close to a whimper.

"How many steps to the top?" Naima murmurs, tipping her head back.

I see her calculating. Measuring the distance with her eyes. Panic claws at my chest.

"Naima Stonehand, I swear to every deity that has ever

existed, if you run up those stairs and we survive, I will kill you myself."

A surprised laugh bursts out of her. Kage snorts. Even Malachi huffs behind me. Before I can yell at them for laughing, warmth floods the bond. It sinks into my bones, loosening the tension in my muscles.

"Send another shadow up," Naima suggests. "Let's see what we're working with."

"And one down," I add. "To see what's beneath us."

Kage scoffs. "Sure, why don't I just drain my entire gift before we even get inside?"

"What's taking so long?" Margot hisses from below.

"The stairs aren't stable."

Her eyes widen as the structure sways. "Goddess."

Draven appears beside her. "How did you miss that, Yosh?"

"Excellent question," I mutter, glaring at Kage.

He has the decency to look uncomfortable.

"This is the only way in," Draven repeats.

I press a hand to my forehead. "Oh my gods. We know that, Professor."

Draven snorts.

"Kage." Malachi's voice is calm. Commanding. "Can you wrap a shadow around each of us?"

"I can. But you know what that could mean inside."

"Do it. Or we never make it up."

Kage summons his shadows. I watch one coil around Naima's torso like a dark serpent. Another wraps around me. I gasp at the coldness of it.

"Naima." Malachi's voice is low, steady. "Slow steps. Distribute your weight evenly."

She nods. Looks up. Looks back at us. "Ready?"

"Go."

The stairs shift the moment she moves. I bite my lip. Hold my breath.

They sway harder when Kage follows.

"How do we get out?" I whisper over my shoulder.

"Side door," Draven calls up. "Every temple has one. We'll meet you there or across the street, depending on how crowded it is out there."

A hand presses against my lower back. "Your turn."

I take a breath. Look up at the darkness waiting above. I climb. Hands on the steps ahead, weight distributed like Naima did. Without a lantern to manage, I move faster, but the darkness pressing in from all sides does nothing to calm my nerves.

The stairs groan. Sway. I squeeze my eyes shut. Force myself to breathe. Then keep climbing. When I finally reach the top, I sag into Naima's arms.

I turn to watch Malachi climb. He doesn't have a shadow around him. Nor is he distributing his weight or placing his hands on the steps. Of course he isn't.

My heart stops as the stairs sway beneath him. He keeps moving as if it's nothing. As if gravity is a suggestion he's chosen to ignore. When he reaches us, he opens his mouth and shuts it when the staircase groans louder.

I grab his cloak without thinking. We watch in horror as the entire structure swings from one side to the other. If any of us had still been on those steps, we would have fallen.

"What the …" Kage breathes.

Malachi grabs me and spins us toward the door. "Open the fucking door!"

We spill through the doorway as the world shakes. Malachi yanks me against his chest and slams us into the wall. Kage wraps Naima in shadows as they crash beside us.

Then, stillness.

I summon flames to my palms. Kage produces four thin torches, and I light them one by one. Malachi and Naima crack the door open, peering into the darkness beyond.

"I was sure it collapsed," Naima breathes.

"It didn't?"

She shakes her head. "Crashed into the wall, but it's still standing."

"We need to move," Kage says. "Now."

The smell hits me first. Decay. Something rotting, though nothing visible to explain it. We step out of the chamber and walk toward the rotunda.

At its edge, we stop. The temple is ruined. What must once have been opulent white stone and gilded columns is now chipped, crumbling, covered in dust. Abandoned. That's the word for this place.

Everything I've heard about the Keep describes elegance. Luster. This is the opposite of that. I can't imagine the Council setting foot here.

Our footsteps echo as we cross toward the dome at the center. Only remnants of a fire pit remain, cold and dark. A prickling sensation crawls up my spine. I remember, suddenly, what else lurks in Council territory.

"Watch for silent guards," I whisper. "The birds."

"Have you ever seen the legion guards use their gifts?" Kage whispers back.

I exchange a confused look with Naima before looking at him. "Why do you ask?"

"He thinks the silent guards are shifters," Mal responds.

I stop in my tracks and spin to face them. "*What?*"

"It's just a theory," he says, but the way he looks at Mal tells me it's more than that.

"We can talk about this later. Right now, we have to find Jordan and get out," Mal says, his tone not leaving room for argument.

Kage nods and sends his shadows spiraling outward, scouting. "No way the scepter is here."

Malachi murmurs something in agreement.

Naima moves to my side. "You're going to have to use your serephony."

Malachi turns sharply.

Kage recalls his shadows and glares at me. "This is what I meant during planning."

"You were talking about stopping time," I argue.

"She doesn't like using it. For obvious reasons," Naima snaps before Kage can respond, and takes the torch from my hand.

Understanding dawns on his face. "Because you're an empath. Both gifts at once …"

He doesn't finish. He doesn't need to. It's a recipe for disaster. I do it anyway. I take a breath, close my eyes, and focus on Jordi's energy signature, that particular hum I'd recognize anywhere.

In my mind, I move through the temple. Out of the

rotunda. Down halls I've never walked. Between columns I've never seen. Searching.

The air grows colder as I search. That strange energy from the tunnels is here too. Watching. Waiting.

Something brushes my arm. I jolt, trying to see, but my mind's eye can only show me places I've been. The darkness beyond is a void.

"Pull back if you sense danger," Malachi warns.

"Unless you can pinpoint its location," Kage adds.

"No." Malachi's voice sharpens. "We don't know what's down here."

Naima hisses for silence.

Cold touches the back of my neck. I spin in the darkness, heart pounding. What if he's not here? What if this was all for nothing? The cold pursues me. I move faster, but it stays at my heels.

I'm passing a chamber when I feel it. Not the cold. Something else. The incessant chatter from Mortiana's summons, loud and painful.

But beneath it, underneath all that noise, a familiar hum. Restless energy. Sharp edges. Scattered warmth.

Jordi.

My eyes fly open. "I found him."

Malachi studies my face as Naima presses the torch back into my hand.

"There's something else here," I say as we move. "Something I can't explain."

"The birds?"

"No." I shudder. "Something ... evil."

"Shroudmaidens?"

I shake my head. "They don't feel evil."

"What do they feel like?" Mal asks. There's hesitation in his voice. Something that makes me pause.

"Grief." I meet his eyes. "They feel like grief."

His expression gives nothing away. I file that away for later as we reach a set of double doors. Malachi and Kage push through together. I follow, torch trembling in my grip.

The chamber is smaller than the main rotunda. And every surface, from floor to domed ceiling, is covered in memory stones. At the center, a raised platform bears the symbol of the Everlasting, crafted from the same dark stones. Above it, a white stone table.

And on the table, my brother.

He's pale. Gaunt. He looks like he hasn't been fed in weeks. A sob rises in my throat. I move toward him without thinking.

Malachi's arm catches me around the waist. Hauls me back. "You stay here." His voice is a low growl against my ear.

"But—"

His eyes pin me in place. "I don't want you anywhere near those stones. Do you understand?" His grip tightens. "We're running out of time."

"He's right," Naima says quietly. "Even I can feel them. And I don't have your gift."

I swallow. Nod at her, then at him. "I'll stay. Just …"

"I'll be careful with him." He releases me and turns toward my brother.

I want to tell him to be careful with himself, too. The

words won't come. I push the feeling through the bond instead. *Be safe. Please.*

If he receives it, he doesn't show it. He and Kage study the room. The stones. The safe paths between them.

They debate whether Kage's shadows can reach far enough. In the end, that's how they do it. Kage's shadows lift my brother from the table and carry him back to us.

Back to me.

CHAPTER TWENTY-EIGHT

I hold Jordi's cold hand as Malachi carries him through the ruined temple. His skin is ice. His breathing shallow. Kage pushes open the side door and noise crashes over us. Music. Laughter. The Moon Festival in full swing. We barrel through fog and drunk revelers, pushing toward Veritas territory.

It strikes me, as we push through the crowd, that it wouldn't matter if we reached Veritas. There is no safety. There never was. I squeeze Jordi's hand tighter, wishing he were awake enough to mock me for believing there ever could be.

We slow when we reach the alley. Margot and Draven rush forward, eyes widening as they take in Jordi's appearance.

Margot presses the back of her hand to his forehead. "He looks ghastly."

I swallow past the knot in my throat and nod. He looks worse than he did after the poisoned arrow. And that nearly killed him.

"Where do we go?" Malachi asks.

"The Whispering Ponds," Naima says. "Where else?"

"Will it be safe?"

Malachi's free hand finds mine. His fingers lace through my trembling ones. "Where do you want me to take him?"

The answer claws its way out of my throat. "There's nowhere. There's nowhere safe."

I press a hand to my mouth, blinking back tears. The hopelessness of it settles over me like a shroud. There is nowhere safe for him. The moment the Council discovers he's gone, they'll come looking. And they will find him.

Malachi squeezes my hand. "Can you treat him at the clinic?"

I nod.

He releases me and starts walking. We follow.

Malachi sets Jordi on the exam table and ushers everyone out. The door closes behind them. I press my forehead against the wood. Breathe. Then turn to face my brother. I don't waste time on tears. I'm not sure I have any left.

I don't reach for ingredients. Don't remove his shirt. I simply place my hands on his chest, close my eyes, and find my center.

Then I focus on him.

The last time I used this gift, I had to dig deep and pull the poison. This time is different. There's nothing to pull. I find the source of his injuries quickly. Heal his ribs first, then his wrists.

Then I turn to his energy. That's where the real damage

lies. I push some of my own into him. And as I do, I remember the prophecy.

What the Flame said about losing my memories. So I push more. Love. Gratitude. Courage. Compassion. Hope. All the things I wish I'd given him sooner. Things I pray I'll give him again, when my memories return. If they return.

A hand covers mine.

My eyes fly open. Hazel eyes stare back at me. Eyes I've missed so much.

"You saved me again," he croaks.

I laugh and wipe tears I was certain had dried up. "Someone has to." I smack his arm lightly. "Gods, Jordi. What were you thinking?"

He laughs weakly as I help him sit up. I watch him drain two glasses of water too quickly, then wait until I'm sure he'll keep it down before speaking.

"We have so much to discuss. And so little time."

His eyebrow rises. "Little time?"

"Draven leaves for Vindariel soon. I need you to go with him."

He blinks. "Are you coming?"

I glance at the door. "I can't. Not yet."

"Then neither can I."

"You have to," I say, drawing out each word in hopes that they sink in. "The Council took you to the Hall of Gratitude to feed the Everlasting. Constantine has a chip of the amber stone. The actual Everlasting. That's how he channels Cato's power."

Jordi's eyes widen. "His ring. I saw it when they brought me in. It was glowing."

"Glowing?"

"Faintly. Like it was …" He shudders. "Drinking something. I thought I imagined it."

I remember the amber flash in Constantine's eyes at the square. I didn't imagine that. And I didn't imagine the wrongness in that temple.

"I don't know what it means for Cato." I swallow the bitter taste in my mouth. "But the Council will come looking for you."

He studies me. "You spoke to Sara."

I nod, blinking back fresh tears. "She told me everything."

"About the Shroud? The stones?"

"Everything."

"Did she tell you I wrote those messages on the walls?"

My eyebrows shoot up. "No." A laugh escapes me despite everything. "Gods, Jordi. You are the most brilliant idiot I know."

He grins. "I try."

"Who else? Just you?"

"A few others." His expression darkens. "It doesn't matter. The 'renegades' stopped. Most of them got scared."

Of course they did. It happens every time. Every rise and fall of civilization. Every time one group deems themselves superior, whether by class, skin color, sex, or the gods they worship, they use the same tactics.

Sometimes they strike at the perceived leader. Other times, they target loved ones. Or silence the loudest voices first. Whatever it takes to instill enough fear that the rest fall in line.

It happens with pack animals. With certain hawks. With raffins. The thought gives me pause.

I think about Cato. His scepter. The way he compels people to follow him, to bend to his will. Constantine doesn't have a scepter. He has something worse. Erasure. Suppression. The Shroud.

He erased the gods from memory. Turned them into costumes for the Moon Festival. Characters to dress as, never beings to worship. No. Worship is reserved for the Everlasting. And even that, he doesn't call a god.

He uses altered incantations to bend residents to his will. Memory stones to feed the Shroud. Amulets as weapons of fear. No one dares remove them. No one wants to be blamed for letting the Shroudmaidens in.

I would call him clever, but there's little convincing needed when you've stripped away someone's memories. His flowery speeches, his posturing. They're for his benefit, not theirs.

"The Sages said you went to the Keep on purpose."

He sighs. "I thought I could spare you some pain. Move the stones so they could no longer feed the Shroud. Give those people a chance to ..."

"Survive once the Shroud is gone?"

"Yes." His eyes are full of sorrow. "But the memory stones can't be moved. I tried."

My stomach drops.

"I'm so sorry, Temp. The older residents, the ones who were here when the treaty was signed, and some who arrived when we did ..." He swallows. "They can't survive without their amulets."

I set my elbows on the table and bow my head. "So when the Shroud falls ... they'll die?"

"I'm sorry."

I shake my head. "Lenora's journal mentioned a reversal elixir."

"It won't work on them." His voice is hollow. "Too many stones have turned black. Those people are already gone. The amulets are the only thing keeping them here. If the Shroud vanishes, it powers them off."

My stomach lurches. I press a hand to my mouth. All those people. So many stones in those tunnels. So many lives, already hollowed out.

"The newer residents should be fine. The ones who arrived after us."

My eyes fly open. "What about Arlo? Cas? Bastian?"

"Arlo and Cas take theirs off regularly. But Bas ..." He looks away. "I don't know."

I think of Margot and bite my lip to keep it from trembling. Gods. It's too much.

"Did you know the Council was using different elixirs?" I whisper.

"I suspected. Draven remembers his life, and he took the same elixir as everyone else."

"Do you know what makes it different?"

"No. But while I was 'recovering' at the Hall of Reflection, I overheard a healer. She said some duelers came in for treatment. The way they described feeling at the amphitheater ..." He pauses. "It was like they were being controlled."

"Controlled how?"

"Their minds." He meets my eyes. "Is it possible an incantation could do that?"

"Only at the amphitheater?"

"I don't know." He starts pacing the small space. "The amphitheater was one of the first structures built in Lunaris. The temple in front of it, too. And according to Arlo, there are no tunnels beneath it. Something is blocking them."

He stops. Turns to face me. "What if that's where the main concentration of stones is? What if that's what makes people susceptible to Constantine?"

"His mind control?"

"Maybe. I don't know." He shivers. "Is it possible to control someone's mind without an elixir? Or is it the elixir he gives them when they arrive? I can't figure it out."

I think of the history we've studied. The patterns. "I don't think it takes much to control someone's mind. They just need to be susceptible."

"Gods." His voice is barely a whisper. "And having no memories makes them more vulnerable."

I nod, horror mounting, and remember something else. "The poisoned arrow that hit you that day. It seemed aimed at you specifically."

Jordi shakes his head. "It was a new legion guard."

"They shot several of them right at you."

"He shot a few people. He shot his own foot, too. He claimed he was seeing things that others said weren't there." His mouth twists. "He was taken to the Hall of Reflection. He didn't survive."

"Are you sure?"

"Fairly sure." He shrugs. "Why else would it only have happened that day?"

I have no answer for that.

"What about the Shroudmaidens? Are they really sacrificed healers?"

"I don't know for certain. But an old Veritas scholar had a theory." He pauses. "He believed the maidens sacrificed themselves for Pia. To help her in the afterlife."

"How? Why?"

"He didn't explain. Just said he saw a pattern."

I think of the Shroudmaidens in the tunnels. Their glowing eyes. Their accusation: *You fed—*

"This is awful," I whisper. "All of it."

"It's not your fault."

I scoff. "Maybe not the oldest residents. Maybe not directly. But it's still my fault."

"You couldn't have known!" He slides off the table and grabs the edge when his legs wobble. "We couldn't have!"

"I should have. I made those elixirs for years, Jordi. Years. How could I not sense something was wrong?"

"You stopped the moment you suspected something was wrong. You didn't even know the full truth." He shakes his head. "I can't believe you didn't tell me."

"It wouldn't have changed anything."

A wave of emotion crashes over me. The curse. The bargain. Everything I haven't told him.

"Jordi. I need you to go with Draven."

"I can't. I read that prophecy. I saw what's coming." His voice cracks. "I can't lose you."

I press my hand to my throat. "Did you actually have a vision?"

He wipes his eyes. "I have Fidus's scepter. *Had*. I buried it in the forest before I went to see you that day."

I stare at him for a moment. "How did you get it?"

"I was looking for Ignata's temple. Found a cave I'd never seen before. The scepter was just ... there." He shivers and wraps his arms around himself. "It was strange, Temp. One moment I was here. The next, somewhere entirely different."

I frown. "Different how? *Where*?"

"I don't know. I just know it wasn't Lunaris."

"And you took the scepter? You didn't think you might end up cursed like every fool in those old texts?"

He shrugs. "I figured at least I'd be a cursed fool with a god's scepter."

A laugh escapes me despite myself. I swat his shoulder. "There's something seriously wrong with you."

He grins. "But you love me anyway."

I press my lips together as emotion rises again. "Jordi. I need you to go. I can't do what I'm supposed to do while worrying about your safety."

He opens his mouth to argue. A knock interrupts him.

I wipe my tears as Jordi calls for them to enter. Malachi steps through the door. Jordi gapes at him, then me, then Mal again.

"I hoped you'd be awake. Didn't expect to find you standing," Mal says to a bewildered looking Jordi.

"Do you know who he is?" I ask warily, studying my brother's expression.

He frowns and shakes his head as he stares at Mal. "I don't think so. You look like someone, though."

I exhale. "Bain carried you all the way from the temple. And you stink. So you should thank him."

"Well, thank you, Bain. Sorry I wasn't awake to enjoy it." Jordi's grin makes me laugh. Even Malachi's eyes crinkle. "Are you the one staying in my quarters?"

"Yes. So I should be thanking you."

Jordi turns to me. The grin on his face makes my stomach drop. "I figured out who he reminds me of. He looks just like those heroes in those romance—"

"Jordan!"

"—novels!"

"I read three of those books! *Three!*"

"Until the pages fell off," he says, laughing, then wincing. "Gods, that hurts."

"Good." I glare at him, then at Malachi, who looks far too amused.

"I don't think I've ever seen you blush," he says, eyes bright.

I groan and turn away to busy myself with tidying the room. There's another knock, and I turn back around to watch Draven enter the room. He greets Jordi with a tight hug and pulls away when Mal clears his throat.

"We need to speak with both of you."

I lean against the table behind me. The cages underneath rattle with my weight.

"Draven leaves for Vindariel soon. You should go with him." Malachi's voice is calm but firm. "If you don't want to stay there, he can take you to Aerathos or anywhere else. But you can't stay here."

Jordi's eyes narrow. First on Malachi. Then on me. "Did the two of you plan this?"

My sigil flares. "When, exactly? While we were saving your life? Or while we were trying not to get caught by the legion?"

He crosses his arms. "I'm not leaving you behind."

My chest tightens. I look at Draven. At Malachi. Back to Jordi.

"I made a bargain with Mortiana," I blurt out.

Draven makes a choked sound.

Jordi stares at me. "You *what*?"

"I made a bargain. I cannot leave until I repay my debt."

"Ada." He sets his hands on his matted hair. Paces the few steps the room allows. Stops. Paces again. When he faces me, his eyes are wide with fear. "This is what I ... *Gods*." His gaze darts to Malachi, then me. "Does he know?"

I stiffen. "No."

Jordi laughs. It's not a happy sound. "Of course not."

"Know what?" Malachi's voice has gone quiet. Deadly.

"Nothing," I say through clenched teeth. I hold Jordi's gaze. "If you know as much as you claim, you understand this is the only way."

His eyes fill with tears. And somehow, that fills mine too. As if we draw from the same well.

"Godsdamn you," he whispers, lip trembling.

"It's the only way." I wipe tears from my cheeks. They keep falling.

He surges forward and wraps his arms around me. As if

he can keep me safe inside them. As if holding tight enough will change what's coming. The sob in his chest loosens the one in mine. Soon we're both crying too hard to speak.

"I figured I should be the hero for once," I whisper against his shoulder.

He squeezes tighter. "You've always been the hero, Temp. I was just trying to be worthy of being your brother."

That makes me cry harder. All the time we wasted on petty arguments. All the time I spent pushing him away. For what? In the end, we were always going to end up here.

Prophecies are more legend than story. They may vary in the telling. But they don't change. And they can't be erased.

We cry for what feels like an eternity. When we finally pull apart, we're alone. Malachi and Draven have slipped out without a word.

Jordi wipes his face. "Now we know what warriors are truly scared of."

I choke out a laugh. "You know what else scares them? The way you smell right now. You need a bath and a meal before you go anywhere with Draven."

"That I won't argue with."

We go home. He bathes. Eats. Packs what little he'll need for the journey north. We only have a few hours. I make every moment count.

I look around my dining table and wish I could freeze this moment forever. Kage, telling some elaborate story with his hands. Jordi, hanging on every word. Naima, rolling her eyes but joining the antics anyway. Margot, smiling despite the sadness in her eyes. Draven, shaking his head and correcting Kage's exaggerations.

And Malachi.

The warrior I never asked to be bound to. The man who has somehow become part of me. He's quiet, as always, listening to Kage's story. But the moment my gaze finds him, his eyes lock onto mine.

I don't know if it's the bond or the Rook in him, but he always senses me. Knows where I am before I move. And despite his perpetual annoyance with everything, despite his ability to perpetually annoy me, I find that he's the best thing to come from all of this.

I can only hope he doesn't hate me when he learns who I am. And that when my memories are taken, the goddess lets me keep these faces. These people. What they mean to me.

CHAPTER TWENTY-NINE

For the first time in three years, I don't go to the clinic. I go through the motions of dressing, then change into a shapeless tunic I normally sleep in. I sit at my desk. And I start writing.

Everything I've learned. From Lenora's journal. From Malachi. From Jordi. From the Sages. From the Flame. I write it all down because I'm certain of only two things now. The first is that at some point, I won't remember any of this.

As I write, I realize why I've always been at odds with the history books. The ancient texts. The carefully curated archives of Veritas. Writing is self-serving altruism disguised as art.

Worse, disguised as fact. We recount history as we perceive it and hope we're remembered for telling the truth. But there are so many sides to every story. So many ways to perceive a single event. In the end, every account is true. And every account is false.

This is why we keep making the same mistakes. Not because we fail to see the signs. We see them. We simply cling to what resonates with our own experiences. Choose what serves our purpose.

In Lunaris, what serves the Council serves the residents. In Veritas, what serves the Order serves us. We tell ourselves otherwise. But the pattern is the same.

We are used, therefore we use.

Maybe that's why every organization, every order, every guild relies so heavily on logic and fallacy. They know it's in our nature to tear each other apart. All they have to do is provide the push. The weapon. Then sit back and watch.

Which makes me wonder about the gods. They invented this hierarchy. They sit above it all. So why intervene now? Why work together, summon mortals, bargain with us? What are they afraid of? I don't know.

What I do know is this: in the end, nothing will matter.

Except, perhaps, everything.

I close the journal as the knock comes. I push away from my desk. Take a breath. Prepare myself for the conversation I've been dreading.

Malachi gave me space after everyone left in the middle of the night. But I've felt his restlessness through the bond all day. A low hum of impatience. Of worry.

I pull open the door. He's wearing a clean navy tunic and matching pants. His hair is damp, freshly washed.

His frown deepens when he sees what I'm wearing. "You didn't go to the clinic?"

"I didn't think I should." I glance past him, checking for Kage. We're alone. "I'm not sure we should stay here much longer."

"We can stay tonight. Tomorrow, we'll go somewhere

else." His jaw tightens as he searches my face. "I can't do this anymore."

My stomach drops. "Do what?"

"This!" He throws his hands up and lets them fall against his sides. "Tell me what changed between that kiss, which I can't stop replaying every second of every godsdamned day, and that meeting with the Sages. Tell me what they said to you."

The breath I take catches in my throat. *Gods*. I've imagined this conversation a thousand ways. Not once did I think he'd mention the kiss. For the thousandth time, I think how much easier this would be if he were just some outsider. A stranger passing through for the Moon Festival.

But if that were true, he wouldn't mention the kiss. Wouldn't want to speak at all. We wouldn't have gotten to know each other. Wouldn't have these feelings between us. This longing. This ache. This *adhoranelo*. I sort through every scenario I prepared. In the end, there are only two choices.

I can tell him the truth. Risk losing his private smiles. The heat in his eyes when he looks at me. His warmth. His kindness. Those moments of possession. His rapt attention.

I'll lose those things eventually. The prophecy guarantees it. The Flame confirmed it. But I don't have to lose them now. I could pull him to me. Kiss him. Get lost in the moment.

The moment the thought forms, I think of all the choices that have been taken from us. From him. The choices I've taken from others, and I know I can't take this one from him. I won't.

I remember what he told me once: *Tomorrow's stories shouldn't diminish today's actions*. I can't ignore this any longer.

Maybe he'll hate me. Maybe he won't. But that will be his choice to make. And mine to live with.

"You're right," I say after a long moment. "We need to talk."

Concern flickers across his face. It almost makes me want to take it back. Instead, I turn and walk to my bed. Sit cross-legged against the pillows.

His eyes widen. "You want to talk in here? In bed?"

"It won't matter. I doubt you'll want to rip my clothes off after you hear what I have to say."

His eyebrow rises. "I'm fairly certain that would never be the case."

I huff out a laugh, tucking my knees into the tunic and hugging them to my chest. "I'm fairly certain you're wrong."

"Should I remind you that I'm rarely wrong?" He kicks the door shut behind him and steps inside.

I shake my head and watch him look around, considering his options. He crosses to the seating area, picks up one of the wing-backed chairs, and carries it to my bedside. He sits. Waits.

I take a breath. "Tell me about your debt."

Surprise flickers across his face. Then his eyes narrow. "Why?"

"Mortiana said she cannot speak of the dead. But you can. If you're willing to tell me about your debt."

He goes completely still. "You answered her summons?"

"Answered?" I raise an eyebrow. "As if I had a choice?"

The lights flicker. "Every time you step into that room, every time you approach the Flame, you're making a choice."

"I don't know how not to answer." My voice is calmer

than I feel. "She gave me things to ask you. Things to tell you. Things I don't want to say."

"What kind of things?" That quiet, dangerous tone again. The one that makes my neck prickle.

"She wants you to take me to her."

He scoffs and looks away. "That's not happening."

"She said she'll give me the scepter herself."

The lights flicker. His hands flex on the chair's arms. "She said that?"

"Her exact words: 'Tell Malachi to bring you home, and I will give you the scepter myself.'"

His eyes narrow. "What does she want in exchange?"

"Nothing." I shrug, though nothing about this feels casual. "She said she already has my soul."

His jaw tics. He looks away. I don't need the bond to tell me he's furious. Don't need my empathy. Don't need the lights, which are flickering differently now. As if they're afraid to stay lit too long. As if they might catch his ire.

"Mal."

He clenches his fists in his lap. Closes his eyes. "I'm not taking you to her."

The words are soft. Too soft.

I hug my knees tighter. But I can't look away from his face. I've seen him under flickering lights before. Seen the hard lines of his jaw, the menacing energy that surrounds him when he's upset.

This isn't that. This is more. If I weren't watching so closely, I might miss it. If I hadn't memorized every line of his face, I wouldn't notice.

But I am. And I have.

Which is why it's impossible to miss the thin lines forming beneath his eyes. Not silver, like the Sages get when their eyes flash. These lines are gold. Or copper. It's hard to tell against his skin.

Then his eyes open.

I thought the Sages were terrifying when their eyes flashed silver. They're nothing compared to this. His beautiful golden-brown eyes, the color of memory stones and my favorite sunrise, flash bronze.

Bronze.

And everything inside me goes still.

CHAPTER THIRTY

"Mal." My voice is barely a whisper. "What's happening to you?"

"I'm not taking you to her," he says, his voice a low growl.

I would never have dared touch the Sages when their eyes flashed silver. But with him, I can't stop myself. My heart pounds. My hands shake. I move to the edge of the bed and lift my palms to his face.

He closes his eyes. Releases a soft sigh as my fingers find his cheeks.

"Does that feel good?"

He huffs a laugh. "What a question."

"Does it?"

"Everything you do feels good." His voice is low. Gravelly. It makes my stomach clench.

"The elixir I used on your wounds has menthol. That's different."

His eyes open. No longer bronze, but the possessive heat blazing in them makes my pulse flutter as wildly as the lights.

"It has nothing to do with the menthol." He holds my gaze. "It's you. Everything you do. Everything you are."

The words cleave into me. I drop my hands. Look away. Bite my lip against the tears that spring to my eyes.

"You don't know what you're saying."

"Will you please just tell me what changed?"

I swallow past the knot in my throat. Nod. "I will. But I need to ask you something first."

"Then ask me, Ada!" His voice rises. "I'll tell you anything. Everything. Just—" He stops. Closes his eyes. Takes a breath. When he opens them again, his voice is controlled. "Just ask."

Ada. Not Menace.

Hearing him use my name shouldn't hurt this much. But I suppose I should get used to it.

"Have you sacrificed healers?"

Surprise crosses his face. Then he looks away. My heart hammers as the silence stretches. It feels like an eternity before he clears his throat.

"Mortiana told you this?"

"Did you kill them or not?" My voice is barely above a whisper. "That's all I'm asking."

The anguish in his eyes almost makes me take it back. Almost.

"Do you think I killed them?" He searches my face. "You must, or you wouldn't ask. You think because I'm a warrior, a Rook, desperate to save his kingdom, I'd slaughter innocent people?"

"Just answer the question, Malachi."

"I will. But I want to know what you think." He leans

forward. "You know me better than Mortiana does. You know me better than …" He shakes his head and lets out a humorless laugh. "What do you believe?"

"I don't believe you'd kill innocent people. But the way she said it …" I exhale shakily. "I know what this curse has cost you. I can't imagine the frustration. And I thought, if I'm going to flay myself open for you, I might as well make you do the same."

He's quiet for a long moment. "I didn't kill them, but they were inhabitants of Tenebris. Under my protection. And I did nothing to stop their deaths." He looks at me. "I suppose that's the lesson Mortiana wants me to learn."

"What is your bargain?"

He sighs. "Do you remember when I told you I'm only woken from stasis during Reckonings? Or when Mortiana needs something?"

I nod.

"I transport souls for her. The souls of loved ones who died because of the curse." His jaw tightens. "I assume healers have been among them. Along with my grandparents. My uncles. Aunts. Cousins." He swallows hard. "My niece."

My breath catches. "Why?"

"It's part of my—"

"No." I cut him off. He looks up, startled. "Why do *you* have to pay these debts? Why not someone else? Why you?"

"Because I'm the prince of Tenebris."

The words land like stones.

"Prince Malachi Bain Malvorathis." He watches my face. "That won't mean anything to you. You don't learn our history. But that's why."

The air leaves my lungs. I scoot back, needing distance. "You're the prince."

He nods. "You know how the Sages give children they visit three fates and a name? I'm Prince Malachi Bain Malvorathis, the Cursebearer." His mouth twists. "Prince Bain the Cursed."

"The prince of Tenebris," I whisper. My vision blurs. I stare at my black-stained fingernails.

"Technically, I'm the spare. My sister will take the throne when ..." He clears his throat. "When the curse is lifted."

Gods. I thought he was just a warrior who'd sacrificed much for his kingdom. That was bad enough. This is worse. So much worse.

"Your sister. The warrior," I say, my voice sounding far away.

"We come from a long line of them."

I nod, reeling. The prince. He's the prince. How can a father I've never met ruin my life so completely? I hate Cato for everything. But I hate him most for this.

"That's why she said you'd never belong to me," I whisper.

The lights flicker. I keep my eyes on my hands.

"She said that?"

I nod. It's all I can manage as shame crashes over me.

"I'm..." My lip quivers. "Oh gods. I can't do this." I press my hands to my face. "I'm such a coward. I said I'd tell you everything, and I can't. I *can't*."

"Ada." He leans forward. Sets his hand over mine. "Look at me."

His touch. His comfort. It's too much.

A sob breaks free. I yank my hands away. "Please don't touch me!"

A myriad of emotions cross over his features. Through my tears, I catch only confusion. Pain.

"Cato is my father." The words fall between us like a blade. I swallow. "The man who cursed your kingdom. Who made you …" I choke on a sob when I see his face.

I would run if I could. Escape the sight of his face. But I'm shaking too hard to move, and I know this moment will haunt me for the rest of my life. I bury my face in my hands. Force a breath. Force myself to look at him again. His expression nearly undoes me.

"I'm the healer you've been searching for." I force myself to breathe. To speak. "I didn't tell you at first because the Sages always warned me I'd be hunted by outsiders. Then you said you needed the scepter, and I thought … I didn't think you needed a healer. So it didn't matter. But then the Sages told me …"

I have to stop. Breathe. Get it together. "They told me Cato and Pia are my parents." My voice breaks. I press a fist to the ache in my chest.

"I'm so sorry, Malachi. I can't even begin to tell you how sorry I am." I force myself to meet his eyes. "And I'm sorry I'm the one you're bound to."

Another sob rises. I bury my face in my hands. It's so unfair. All of it.

Who my parents are. What my father did. Everything Malachi has sacrificed. But after all he's been through, the fact that Mortiana bound him to me may be the cruelest blow of all.

I've avoided reaching for the bond out of cowardice. But now I do. And gods, the pain on his end cuts so deep I think it might rip me apart. I wipe my face. Lower my hands.

"I'm sorry," I repeat, calmer now. "If you take me to Noktemore, I can fix this. I know what it means for me. For us. I know I'll have to sacrifice—"

The flickering lights should have warned me. He moves so fast I don't have time to react. His hand catches my chin, tilts my face up. His eyes are hard. Brutal.

"You have no idea what this means for us." His voice is low. Dangerous. "You will not sacrifice yourself. I don't care who your parents are. I don't care what Mortiana says, or the prophecy, or anyone else." He swallows hard. "I will not lose you to this curse."

I stare at him. "What?"

"I won't allow it."

"But I ... and you ... did you hear what I said? My father cursed your kingdom. He's the reason—"

"I don't give a fuck!" He releases my chin and looks away. His eyes flash bronze before returning to golden brown.

"Malachi." I keep my voice gentle. Careful. Like calming a wounded animal. "This is an entire kingdom. Your kingdom. I'm one person. It's not—"

He spears me with a glare. "No one is just one person. Least of all you."

"The prophecy—"

"Don't." His voice is low. Thick with fury. The air crackles around us. "Do you remember when you asked what Noktemore was like?"

I swallow. "You said it's a kingdom like any other."

"It is. A kingdom where Mortiana rules as queen. Where her court is filled with souls indebted to her. People who would do anything to gain her favor." His smile is sharp. Cold. "A court where princes and princesses and demigods are humbled."

My breath hitches. But I stay quiet.

"The gods reserve stasis for worshippers. People they favor. It's not something you ask for. It's something you're granted, if you're found worthy." His jaw tightens. "I walked into her court on my first day and demanded it."

My eyebrows rise. I stay silent.

"She didn't know what to do with me. Hated me the moment I arrived. A Rook." His lips twist. "I'm Lugal's warrior. Serve Maia. Mortiana loves her husband and sister-in-law, but she's a goddess. And there's nothing gods love more than power."

I inch closer. I can't help it. His lips twitch as he tracks my movement. A predator watching prey. And I would let him catch me.

"But she loves her family. So instead of sending my soul to Oblivion, she agreed to bargain." He raises an eyebrow. "I told her if she could find something I truly wanted, I'd accept any punishment. If she couldn't, she'd grant me stasis."

A dark smile crosses his face. "I knew her games. Knew the Nightmares she unleashed on her court. I knew she couldn't resist."

"Nightmares," I whisper. "They're like sirens? Compulsion and beguilement?"

"More powerful. They can show you your worst fears. But in Noktemore, they prefer to show your greatest temptations." His voice drops. "They create mirages. By the time you realize it isn't real, Mortiana knows what you want. It's how she traps people into making more bargains."

"How does it work?"

A dangerous gleam enters his eyes. "Do you want a demonstration?"

I rear back. "You can do that?"

"Being in stasis in Noktemore has benefits. Transporting souls, too. Over time, you acquire gifts from the goddess." His lips curl into a slow, dark smile. He leans closer, stopping inches from my face. "Don't worry, Menace. I won't use my gifts on you unless you ask."

My eyes narrow. "What did the Nightmares show you?"

He leans back. "Everything an arrogant twenty-eight-year-old prince could wish for."

"And?"

"After a year of games, Mortiana realized she couldn't win."

"What does that mean?"

He rises from the chair. Plants his hands on either side of me, caging me with his body.

My pulse thrashes. "Mal. What does that mean?"

"Do you remember when Kage asked if you'd ever thought about having children?" His voice is low. Raspy. "Your answer was immediate."

"Of course," I whisper. "I've never even met a child. How could I want one?"

"It's the same for me. I was named Cursebearer the moment I opened my eyes. By the time I could walk, Tenebris and Arusha were at war." He holds my gaze. "The Nightmares can only show you what you truly want. Not your duty. Not what you've been told will fulfill you."

I nod. Lick my lips without thinking. He tracks the movement. When his eyes lift to mine, they're molten. Crackling with a need that rivals my own. A fire that can't be extinguished. Like the Flames ignited by gods.

"They couldn't show me anything." His voice drops to a whisper. "Because I didn't know what it was to want until I met you."

And then he strikes.

His mouth claims mine in a kiss that makes everything else vanish.

CHAPTER THIRTY-ONE

There's no softness in this kiss. No careful exploration. Only determination. Plunder. His tongue sweeps into my mouth and tangles with mine, hungry and demanding.

I fist my hands in his hair. Wrap my legs around his waist. When he grinds into me, the moan that escapes is shameless.

He does it again. Harder. Growls against my mouth when I meet his thrust. Bites my lip when I do it again.

He tears his mouth away long enough to yank the tunic over my head. Stops. Stares. I'm bare beneath it. Nothing between us but air and heat.

"Temptation." His voice is raw. "That's what it stands for."

Every other time he's asked, I've had a quip ready. Now I can't think of a single word. Not with his eyes on me like that. Wild. Ravenous.

His gaze traces my jagged scars. Travels up the sigil on my torso. He releases a shaky breath when his eyes reach my breasts. My nipples are peaked, aching for him. When his gaze finally lifts to mine, I'm trembling.

We stare at each other. Chests heaving. Wanting. Needing.

Holding his gaze, I rise onto my elbows. Stretch out my leg. Press my foot against the hard length straining his pants. I bite back a gasp.

Gods, he's impossibly hard. His eyes flare and darken as he takes a step back and begins to undress. His eyes stay on my face, tracking every shift in my expression as he reveals himself inch by inch.

Hard muscle. Golden skin. Scars that tell stories I want to learn. When he stands fully naked before me, I don't bother hiding my admiration. Don't bother pretending my mouth isn't watering.

"The way you look at me." His voice is gravel and smoke.

He steps forward. Drops to his knees. I gasp as his mouth finds my ankle. He presses hot, open kisses up my calf. My knee. The inside of my thigh.

The combination of his tongue, his teeth, the scratch of his beard against my skin makes it impossible to stay still. By the time he reaches my inner thighs, I'm shaking. He groans against my skin like I'm the best thing he's ever tasted.

He worships my scars with his mouth. Traces my sigil with his tongue. Finally, finally, he reaches my breasts. I stop breathing when he licks my nipple.

Arch off the bed when he draws it into his mouth and sucks deeply. The deep moan he releases vibrates through me, settles between my thighs, makes me clench around nothing.

I sink my fingers into his hair, writhing beneath him as he moves from one breast to the other. Licking. Sucking. Biting just hard enough to make me cry out. I could shatter from this alone.

Then he starts kissing his way down. Nipping. Tasting. Until his face is between my thighs and I forget how to think.

His rough fingers part me gently. The glazed, reverent look in his eyes as he stares at the most intimate part of me ... that might be my undoing. And then he licks me. Just once. A slow, deliberate stroke that makes every thought in my head scatter like ash.

"Gods, Menace." His breath fans over my sensitive flesh. "I've dreamed of this, but ..."

He doesn't finish the sentence. His mouth closes over that bundle of nerves instead. My hips bow off the bed and he presses me back down against it. I fist the sheets at my sides, desperate for something to anchor me.

"Oh my gods, Malachi—"

He uses his tongue the way a painter would use a brush, his mouth the way a starving man devours his last meal. My hips undulate on their own accord, chasing a release on his tongue, and he growls in approval, gripping my thighs hard as he sets to demolish me.

Even through the haze of pleasure, I know this man is going to ruin me. And I'm going to let him. He groans against me like he's the one losing his mind. Like he's the one unraveling.

He uses everything. The bond. The hitch in my breath. My writhing. The sounds spilling from my lips. He takes it all and uses it against me until he's found every spot that makes me scream.

Until I shatter. Convulse. Until my voice is hoarse from screaming his name. A ragged groan tears from his chest as he lifts his head. He slides two fingers inside me and starts pumping slowly, stretching me.

"Oh my—" I arch off the bed, unable to form words as his fingers work me and his thumb circles that sensitive bud.

"Look at you. So fucking beautiful." His voice is wrecked as he continues his torture.

Somehow, I manage to open my eyes and look down at him. Gods, I shouldn't have. He's watching me with such wonder. Such awe. Like I'm something precious. Something sacred. The emotion that rises in my chest is too much. I bite my lip hard to keep it from spilling over.

"Mal." My voice breaks. "I need you inside me. Please."

His eyes smolder. He holds my gaze as he latches his mouth over me again, hooks his fingers, and sends me over the edge once more. I come screaming again. I hear him murmur something as he kisses my leg. Feel the bed shift.

When my vision clears, he's hovering over me, one hand cupping my face as he starts to slide inside. I gasp at the stretch. Spread my legs wider to take more of him. My eyes squeeze shut as tears threaten to spill.

"You okay?" His voice is rough. Strained.

I nod, eyes still closed.

He stops moving. "Ada."

"Don't stop." I force my eyes open. "Please. It's just been a long time. I'm fine. Keep going."

He huffs a laugh. It's strained, barely controlled.

"It's been much longer for me." His forehead drops to mine. "Taking myself in hand every night, thinking of you … it's nothing compared to this. Nothing compares to you."

My heart stutters at the admission. I slide my hands back into his hair, and something in his expression softens.

"Go slow," I whisper.

He lowers his mouth to mine in answer.

"Keep your eyes on me." He pulls back just enough to hold my gaze. "I want to watch you fall apart around my cock."

My breath catches. I nod.

He sinks all the way in with a thrust that knocks the air from my lungs. Both of us make a sound. His is strangled, barely contained. Mine is something closer to a sob.

He holds there for a moment. Lets me adjust. Then he finds his rhythm. I can't look away. Can't do anything but feel as he moves in slow, languid strokes. Each thrust hits that spot inside me that makes stars burst behind my eyes. Each retreat leaves me aching for more.

He braces on his forearms. Claims my mouth again. His tongue finds mine in a slow, sensual rhythm that mirrors the movement of his hips.

"So close." I whimper against his mouth. "Mal, I'm so close—"

"Gods, yes." He increases his pace, tongue stroking into my mouth in time with his thrusts. "Give it to me. Give me everything. Let me feel you."

He breaks the kiss. Pulls back. There's something wild in his eyes as he grips my hips. Then he unleashes.

Harder. Deeper. Relentless. I'm speaking words that make no sense, screaming for him not to stop, and then I shatter, clenching around him so hard he groans.

"Oh, fuck. Fuck, Ada." His thrusts stutter.

Then speed to an impossible pace as he chases his own release. He roars as he comes undone. Shudders so violently that I shudder with him. He collapses forward but catches himself on his forearms before his full weight crushes me.

I wrap my arms around him. Take the first content breath I've drawn in longer than I can remember.

After a long moment, he pulls back. Searches my face. I watch his throat work as he swallows.

"What you said earlier, about flaying yourself open." His voice is rough. "You've been doing that to me every second of every day since we met."

He claims my mouth again before I can respond.

"How did you get these?" he asks, tracing the larger scars on my torso.

"That one is from my bargain. Jordi was shot by a poisoned arrow and I didn't know how to use my healing gifts."

His eyes flick to mine. "Your desperate bargain."

I nod, smiling softly as I brush his hair away from his eyes. "I guess when I heal people, I end up taking their scars."

"You guess?"

"I didn't see Jordi's chest afterward. I forgot to ask if he ended up with one."

He nods and traces the larger, jagged scar. "What about this one?"

"I don't know."

He frowns as he searches my face, waiting for an explanation.

"I had it when I arrived. That's what the Sages told me, anyway."

He stares at me for a long moment before he presses a kiss to each scar, then my sigil, then my throat, and finally, my lips. I smile as I sit up higher against the headboard, pulling the sheet up with me as I turn my face towards him.

"Why do your eyes flash like that?"

He settles beside me. "Because I'm a Rook."

"Freida told us stories about raffin wielding different colors of lightning. She never mentioned the riders' eyes flashing."

"Not all raffin wield lightning. Some control cloud formations. Create storms. It helps them travel unseen." He stretches his arm behind me. "Others can disappear entirely. My raffin happens to wield bronze lightning."

"That sounds incredible." I pause. "And terrifying."

His lips twitch.

"Have your eyes flashed before tonight? I can't imagine I'd miss something like that."

"Once." He casts me a sideways look. "At Siren's. When I learned you were in a private room with that legion guard."

A smile spreads across my face before I can stop it. "Because you were jealous?"

He chuckles. "Are you so cruel that my agony excites you?"

"Your agony doesn't excite me." I trace a finger down his chest. "Knowing you want me does."

He cups the back of my neck. Gods. Even after everything

I've told him, he looks at me like I'm the only one who can satisfy the hunger banked inside him.

"I always want you, Menace."

The yearning in his eyes undoes me. I shift, straddling his stomach, and shiver when I feel him hardening between my legs. I lean in, holding his gaze, and press a soft kiss to the hollow of his throat. The choked gasp he makes sends a thrill through me.

"Merciless." His fingers dig into my thighs as I lick up the column of his throat. "That's what you are."

"You said you like everything I do."

"I love everything you do." His grip tightens. His voice is hoarse. "Everything."

I pull back to say something. The words die on my tongue when I see the hunger blazing in his eyes. Instead of speaking, I rise up. Position him at my entrance. And slowly sink down.

My breath catches at the stretch.

"Gods—fucking—damn." Each word is punctuated by a strangled sound as I seat myself fully.

When I start to move, he makes another sound. Something between a groan and a prayer.

"The meeting with the Sages." His fingers trace slow circles on my back. "That's when you learned about your parents? That's why you wouldn't let me comfort you?"

I nod against his chest.

"Gods, Ada." He pulls back to see my face. "Why didn't

you tell me? Did you think I'd drag you to the Bratus? Did you think I'd—"

"No!" I push up on my elbow to face him. "I didn't want you to look at me and see a monster. That was before I knew you were the prince!"

He chuckles, hand settling on my hip. "And we know how you feel about monarchs."

"Oh gods." My eyes widen. The twinkle in his only grows brighter.

"Don't worry. I won't tell the king."

"Goddess strike me." I bury my face in the pillow. "You couldn't have stopped me from putting my foot in my mouth?"

"And make myself a target of your ire?" He laughs. "No, thank you."

He brushes the hair from my shoulders. Turns my face toward him. Cups my cheek, eyes soft. "You're so beautiful."

"So are you." My chest tightens as I shift closer. "What are we going to do?" I whisper.

"Figure it out." His thumb strokes my cheek. "Together."

"What if we can't?"

"We will."

I swallow. "The Flame said I won't lose my life to the curse."

His eyebrows rise. "She said that?"

"She said I'll lose my memories." I look away.

"That's not going to happen."

My eyes snap to his. "Mal. We can't change fate."

"I'll speak to her. I'll—"

"No." I sit up, cross my legs, face him fully. "You are not making another bargain."

He sits up, shoulder against the headboard. "You can't make that decision for me."

"And you can't fix everything with bargains." My voice sharpens. "*I* won't allow it."

He stares at me. Eyes narrowed. Jaw tight. "We'll leave the night after tomorrow."

"What about the ivory weapons?"

"Kage will handle it." His voice brooks no argument. "Our priority is the scepter. And finding a way to lift this curse without endangering you or losing your memories."

I nod.

"I meant what I said." His eyes hold mine. "I won't let you sacrifice yourself."

We both know the prophecy can't be changed. But I place my hand over his and squeeze, hoping it's enough. Cursebearer. What a terrible thing to name a child. What a terrible weight to carry for three hundred years.

I refuse to add to it.

CHAPTER THIRTY-TWO

THE TRANSITION BETWEEN SLEEP AND WAKING CARRIES ITS OWN kind of magic. But it's never felt like this. If I could bottle this feeling, the warmth of Malachi's arms, his heartbeat steady beneath my ear, I would drink it every day.

I'd drink it now, just to quiet the warning coiling in my gut. My eyes open with the sun. Golden-orange light spills across the sky, the same shade as his eyes at dawn. I exhale slowly.

"Something wrong?" His voice is low, rough from sleep.

"No. Yes." I huff a laugh. "If I ignore everything we're facing and stay like this all day, things would be perfect."

He presses a kiss to the top of my head. "When this is over, we'll have all the time in the world to stay like this."

I start to respond. Stop. When will it be over? When my memories are gone? When the curse is lifted? When Cato is dead? Even if all of that happened at once, I can't picture what comes after. What it means for us.

"Once the curse is lifted, will you go back to Vindariel?"

He sighs. "Yes. Lifting the curse won't resolve everything,

but it will stop the rot. My parents and sister will wake from stasis. And I'll be free of Noktemore for good."

I pull back to lie beside him, facing him. "Where are they now?"

"My parents are in Noktemore. Part of my bargain." His expression darkens. "My sister was supposed to join them, but she went to Arusha to bargain with Cato. Stasis took her before she could leave."

"She's with Cato?" My voice drops to a whisper.

"Yes." His jaw tightens. "He was my father's right-hand man for years. Doted on my sister when she was a child. Taught her to wield a sword." His lips twist bitterly. "Right before I went to Noktemore to plead with Mortiana, she went to Arusha to beg Cato to stop. He kept her there. Warded the entire kingdom so no one could reach her."

"Gods." I stare at the sheets between us. "I'm so sorry."

"I heard he wept when she collapsed and never woke." His voice is so quiet I barely hear it. "They say he keeps her in a glass coffin in his palace."

My stomach turns. I remember what Freida said about the princess of Arusha. The sleeping princess. The glass box.

"Your parents must hate Pia," I whisper. "After everything that happened because she fled there."

"Not at all." He takes my hand. "How could they? Cato is the monster. Pia was trying to escape. Trying to give her unborn children a chance at something better."

I keep my eyes on his chest. If I look at his face, I'll cry.

"Pia was the only person my mother allowed in the room when I was born. She loved her like a sister. She never blamed her for anything. And she would never have let her return to Cato."

The knot in my throat tightens. But something in my chest loosens. I have no concept of Pia as my mother. I never will. But knowing she had someone, that she wasn't alone through all of it, makes the ache a little easier to bear.

"No one in Tenebris blames her." His thumb traces over my knuckles. "When people learned what she did, that she went to the Bratus while heavily pregnant because she couldn't bear to watch them suffer, she became a legend. There's a statue of her near the palace. For years, people traveled from across the kingdoms to visit it. To pray for fortune and health."

I blink hard to keep the tears from falling. "Really?"

He nods. "Hers is the most beloved legend across all the kingdoms. But not everyone knows the full story."

My eyebrows rise. "And you do?"

He tilts his head. "Of course."

I can't help but smile. "Tell me the part no one else knows."

He pulls me closer.

"She'd been staying in Vindariel for months. She was part of the family. Everyone loved her, from the stable hands to the kitchen staff." His voice softens. "But near the end, they started to worry. She kept talking about finding the scepter. Taking it to the Bratus. She was heavily pregnant by then.

"She waited until King Runerth left the city. Then she wrote a letter to the king and queen, left presents for the prince and princess, and disappeared into the night." He pauses. "The rest, you know from the legend."

"What did she leave them?" My voice is barely there.

He cups my face. His smile is soft. Sad.

"A divine sword for the prince. And a divine dagger for the princess."

My breath catches. "You were just a baby."

He chuckles softly. "I was. But Pia Vida must have known what I would become and that one day that sword would come in handy."

My eyes fill as I fully process what he's saying. "Your sword." My voice breaks. "Vida. That's why…"

I can't finish. The sob that escapes is raw, wrenched from somewhere deep.

His smile is sad as he gathers me into his arms. Holds me against his chest while I cry for a mother I never knew, who loved me before I was born, who left pieces of herself behind for a family that wasn't hers to claim.

But claimed her anyway.

CHAPTER THIRTY-THREE

My heart is heavy as I move through the rooms I've called home for the past three years. I always knew I'd leave eventually. But not like this. I don't know what happens after we get the scepter.

But I know I'll never live here again. I may never come back at all. Mal comes up behind me. His arm bands around my chest. I inhale his scent and grip his forearms, sagging against him.

"We can stay here tonight, Menace." His voice is low against my ear.

"It's safer if we stay at one of Tilda's cottages. Pretend we're visitors." I press back against his chest, wishing I could disappear into him. His answering growl vibrates through me.

"It feels impossible to want someone this much." He slides my hair aside, exposing my neck. His teeth graze the sensitive spot beneath my ear. Then his tongue.

"Kage will be here any second," I whisper, even as I tilt my head to give him better access.

He groans against my skin. Keeps exploring anyway. It does feel impossible to want someone this badly. Maybe the uncertainty is what makes the wanting sharper. More urgent. His arm loosens as I turn to face him. My stomach pitches at the need blazing in his eyes. He grips the back of my hair, tilts my face up, and—

Keys rattle at the door.

I jump back. Whirl toward the bookshelf. My heart races, though I'm not sure why. We're adults. We're not doing anything wrong.

"I got Tilda to upgrade us to a three-bedroom cottage. Free of charge." Kage holds up two keys triumphantly.

"Only because you mentioned Ada's name," Naima adds.

He hands me a folded piece of paper. "We need to move. Legion guards are going door to door."

My blood chills. "What?"

"They're asking about the children the Sages raised," Naima says. Her voice shakes.

"Has anyone talked?" I'm already moving toward the door.

My hands tremble as I lock the door behind us. I unfold the paper as we descend the stairwell.

I'm sorry we haven't been able to catch up. It's been busier than usual. I'll try to come by tonight. -Tilda

I stumble on the last step. The little x's dotting her i's. Tilda was part of the renegades. I shove the note in my pocket. The renegades are the least of our concerns right now. If the legion guards are in Veritas, we're running out of time.

"Did you and Margot pack?" I ask Naima as we walk.

She sighs. "Not yet."

"Naima, this isn't—"

Kage's shadows whirl around us without warning.

Mal throws an arm out, pressing us against the wall.

"Legion guards," Kage murmurs. His shadows cocoon us in darkness.

Mal glances at Naima. "Is the Veritas Estate safe?"

"I don't know." Her voice wavers. "It has wards, but those won't matter if the Council knows about the hidden halls."

I take her hand. Squeeze. I wish I had something reassuring to say, but I've never been a good liar. None of the Sages' training prepared us for this.

They taught us to lie about our gifts. To suppress them. To fear using them. But training only goes so far when you know, deep down, that the person teaching you won't actually hurt you.

"So the estate is out," Kage says.

The grim look they exchange does nothing to calm my nerves.

"Where's the cottage?" Mal asks.

"Behind Ada's clinic. More secluded than the others."

Hearing him call it mine makes my throat tighten. I push the feeling down, along with the dream that once seemed just out of reach and now seems impossible.

Mal crosses his arms. "Where are the other cottages?"

"Near Veneficia Alley. A few streets from mine." Naima's grip tightens when he turns that sharp, calculating gaze on her.

"Visitors are renting there?"

She nods. "The hunters Kage identified are staying nearby. That's probably why Tilda gave us this one instead."

His eyes narrow. "Pack a bag. Stay with us tonight."

"I've told them they can't stay in Lunaris," Kage says. "Neither wants to hear it."

"It's not that we don't want to hear it." Naima's voice cracks. She releases my hand. "Where would we even go? How would we leave?"

I wrap my arms around myself. Look away. Her emotions threaten to slip into mine, and I can't afford that right now. I reach for the bond instead. Lean into Mal's unwavering resolve. His eyes flick to mine for a moment before he turns back to Kage.

"Do you have everything we need?"

"Not yet. None of the receipts have names or places of origin. They only have the House of Justice as the point of delivery. My contact at the docks says there's a shipment coming in tonight, so I'm planning to get on that ship and find some answers."

"You trust this contact?"

Kage huffs a laugh. "You know me better than that. I trust three people, and one of them is standing in front of me." He winks at me. "Don't worry. We'll work on that before we're married."

"When does the ship arrive?" Mal asks, ignoring him.

"Ships dock at the second dog watch. I'll head out when the Veritas clock strikes five."

"You're boarding a ship carrying weapons designed to kill Rooks?" I stare at Kage.

"We need to find out who's making them. Where they're coming from." His expression darkens. "Though we have a good idea about the latter."

"They're not just Rook killers." Naima straightens. "The ivory temporarily weakens all gifts."

I frown. "How do you know?"

"I tested it on interns." She adds quickly, "Minor cuts. Nothing they don't already do at the forgery."

Malachi raises an eyebrow. "And?"

"They couldn't use their gifts. Neither could I. A minor cut was enough to block everything except the most basic abilities."

"Godsdamn it." Mal looks at Kage. "We'll have to be quick. Save your shadows."

Kage's shadows, already thinning around us, fall away completely. He scowls. "I can't wait to be rid of this curse."

"Pack a bag," Mal tells Naima. "After we search the ship, Kage takes you to Vindariel."

Her eyes widen. "What about Margot? We can't leave her."

"Then take her by force."

If things weren't so dire, I'd balk at his bluntness. But he's right. When Jordi mentioned leaving, Margot withdrew completely. She hasn't spoken about her vision since, but I haven't stopped thinking about it.

"Bain is right," I add. "We can't give her a choice. Bring her to the cottage and tell her I need to speak to her or something and we'll find a way to keep her there and convince her."

Naima nods rapidly and exhales. "Okay."

Kage steps out first. We follow, blending into the groups of visitors heading toward Veneficia Alley. Naima grabs my hand to slow me down.

"If Vindariel is cursed, how will we survive there?" she whispers.

"Mal says we can keep going north to Aerathos. But for now, Vindariel is safer than here."

Her eyes narrow. "You know you're the only one who calls him Mal?"

I sigh. "Naima."

"I'm just saying. Everyone's noticed."

"Everyone?"

"Me. Margot. Kage. Draven. Even Jordi mentioned it."

I roll my eyes. "You'd think we have bigger things to worry about."

"That's exactly why it comes up. We only talk about our worries." She squeezes my hand. "You two give us something else."

I huff a laugh. "There's nothing to talk about."

"The way he looks at you says otherwise."

I try not to take the bait. Fail. "How does he look at me?"

"The way you look at Milly's pastries."

A laugh escapes before I can stop it. Both men glance back.

Naima grins.

"I have nothing to say about that," I mutter, earning a laugh from her.

We reach the corner before she can press further. Kage turns, key in hand.

"Number four. Tilda said if anything goes wrong, there's a hidden door under the rug in the back bedroom."

My pulse spikes at the implication. I take the key without comment.

"Pack and come straight back," I tell Naima.

"I will. I just need to find Margot."

"Tell her I need to speak to her. We'll convince her together."

She nods sharply, then disappears into the crowd.

I don't know how long I've been alone. The sky bleeds redder by the minute, and my restlessness grows with it. I peer through the gap in the curtains. Pace the sitting room. Peer again.

Naima and Margot should have been here by now. After what feels like an eternity, I can't take it anymore. I scribble a note in case Malachi returns first and grab one of Kage's dark cloaks.

A cold finger of dread traces my spine as I lock the door. I try to shake it off.

Then I turn. Dark fog waits on the corner. Still. Patient. As if it's been expecting me.

I clench my fists and wait.

Empath. The voice is in my ear, cold as death. *Feel us. Hear us. You are ours to claim.*

The air vanishes from my lungs as glowing eyes appear in the fog. Then the darkness retreats, and air rushes back into my chest. I'm still staring at the spot when the sound of screams pulls my attention away.

I run toward the sound and round the corner to find Veritas in chaos. Not the chaos of the Moon Festival, with drunk visitors stumbling through the streets. This is something else. Something worse.

Legion guards shoving people aside. Residents and visitors screaming and running. A woman in a purple cloak falls. Two men rush to help her while the guards dressed in dark green march on without a backward glance.

I stand frozen. Disbelieving.

Then I see Tilda.

Tilda, who is always impeccable, always composed, is shoving through the crowd in a red dress torn at the shoulder. Her lipstick is smeared. Her eyes are wild with terror. I sprint toward her, meeting her in the midst of the screaming. She bellows as she wraps her arms around me and starts to sob uncontrollably.

"What happened?" I try to pull back. "What is this?"

"They took them!" She squeezes tighter, shaking, sobbing. "They just came and took them!"

"Who?"

She pulls back but keeps her grip on my shoulders. Eyeliner streaks down her face. Her eyes are glassy, unfocused.

"They took them!"

"Who?" I shout.

"The children!"

I go cold. "Wh ... what children, Til?"

"Naima! Margot! They took them!"

Everything stops. My vision tunnels. I stop breathing. Stop listening. Stop thinking. And suddenly, it all comes roaring back. I shove past her. She grabs me, but I keep moving, dragging her with me until I see him.

And I stop.

Arlo moves through the crowd like a shark through water. Sharp. Powerful. Untouchable. Behind him, legion guards flank Naima and Margot. Both in manacles.

The scream that tears from my throat doesn't sound human. Tilda's arms wrap around me from behind. I thrash, trying to break free.

"Godsdamn it." She jabs the base of my spine with her finger. "Stop. Moving."

The compulsion hits instantly. It spreads from the point of contact, through my organs, into my brain. My body goes slack. I grit my teeth. Fight it. She taught me how. She trained me for this.

My friends disappear from view. And then I see another face. Casimir. Also in chains. I stagger. Tilda tightens her grip.

"This is against the treaty!" someone screams.

"The Sages broke the treaty long ago!" A legion guard's voice cuts through the chaos. "Their residents refuse to wear amulets! Because of them, our borders are no longer secure from the Shroud!"

"Because of them, the land rots! The curse spreads! Our guards have been poisoned by their forbidden gifts!" The guard raises his voice above the crowd. "Tomorrow, these renegades will be dealt with! Bring us Jordan the Mapmaker!"

"The Council took him!" someone shouts. "You already have him!"

"Bring us Jordan, or we deliver death to these traitors!"

The crowd follows the procession. I'm trapped by Tilda's compulsion, her arms locked around me. By the time I break free, they're gone.

There's nothing left to chase.

CHAPTER THIRTY-FOUR

We make it inside before Tilda's legs give out. We crumple to the floor together. I don't know how long we stay there. She murmurs "What a mess, what a mess" like a prayer. I sit in silence.

I'm out of words. Out of thoughts. Out of tears. All I can see is Arlo leading the charge. *Arlo.* Of all people. I would have believed it of anyone but him.

"He wasn't himself," Tilda whispers when I say it aloud. "He just wasn't."

"How did this happen?"

She opens her mouth to respond. The door crashes open. The lights flicker as Malachi steps inside. His eyes sweep the room, land on Tilda shielding me, and go cold.

He prowls toward us with an expression I have no doubt many have seen in their final moments.

"Stop." Her voice shakes, but the compulsion drips from it.

My teeth grit against the pull. Kage freezes by the door.

Malachi doesn't even slow. He keeps his eyes on mine as he crouches before me.

"Let go of her," he says, his voice barely a whisper, but Tilda's arms fall away instantly.

Then he's lifting me off the floor, cradling me against his chest. I bury my face in his neck. Breathe in the lingering scent of the ocean and him.

"Who are you?" he rumbles.

I blink and pull away. "This is Tilda. Tilda this is—"

"Prince Malachi Bain Malvorathis," Kage announces as he walks over.

"Oh my goddess." Tilda's eyes go wide. She curtsies.

"Oh gods," I whisper. Mal stiffens.

"My apologies, Your Highness." Tilda straightens. "My name is Carla Matilda Ocasio. I—"

"She's a friend," I say, trying to push away. His grip tightens. I shoot him a look. "Bain."

His eyes snap to mine and narrow.

"She's a friend," I repeat. "Set me down."

He does. Slowly.

"They took Naima and Margot." I look at Kage, then Malachi. "Tilda tried to help them. She stopped me from doing something stupid."

Malachi glares at me, then turns to Tilda. "In that case, thank you, Carla Matilda Ocasio, for preventing a slaughter."

I frown. "They took—"

"I heard you." His voice is steel. "We will get them back."

I narrow my eyes but don't argue. I turn back to Tilda.

"Is that what they were talking about out there? The amphitheater tomorrow evening?" Kage asks.

Tilda nods. "They stormed in from nowhere. Margot was dropping off a dress. Naima came looking for her." Her voice breaks. "She didn't even make it inside before they grabbed her."

I squeeze my eyes shut. The scene plays out behind my lids.

"Why them?" Malachi asks.

"Someone said Bastian told the Council who the children at the estate were." Tilda frowns at me. "But he was one of them. One of you. Why would he do that?"

I stare at her. It's all I can do.

This is what Margot saw. Or part of it. Bas being executed. But did she see the wrong person? Did she misread her own vision? Gods, what else did she see? My stomach coils with questions I can't answer.

"Naima had a container of water." Tilda's eyes widen, as if remembering. "She threw it up, tried to wield it, but the water just… fell. Like she couldn't access her gift. She started screaming about Rook killer weapons."

My heart stutters. "What about the weapons?"

"I don't know. The guards didn't draw any weapons."

I wrap my arms around myself. Look at Malachi. "Did you find the ship?"

A sharp nod. Nothing else.

I replay the scene in my mind. Their faces. The way they walked between the guards. The manacles—

"The handcuffs." I drop my hands and round my shoulders back. "Did you see them clearly?"

"I was too busy trying to compel them to stop, but they just…" She trails off. Her eyes go wide. "My compulsion didn't work."

My pulse pounds in my ears.

"The manacles could be made of the same ivory," Kage says.

I nod. "I think the ones they took Jordi away with that time may have been as well."

"But why wouldn't my compulsion work on the guards?" Tilda's voice drops. "That's never happened before." She pauses. "And why do they want Jordi?" her voice breaks. "Please tell me he got away."

"He's safe," Mal says. "Naima and Margot will be too. We'll make sure of it."

"Will your people come? Will they fight?"

"We've sent word."

"Thank the goddess." Her lip trembles. "Gods, Temp. Arlo."

I hug myself tighter. Nod.

Malachi shoots Kage a look.

"Come on, Tilda." Kage's voice softens. "You need rest. Let me walk you back."

She pulls me into another fierce hug. "Please be careful."

I hug her back. But all I can think is, we're past that now.

We wait for them to leave. For the door to close. For the lock to click.

I turn to Malachi. "The handcuffs must be made of the—"

He swoops down and claims my mouth before I can finish. It's a desperate kiss. Fear and devastation poured into one another. The bond hums between us, a reminder that these moments are stolen.

Maybe that's why I respond with such urgency. Tugging

him closer. Wrapping my legs around him when he lifts me. When we break apart, we're both panting.

He presses his forehead to mine. "Damn it, Menace. I felt your fear from the ship. I couldn't get here fast enough."

"I'm so scared, Mal." My voice shakes. "I've never been scared like this. Not even when Jordi was taken."

Constantine has never done anything like this. If he has the Sages too, I can't imagine what it means. According to Veritas teachings, when the Undying Flame of a kingdom snuffs out, the kingdom dies. The Sages are the only ones who can tend that Flame.

If they die, lifting the curse won't matter. There will be no kingdom left to save. Constantine must know this. If he's truly trying to serve Cato, if they want Tenebris, they must understand they can't destroy the Flame. But my friends. My family. What are they to him?

"We'll get them back." His expression is fierce. Certain. "We'll get them."

"What if this is just the beginning? What the Flame said…"

He silences me with a hard kiss. "We will get them back."

He carries me to the back room. Shuts the door. Sets me on the edge of the bed before disappearing into the bathroom. I fall back and close my eyes. The air is thick with citrus and eucalyptus.

The scent unlocks something. A memory I'd forgotten. The soap maker's shop. The Sages sent me there to intern, years ago. The soap makers spoke of their work as if it were the most important in the Order. Everyone does. That was when I first noticed the Veritas pin on their coats, the gold signet ring with the symbol.

I smile, remembering when we ran out of soap at the estate and Cas convinced me to share his. The memory curdles. Becomes the image of him in chains tonight. I force myself to breathe.

I breathe until I find my center. And then I'm somewhere else. Not physically. In my mind. Walking through the dark forest behind the cottage. Toward the Shroud. Toward the whispers and the glowing eyes that call to me. I don't run. I stare back.

"Tell me what you want," I whisper.

You.

I clench my trembling fists. "Why?"

You are owed to us. You kept this place fat with grief, and loss, and memory.

My chest tightens. "Are you the healers? The ones sacrificed to the Bratus?"

We are a collection. Memories. Grief. The last word comes as a hiss. *Rage. Only you can free us. Only you can feel us.*

"Will you be free when the curse is lifted?"

Some. Others will wait. To remind you.

"Remind me of what?"

What was taken from us. What was taken from you. What is owed.

The voice fades, growing distant.

My eyes fly open.

Mal sits beside me, rubbing my arms, worry etched into his face.

"You're still shaking." His voice is gentle. "I ran you a bath."

"I can't—"

One look from him silences the refusal.

"I'm not asking you to soak for hours. But you need to calm down. Go. I'll get you when Kage returns."

I nod and take his hand.

As I step into the bathroom, I glance toward the forest. The darkness seems closer than before.

As if to say: *It won't be long now.*

Kage spreads a creased, stained map across the table. Lines crisscross the yellowed paper. "These are the old tunnels. The old tunnels." He taps the map for emphasis.

"Where did you get this?"

"Tilda. She's been hoarding old documents for years. In case something like this happened."

He traces a line on the map. "The hidden door in the bedroom leads to this tunnel." His finger slides through the forest, past the Shroud, and keeps going. "All the way up here."

My eyes widen. "To Vindariel?"

"As long as the passages haven't collapsed. Tilda says this is the only entrance, so I doubt anyone's touched them."

I slump back. A direct path out of Lunaris. This whole time. And Tilda knew.

"It could work as an alternative route for the Rooks," Kage says.

"According to the texts, the Shroud should clear a better pathway soon."

I sit up. "Didn't Jordi and Draven take that route?"

"The path is safe to reach the other side where the Rooks are waiting," Kage explains. "It's the route from there to here that normally poses a problem."

I sink back in my seat, wondering if it poses a problem because the Shroud is being fed from this side. I push the thought away.

"Did you hear anything about the Sages?"

"Only that they haven't been seen. Everyone assumes they're at the Keep. That they'll be at the amphitheater tomorrow."

"A show of power," Malachi says.

"Or he doesn't believe in the Flame," Kage suggests.

"Even so, he can't be stupid enough to publicly execute a Sage."

I suppress a shiver. "What's the plan for tomorrow?"

Kage and Malachi exchange a look. When Malachi turns to me, his expression is calculating. My stomach drops before he even speaks.

"We're going to remove as many amulets as we can."

I stare at him. "That can't be the whole plan."

"Draven said the amphitheater is usually warded, but we haven't felt any wards since we arrived. They're relying on the ivory." He leans forward. "There are only three of us. Our gifts are limited by the curse. Yours aren't, but I don't want you anywhere near Constantine."

I cross my arms. "So I'm supposed to do what? Stand back and watch you fight?"

"Of course not." His eyes hold mine. "You'll be taking amulets off people's necks."

I gape at him. "You want me to do that? I told you what the Sages made me do. Those amulets are the only things keeping some of those people alive!"

"Temporarily!" His voice rises, then drops. "The ones who are going to die will die the moment the Shroud breaks. Jordi confirmed that."

"Right, so let me just kill them faster," I huff, shaking my head. "Great plan, Bain."

His jaw clenches. He sets his hand on my bouncing knee. "That's the second time you've called me that today."

I raise an eyebrow. "Isn't that what your friends call you?"

"I think we're a little past being friends, don't you?" He squeezes my knee.

Kage chuckles and presses his lips together when we turn in his direction. "For once, I'm not trying to eavesdrop. I'm just ... right here." He raises his hands and looks at me. "Just so you know, only his mother calls him Mal. I'm only telling you this so you know he's not the type to mess around and leave you or anything."

My head snaps to Mal, who has a bewildered expression on his face as he looks at Kage. He shakes his head and turns to me. For a long moment, we simply stare at each other, at a loss for words.

Then, he says, "I would do anything for you, but I can't spare you from this. The people who are going to die without the amulet, aren't truly alive. You have to know that. You said yourself you saw those laborers."

I swallow. He's right. I know he is. But gods, it hurts.

I nod. "Fine."

His eyes soften. He squeezes my knee, then turns to Kage, all business again. "Is there a tunnel that leads to the amphitheater?"

We plan until there's nothing left to plan. I don't feel any better. All I can think about is Constantine. The Shroudmaidens. What Jordi believes lies beneath the amphitheater. And what all of it might mean for my memories.

CHAPTER THIRTY-FIVE

The tunnel spits us out beneath the amphitheater. A narrow corridor reeking of blood and animal musk. I press my hand against the damp stone to steady myself. The roar of the crowd pulses through the wall like a second heartbeat.

It sounds like the ocean during a storm. Relentless. Hungry. Alive.

"This way." Kage's shadows snake ahead to scout.

We follow through arched passageways, past iron gates and holding cells I force myself not to look into. The amphitheater was built for spectacle. For blood sport. During the Moon Festival, death dresses up as entertainment.

I've only been here twice. Once for Arlo's first duel. Once for Casimir's. Both times left me drained. I blamed my empathy.

I was wrong.

It wasn't anguish from watching people I love get hurt. It's anguish—period. There's so much of it trapped within these walls, it's stifling.

Mal's hand finds the small of my back as we climb the stairs. It's light and brief. A small reminder that I'm not alone.

I cling to that as we emerge into the lowest tier of seats and are met with the deafening noise.

The amphitheater stretches in tiered crescents of limestone and marble, rising story after story toward the open dome. Every seat is filled. The entire island must be here. Lunarian residents in green. Veritas in maroon. Visitors in purple, blue, and gold.

My eyes sweep the arena floor. Guards. Officials. A wooden platform at the center. My knees nearly buckle when I find them. Naima. Margot. Cas. Wrists bound in ivory that gleams under the torchlight. Cas's face is bloodied, but defiant. They all are.

Kage's hand closes on my arm. "You okay?"

I nod and force myself to keep looking. To take in the full horror of what Constantine has planned. The platform sits directly beneath the open dome. I look up at the blood-red sky above, at the moon that looks down on all of this as if it's savoring the promise of what's to come. Waiting. Salivating.

Behind my friends, a massive dark green banner bearing the Everlasting's symbol hangs between two columns—the eye inside the heart. I see Arlo standing at the edge of the platform in his gold-winged uniform, the bow Freida gifted him all those years ago hanging from his hand.

The torchlight catches on his blond hair, his sharp cheekbones, the strong line of his jaw. Even from here, his eyes look flat. "What did they do to him?" The words scrape out of my throat.

"Compulsion," Kage says grimly. "Strong. Probably tied to that amulet he's wearing."

My eyes drop to the amulet. Not green, but amber. I

recall Jordi's words about Constantine and this place, and look at the ground, wondering where the center of this place would be, and what exactly is down there.

My eyes dart around in search of Constantine. I find him walking up to the platform. People start cheering, others booing. He's dressed in his typical ceremonial green and gold. His silver hair gleaming as he prepares to address the crowd with his arms spread wide.

The amber chip on his ring catches the torchlight. Or maybe it's glowing on its own. Pulsing, like a heartbeat. Like it's feeding. My stomach churns.

At first, his voice is low, then it carries through the amphitheater, amplified by the acoustics the original builders designed for this exact purpose. To make one man's words feel like the voice of a god.

"—betrayed us all! These renegades, these traitors, have been hiding among us, using their forbidden gifts against us, weakening our borders, inviting the very darkness we've spent generations protecting ourselves from!" The crowd roars. Some in agreement, many in protest. It doesn't matter. Constantine has the stage, the spectacle, and he has my friends in chains.

"Tonight, we cleanse Lunaris of this poison! Tonight, we prove that the Everlasting only protects those who are faithful!"

I start moving closer to get a better look. Mal's hand closes around my wrist and yanks me back. "Wait," he growls.

"I just want to see!"

My gaze travels upward, following the columns that rise like bones toward the sky. My heart stops when I see the

Sages. They're suspended from the third story, wrists locked in cuffs that gleam white. Their bodies hang limp, feet dangling over the void.

Anala's dark hair has come loose from her crown braid and falls around her face like a veil. Freida's armor is gone. She's wearing only a thin shift, her muscular arms trembling. Their eyes are open, flashing, defiant, but Sara is staring directly at me.

"Oh my gods, Mal," I whisper, gripping his hand tighter. "The Sages!"

"The cuffs are draining them," Kage says quietly to my right. "He really is out of his mind."

"They'll kill them!" I hiss, twisting in Mal's grip. "If we don't—"

"I know." His eyes bore into mine, and I see the impossible calculation he's running.

There are too many people to save, and not enough time. Not enough hands. I look at the Sages' lives withering away above. My friends in chains below. At Arlo with his empty eyes and that arrow in his hand, as if he's waiting for Constantine's command.

I take a deep breath and turn to Mal. "What can you do that won't deplete you completely?"

"I can create a distraction, but the illusion will only last so long."

"And once we touch those cuffs, we don't know what will happen," Kage adds.

"Which is why we need to focus on taking off the guards' amulets," Mal says pointedly.

"I'll take the amulets," I say. "You two get the Sages. You can actually reach them in time."

"Ada—"

"I won't—"

"I know you." His jaw is tight, eyes blazing. "The second we turn our backs, you're running down there."

I open my mouth to argue. Close it. Because he's right. I won't be able to watch my friends die and do nothing.

I grab the front of his tunic. "If the Sages die, the Undying Flame dies with them. Everything dies. We need them alive."

"And I need you alive!" His voice is raw. Guttural.

"Listen to me." I cup both sides of his face, and he automatically wraps his hands around my wrists. "I'm not going to die here. We know that much."

"We don't know that, Ada. Nothing is written in stone."

"Bain," Kage says hesitantly. "We need to do this while they're distracted."

"Wait!" His eyes pierce mine. "Did you see this? Did the Flame—"

"No! I told you everything I remember!"

"I don't like this." He turns toward the spectacle.

I grab his face harder. Force him to look at me. "We are fated, Malachi Bain. We are written in stone."

His eyes darken. "Fuck this. You're coming with me."

He grabs my hand and hauls me toward the stairs.

I yank free at the corner. "I'll slow you down and you know it!"

"Godsdamn all of this." He glares at me.

"Bain."

"Go!" he roars at Kage. "I'll catch up!"

My heart pounds. "You need to get up there before anyone notices."

"Then come with me. I'll carry you." He lunges. I jump back instinctively.

I close my eyes. Breathe. Roll my shoulders back.

"I need to get to the ground level."

"Why? To run out there and—"

"No." I grab his tunic. "I need to feel what's beneath it. I can't explain, Mal. I just... need to."

"You're going to use your gift of serephony here, of all places?" He seethes, bringing his face closer. "Are you out of your godsdamn mind?"

"Maybe." I hold his gaze. "Maybe I get down there and nothing happens. Maybe I run toward that platform and try to stop something I can't stop. I don't know. Neither do you. That's the point. We don't know anything except the prophecy."

He scowls and looks away.

I pull his face back to mine. "You asked me once if I regretted making my bargain. I told you to ask me when this was over." My voice breaks. "I don't need to wait. I'd make a million bargains if they'd tether me to you. If anything happens..."

"Ada," he warns, eyes wary.

I swallow past the knot in my throat. "Remind me. Remind me you once made me feel like the most important woman you'd ever met. The most powerful. The most beautiful. Even though I was only an apprentice. Only an empath."

"Menace." A whispered plea. "Please—"

I rise on my toes and haul his mouth to mine. He makes a sound against my lips, something broken and desperate, and kisses me back like it might be the last time.

My knees are shaking when we pull away, but somehow, I will myself to start running. The last thing I hear before the crowd swallows me is Mal's roar of fury, but it's not what I feel through the bond. There, I find warmth and strength, and that's enough to keep me going.

Heart pounding, I raise my hood and start snatching people's amulets as I push through the crowd. When I get back to the edge of the tunnel, I set my foot on the sand and jerk back. The onslaught of emotion nearly drives me to my knees.

"That's her!"

The voice cuts through the roar like an arrow. Ronnie. I hold my breath, praying I misheard. But his voice comes again. My sigil flares. I turn and find him a few rows up, pointing at me with pure triumph on his face.

"That's the healer! Jordan's sister!"

My ears ring. I whirl and come face-to-face with two guards. I snatch their amulets. Toss them aside. One guard's eyes widen. He falls. I force myself to move, but hands grab me from behind before I can take a step.

I kick. Thrash. The guard's grip doesn't loosen. He drags me toward the platform.

"She's one of them!" Ronnie screams.

My sigil flares at the sound of his voice and accusation. My feet pedal against the ground, kicking sprays of sand as I try to get out of the guard's grip and turn toward the agitator at the same time.

"One of whom, Ronald?" I shriek. "The children the

Sages raised? How would you know that? Want to tell everyone where you grew up? Which room you slept in at the estate?"

He pales.

Sara would call this unbecoming of an empath. Cruel, even. I don't care. I'm dragged to the front of the platform, forced to my knees. A blade presses to my throat. I stop breathing. I don't dare look up toward the Sages. Can't risk drawing attention to Malachi and Kage.

Constantine's lips curve. "You are Ada, then. Jordan's sister. A healer, if that man is to be believed." His smile sharpens. "I'm sorry there's no room for you on the stage with your friends. *Yet.*"

My eyes narrow, then fly to my friends. Naima and Cas are livid. Margot is panicked, staring at someone near the stage. I follow her gaze to Bastian, who's standing there, shoulders back, expression drawn.

My sigil burns again. He doesn't look happy. But his eyes aren't empty like Arlo's. And he's not doing anything to stop this.

"The next traitor pains me, truly." Constantine's pout is theatrical. Disgusting. "This one has a gift he tried to bury. Every touch reveals recent memories. Every intimate touch…" He pauses for the crowd's murmur. "Reveals everything. Fortunately, Nicolas has a similar gift. And has been very thorough in his service to the Council."

My stomach drops. Nicolas. The Council member Bas was in love with. Bas, who has always had a poker face that could fool anyone, looks like he's fighting tears.

Guards close in. People he probably knows. People he called friends. All of this is sickening.

"I thought gifts didn't exist!" The words tear from my throat. "I thought the Council was against them! Why is Nicolas allowed to use his?"

The crowd stirs. Agitated. It doesn't matter whose side they're on. Noise is good. Distraction. Time. Anything that will help us.

Constantine's eyes narrow. "Silence!" He gestures to the guards. "Bring him up."

"Nicolas!" Bas breaks free, makes it halfway across before they catch him again. They cuff his wrist with ivory. He keeps fighting.

I reach for the bond, grasping for anything that'll keep me grounded. I let out a breath when I find it and feel the warmth. Then I hear gasps. Even Bas stops fighting and looks to the left. I turn and frown when I see a man in dark green and gold, like a Council member, walking over.

Constantine's strangled gasp beckons my attention. There's a look of awe on his face when he whispers, "Everlasting?"

My stomach lurches so hard, I double over. I hiss at the bite of the blade slicing into my neck. My hands land on the sand before my face hits.

I turn to look at this Everlasting. I don't know what I expected evil to look like. Not this. Not a regular man. There's nothing remarkable about him. And yet I can't look away.

"Why don't you tell him how you're his true heir?" someone shouts.

"Isn't that what you've been claiming?" yells another.

Constantine blanches. "No, no. I said I wished I were his heir!" His laugh is shaky. Desperate.

I look at Cato again. Watch the bottom of his cloak slowly fade. A mirage. Malachi's mirage. I bite back a laugh and push gratitude through the bond.

"Who did this?" Constantine roars, pointing at the spot Cato's image vanished from.

"Maybe it's the Everlasting punishing you for your lies!" someone yells.

"Who said that?" Constantine bellows, face red as he looks up at the crowded stands. "Traitors!" He whirls on Bastian.

"I've done nothing wrong!" Bastian spits. "I gave you everything! My whole life!"

Constantine's grin wavers. The crowd is turning. He feels it.

"What kind of leader uses his guards' thoughts against them?" someone yells.

"A cage!" I shout. "This whole place is a cage built on lies!"

"Silence!" Constantine's face contorts with rage. "SILENCE!"

I take a deep breath and try to focus on my serephony as Constantine looks around wildly. I lift my hands from the sand as if burned. There's so much anguish, so much anger, the ground is practically vibrating with it.

I think of what Kage said about the Bratus. What Jordi said about memory stones. Maybe both are down there. Maybe something worse.

"You were useful to me. That's all any of you ever were!"

Constantine snaps at Nicolas. "Would you like to say anything to your former lover?"

Nicolas presses his lips together. Shakes his head.

Bas's shoulders shake with rage. The rage he was allowed while we were forced to swallow ours. I think of how angry he was as a child. How quiet he became after the Dueling Estate. None of it matters now. I may not care for him, but he doesn't deserve this.

No one does.

"Arlo," Constantine barks.

Arlo walks over with his bow and arrow and stands in front of the platform, just feet away from me, feet away from Bas.

I stop breathing when I realize what's about to happen. Still, I shake my head in denial. Arlo lifts his bow and nocks the arrow on the string, pointing it directly at Bas' chest.

"Arlo!" I shriek. "No!"

Margot lets out a guttural scream and crumples. The guards at her sides hold her up before her knees hit the ground. Naima and Cas yell at the same time.

"Arlo is a master archer," Constantine announces. "And he will bend to my will."

The guards haul me to my knees. I can't stop myself from looking up. Mal and Kage are there. Far above. Working on Freida's manacles. Anala and Sara are already free.

I see his face turn towards me. I hear loud thumps on the stage, the sound of everyone's gasp, and look to find two guards on the ground with their amulets nearby. I look at Mal again, knowing he's responsible somehow, and again, send him a burst of gratitude.

More time. Constantine claps his hands. New guards rush forward. They fall too. Again. And again.

"Who is responsible for this?" Constantine roars.

He looks up at the Sages' chains.

Empty.

I look up. No sign of Malachi or Kage either. Relief floods me.

Constantine screams for more guards. More drop. More rush in. A sick, endless game.

He turns back to the crowd, trying to regain control. Shouting something about Arlo's skills. About justice. My friends are shaking. Sweating. Bas's pants are stained at the front. My sigil burns at the sight of it. Arlo lifts his bow again. Nocks an arrow. Points. His movements are smooth. Mechanical. Empty.

"Arlo!" I shout, managing to crawl two steps before the guards catch me and plant me on my knees again. The blade knicks me again, spilling more drops of blood onto the sand.

"Remember who you are! He's using you! Lo! Please! Lo! Please remember!" I yell over, and over.

"Lo! This isn't you!" Bas shouts, his voice breaking.

Naima. Cas. Margot. All screaming his name. The crowd takes it up. A chant. A plea. Arlo's hand trembles. Something flickers behind those empty eyes. Horror, maybe. The horror he'd feel if he could feel anything at all.

"Please," I beg. "Please, Lo. Don't do this. Don't—"

Constantine waves his hand. "Release."

The arrow flies.

Bastian doesn't have time to scream. One moment he's

standing. The next, he's falling backward, an arrow buried straight through his heart.

Margot howls.

The amphitheater erupts.

My sigil burns. Brighter than it ever has. So bright I think it might split me in half.

A scream rips through me as I dig my hands into the sand again.

And then I hear Constantine's voice again. "Get her up! Arlo. Your next mark."

When I lift my head, he's pointing the arrow at Margot's chest, and something inside me hollows.

I look up and see Mal fighting off guards near the tunnels. Kage's shadows are dimming, thinning from overuse. Then I feel it through the bond. A stab of pain. I look back at Malachi. See the gleam of ivory protruding from his side. He sways. His eyes lock on mine.

I tug the bond. Pour everything I have into him. Strength. Love. Whatever's left. A scream tears through me. My fingers dig into the sand. My sigil burns with the unfairness of it all.

It burns at Constantine's voice. At Naima's screams. At the sound of Veritas residents fighting their way out of the tunnels, joining the battle around Kage and Malachi.

I close my eyes and I open myself to everything. Every emotion buried in this ground. Every memory I helped erase. Every scream I helped silence.

I don't reach for a weapon. Don't reach for Malachi or the bond or the gifts I've spent my life hiding. I reach for the anguish. For the anger.

For every memory stone beneath this amphitheater.

Every suppressed sob. Every swallowed scream. Every woman in Lunaris who bit her tongue until it bled because the sigil on her chest told her anger was forbidden.

That silence was safer. Every time she was told to follow rules without questions. Every time she smiled when she wanted to scream. I take all of it, until I feel like I'm burning inside.

Until the skin on my chest feels like it's splitting open and something is clawing its way out. And all that rage contained, that I've never been allowed to have, bursts.

The ground shakes. Cracks. I hear screaming. The crowd. Me. Something older.

"What is she doing?" Constantine's voice. Distant. Afraid. "Stop her! STOP HER!"

But no one touches me.

Deep in my chest, something ancient stirs. I feel the Shroud. Feel it lifting. Shifting. And then it's too much. Too much grief. Too much sorrow. Lifetimes of it.

Menace. Malachi's voice. In my head.

Mal? How?

The bond. He sounds tired. I try to open my eyes to look for him, but my eyes are burning. *Ada, you need to stop. You're taking too much. You'll drain yourself.*

I can't! I don't know how.

The ancient thing inside me stirs again. My eyes pop open. I look up and see shadows floating. And then my body rises.

Menace? He sounds drained. Wary now.

I try to find him in the crowd. I can't.

"Her eyes are flashing blue!"

"The true heir!"

"Impossible!" Constantine's voice cracks.

I don't mean to move, but that ancient thing guides me, and suddenly, I'm gliding onto the platform.

"Temp!" Naima's voice. "Your eyes!"

"Something is happening," Cas croaks out as he falls to the ground.

"No, no, no!" Margot cries. I see Arlo's bow and arrow, and his figure on the ground. His amulet. Was Mal able to take off his amulet?

Deep down, I panic. But the ancient thing is stronger. It won't let me waver.

This is Mortiana's message, I realize.

I open my mouth. Hear myself speak in a voice that isn't mine. Clear. Rhythmic. Commanding.

"If I am to become a legend, let it be known: I am Ada the Tempest. Chosen by the gods, along with seven others, to restore the balance."

I turn. Lock eyes with Constantine.

"I am Ada, the Wielder of Wrath. Daughter of Pia of Larimar. Liberator of the Shroud. Killer of the Everlasting."

The gasps wash over me. My vision darkens. My mind slips.

But I fight the current. Reach for the bond. It's weakening, thinning, but I tug hard. Find Malachi's eyes in the crowd.

And I add my own message to Mortiana's. "I am …" I pause. Darkness closes in, but I push past it. "I am Ada Temperance Acevedo. Cursebreaker of Tenebris."

And then, nothing.

CHAPTER THIRTY-SIX

Malachi

A MYRIAD OF THOUGHTS CRASH THROUGH ME AS I WATCH ADA hover over the platform. But three rise above the chaos, louder than the rest.

Nothing could have prepared me for this.

I've never been so scared in my life.

And I'm going to kill Mortiana for this.

She must have known. Must have known Ada's eyes would flash bright blue, like the hottest part of a flame. Something I've only read about in ancient texts. Something I never thought I'd witness. Ada is not just an empath. Not just a true healer. A true siphoner.

Worse, Mortiana must have known heralding this message would put Ada in imminent danger. Must have known and sent her anyway. I clutch my injured side and force myself toward the stage, muttering a protective incantation as I drag my sword behind me. The glyphs activate, humming against my skin, and I pray to every god listening that the protection reaches Ada before she finishes.

"—Killer of the Everlasting."

I stop walking.

My pulse crashes in my ears. The words echo through the amphitheater, through three hundred years of waiting. I watch Constantine stumble backward as if the declaration itself has struck him.

An arrow grazes his ear and clatters to the ground beside him. My gaze flicks behind him, to where Freida stumbles out of the tunnel with a bow in hand, already nocking another arrow. Constantine's hand flies up instinctively, but his wide eyes remain fixed on Ada. He drops his bloody hand as if he hasn't felt the wound at all.

Near the tunnel, a legion guard shoves Freida sideways. She's forced to abandon her mark and fight. I clutch my side harder. Force myself to keep walking.

The Shroud is lifted. Kage's voice slams into my mind. *The Rooks will be here soon.*

I let out a ragged breath. Good news, at least. *Are you injured?*

A pause. *Yes. I can't summon my shadows. I can barely stand. How the fuck are you walking?*

I don't respond. The fear of losing Ada is the only thing keeping me upright, and that's not something I want to admit right now. I swallow hard and keep going. Keep staring at Ada.

Keep praying to Maia and Lugal that I'll reach her before another wave of guards descends with those ivory weapons. Praying that if I fall, she'll at least be protected.

As if she senses me, she turns. Those burning, unblinking blue eyes lock onto mine. Even through the chaos, even through the fear, I feel the bond flare between us. Feel her reaching for me.

"I am," she starts, in her own voice this time. This is no longer Mortiana's message. This is Ada. My Ada. I hold my breath as her lips move again. "I am Ada Temperance Acevedo. Cursebreaker of Tenebris."

The proclamation grabs me by the throat.

And then she crumples.

Fuck.

I use the sword as a crutch and try to move faster. *Menace! Ada! Stay with me!*

I shove the words through the bond. Shove whatever strength I can muster after them. The effort makes my head spin so fast my knees hit the ground. Sand billows around me like smoke.

Bain. Kage's voice makes me blink.

I grip my sword tighter. Use it as leverage to haul myself up. Stumble back down, crashing so hard my teeth rattle.

The Veritas guards are on their way to you. You need to wait. You're going to get yourself killed.

I ignore him. I don't have the energy to respond and focus on the bond at the same time. I squint through the dust, trying to make out the stage. Reach for the bond and find it thready. Flickering.

Panic seizes my chest.

I tug harder. Feel her confusion. Her fear. I summon what's left of my strength, bury the sword in the sand, and drag myself upright. My legs threaten to buckle.

Then I see a flash of green uniforms carrying Ada's limp body toward the tunnel on the right side of the arena. A roar rips from my throat as I limp after them. Most of the legion guards are down, scattered across the sand. We were certain without their amulets they'd shift. We were hoping Ada's friends would too.

Now I wonder if they even know they have the ability. On the opposite side of the amphitheater, Freida is still fighting. I keep walking toward the tunnel instead.

"It leads to the dock!" Naima shouts, sprinting toward me with those ivory manacles still clamped around her wrists.

Margot stumbles after her, sobbing so hard she trips over her own feet. I keep walking, barely avoiding tripping over myself.

They're headed for a ship. Kage's voice again, urgent and raw. *They're taking her to Arusha.*

Another sound tears from my chest.

Naima flinches and raises her bound wrists. "If I can get these off, I can reach her!"

My head whips toward her. "How?"

"Water," she says, as if that's the most obvious answer in the world.

Maybe it is. I don't care. All I know is if that ship leaves for Arusha, I won't be able to reach Ada. Not in time. Not like this.

I keep hobbling toward the tunnel. "I can't break them. My gifts won't work on the ivory."

"Can I use your sword?"

I stop. Clutch my side. Give a sharp nod.

She crouches down and slides the manacles along the blade, sawing back and forth. They snap in half but remain clamped on her wrists. She shrieks in frustration, glances toward the tunnel, then surges to her feet and takes off running.

She stops beside Arlo's unconscious form long enough to grab his bow and arrows. Keeps going.

"Naima!" Margot screams, stumbling after her.

My head swims. I take another step. Another. I crash to my knees.

My chest rattles with each breath. I yank my hand away from the stab wound and try to haul myself up again. That stupid fucking ivory. Poisoning me from the inside.

I reach for the bond.

The protection I placed on her is holding. That lets me breathe a little easier, but it's not enough. Nothing is enough. Through the bond, I feel her confusion.

She's reaching for it. Grasping for a thread she can't name, can't follow. She doesn't know what the bond is. Doesn't know who's on the other end.

An ache settles deep in my chest. I squeeze my eyes shut. "Menace," I breathe. "Please."

It's the last plea I make before darkness crawls in from the edges of my vision and my world tilts sideways. The last thing I feel before the darkness takes me is her heartbeat, faint and frightened, pulsing alongside mine.

I'm coming for you, menace.
I'll make you remember.

EPILOGUE

THE ROOM IS BEAUTIFUL.

That's the first thing I notice when I open my eyes. The way the light falls through gauze curtains, turning everything soft and golden. The ceiling is painted with stars, silver and white against deep blue, and for a moment, I just stare at them. Trying to remember if I've seen them before.

I don't think I have. But I'm not sure.

The bed beneath me is impossibly soft. The sheets smell like lavender and something else, something sharp and green that I almost recognize. When I push myself upright, my body aches in ways I can't explain. My hands are bandaged. There's a tender spot at the base of my throat.

The room is large and bright and filled with beautiful things. A vanity with a silver mirror, fresh flowers in a crystal vase, a wardrobe carved from pale wood. None of it feels familiar. But none of it feels *wrong*, either.

A man stands at the window wearing a long green robe with gold stitching. He has black hair, and when he turns to look at me, I notice his light brown eyes and warm smile.

"You're awake," he says, his voice warm. "How do you feel?"

I open my mouth to answer and find I don't know. I feel hollow.

"Confused," I whisper hoarsely.

"That's to be expected." He crosses to the bed and sits at the edge, careful to leave space between us. "You've been through an ordeal. Do you remember what happened?"

I try to reach for it and find nothing but fog. Shapes moving in the dark. A roar of sound. Red light. The taste of something metallic on my tongue.

"No."

"What *do* you remember?"

I close my eyes and search for solid ground. Facts. Things I know.

"My name is Ada." The words come slowly, like pulling thread through a needle. "I'm a healer. I live in ... in ..." The fog thickens. "Lunaris. I lived in Lunaris."

"Good." He sounds pleased. "What else?"

I frown. "I think I have a brother."

"You do. Jordan. He's safe. I've made sure of it."

Relief flickers through me, though I couldn't explain why. I can't picture his face. Can't remember the sound of his voice. But the word *brother* feels true, and right now, that's enough.

"Anything else?" the man asks.

I push harder. Try to find the edges of the emptiness. There's something there. Something important, but every time I reach for it, it dissolves.

"There was ... someone." The words feel dangerous in my mouth. "I think there was someone."

"Someone?"

The ache in my chest sharpens. That absence. "I don't know. I can't—" I frown, pressing my hand against my sternum. "I can't remember."

"That's alright." He smiles. "You're safe now. That's what matters."

Safe. The word feels wrong somehow.

"Who are you?" I ask.

Something flickers across his face. There and gone.

"My name is Cato," he says. "And I've been waiting a very long time to meet you, Ada."

He reaches out and brushes the hair from my forehead. His hand is cool. Careful. The gesture should feel comforting, but something in my chest recoils from it. Some instinct I can't name.

"Where am I?"

"Somewhere safe. Somewhere no one can hurt you." He stands, smoothing his green robe. "Rest now. You need to recover your strength. There will be time for answers later."

He moves toward the door, and panic spikes through me, sudden and sharp. "Wait."

He pauses. Turns.

"Will you ..." I don't know how to finish. Don't know what I'm asking for. "Will you come back?"

His smile widens. "Of course. I'm not going anywhere, Ada. Neither are you."

The door clicks shut behind him, and I'm alone.

I sink back into the pillows and stare at the painted stars

on the ceiling. They blur as my eyes fill with water I don't understand. I'm not sad. I don't think so, anyway, but something in me is grieving anyway. Mourning a loss I can't name.

The tug comes again.

Sharp. Insistent. A thread pulled taut in the center of my chest.

I press my hand against it and try to follow it. Try to trace it back to wherever it leads, but there's nothing on the other end. Just fog and silence.

Someone, I think. *There was someone.*

But the thought dissolves before I can hold it, and by morning, I've forgotten it was ever there.

ACKNOWLEDGEMENTS

I hate forgetting to thank people (and I always forget to thank people), but these last couple of years have been a lot. At the risk of forgetting some, I want to properly acknowledge those who checked in on me without knowing how bad I was doing. Sometimes a simple, "Hey, you alive?" or "Haven't seen you around, just checking to see how you're doing" have the power to pull you out of the dark before you fully immerse in it. So, thank you. <3

First and foremost, I want to thank the people who worked on this book. Gina Licciardi (thank you for your patience!), Stacey Blake (thank you for your incredible attention to detail and your patience!), Hang Le (the magician! I'm in awe of you), Travis from To The Moon and Back Design (thank you for putting up with my terrible math and changing the dates on the maps -amongst other things- 1000x LOL), and Angela Rizza (for the BEAUTIFUL ravens!). Special shout out to Jan Corona, Anna Page for beta reading it (on such short notice) and Amanda Cantu, and Karinna Baez for reading it early <3

In no particular order: Charleigh Rose, Nana Malone, Melissa Gaston, Adriana Herrera, Kennedy Ryan, Dylan Allen, Adriana Locke, Gina Azzi, Tarryn Fisher, Willow Aster, Riley Page, Corinne Michaels, Laurelin Paige, Shanora Williams, Kandi Steiner, KA Linde, J Sterling, Georgana Grinstead, Bobby Kim, Melissa Saavedra, Mandy (Books and Lyrics),

Jan Corona, Happy Driggs, and gods, I know there are more, but I'll just have to personalize your book :/

Special shout out to all of the indie and romance bookstores that keep my books in stock (including, but not limited to: SteamyLit, Novel Grounds, The Last Chapter,

Under the Cover, Fred & June, Flutter, and Bookmarks). You are so important to the book community and your reach is wider and more powerful than you know.

Mami, gracias por creer en mí y por ser una campeona de mis libros. Te quiero!

Jay & Kaylee, the best brother I could ever ask for and the best sister-in-law. I love you guys.

AJ—the light of my life. I love you more than you love Miss. Vale.

My in-laws, for everything. Your willingness to drop everything and help us whenever we need you is invaluable. *You* are invaluable. We're so lucky to have you. I love you.

Ana y Luis, los quiero muchísimo. Luis- gracias por los libros y los videos de la historia de R.D. Tus cuentos son una inspiración.

Diana & Anabelle, my friends, cousins, sisters, who are always there when I need them and always proud of every book I write, I love you so much.

Lidia, who's always willing to answer my questions and learn the most RANDOM THINGS alongside me –your incessant mind, willingness to learn and research things give me life. I love you so much.

Katie, for getting me out of the house more often than I otherwise would lol. Your friendship means the world to me.

Christian, I don't even have the words to express my

gratitude to and for you. I don't say it often (not nearly as often as I should), but the best thing that ever happened to me was meeting you on my first day of college (even if I did try to fight the inevitable as long as I could lol). Pieces of you are scattered in every romance hero I've ever written, but none will ever compare to the reality of you. 20+ years later, you're still my favorite person in the world. I love you x infinity.

Abraham & Moses—my biggest cheerleaders and haters (lol). Most days, I wish I could turn back time and erase my years of cancer and treatments so you never have to know what it's like to have a sick parent and deal with the things that come with it. But then I see the young men you've become and think it was meant to be that way. You are the most caring, selfless, loyal, strong, resilient young men I've ever known. I'm so proud I get to walk the earth alongside you, and so fortunate to call myself your mother. No matter what you do (or don't do), I hope you know the world is a better place because you're in it. Your existence is enough. I love you more than anything (even silence, and books, and pizza, and Disney, and dogs lol).

ALSO BY CLAIRE

Romantic suspense/Romantic thrillers...
Until I Get You (spicy)
When We Lied (spicy)
Half Truths (low heat)
Twisted Circles (low heat)
Because You're Mine
Because I Need You
Because I Want You
Because I'm Yours

Contemporary romances...
The Player
Kaleidoscope Hearts
Paper Hearts
Elastic Hearts
The Heartbeaker
The Rulebreaker
The Troublemaker
Catch Me
The Trouble With Love
The Consequence of Falling
Then There Was You
The Sinful King
The Naughty Princess
The Wicked Prince
Fables & Other Lies

ABOUT CLAIRE

Claire Contreras is a *New York Times* Bestselling author, mother, wife, and breast cancer survivor. She was born in the Dominican Republic, raised in Miami, Fl, and currently lives in North Carolina with her family.

You can find her on FB (in her group—Claire Contreras' Crew)

On IG: ClaireContreras

Or sign up for her NL (for the latest): geni.us/ClairesNewsletter

www.ingramcontent.com/pod-product-compliance
Lightning Source LLC
LaVergne TN
LVHW091700070526
838199LV00050B/2219